'Shall we dance?' Vittorio asked. 'And couldn't you smile at me as though I was your heaven on earth?'

'But what would that prove?' Jackie asked. 'Only that I'm one of the crowd chasing you. Now, if *you* smiled at *me* that would be better. But don't worry. I do understand why you don't want to.'

'Don't I?'

'Your heaven on earth? Me? More like purgatory, driving you mad.'

'Which is just how you like it.'

'I can't deny that.'

They laughed together. Those dancing near them observed that they were in perfect accord and exchanged significant glances.

'Now we've *really* given them something,' she teased.

'And if they heard me tell you that you look wonderful tonight they'd enjoy that even more.'

'No, don't say that.'

'But I want to say it.' H̶e̶ ̶̶ ̶̶ ̶̶ ̶̶voice. 'Y̶̶ lovelier than ever tonigh̶̶

A PROPOSAL FROM THE ITALIAN COUNT

BY
LUCY GORDON

First Published in Great Britain 2017
By Mills & Boon, an imprint of HarperCollins*Publishers*
1 London Bridge Street, London, SE1 9GF

© 2017 Lucy Gordon

ISBN: 978-0-263-92337-7

23-1017

Lucy Gordon cut her writing teeth on magazine journalism, interviewing many of the world's most interesting men. She's had many unusual experiences, which have often provided the background for her books. Once, while staying in Venice, she met a Venetian who proposed in two days. They were married for forty-five happy years, until his sad death. Naturally this has affected her writing, in which romantic Italian men tend to feature strongly. Two of her books have won a Romance Writers of America RITA® Award. You can visit her website at www.lucy-gordon.com.

I dedicate this book to my Italian husband, Roberto,
who taught me so much about Italy,
and whose love inspired me to set so many books there.

PROLOGUE

'I DID WRONG. I didn't mean to, but I couldn't help it. All in a moment I found that I could be wicked.'

The old man lying on his deathbed spoke weakly, for his strength was fading fast. Vittorio, the young man sitting beside him, grasped his hand and spoke urgently. 'Don't say such things, Papà. You're not wicked. You never could be.'

'Try saying that to George Benton. He was the man I robbed of a million, whose life I ruined, although he never knew it.'

Vittorio rubbed a frantic hand over his eyes and said fiercely, 'But that's impossible. How could he not have known?'

His father's eyes closed and he turned his head, as though too full of despair to say any more. Vittorio rose and went to the window, looking out onto the grounds. They were lavish, extensive, perfectly suited to the Counts of Martelli, their owners for five hundred years.

Franco, the present Count, lay still as his life slipped away. Vittorio knew that his father's mind had often been confused recently. And surely this was merely another example. Yet there was a desperation in the dying man's manner that warned him of something different; something fearful.

'Don't worry about it. Papà,' Vittorio urged, sitting by the bed again. 'It's all in the past.'

'It will never be in the past until it's put right,' the Count murmured. 'We were friends. We'd met here, in Italy, when he came on holiday. We became friends, and when I went to England a few weeks later I visited him. He was younger than me, and that made him fun to be with. We enjoyed a good time, going out for the evening, having a drink, charming women. And we placed a bet. It was just innocent fun—until his gamble paid off! He didn't know. He was too woozy with drink by then. So I cashed in his winnings, then supported him home and put him to bed.'

'What did you do then?' Vittorio asked quietly.

'I'd had the bank draft made out in my name. I did intend to cash it, and pass the money over to George once he was sober, but I fled before he could wake up.'

'And he never suspected?'

'How could he? I never told him about winning. The next day I cashed the draft and returned home to Italy. I never meant to do wrong. I'd just succeeded to the title, but my pleasure was tempered by the discovery of the debt hanging on the estate. Now suddenly I could clear the debt. The world was bright again. It was wonderful to have people showing me respect, calling me Count Martelli.' He managed a wry smile. 'Vittorio—my son—you'll soon know that feeling.'

'Don't, Papà,' Vittorio said with soft violence. 'I don't want you to die.'

The elderly Count squeezed his hand. 'You're a good son. But my time has come.'

'No,' Vittorio said fervently. 'You must stay with me a little longer.'

The thought of losing the father he loved was intolerable. His mother had died giving birth years ago. His father had raised him since then, and together they had been a team, each meaning more to the other than anyone else ever could. Now the man who was the centre of his life was to be snatched from him, and the pain was agonising.

'Fight it, Papà,' he pleaded. 'Another day, another month, another year. I'm not ready to do without you.'

'You won't have to. I'll always be there with you—in your mind, your heart, wherever you choose.'

'I choose to keep you with me in *every* way,' Vittorio whispered.

'My son—my son—there's just one thing I would ask of you.'

'Whatever it is, I'll do it.'

'All these years I've got away with what I did, and now that the end is near—' he shuddered '—I must seize my last chance to make amends—with your help. Promise me—swear.'

'I'll do anything I can. My word.'

'Find Benton. Ask his forgiveness. If he needs money—'

'I'll give him whatever he needs. He'll forgive you and you can rest in peace.'

'Peace? I can no longer remember how that feels.'

'But you will have it, Papà. Wherever you are. I promise.'

'Thank you—thank you.' Franco whispered the words over and over.

Vittorio rose quickly to pull the curtains across the window.

'Don't do that,' his father begged. 'You'll shut out the light.'

'I was afraid the sun was too dazzling for you.'

'It won't be for long.' He gave a sigh. 'Sunlight never lasts. You think it will. You think the light has come into your life for ever. But suddenly it's gone and there's only darkness.'

Vittorio sat down again, taking his father's hands in his. 'Darkness can be fought,' he said. 'I'm going to fight this for you.'

'One day you'll have your own darkness to fight. You

can never tell when it will come, or what will cause it. You must always be ready for what you've never expected. Take care of yourself, my son. Take care—when I'm no longer with you…'

His voice faded.

'But you will always be with me. You must be. Can you hear me? Can you hear me Papà? *Papà!*'

But there was no response. Franco's eyes had finally closed and he lay still.

Vittorio dropped his head against his. 'I promise,' he whispered. 'I gave my word and I'll keep it. Wherever you are—hear me, believe me, and rest in peace.'

CHAPTER ONE

THE WORLD WAS full of light and glamour. Excitedly Jackie danced this way and that, rejoicing in the vision of her beautiful self that appeared in the mirror. Music played in the distance, inviting her into a universe in which she was the heroine.

But abruptly the dream ended. As she opened her eyes the real world fell back into place. The mirror's reflection showed not the luscious beauty of her fantasy but Jackie Benton, a slender young woman with a face that was intelligent, but not beautiful.

She sighed, easing herself out of bed.

Surrounding her was the austere bedroom where she spent every night. By now she had hoped to leave it behind, move to a new home and a more exciting life. But fate had arranged things differently, confining her to Benton's Market—the little shop where she lived and worked.

She'd spent most of her life in the tiny apartment over the shop that her father, George Benton, had started twenty years earlier. He had fought to make it a success, always struggling with money worries, and raising his daughter alone when his wife had left him.

In his last years Jackie had been forced to run the shop alone—something that had given her an unexpected satisfaction.

She was clever and hardworking, able to retain information about all the stock, and produce it at a moment's notice. Something which had at first impressed her father.

'You really remembered all that?' he would exclaim. 'Well done! You're in the right business.'

'I get it from you,' she had reminded him. 'I remember when I was a child there were lots of times you made people gulp at what you could remember without having to look it up.'

It had been a happy moment, uniting father and daughter. He had been proud—not only of her memory but her ability to choose the best stock. Knowing this, she had felt her confidence grow, and she had begun to see herself as a serious businesswoman.

Just occasionally her father had given her a little warning advice. Once, when a temporary employee had flounced out in a temper, he'd said, 'Did you have to be so hard on him?'

'I wasn't hard on him,' she'd protested. 'I just pointed out that he'd got something wrong. And he had.'

'You might have been a bit more tactful.'

'Oh, come on, Daddy,' she had said, in a teasing voice. 'What you mean is that a woman mustn't tell a man that he's wrong in case he's offended. But we're not living in the nineteenth century.'

He'd patted her hand. '*You* may not be, darling, but a lot of men are. You're a bit too fond of giving orders.'

'Too fond for a woman, you mean? You think I should just go along with him? Even when I know he's an idiot?'

They had laughed fondly together, but she'd come to understand that he had been making a fair point. She had learned to speak with more care, but it was still exasperating to have to do so when she knew she was an expert.

She had gradually come to enjoy the feeling of being in command—not merely of their employees but of the whole running of the place. She had chosen stock and it sold well. She'd had the instincts of a talented businesswoman, and they had given her hope for the future.

But her hard work had come too late. Matters had started

getting worse, owing to the mountain of her father's debts that had piled so high that even her commercial success could not completely deal with it. Finally her father had been forced to sell the shop.

By then his life had been drawing to a close. Rik, the new owner, had reluctantly allowed them to stay in the little apartment upstairs, and Jackie had continued to work in the shop—but only part-time, so that she could always hurry upstairs to check that her father was all right. She nursed him gladly, giving him everything in her power in return for the loving care he had always shown her.

'It's so hard for you…to be caring for me and working downstairs as well,' he had said once. 'Such a burden.'

'Stop it, Dad. You could never be a burden to me. *Never.*'

'Bless you, darling. I wanted to leave the shop to you. I'd have been proud to give you a legacy. I hoped once— But there. It just didn't work out.'

She would have loved to own the shop. So much of its success was due to *her* work, and it still held the atmosphere created by her beloved father. But she had known she must abandon that dream.

Her father had died a few days later. And then Rik had offered her a lifeline.

'You're welcome to stay if you become full-time. You can go on living here.'

She'd thought carefully before agreeing. She disliked Rik— an ill-tempered man in his forties—But she had accepted the job because it would give her a little time to work out her plan to escape into a new life—one in which she would have her own business, organising everything, using the talents she'd so gladly discovered.

Her dislike of Rik was well-founded. He had a high opinion of his own knowledge and skills, but Jackie felt that he actually knew very little. He made silly mistakes for which he blamed *her.*

She had tried to save money, hoping that soon she would be able to afford to leave and explore new possibilities. But it had been a hopeless task. Following George's death had come the discovery of more debts that he hadn't managed to pay, even with the money he'd made from selling the shop. Her savings had soon been swallowed up by them. And she had no hope of saving much more, given the meanly low pay Rik allowed her.

'I give you a fair wage,' he would say. 'You live here for nothing. If you worked somewhere else you'd have to pay for accommodation.'

It was true. Frantically she had hunted for another job, but hadn't been able to find one that paid enough to solve the problem. Now she felt trapped, and with no obvious way out she just had to hope for a miracle!

She showered and dressed carefully. She presented a picture of efficiency—ideal for the work that consumed her life—but her looks didn't please her. She considered herself far too plain.

She opened her laptop and logged on to her bank to check the state of her account. The result made her groan with despair. She had very little money, despite her attempts to live frugally.

Dispirited, she opened an astrology website, and read her prediction.

The fates are planning a startling new beginning for you. The sun in Jupiter will bring things you never anticipated, and decisions that will change your life.

In her dreams, she thought wryly. Last week it had said she was going to be a millionaire. And look how *that* had turned out.

She read the prediction again, trying to see it as the approach of the miracle she longed for, and then hurried downstairs and opened up the shop. She served a couple of customers, then spent some time looking around.

The shop had a variety of stock, including home wares and groceries. She often wished she could persuade Rik to show a little more imagination about the stock. But he had no sympathy for her ideas.

'This is a practical place, full of practical items,' he'd once told her sternly. 'You're too fanciful, Jackie. That's your trouble. You want life to be fun, and it isn't designed that way.'

'Not always fun,' she'd protested. 'Just a little bit of excitement now and then. I remember Daddy felt the same.'

'You father spent too much time looking for fun. It was his ruin.'

'*Something* ruined him…' She'd sighed. 'But I don't think it was that.'

'Get on with your work and stop wasting time.'

On the flight from Rome to London, Vittorio sat sunk in thought, wondering where the search for George Benton would finally lead him. Common sense told him he need not search at all. If he simply refused, who would ever know?

But his conscience would know. His promise had brought his father peace in his final moments. If he broke his word the knowledge would be with him for ever. And somewhere in his heart he sensed that his father's reproaches would always haunt him.

Everything had changed with Franco's death. He'd spoken of the pleasures of being Count Martelli, and Vittorio had soon discovered that it was true. The first time someone addressed him as 'Signor Conte' he had hardly been able to believe he'd heard correctly. His employees now treated him with deference, almost awe.

But his father had also spoken of other things—of the

hidden problems behind the glamour, that the rest of the world knew nothing about. And here, too, he had been right.

Vittorio had gone through Franco's things, seeking clues about his father's past life and George Benton. He'd found a photograph of the two men together, which must have been taken during their meeting in England many years before.

How old would Benton be now? Middle-aged? At the height of his powers? Ready to take revenge on the family that had cheated him out of a fortune? He wasn't looking forward to their meeting, but there was no choice.

Franco's papers had also included a newspaper cutting, mentioning a shop called Benton's Market. There was a picture of a small, shabby-looking shop, and one of George Benton, looking older than in the other picture.

That was Vittorio's clue. He had a lead.

At the airport he hired a taxi and spent the journey studying a map of London. The area he sought was just north of the River Thames in the east of the city. As they approached the area Vittorio asked the driver, 'Is there a hotel near here?'

'There's one just around the corner. Mind you, it costs a lot.'

'Fine. Take me there.'

The hotel was pleasantly luxurious. He booked a room for the night, then went out to explore.

Almost at once he saw a corner shop with its sign proclaiming 'Benton's Market'. He took a deep breath, clenching his fists, vowing not to lose his nerve now.

Nearby was a small café, with tables outside. He found a seat, ordered some coffee and took out the photograph of Benton. From this angle he could see through the shop windows clearly enough to know if the man was there.

But time passed and there was no sign of him—only a young woman arranging stock in the main window. Much of it was already in place, but she was intent on reorganising it, giving it all her concentration.

He admired the woman's dedication and artistic flair. He would value such an employee himself, to work in the department store he owned and managed in Rome.

Suddenly he tensed as a man appeared from the rear of the shop. Could this be Benton? But he looked nothing like the picture. His face was thin and severe. His manner to the woman suggested ill temper. When he spoke Vittorio could just make out the words through the open door.

'*Must* you waste time faffing about over this? There's a pile of stuff at the back needs unpacking.'

'But I thought we agreed—' she began to say.

'Don't argue. Just do as I tell you. Get going.'

Looking exasperated, she retreated to the back of the shop.

Vittorio approached the shop, entering with the air of an eager customer.

'I'd like to buy some apples,' he said.

'We've got some here,' the man said. 'No—wait. They *were* over there. What has that stupid woman done with them?'

'I'd also like to talk to Mr Benton, please.'

The man glanced up, scowling. 'What do you want with him?' His tone became suspicious. 'You're not another debt collector, are you?'

'No, it's a personal matter.'

'Well, you can't see him. He's dead.'

'Dead?' Vittorio froze, feeling as though he'd heard a thunderclap. 'When?'

'A year ago. But his daughter still works here.'

'Was that her I saw? Can I talk to her?'

'You can, but not just yet. She's got work to do. You'll have to wait until she's finished for the day.'

Feeling depressed, Vittorio departed. Returning to the

café he settled again to watch the shop, trying to get his thoughts in order. Everything he'd planned was in a shambles. He must talk to Benton's daughter and just hope that she was a sensible woman who would accept financial compensation and let the matter end.

Throughout the afternoon he saw many customers go into the shop. The young woman dealt with them efficiently, always smiling and friendly. Every one of them bought something from her.

Benton's daughter was a natural saleswoman, it seemed.

He stayed there for four hours. He read the paper and then busied himself sending and receiving emails from his smartphone. The frustration of waiting was hard to endure but he forced himself. So much depended on this.

Inside the shop Jackie was working hard. Often she glanced out of the window, puzzled to see that the strange man was still there, sitting outside the café. She concluded that he must be a tourist, albeit a very well dressed one!

At last it was closing time. As she was preparing to leave, Rik arrived.

'Don't go yet,' he said, scowling. 'We need to have a talk about making new orders.'

'But I can't stay,' she protested. She gave him a wry smile, saying, 'And, let's face it, you don't pay me enough to make me want to do overtime.'

'Don't be impertinent. I pay you a fair wage. If you did better I might pay you more.'

'It's not *my* fault profits are low,' she said indignantly. 'I don't think you're buying enough of the right stock.'

'And *I* don't think you're making a big enough effort,' he said coldly.

In his anger he spoke with a raised voice.

Vittorio, a few feet away, heard him through the open

door. He rose and headed for the shop, from where Rik's grouchy voice could still be heard.

'I'm not asking. I'm telling you to stay where you are so we can discuss these orders.'

'*No!*' Jackie said furiously.

Once before she'd agreed to this demand and it had stretched to two hours, without so much as a penny being added to her wages.

'Now, look, Jackie—'

'We can talk tomorrow,' she said desperately.

Unable to bear any more, she fled blindly—and collided with a man entering through the front door. She began to fall, nearly taking him down with her.

'I'm sorry—' she gasped.

'No, *I'm* sorry,' Vittorio said, holding her firmly.

'Come back here,' Rik snapped, reaching out to take her arm in a fierce grip.

'Let me go!' she cried.

'I'll let you go when you do what you're paid to do.'

The last word ended on a yelp that burst from him at the feel of Vittorio's hand gripping his wrist.

'Let her go,' ordered Vittorio.

'Who the hell do you think you are?' Rik wailed.

'I said let her go, and you'd better do so if you know what's good for you.' Vittorio's voice was harsh and unrelenting.

Jackie felt Rik's painful grip on her arm loosen, until she was able to free herself.

A glance back at Rik showed he was scowling. She hurried away, following Vittorio, who put his arm protectively around her.

'Sorry about that,' he said. 'I didn't mean to get you in trouble with your boss.'

'Don't blame yourself.' She sighed. 'He's always like that.'

'I'm afraid I tripped you.'

'No, I tripped *you*. I wasn't looking where I was going.'

'But you stumbled. Are you sure you aren't hurt? I thought you might have twisted your ankle.'

'Just a little.'

'You should sit down. Let's go into the café.'

Once inside, he took her to a table in the corner, summoned the waiter and ordered coffee. When it was served he took a deep breath.

'*Signorina*—'

'My name's Jacqueline Benton. People call me Jackie.'

'Thank you—Jackie.'

'You called me *signorina*. Are you Italian?' She sounded hopeful.

'Yes, my name is Vittorio.'

She seemed pleased at the discovery. Smiling, she offered her hand. '*Buon giorno*, Vittorio.'

'*Buon giorno*, Jackie.'

'I really thank you for what you did—rescuing me from Rik.'

'He must be a nightmare to work for. But I guess you're out of a job now.'

'Probably not. You're right—he *is* a nightmare. But things like that have happened before. He always apologises afterwards.'

'He *what*? I find that hard to believe.'

'So do I, in a way. But if I left it would be hard for him to find someone who'd put up with his horrible behaviour while knowing the place as well as I do.'

'So he knows how to act for his own benefit?' Vittorio said wryly.

'Oh, yes. Mind you, I suppose you could say that of everyone. We all do what suits us, and we don't really think about anyone else's feelings.'

He knew an uneasy moment. Was it possible that she suspected the truth about his arrival?

But she was smiling pleasantly, and he told himself not to panic.

'I find it hard to believe that of you,' he said gently.

'Oh, I can be selfish when it suits me.' She gave him a cheeky smile. 'You wouldn't *believe* the lengths I go to just to get my own way.'

He smiled back, charmed by her impish humour.

'I'll believe whatever you care to tell me,' he said. 'But you don't need to go to any great lengths. Just say what you want and I'll take care of it.'

That could be quite a temptation, she thought, remembering what she had read on the astrology site.

The fates are planning a startling new beginning for you. The sun in Jupiter will bring things you never anticipated...

Certainly she hadn't anticipated a charming, handsome man declaring himself at her service.

Watching her face, Vittorio managed to read her expression fairly well. He guessed she was trying decide how much fun they might have teasing each other.

And it might be *really* good fun, he thought. As well as humour there was a warmth in her eyes that tempted him to move closer.

'Rik said a man was asking after my father,' she said. 'Was that you?'

'Yes. I was sorry to hear that he was dead.'

'Why are you looking for him?'

Vittorio hesitated, sensing the approach of danger. Suddenly he was reluctant to disturb the delightful atmosphere between them.

'My own father knew him several years ago,' he said carefully.

'How did they meet? Did your father try to sell him some Italian goods for the shop?'

'No, he wasn't a salesman. He was Count Martelli.'

He waited for her to react with delight to hearing his status, as he was used to, but she only said ironically, 'A count? You're the son of a *count*? Are you kidding?'

'No, I'm not. And, since my father has died, I *am* the Count.'

She burst into a delicious chuckle. 'You must think I'm so gullible.'

'Why don't you believe me?'

'Because my father never once mentioned knowing a *count*—or even admitted meeting one. I just can't imagine that my father was ever friends with an aristocrat, not when we were so poor.'

'Was he really poor? He managed to start his own business.'

'He borrowed a lot of money to buy the shop. And it was a big mistake. He never really made the profit he needed, and we always lived on the edge of poverty.'

'That must have been a very sad life for you,' Vittorio said uneasily.

'Not for me as much as for him. It destroyed his marriage to my mother. She left him for another man. For years Daddy and I had only each other. I adored him. He was a lovely man…sweet-natured, generous. I went to work in the shop, to help him. It wasn't the life I'd planned—I'd dreamed of going to university. But I couldn't abandon him. And in the end he was forced to sell. Rik beat him down on the price, but he offered me a job and let us go on living there. I did all I could for Daddy, but it wasn't enough. A couple of years ago he had a heart attack.'

Vittorio dropped his head, staring at the floor. In his

worst nightmares he'd never imagined anything as bad as this. If George Benton had received the money that should have been his everything would have been different for him. He might even be alive now.

What would she say when he told her?

He clenched his fists, trying to find the courage to do the right thing.

But his courage failed him, and to his relief the waiter appeared.

'We're about to close, sir.'

'Then I guess we have to go,' he said hurriedly, trying not to sound too relieved.

It was dark outside. He walked Jackie to the shop door and waited, wondering if she would invite him in. But she only said, 'I'm glad we met. It was nice to have coffee.'

'Yes, it was. Jackie…' He hesitated, uncertain how to go on.

'Yes?'

'Nothing. Perhaps we can—see each other again. I'd like to talk.'

'So would I. Tomorrow?'

'I'll look in.'

She went inside, locking the door behind her. For some moments Vittorio stood in silence, trying to come to a troubling decision.

He should have told her everything, but he knew the truth would hurt her greatly. He felt that in his heart, and flinched from striking that blow.

He'd planned every step of the way how he would confront George Benton, explain, apologise, and draw a line under it. Instead he found himself confronted with a woman whose sweetness and vulnerability touched his heart. And the truth was he didn't know how to respond.

After standing there hopelessly for several minutes he turned and hurried away into the darkness.

CHAPTER TWO

NEXT MORNING VITTORIO awoke early. The clock said half past five and suddenly there seemed no point in staying in bed. Showering and dressing quickly, he headed straight out.

It felt good to enjoy the fresh air and the fast-growing light. But then he saw something that alarmed him. A young woman walking away in the distance. It was hard to be certain of details, but she looked strangely like…

Jackie.

Wanting to be sure, he hurried after her, but she turned a corner out of sight.

Cursing, he ran desperately through the streets. He didn't know London at all. It was hopeless, he thought frantically when he found himself by the River Thames. She must be walking along the embankment—but in which direction?

Then luck was with him. After a hundred yards he could see her, sitting on a bench, staring out over the water. He moved closer, struck by the way she seemed sunk in another world. It reminded him of himself the night before.

He stayed silent, unsure whether it was right for him to disturb her, but after a moment she glanced up.

'Vittorio? What are you doing up this early?' she asked.

'I couldn't sleep so I thought I'd stretch my legs. How are you this morning, Jackie? Are you worried about facing Rik today?'

'I'm fine—honestly.'

'Forgive me, but I don't think you are.' He lifted her chin with his fingers, looking at her face. 'You've been crying.'

'Just a little.'

He put his arms round her, overtaken by a desire to care for her. Protectiveness was a feeling he'd seldom, if ever, known before, and now it was almost alarming. He had to tell her something that would break her heart, and suddenly he wasn't sure that he could do it.

'Hold on to me,' he whispered. 'It'll be all right.'

'Sometimes I think things will *never* be all right,' she said. 'I'm sorry to dump all this on you, but I can't talk about Daddy without—'

'Without remembering all the bad things that happened to him?'

'I don't know why, Vittorio, but I feel I could tell you anything.'

She looked up again and the sight of her vulnerable face swept him with a desire to kiss her. He yielded—but only to lay his lips on her forehead.

'Do you want to tell me any more?' he murmured.

'You can't want to hear such a terrible story,' she said.

She was more right than she could imagine, he thought wretchedly. But he owed it to her to listen.

'You can tell me *anything*, Jackie.'

She brushed the tears aside from her face. 'I don't really know what to say… It isn't my tragedy.'

'In a way it is. You lost too. You wanted to go to university. What did you want to study?'

'I wanted to study languages. They just seem to come easily to me.'

He regarded her wryly.

'Buon per te, signorina. La maggior parte delle persone non possono far fronte con le lingue.'

He spoke in Italian. His words meant, 'Good for you *signorina*. Most people can't cope with languages.'

'Italian is the language I manage best,' she said. 'I took a few classes at night school, because we were planning to take a holiday there together. My father longed to travel to Italy. He'd been there once as a young man.'

'Did he tell you a lot about his visit?'

'Yes, he said it was such fun.'

'Did he never mention meeting my father?' he asked.

'He mentioned an Italian friend, but said nothing at all about him being a *count*! They met in Italy and then again in England a few weeks later. From what Daddy said I gather they got on really well and enjoyed each other's company.'

Vittorio nodded. 'Yes I remember Papà saying something like that—I gather they had quite a few adventures together whilst he was there.'

'Daddy said things like that too. He had such a lovely time with his Italian friend. Only then—' She checked herself.

'Then?' Vittorio said tensely. He had an uneasy feeling that he knew what was coming.

'Then suddenly it was all over. One day they were close buddies—the next day his friend disappeared. He left a note but it didn't say much. Just *Goodbye my friend. Franco*'. No address, nothing. Daddy couldn't contact him and he never heard from him again. It left him very unhappy after what they'd been to each other.'

'He told you that? Didn't he tell you any more about who the man was?'

'No, just that his name was Franco. If he'd known more he'd have told me, I'm sure. Maybe your father never let him know that he was a count?'

'Maybe…' he murmured.

Their eyes met, and what Jackie saw took her breath away. There was an intensity in his gaze as though nothing but herself existed in the world. It was something she'd never seen in any man's eyes before, and she became suddenly conscious of the soft thump of her own heartbeat.

'Jackie—' Vittorio checked himself, unsure how to continue. This was taking more courage than he had anticipated.

'What's the matter?' she asked. 'Are you all right?'

'I'm fine—but there's something I must—'

She felt a sudden sense of brilliant illumination—as though the clouds had parted on a rainy day. She'd hardly dared to hope that the vibrant attraction that possessed her possessed him too, but now she let herself wonder if perhaps it did.

A memory returned to her. That astrology prediction had said, *The fates are planning a startling new beginning for you. The sun in Jupiter will bring things you never anticipated, and decisions that will change your life.*

It was happening. This was the great moment that fate had planned for her. Now surely he would tell her how their meeting had affected his heart, and that was something her own heart longed to know.

She clasped his hand between hers.

'Whatever you have to say, I know I'll like it,' she breathed. 'We've understood each other from the first moment, and—'

'Yes…' he murmured. 'Yes—*yes*—'

He knew the next few minutes would be tense, but something in her seemed to reach out to him, drawing him into a circle of warmth such as he'd never known before. It was what he needed most in all the world, and he knew a moment of fear lest his revelation ruin things between them.

He raised her hands and brushed his lips against them. 'I hope so much that you're right,' he said. 'But you can't imagine—'

'I think I can. Daddy always said you had to be ready for the unexpected.' She met his eyes, her own full of happiness and hope. 'And I'm ready for anything. Say it, Vittorio, and you might like my answer.'

He drew a sharp breath. Now the moment had come when he must find the courage to tell her everything.

But the sight of her eyes shining up at him caused his courage to fail. Suddenly he could see how that light would fade when she knew the terrible truth behind her father's suffering. The thought of her pain made him shudder, and he knew he could not force himself to speak.

'I have to go,' he said uneasily.

'What? But—'

'I'm expecting an important phone call. I have to get back to the hotel.'

He rose to his feet and she followed him reluctantly. Suddenly a moment filled with magic had dissolved into nothing, leaving her desolate.

As they walked back beside the river it began to drizzle.

'Better get back quickly, before it really starts to rain,' he said.

They hurried the rest of the way, until they reached the shop.

'I'll see you again soon,' he said. 'We'll talk then. Take care of yourself.'

Then he fled, devoured by thoughts whose bitterness was aimed accusingly at himself. He was no better than a coward!

His own words came back to him.

You can never tell what fate has in store for you.

It was more true than he could have dreamed. His plan for this meeting had never included the desire to hold her, comfort her, protect her—do anything rather than hurt her. It had overtaken him without warning, reducing him to helplessness. And there was no turning back.

Inside the shop, Jackie hurried up the stairs and looked

out of the window in time to see Vittorio vanish around the corner.

She sighed sadly. It was obvious what had happened. He'd been about to kiss her but had changed his mind at the last moment.

Did he want her or not? He had seemed to be trying to tell her something without words. Had she misunderstood him? But he *had* seemed on the verge of telling her something.

What could it possibly be?

She busied herself opening up the shop. Saturdays were always busy. But somehow she couldn't get stop thinking about him. He was there in her mind, his eyes glowing with a look that made her heart beat faster.

Next day was Sunday, which meant the shop was closed. Fearful of missing her, Vittorio hurried there early. He'd lost his nerve the day before, but he couldn't risk losing it again.

A window opened above him and a voice said coolly, 'Good morning, Vittorio.'

Jackie was looking down at him.

'Morning!' he cried, smiling brightly. 'Can you come down?'

'I'm not sure—'

'Please, Jackie, it's important. We really have to talk.'

'We could have talked yesterday.'

'*Please.*'

'All right. I'll just be a moment.'

She hurried down, full of hope that her tense wait would be over. He seemed to have come close and then retreated, and now she couldn't bear any more. It *must* be the dream she'd longed for. They had known each other such a little time, but what did time matter when their hearts reached out to each other?

Perhaps his feelings were stronger than he'd known before, which was why he feared expressing them. But she would open her arms and her heart to him and they would both know happiness.

As soon as she appeared downstairs he put his arm about her shoulders.

'Let's have some breakfast in the café. It's nice and comfortable in there.'

'And we can talk,' she said eagerly.

When they were settled she waited for him to speak, but again he felt silent, as though attacked by doubt at the last moment. Her heart sank. Her hopes had risen so high. She couldn't bear to lose them again.

'Vittorio, please tell me,' she said. 'Whatever is on your mind I can tell it's important.'

'Yes, it is…' he said hesitantly.

'Then please be brave and say it. Are you afraid of what I'll say?'

'I might be,' he said. 'I don't think you can imagine—'

She touched his face. 'Tell me, Vittorio. Let's get it out between us and then tell each other how we feel.'

'Yes,' he murmured. 'You're right. Do you remember—?'

'Remember?'

'How we talked about our fathers yesterday.'

'Yes, I remember, but—'

'I should have told you then. It's a terrible story, Jackie, but I have to tell you. Your father once placed a bet that won a million pounds.'

'But that can't be true! He'd have told me—we'd never have been in the situation we found ourselves in if that had been the case.'

'He didn't know. My father and yours were out together one night. Your father got tipsy, and he was dozing when the results were announced. When he awoke my *papà* had taken the winnings and kept them.'

Jackie had a terrible feeling of having crash-landed. The words reeled in her head. Only one thing was clear.

This wasn't what she'd expected to hear.

'What on earth are you saying?' she demanded. 'You *can't* mean that he didn't tell Daddy he'd won? That would be dishonest, and surely—'

'It was the only dishonest thing he ever did, and it tormented him. He told me about it just before he died.'

'Is this—this what you've been trying to say?' she stammered.

'Yes, it took me this long to pluck up the courage to tell you that my family has damaged yours. I'm sure you'll find it hard to forgive. Right at this minute you probably hate me.'

That was closer to the truth than he could possibly know. As her dreams collapsed, leaving her in the middle of a desert, she felt a terrifying rage begin to take her over.

'There's something else I have to tell you,' Vittorio said. 'I'm not sure how it will make you feel.'

'Try me,' she whispered, with a faint flicker of renewed hope.

'Papà made me promise to find your father and sort things out.'

'Sort things out? What do you mean by that?'

'I planned to give him the money Papà took from him. A million pounds. I hoped it would make everything all right.'

She stared at him, barely able to believe what she was hearing.

'You hoped *what*?' she said furiously. 'You really hoped things could be made *"all right"* after so many years? After Daddy suffered so much from poverty and it made his wife abandon him? After the way he died in despair? You can't give him your money *now*.'

'But I can give it to you.'

'You think that will make his suffering *all right*?'

'I didn't mean it that way,' Vittorio said tensely.

'Oh, yes, you did. You think money can solve everything—but when a man's dead it can't solve anything at all. You don't understand that, do you? Hand over a cheque and everything's settled! Maybe that's true in business, but not in real life. But you don't know anything about real life.'

'Jackie, please—let me explain. I only want to—'

'You only want to make yourself feel good.'

'I don't think money solves everything, but I'd like to pay the debt my family owes.'

'This is a con. Do you *really* expect me to believe that you can hand over a million pounds, just like that?'

'You think I don't have that much? You're wrong. My father didn't waste the million he gained.'

'You mean the million he *stole*,' she raged.

'Very well—he stole it. But he wanted to pay it back. He invested it successfully, so that it made several more millions. I can give you back every penny—plus a few thousand for interest.'

'Oh, you think it's so easy, don't you? I wouldn't take money from you if I was starving. This conversation is at an end.' She stood up. 'And don't you dare follow me.'

He'd reached out a hand to stop her, but something fierce in her manner made him draw back.

'Please—' he began.

'No. Don't you understand? *No!*'

She fled, fearful lest her true feelings become too plain. Instead of the loving emotion she'd hoped for he'd offered her *money*. If she'd stayed a moment longer she was afraid she might have done something violent.

Her departure left Vittorio in a state of total confusion and misery. Nothing had worked out as he'd intended. He'd failed to fulfil his father's dying wish. Guilt tore at him.

He paid his bill and went out into the street, walking back in the direction of the shop. There was no sign of her.

There was nothing to do but return to the hotel and do some serious thinking about what he was going to do next.

But he found that serious thinking was very little help in a situation he didn't understand.

The rest of Jackie's day and night was tormented. The incredible events of the morning whirled through her brain, and at the end of the day—even though she was exhausted and wrung out when she finally got to bed—she couldn't sleep. Instead she sat up in bed and opened the laptop she always kept with her.

She did a search on 'Count Martelli'. She was half ready to learn that he didn't exist, that the whole thing had been a con, and for a moment it seemed that her suspicions were correct. The picture that appeared on the screen was of a man in his sixties.

He's lying, she thought furiously. *That's the real Count.* But then she saw the text.

Count Franco Martelli, taken just before his death four weeks ago. His heir is his son, Vittorio Martelli, latest in a line stretching back five hundred years.

She clicked the link marked 'Count Vittorio Martelli' and and at once saw a photograph of the man she recognised. There was no doubt.

Her temper surged once more at the memory of Vittorio trying to pay her off to assuage his family's guilt. But had she been too hasty? Had she let her temper get the better of her once again?

Vivid in her mind was the memory of her father's suffering. He'd tried to put on a brave face for her sake, but he hadn't always been able to manage it. Often she had found him in tears. He'd smiled and reassured her, but over time she had come to understand the problems. Her heart had broken for him. She had become his comforter, intent on giving him some kind of happiness.

But the last year of her father's life had been the saddest she had ever known. She still wept when she remembered his suffering.

Vittorio thought money was the answer to everything!

And yet she knew there was another reason for her rage. When she remembered how her hopes of winning Vittorio's feelings had risen, and then been smashed to the ground, she felt capable of murder.

He had just been playing a game until he had what suited him. He hadn't spared a thought as to what it was doing to *her*.

So accept the money, said a voice in her head. *He offered you a million—more than a million with interest.*

Because he thought it would put right what his father had done. If he wasn't such a heartless monster he'd know that nothing could *ever* make it right.

What would her father have done? If he were still alive it would be so different. Then of course they would have accepted the money. It would have been his due. But now he was gone would it be right for her to accept it on his behalf?

She closed the laptop and went back to bed. At last she managed to nod off, sinking into a deep and dreamless sleep.

Vittorio's night had also been troubled. He'd fallen asleep easily, but found his dreams haunted by Jackie's contempt until they were practically nightmares that woke him in a cold sweat.

He rose out of bed. He had no desire to go back to sleep lest the alarming female return to torment him. Day was breaking and he felt the need of a fresh air. Dressing hastily, he went downstairs and out into the street.

His thoughts were full of the promise he'd made to

his beloved father. Come what might he *had* to make this right—for everyone's sake.

Almost at once the shop came in sight. It was time for it to be open, so he went closer and looked through the glass door, but he could see no sign of anyone. Moving quietly, he opened the door and slipped inside. At once he heard the sound of voices coming from deep within. One was Jackie's, and the other he recognised as the weasely boss who had appeared during his first visit. His voice was raised in annoyance.

'Jackie, you're *mad*. You should have got all you could out of the Count and then invested in this place. I could do with some money to cover the debts. You could have helped me out and you just turned it down? How could you be so *stupid*?'

She replied in a voice filled with rage that reminded Vittorio of the way she'd spoken to him with equal fury during last night.

'You think I should have taken his money and used it for *your* convenience?' she raged at Rik. 'I'm not *that* stupid.'

Vittorio stepped a little closer, careful to keep out of sight but wanting to hear everything.

'You just can't recognise reality when it's under your nose,' came Rik's reply. 'You had the chance of a fortune. You could have taken it. But perhaps your fantasies are fixed on something else.'

'What does that mean?'

'It's *him*, isn't it? You refused his money because you're hoping for a better offer! You think you can lure him into marriage, but you're wasting your time. A man like that wouldn't marry *you* in a million years.'

'And I wouldn't marry *him* in a million years. He's cold—and arrogant enough to think that money can solve anything.'

Vittorio made a wry face. A wise man would have slipped

away at this moment, but he didn't feel wise. He felt as though Jackie had seized him and was holding him at her mercy in whirls of confusion.

'It can solve a great deal,' he heard Rik say. 'It could pay a lot of my debts—many of which are *your* fault.'

'How can you say that?'

'If you did a better job this shop would be doing well, instead of sinking into debt.'

'The shop was in a bad way when my father sold it to you. That's how you got it so cheap. I heard you—beating him down on the price when he was too weak to fight you.'

'Don't try to blame me for your father's failings. Luckily it's not too late. You've still got time to find this Italian Count and tell him you'll take the money.'

'You think I'd—? You're mad.'

'I'm *telling* you to do it.'

'And I'm telling *you* to go to hell.'

'I warn you, Jackie, you're walking a very fine line. Perhaps I'd better see him myself—'

'Perhaps you should,' Vittorio said, stepping out so that they could see him.

Rik noticed him first, and the shock on his face alerted Jackie, so that she looked behind her, also appalled at the discovery.

Rik assumed a severe manner. 'We have business to discuss,' he said.

'The only business we have is for you to listen to what I have to say,' Vittorio said bluntly. 'For you—not a penny.'

'But you have a debt to pay,' Rik squealed.

'Not to *you*.'

'Jackie, tell him,' Rik whined. 'Tell him he's got to pay you what he owes you.'

Jackie looked intently at Vittorio, but did not speak.

'Do it now,' Rik snapped. 'Let me hear you say it.'

'I have nothing to say,' she replied coldly. 'The Count's

debt is impossible to repay.' She met Vittorio's gaze and said emphatically, *'Ever!'*

Rik looked from one to the other, scowling.

'So *that's* it,' he raged. 'You two are in this together. As soon as I'm out of earshot you'll take the money and cut me out.'

'You can't be cut out because you were never *in*,' Jackie said fiercely. 'You bought this business fair and square, and any debts are now your responsibility. Besides, I will never take a penny of his money.'

'You're insane!' Rik seethed. 'What kind of fool turns down that sort of money? Well, if money's of no importance to you then you won't be needing this job. *Or* the accommodation I've provided for you. You're fired. I'll give you one hour to clear out your stuff from upstairs.'

Rik stormed out, pausing at the front door.

'One hour!' he yelled. 'I mean it.'

Then he was gone, slamming the door behind him.

Vittorio turned swiftly to Jackie. 'Good riddance.' he said. 'Forget him. He isn't worth bothering with.'

Jackie was shaken, but determined to maintain her dignity. 'How long were you there, listening?'

'I came to see you and arrived just as you were telling him what had happened.'

'I never meant to tell him, but he made me so angry that I said it to knock the smile off his face. I could have strangled him.' She gave a bitter laugh. 'I'd have enjoyed that.'

'Don't worry. He's bound to give you another excuse. He's a pig, Jackie, and you're better off without him.'

'But this isn't just my *job*. I've lived here all my life and now I've lost my home, too.'

'Then we must find you another one. Get packing and we'll be out of here—fast.'

'I've nowhere to go.'

'Trust me to arrange that.'

She knew an instinct to rebel against him. This catastrophe had happened only because he'd come to England and caused trouble. Now she'd lost her job and her home, and he was to blame.

But was he really? If she hadn't been silly enough to tell Rik about the money this wouldn't have happened. When was she going to learn to control her temper?

Never, she thought fiercely.

'Let's get you out of here,' Vittorio said. He took her arm and ran up the stairs with her and began opening drawers and cupboards, working hard to help her.

'Is that your only suitcase?' he asked, regarding the one she had produced.

'Yes, but I've got some plastic bags.'

Luckily the bags proved enough to take her few possessions.

'Anything else?' he asked at last.

'No, that's all.'

'You have nothing else?' he asked, looking astonished.

'This is all I need,' she said defiantly.

He gave her an odd look, as though wondering what madness had made her refuse his money when she seemed to own so little, but all he said was, 'Then let's go.'

She looked around nervously as they went downstairs, but there was no sign of Rik.

'Where are we going?' she asked as they went out into the street.

'I'm staying in the Davien Hotel, a couple of streets away. We'll get you a room there for tonight, then make our plans.'

She knew the hotel. It had a reputation as being costly.

'I don't think it's quite the right place for me,' she said uneasily.

'If you're worried about the money, don't be. I'm paying. I landed you in this mess and it's my responsibility to get you out.'

Suddenly she recalled Rik's warning to her. He'd suggested that Vittorio was hoping to lure Jackie into bed with the empty promise of a great fortune.

Suddenly she was uneasy. Was that why Vittorio was taking her to his hotel at his own expense? Did he mean her to share his bed?

Only recently that thought would have excited her. Vittorio attracted her powerfully. The thought of lying with him in bed would have been a pleasure. But now everything was different. Was he trustworthy? Could she be sure?

A short walk brought them to the hotel. Vittorio went to Reception and chatted with the woman there as she typed something onto the keyboard. Nodding to her, he headed back to Jackie.

'I've managed to secure you a room on the second floor.'

He escorted her upstairs, leading her to a door for which he had the key. She held her breath.

But when the door opened she knew she'd done him an injustice. There was only one single bed.

'Th-thank you,' she stammered.

'If you need me I'm three doors along the corridor.'

He departed at once, leaving her standing alone, trying to take in everything that had happened. Only yesterday she had quarrelled with this man, and today he had come to her rescue and she had accepted his help gladly.

It doesn't make any sense, she mused.

But nothing had made sense since she'd met him. Perhaps nothing ever would again.

He returned just as she finished putting her things away.

'They do a good lunch here,' he said. 'I'll have some sent up.'

'Couldn't we eat downstairs in the restaurant?'

'Do I make you feel nervous, Jackie? Are you afraid to be alone with me?'

'Of course not,' she said uneasily. 'I have no feelings about you one way or the other, actually,' she lied bravely.

'So you didn't mean it when you said you wouldn't marry me in a million years? Or the bit about me being cold and arrogant and a person who thinks money can solve anything?'

For a moment it was as though her worst nightmares were coming true. But then she saw he was grinning, and that his eyes were full of friendly humour.

'Forget it,' he said. 'People say things in the heat of the moment. And it's not far different from what you said to me yesterday. But it's time we drew a line under that. We have to work matters out between us and be friends—if that's possible.'

It was still embarrassing to know that he'd heard her, but his unexpected humour made it bearable.

'So—can I have some food sent up?' he asked.

'Are you asking my permission?'

Again he gave her a cheeky grin. 'Isn't that what you prefer a man to do?'

'Stop trying to make me sound like a bully.'

'Not a bully. Just a woman who knows her own mind— as Rik would tell us after the way you stood up to him. He's a nasty bully, but you really dealt with him.'

'Yes—and that was so successful that now I've got to start looking for another job and a home.'

'But where? You'll never get another job around here. He'll make sure of that.'

She groaned, recognising that Vittorio was right. Rik would spread the word that she was unreliable, destroying her prospects.

'I still feel that I owe you any help I can persuade you to accept,' Vittorio said.

'You have a job to offer me?'

'Not here, but in Italy. I could find many opportunities for you there. Why not come back with me?'

CHAPTER THREE

JACKIE STARED AT him in disbelief. 'Italy? Did I hear right?'

'Dead right. I want you to work for me in my family's department store in Rome. Your talents will be valuable.'

'But I've only ever worked in a little shop. I'd be useless in a department store.'

'Not in our glass and china section. It's a new department, and it isn't doing brilliantly because nobody really understands it. But you could bring it to life and make it profitable.'

'According to Rik, I was lousy at making profits.'

'Were you? Or did *he* make a lot of stupid decisions?'

'Yes, he buys all the wrong stuff.'

'So I can rely on you to buy all the *right* stuff?'

'Mightn't the language be a problem? I never got to finish my Italian course at night school. I had to stop when Daddy became ill.'

'A lot of people there speak English. Some of our customers are tourists, and your English would be a blessing to them. Your Italian seems already pretty good, and you can work to improve it.'

'It's very kind of you—' she began uneasily.

'No, it isn't. I'm not being kind. I'm a businessman and I'm doing what any sensible businessman does—turning the situation to my own advantage. I could make a lot of money out of you, and I'm not passing up the chance to do that.'

'But how—?'

'You won't just have that one department. I want you to cast your expert eye over the whole store and tell me how it looks to you—because that will tell me how it looks to our customers. Tourists are profitable, and you can help me attract plenty of them. And it could open some new doors for you, Jackie. I'll pay you a decent wage—far more than Rik paid you—and you'll have a position of authority.'

Authority. The word seemed to sing in her ears. This would truly be a new, more satisfying life—exactly what she had longed for. Again she had the mysterious feeling that Vittorio could read her mind.

'Authority?' she echoed. 'Do you really mean that?'

'You'd be in charge of your department. You'd have a team that would take your orders. Or don't you feel up to giving orders?'

'Oh, yes, I do. That was always my problem with Rik. And with my father too sometimes. He complained that I argued with him too much.' She gave a brief laugh.

'Don't worry. When you're working for me you can give all the orders you want. I'll make it clear to the team that *you're* the boss. You need never fear another bully like Rik.'

It sounded too good to be true, she thought, trying to suppress a flicker of confusion. Knowing the terrible truth about how her father had been treated had made hostility flare between them, but there were other feelings too— some warmer, some interested, all confusing.

But what else could she do? Where else was there for her to go? What other life was possible for her? It was as if all other doors had slammed shut and fate was driving her irresistibly into this man's power.

Surely she could take advantage of the situation, just as *he* planned to do?

Here was a chance to learn new skills and gain new experiences that might open up a world of fresh opportunities for her.

'All right,' she said in a daze. 'I'll go to Italy with you.'

'Good thinking. I knew I could rely on you.'

She ventured to say, 'You mean because I've agreed with you?'

'What else? That's my definition of good thinking. So, now there's nothing to hold you back we can go tomorrow. I'll book two tickets.'

After booking the tickets Vittorio ordered a meal and a bottle of wine from room service.

'After this I must attend to some business matters. I suggest you relax for the rest of the afternoon, and then I think we should both get an early night,' he said, adding in a teasing voice, 'In our separate rooms, I promise.'

'Stop teasing,' she said cheerfully. 'I wasn't thinking that.'

'Good. Then we can both relax.'

'Of course. We agree to be friends. That's all.'

'Friends…' he mused. 'What kind of friends? Best friends?'

'We'll have to wait and see.'

She was right. Friendship was their only hope. Had she really feared lest he come to her door? After their argument the day before he could well believe that she didn't want him. His own feelings for her were less clear.

Officially they were enemies, and his instinct to protect her was troublesome.

She was becoming important to him in ways that confused him. Perhaps soon he would understand them. For the moment he preferred to wait and see what fate had in store.

He lifted his glass of wine in her direction.

'Here's to you,' he said. 'You don't know how much I'm going to rely on you.'

And it was true, he thought. She didn't.

It was a quiet meal, with very little talk. Instinctively

they both knew that for the moment enough had been said. Perhaps too much.

At the earliest moment they finished eating.

'And now I really must get on with some work. I'll head back to my room, but if you think of anything else you need today please call through.'

He bade her a polite good day, and left.

Returning to his room, he recalled something he'd meant to say to her, and hurried back to see her.

A surprise awaited him. He looked out into the corridor just in time to see her getting into the elevator and the doors closing.

Where on earth could she be going? he thought frantically. Surely not to talk to Rik?

There was no hope of catching up with the elevator. He went to his window and looked down. There she was, walking away along the road, and then turning through a large gate that he knew led to a church.

Every cautious instinct told him to stay where he was—not to follow her. But something about Jackie always overcame caution.

In a moment he was out of the door, hurrying until he reached the church gate.

Inside was a cemetery. As he watched she approached a tombstone and knelt before it. He was too far away to make out the name, but he could hear Jackie saying urgently, 'I'm sorry, Daddy. I really am.'

So this was Benton's grave, and she had come here to talk to him. Vittorio backed away, unwilling to invade her privacy, but he couldn't help hearing her next words.

'I don't really trust him. I'd like to, but he doesn't understand what a terrible thing was done to you, and that makes him almost as much of an enemy as his father. But I must go to Italy. I'll come back, I promise. Only forgive me. Please, *please* forgive me.'

As watched she pressed her lips to the stone, then leaned against it, sobbing.

Torn by the instinct to comfort her, he took a step closer—but stopped just in time. Whatever happened, she mustn't know he was there. He had an unnerving feeling… as though he'd been suddenly stranded on a desert island. He hadn't expected this, and the sensation of being caught unprepared was alarming.

He backed off and hurried away, haunted by her words—

I don't trust him… Almost as much of an enemy as his father…

If that was how she thought of him he supposed he couldn't blame her. But it hurt more than he would have expected.

Back at the hotel, he returned to his room and went to the window, hoping to see her return. But hours passed with no sign of her and his heart sank. Where had she vanished to *now*? What trouble might she have fallen into? Had she changed her mind about accompanying him to Italy?

Then a noise from the corridor made him hurry outside. She was there, turning the key in her lock.

'There you are,' he said with relief.

'Were you looking for me? I'm sorry I vanished. I just had to— Well, never mind.'

He hesitated. All his cautious instincts warned him to keep the secret, but the need to be honest with her was greater.

At last he said, 'You just had to say goodbye to your father.'

She stared at him. 'How do you know?'

'I saw you.'

'But how?'

'I followed you to the cemetery.'

She gasped with outrage. 'You *followed* me? How *dare* you?'

She stormed into her room and tried to close the door, but he reached out to keep it open.

'Let me come in,' he said.

'I'd rather you didn't. In fact I'd rather you vanished off the face of the earth.'

'Well, I'm sure you'll eventually think of a way of making that happen. But for the moment we need to talk. Let me in, Jackie. *Please.*'

Furiously, she turned away. He followed her in, closing the door behind him.

'Don't judge me, Jackie—please. I'm not stalking you. I followed you because I'm concerned about you. You seemed so lonely, walking, and when you reached the grave…' He paused, feeling desperate. 'You cried so terribly. I wanted to take you in my arms and comfort you. I didn't because I knew you'd be angry that I was there. I went away. I wasn't sure that was the right thing to do, but I don't seem to get anything right these days. The more I try, the more wrong I get it. But I'm glad I was with you for a few minutes. I think I understand you better now.'

He saw a strange, slightly puzzled look come into her face.

'Yes, that surprises you, doesn't it?' he said. 'I'm the last person you'd expect to understand you.'

'People don't easily understand other people,' she murmured.

'But I think we manage it. We must talk about that another time. For now, please just tell me that you believe I meant no harm and you forgive me.'

'All right,' she said reluctantly. 'I realise you didn't mean it badly.'

'And I'm forgiven? Please Jackie. Let me hear you say it. *Please.*'

She drew a sharp breath, stunned by the desperation in

his voice and the intensity in his eyes. There was no way she could refuse this man anything he asked for.

'I forgive you,' she said.

'And you mean it?'

'Yes—*yes*—'

'As long as you *do* mean it. Things could so easily go wrong between us—but we won't let that happen. Best if you go to bed now and have a good night's sleep. Tomorrow will be a busy day. Goodnight.'

'Goodnight.'

Before leaving he turned to look back at her once more. Jackie tried to understand his expression, but there was something about it that confused her.

Nor was that the only thing about him so unexpected that she could hardly believe it. The way he'd almost begged her for forgiveness had startled her, revealing a side of him she'd never suspected.

She was glad to lie down. She needed sleep, but for some reason it didn't come. It was alarming that he'd been there while she spoke to her father. Had he heard her say that she didn't trust him?

She lay still, listening for the sound of his footsteps outside, wondering if they would return to her door. But nothing happened.

At last the silence seemed to overwhelm her and she fell asleep.

As Vittorio had said, they rose early next day and were soon ready to leave.

'You won't be insulted if I pay your bill, will you?' he asked as they went downstairs.

'Would it make any difference if I was?'

He grinned. 'Not the slightest.'

'Then I'd better give in—until I find a way to make you sorry.'

'I'll look forward to that,' he said ironically.

She watched as he went to the reception desk and paid. Then all was ready and they headed for the front door.

But as soon as it was open she saw something that made her stop, frozen with dismay.

'Oh, no!' she groaned.

'What is it?' Vittorio asked. 'Ah, I see. *Him!*'

Rik was standing there, barring their way, his face full of spiteful hilarity.

'So there you are!' he jeered. 'Just as I thought—you stupid woman!'

'You told me to leave so I went,' she said coldly.

'Yes, you went running to *him*. Think you're going to be a countess, do you? Don't kid yourself! He's playing a clever game to stop you suing him for the money his family stole. He'll use you, then throw you out.'

'The only one who's being thrown out is you,' Vittorio said coldly.

Rik gave contemptuous laugh. 'Don't tell me you're taken in by her—? *Argh!*'

The scream was dragged from him by the feel of Vittorio's hand about his neck.

'I know all I need to know about this lady,' Vittorio said harshly. 'But let me tell you something about myself. I'm a man who won't tolerate an insult to a friend, and who'll do anything necessary to make someone sorry they caused trouble. Do you understand me?'

'Yes…' Rik choked.

'Then get out of here while you still can. Otherwise I might do something we'd both regret.'

He released Rik, who staggered away, looking terrified. He gave one last appalled glance at Jackie. Then he fled.

'Are you all right?' Vittorio asked her.

'Yes—fine—thank you.'

In truth she was far from all right. She'd seen yet another

side of Vittorio—one that shocked her. The look in his eyes had been that of a man who would go to any lengths to punish someone who had defied him. She knew it had been in her defence, but that couldn't ease her horror.

'Would you really have hurt him?' she whispered.

'No, of course not. But I had to make him believe that I would. Scare someone enough and you don't need to do anything else to them. Being frank. Isn't that something you've tried yourself.'

'Now and then,' she admitted. 'Not violently, but—'

'But making him believe you know something he doesn't want you to know? I'd give a lot to know how often you've used *that* one.'

'You'll just have to wonder,' she said lightly.

'Congratulations. You're as bad as I am. Shake.'

He held out his hand.

Laughing, she took it. 'I'll never be as bad as you are,' she said. 'But I'm working on it.'

'Perhaps he was right about one thing. *Should* I be afraid of you suing me?'

'Of course not. How can I?'

'I've admitted the theft.'

'It was your father's theft, not yours. And there were no witnesses when you told me. You could just deny it and there'd be nothing I could do.'

'Maybe Rik overheard me?'

'Don't believe anything Rik says—especially that nonsense about me wanting to be a countess.'

'Of course. I know you wouldn't marry me in a million years. I heard you say so yourself, remember?'

'Look, about that… I really am sorry—'

'Don't be sorry. You're not the first woman who's said that about me.' He grinned wryly. 'As you can probably imagine.'

'I'm not going to be tricked into answering that!'

'Very shrewd. I can see you're a real discovery.'

'Because I'm not trying to trap you into marriage? Never fear. You're quite safe from me.'

Was he safe? he wondered. Despite the circumstances, and the fact that she wasn't beautiful, he found her fascinating. She was intriguingly clever and her sharp humour appealed to him.

But more than that was the intense emotion that seemed to reach out from her in a way he couldn't understand. They never spoke of it. There was just a feeling that their mysterious closeness was inevitable, and that it was bound to grow.

The thought made him cautious. Developing warmer feelings for her would put him in her power, and that was something he always strove to avoid.

As the son of a count, he was used to young women pursuing him for the sake of his title. He'd thought himself well protected until the girl who'd once won his heart had betrayed him with the son of a duke. He would never forget the moment he'd discovered them in bed together—or the look she'd bestowed upon him, as though she despised him for daring to hope for her.

That had been several years ago, but the memory stayed with him. Love was unsafe. It caused danger and pain, and a wise man kept his distance.

But life without love did not mean life without marriage. One day he would have to take wife for the sake of producing an heir. His father had spoken of it in the last moments of his life.

'Marisa,' he'd murmured. 'She's perfect for you.'

Marisa was the daughter of a *barone* and an ideal choice for Vittorio's wife—at least according to his father. For a year he'd made his wishes plain. But Vittorio had resisted. He was on good terms with Marisa, but only in a brotherly way. Despite her youth and beauty, she did not attract him. Nor did he want a wife he hadn't chosen for himself.

When he returned to Rome he knew that Marisa and various similar problems would be waiting. But with Jackie's friendship to support him he felt more at ease.

The taxi was waiting to take them to the airport.

'You'll like Rome. Your Italian is good enough to help you feel at home.'

'Do you spend a lot of time in the city?'

'Yes—plenty.'

'But isn't your time taken up with managing your estates?'

'I have to do that as well, of course, but I have an estate manager who handles the difficult stuff. Mostly my time is taken up with the department store.'

'You actually *work* there?'

'Does that surprise you? You think I'm useless for anything except lying around enjoying my title while others do the work?'

'After the way you've rescued me I'm not likely to think you useless.'

He gave her a teasing glance. 'Very tactfully said.'

'Yes, I've got to stay on your right side, haven't I? Why don't you tell me some more about the store so that I can flatter you further?'

'It sells a wide range of goods which I buy from all over the world. You're going to be very valuable to the business. But I've already told you that.'

'Yes, you grabbed me because I could be useful. Sheer cynical self-interest. Just what a businessman needs. Well done.'

They shared a laugh.

'Glad to see you're a realist,' he said. 'Would it be insulting to suggest that you too have some cynical self-interest?'

'No, I'd take it as a compliment.'

'Good for you.'

'Working for you is going to teach me a whole lot of

things that I can use in my future career.' She gave him a thumbs-up sign. 'Here's to cynical self-interest.'

'The most useful motive in the world,' he agreed, making the same gesture.

'Cheers!'

They shook hands.

At last the airport came into view. Soon they were queuing for their flight and boarding the plane.

Jackie was taken aback to discover that Vittorio had booked the most expensive first class seats. But then, why wouldn't he? He was a count and a successful businessman, wasn't he?

'Take the window seat,' he said. 'It's more interesting that way.'

'Is it a long flight?' she asked as the plane began to move slowly down the runway.

'Only two and a half hours.'

Never having flown before, she was nervous. But she managed to stay at ease until take-off, and then gazed out of the window as the ground fell away.

'What will happen when we get there?' she asked.

'We'll be met at the airport by my Aunt Tania. She lives with me and looks after the house. I called her this morning and asked her to prepare a room for you.'

Before she could reply, the plane quivered. She took a sharp, nervous breath and clenched her hands.

'It's all right,' Vittorio said. 'Planes always shake when they go through clouds. We're not going to crash.'

'No—I realise—it's just that—'

'It's just that you're afraid of flying.'

'I've never flown before.'

'Is there anything else bothering you?' he asked, regarding her with concern.

'Just a little headache. It's not too bad.'

He took her hand in his. 'Probably caused by nerves. Don't worry. We'll soon be there.'

CHAPTER FOUR

AT LAST THEY landed at Leonardo da Vinci Airport. They spent a few minutes collecting their bags and then they were able to make their way out. Jackie looked around, trying to come to terms with what was happening.

'Ah, there she is,' Vittorio said suddenly.

He began waving into the distance at a middle-aged woman who was waving back to him. The woman began to run forward and he hastened towards her until they were in each other's arms. Jackie reckoned this must be the Aunt Tania he had mentioned.

She moved a little closer, waiting for him to introduce them. But then his aunt turned aside, revealing a young woman who ran forward and threw herself into Vittorio's arms.

Jackie could see that he was tense. He embraced the girl formally, before standing back and turning to indicate Jackie. She couldn't make out exactly what he was saying, but she gathered it wasn't revealing.

'This is my Aunt Tania,' he told Jackie. 'And my friend Marisa. I've told them that we are planning a business arrangement that has made it necessary for you to see Rome.'

'Welcome to our city,' Aunt Tania said politely. 'Vittorio says you will be staying with us. That will be lovely.'

'Did you give her the best guest room?' Vittorio asked.

'Yes, just as you said. Now, let's go home.'

'Have you got a taxi waiting?'.

'No, Marisa drove me here.'

'And I can drive you home,' Marisa said quickly. 'This way.'

When they reached her car she pulled open the door next to the front passenger seat, indicating for Vittorio to get in beside her. He did so, leaving Jackie and Tania to sit together in the back.

It was a lengthy journey out of the city and through the countryside to the Martelli estate. Jackie studied the scenery, occasionally looking round to find Vittorio's aunt regarding her with curiosity.

'So you're here on business,' Tania said. 'What kind of business are you in?'

She took a sharp breath, caught off-guard, and felt troubled about how to answer.

Vittorio came to her rescue.

'Jackie's a specialist in merchandising,' he said, glancing back over his shoulder. 'What she doesn't know about display and point of sale isn't worth knowing.'

Jackie suppressed an ironic smile at his way of describing her work behind the counter in a little shop.

'So you're going to help my nephew run his business?' Tania queried.

'If I can. And I hope he can teach me something that will be useful,' she said.

To her relief, the subject was allowed to drop. Soon they reached the estate and the car swept through extensive grounds up to a great house.

'We're nearly there,' Vittorio said, pointing out of the car window. 'A little further and you'll see my home.'

As he spoke a large building came into view. Jackie gasped at its elegance and beauty.

'My goodness, it's like a palace!' she gasped.

'My ancestors had rather grandiose ideas. It was a matter of pride for them to live in a splendid home.'

And I bet it took a lot of money to maintain, she thought, forcing some of them into acts of dishonesty.

Perhaps the same thought had occurred to Vittorio, for he fell silent then.

'We only live in small part of it now,' Tania said. 'But we still relish the rest, which has a marvellous history.'

A woman whom Jackie took to be the housekeeper was waiting for them as they left the car and climbed the steps to the front door. Vittorio took the bags.

'I'll take these up to Jackie's room,' he said. 'Come along, Jackie.'

Inside, the building was just as luxurious. In a daze she followed him up the stairs and along a corridor until they reached her room. Like the rest of the house it was luxuriously appointed. A large bed took up most of the space, and the walls were lined with elegant wardrobes.

'The maid will be here to help you unpack,' he said. 'Are you all right? You look as though something's the matter.'

'I'm just confused. I can't get my head around everything that's happening. I've never been anywhere like this before.'

'Don't worry—you'll soon feel at home. I'll see to that.'

The words were kindly spoken, but it flashed across her mind that she could never feel at home in this place, surrounded by a luxury that haunted her with memories of her father's impoverished home.

Marisa appeared in the doorway, followed by a maid.

'This is Gina,' she said. 'She speaks English and she will help you.'

Vittorio patted her shoulder. 'I'll leave you to unpack now and I'll see you at supper.'

He followed Marisa out of the room.

Gina immediately got to work, unpacking the bags and putting things away.

Jackie watched her, trying to believe what was happening.

'Here you have a little bathroom,' Gina said. 'And through these windows you have a wonderful view.'

It was true. She was only one floor up, but looking out onto lawns that soon vanished into trees. The sun was setting, casting a glow ever everything.

'No, no, no!'

The cry from a female voice streamed upwards from below. Leaning out, Jackie was unable to see anyone, but she could tell the sound had come from behind a wall.

'Marisa—'

That was Vittorio. But after that one word he got no further for Marisa exploded again.

'Perche, Vittorio? *Perche?'*

Marisa was talking too fast for Jackie to understand much, but she knew that *perche* meant *why*. It was clear that Marisa was demanding an explanation and Vittorio was trying to make her be quiet.

Jackie recalled the suspicious glances Marisa had given her. Plainly her arrival was unwelcome.

The sound died and she turned back to the room. Gina was a skilled maid with a shrewd eye. She studied Jackie's appearance before casting her glance over several of the clothes.

'You are lucky, *signorina,*' she said. 'You have a slim figure. That is a blessing.'

'Slim?' Jackie brooded. 'That's one way of putting it. In England I've been called skinny—even scrawny.'

'Scusami, signorina. Scrawny?'

'In English it's a way of telling someone they're too thin.'

'No, no,' Gina protested passionately. 'You cannot be too thin for fashion. Rome is a city of great fashion. Everything will be fine for you here—especially when you've bought some new clothes.'

'Oh—well—I don't think I'll be buying new clothes,' Jackie said uneasily.

The maid's words were like a blow, reminding her how little cash she had.

'But you *must*. Everyone will want to meet you.'

'That's true,' said Vittorio from the doorway.

How long had he been standing there? Jackie wondered. How much had he seen and heard?

'My new business associate will make quite an entrance,' he said.

With a slight gesture of his head he dismissed Gina, who left the room.

'New clothes,' he said. 'You do need them. We can make arrangements tomorrow.'

'But I can't. I haven't got any money to buy clothes.'

'You crazy woman! I offered you a million pounds and you chucked it back in my face. Now you're complaining about poverty.'

'I'm not complaining,' she said defiantly. 'I'm being practical.'

'So be practical and accept my offer.'

'*No!* Not that. You don't understand, do you?'

'No—and I don't think you understand your own actions.'

He was wrong, she thought. She completely understood the reasons for her stubborn refusal to yield.

If she accepted the money he would consider the debt settled. And that idea was agony to her. For the sake of her father's memory she would never allow him to do that—however much she might need the money.

'Oh, you really *are* contrary, woman,' he growled.

'What's that supposed to mean?'

'You've hardly got a penny to your name but you turn down the best financial offer you'll ever have and treat me as a villain for making it. That's carrying illogicality to new heights.'

'Not illogicality. Pride. Memory of my father's suffering.'

'You think your father would want you to refuse?'

'Yes, because accepting would be like saying what happened to him doesn't matter.'

'I think he loved you too much for that. I think he'd have been glad to see things get better for you.'

'You— How dare you speak of him like that?'

'I only said he loved you. Didn't he?'

'Yes—with all his heart. But you have no right to make use of him like that.'

'All right, I'll say no more. But think about it, Jackie. What sort of future would he have wanted for you? Prosperous? Or living on the edge of poverty? If he was here now, listening to us, what do you think he'd say to you? *Take every penny and live well.* Or, *Tell him to keep his money and get stuffed. Give yourself the pleasure of kicking him in the teeth. Then live on the edge of poverty.*'

'Stop it!' she cried, backing away from him, hands over her ears. *'Stop it!'*

He reached out and for a moment she thought he would take hold of her. But then he dropped his hand, moving quickly away.

'I'll see you at supper,' he said, and left without another word.

As he closed the door she struggled with the desire to hurl something at it. It was shocking for him to put words into her father's mouth just to suit himself. But there was no doubt that he *was* baffled by her refusal to take his money, and she reckoned the reason was plain. A man so wealthy was used to being able to buy whatever he wanted.

Not just wealthy, she mused. He was handsome also. *Too*

handsome. He must be used to women collapsing at his feet and promising to do anything he wanted.

But not me, Vittorio. You've met the one woman who'll gladly tell you exactly where to go.

She wondered if she'd been wise to come here when their hostility was still acute. But he'd saved her from Rik. She would just have to cope as best she could.

To distract herself, she began going through her possessions.

She soon realised that Gina had put her finger on an unexpected problem when she'd spoken of Rome as being a city of great fashion. None of her clothes were fashionable. At best they might be described as serviceable, with several pairs of jeans and dresses that were plain.

Hurriedly she went through the clothes and found something that might do for the evening meal. It was pale grey, neat and slightly elegant. A few moments in front of the mirror gave her a chance to work on her hair, but she wasn't pleased with the result. Drawn back tightly it merely looked dreary. Left to fall around her face it seemed neglected.

There was a knock at the door and Gina appeared.

'Ah, *signorina*, I know what I can do for you. It will soon be time for supper, so I will take care of your hair.'

She had come prepared with hair tongs, and Jackie watched in awe as Gina turned her severe locks into a bundle of delightful curls.

'Thank you,' she said with feeling. 'It's so nice of you to take so much trouble for me.'

'Signor Vittorio said I was to do everything you needed to help you be at your best. He wants you to be happy.'

'How kind of him.'

Was he being kind, or did he just want to keep her quiet and uncomplaining? she wondered.

A moment later there came a knock on her door, and Vittorio entered.

'Excellent,' he said, regarding her. 'Our guests will be impressed.'

'Guests? Are there many coming?'

'Yes, we've had a few phone calls from friends who want to drop in. It's going to be quite a busy party. Shall we go?'

He held out his arm to her and she took it. Together they left the room and headed along the corridor to the top of the stairs. As they arrived she saw a little crowd gathered in the hall below. There were three middle-aged men and several young women. Most notable among them was Marisa, who stood looking up as they descended.

'Our guests are here already,' Vittorio observed.

When he began the introductions Jackie could hardly believe her ears. Every man seemed to have a title. She managed to pick up the words *duca, visconte, barone...* They exchanged greetings with them, their wives and their elegant young daughters.

Wow, she thought. Cinderella certainly had come to the ball tonight.

She wondered why they were all here. But when she saw how she was being regarded by the younger women a suspicion came over her. It was no accident that they were here. Marisa had clearly spread the word of her arrival, alarming all those who aimed to be the next Contessa.

'Let's go and have something to eat,' Tania said, leading the way into the dining room.

A long table dominated the centre of the room, with twenty places laid out. Vittorio escorted Jackie to a chair and sat beside her. She had the impression there was a faint disagreement on his other side, as two young women sought the chair beside him. But it was over in a moment.

The other seat beside Jackie was occupied by Aunt Tania, who was clearly still regarding her with interest. She had a thin, sharp face, which had a disconcerting habit of flashing into a brilliant smile.

'You must tell me all about yourself,' she said now. 'I'd never heard of you until Vittorio called me this morning to say he was bringing you. You're obviously a very significant business associate.'

'I'm afraid he makes me sound too important.'

'Jackie is too modest about her abilities,' Vittorio said. 'When I expand my English business in Rome I'll be doing everything she says.'

Tania raised her coffee cup in salute.

'Congratulations, *signorina*. If you knew how rarely he follows anyone else's advice—or even listens to it—you'd realise what a unique position you hold. Believe me, I'll do all I can to make you feel welcome here.' She smiled. 'My nephew would be very annoyed with me if I didn't.'

'Of course. I'm here to help him make a profit. That's what really matters.'

The two women shared a laugh. Vittorio noticed and nodded with pleasure.

Servants appeared with the supper. Between the excellent food and the friendly talk Jackie had an enjoyable evening.

At last the younger women began to leave the table and settle on sofas. Two of them seized Vittorio and playfully forced him to join them. He was immediately surrounded by admirers.

'I look forward to showing you our house,' Tania said. 'There has been much history here—many notable people. Sometimes we have even opened it to tourists.'

'That sound fascinating,' Jackie said. 'I love history. In England I used to like visiting great historical buildings where dramatic things had happened in the past.'

'Then you'll enjoy Castello Martelli. We've had our fair share of excitement there.'

'Lovely. I even—'

She was checked by a shriek of laughter that came from a nearby sofa.

Glancing over, she saw that Vittorio was deep in conversation with Marisa and the other young women who crowded round him. All of them were rocking with laughter.

'Some more wine?' Tania asked.

'No, thank you,' Jackie said. 'Would you mind if I went to bed? It's been a long day. It was my first flight and it's left me a bit shaken.'

'Yes. It can take it out of you, can't it? Especially if you're nervous.'

'That's very true.'

'You look as if you've got a headache. Go to bed now. I'll send Gina up with something to drink.'

'Thank you.'

At the door Jackie looked back to wave goodnight to Vittorio, but he was still enjoying himself with his female companions, managing to be enfolded in three pairs of arms at once. He seemed to have forgotten that she existed.

As she watched Marisa intervened, pulling the others away but doing it with laughter, as though claiming Vittorio as her property was no more than a joke to her.

Vittorio looked up, noticed Jackie in the doorway and waved. She gave him a slight wave back and departed.

As promised, Gina brought something up to her room.

'English tea,' she said. 'My mistress said you were to have the best.'

'She's being very kind to me.'

'She likes you. She doesn't like that other one, but if the Count marries her—well, what can we do? Goodnight, *signorina*.'

Gina slipped away, leaving Jackie to brood. And there was a great deal to brood about. However she had thought this visit would work out, it was happening very differently, and somehow she would need to find a way to deal with it.

She tensed suddenly, alerted by a noise from the corridor outside. There was the sound of a door being opened, and then Marisa's voice.

'Perché non si può solo ascoltare me?'

Jackie just managed to make out the meaning. 'Why can't you just listen to me?'

Vittorio's reply was also in Italian, but his meaning was blindingly clear. 'Because there's no point. We talk too much and it gets us nowhere. *You* won't listen to what *I* say.'

'Because I don't believe you really mean it. Listen to your *heart*, Vittorio—'

'I *am* listening to it, and it's saying no. There's nothing there. Goodbye, Marisa.'

Quietly Jackie looked out, just in time to see Marisa storming away down the corridor as the door opposite was closed.

So that was his room, she thought.

Glancing around to make sure Marisa was no longer there, she went and knocked at his door.

He opened it at once. 'Marisa, *per favore*— Oh, it's you.'

Looking shocked, he checked himself and drew back to let her in.

'Yes, it's only me,' she said, following him. 'I reckon it's time for you to come clean, Vittorio. You've concealed the truth for long enough.'

'What truth? What are you talking about?'

'I mean the reason you brought me here. You played the gallant knight, rescuing me from Rik, but it was actually about Marisa, wasn't it? You wanted to stop her troubling you and I'm a handy excuse.'

Vittorio closed his eyes like a man wondering how to cope with another disaster.

'It's a bit more than that...' He groaned. 'It's not just Marisa.'

'So it's all the others who hunted you down today?'

'I don't think it's an accident that so many people—women—turned up. They came to see *you*.'

'You think they're all competing for *you*? I've heard of conceit, but that takes the biscuit.'

'You're wrong. I'm not vain enough to think girls are after me for myself. It's the title they want, and they're not the only ones. My father tried to arrange a marriage between myself and Marisa. I told him I wasn't keen, but he wouldn't listen. He was so certain he could persuade me that he let her think it was all arranged. She reckons I'm her property, and if I so much as look at another woman she acts like a betrayed wife. It's getting more than I can stand. Why do you think they came today? Marisa spread the word that I'd arrived with you and they all descended on us to get a look at you. So, yes, I thought your presence here might help me, and I seized the chance because I'm going crazy with this situation.'

'But you didn't think to tell me?'

'I was going to but—well—I just lost my nerve. Suppose I *had* told you? What would you have done? Agreed to help me? I don't think so.'

'You're wrong. After the way you helped me deal with Rik I'll do anything I can for you.'

His eyes gleamed. 'Anything?'

'Anything at all.'

'You'll help save me from Marisa?'

She smiled. 'I'll go into battle against her and you'll be quite safe.'

'That would be wonderful. Just keeping her thinking we're an item. It may just work.'

'But why does it have to be me? Why couldn't you pick someone else?'

'Because you have one great advantage that makes you a better choice than anyone else.'

'What could that possibly be?'

'You've made it plain you don't like me or trust me. Another woman might take my attentions seriously, think I meant them, and then be hurt when she learned the truth. But *you* see me as a cold and arrogant—mercenary, even. That's fine. There's no danger that you'll ever fall in love with me. I know we've decided to be friends, but it's a cautious friendship with suspicion on both sides, and that makes us both safe.'

She regarded him ironically.

'So you chose me because you knew I'd never embarrass you by indulging in romantic thoughts about you? Oh, were you right about that!'

'That's what I reckoned. You'd sooner swoon over a slimy octopus than me.'

'I wouldn't go so far as to say *that*.'

'But you were thinking it?'

She regarded him with her head on one side. 'Maybe. Sometimes it's best to keep your thoughts to yourself. I'm sure you know all about that.'

'It's been useful. Let's shake on it.'

They clasped hands.

'Your aunt doesn't like Marisa, does she?' she observed.

'No, but she's my father's sister, and as such she feels bound by his wishes.'

'Nonsense. The only wishes that matter are yours.'

His face brightened. '*That's* what I like to hear a woman say.'

'Aha! You think it shows I have a submissive nature?' She rubbed her hands. 'I could have a nasty shock waiting for you.'

'I'm sure you will. And I'm equally sure it will be interesting.'

From outside the building came the sound of voices. Vittorio opened the window and looked down.

'They're leaving,' he said. 'Come here.'

She went to stand beside him and he put his arm around her. Down below, Marisa was approaching her car while the other guests streamed out around her. Suddenly Marisa turned her head, gazing up at them.

'Shall we try to convince her now?' Vittorio murmured.

'Yes—what shall we do?'

'Rest your head on my shoulder.'

She did so, and he tightened his arm about her.

'Look up at me,' he murmured.

As soon as she did he leaned down and kissed her forehead.

Jackie drew a slow breath, waiting for him to drift lower until his lips touched hers. But he stayed as he was.

'She's there…watching us,' he said. Let's make this look good.'

His arms tightened, drawing her closer. His free hand caressed her cheek before drifting down, briefly touching her breasts. Jackie trembled, longing fiercely to take things further.

'You said you wanted me to help you…' she whispered.

'Yes—what are you going to do?'

'This,' she said, and reached up so that her arms went around his neck, drawing his head down so that she could caress his mouth with her own.

She could sense the surprise that shook him, then felt his grip on her tighten as he took control, moving his mouth against hers with growing urgency.

Caution told her that she shouldn't do this, but she couldn't make herself be cautious. Desire stormed through her, destroying everything but the need to be his and make him hers.

At last he spoke, his voice shaking. 'I think—I think we've done almost enough to convince her.'

'Yes—yes—'

'Just a few moments more…' His mouth brushed hers again.

Down below, Marisa got into her car. At the last moment she glanced up at them, made a sneering face, then started the car and drove away.

CHAPTER FIVE

'SHE'S GONE,' VITTORIO WHISPERED.

He could almost hear his own voice shaking. The last few minutes had affected him intensely, making him yearn to go further. But he struggled for control, fearful of driving Jackie away.

Reluctantly he released her. 'You did it. Marisa saw enough to get the message. Perhaps I should be grateful to you for taking command.'

'I didn't take command—'

'Didn't you?'

She thought she could guess his meaning. When she had reached up to draw his head down closer to hers, he'd known that her desire was as strong as his, and there was no way she could deny it. He had probably read the message in her eyes.

'You found the right way for both of us,' he said. 'You could say I followed your lead.'

'It was necessary for the performance,' she reminded him. 'Anything's worth doing for an effective performance.'

'Well said! A woman with efficient instincts.'

'And efficiency is everything,' she said lightly.

She met his gaze, both of them knowing that the real message was something quite different.

'Sometimes efficiency really *is* everything,' he said softly. 'But then—things change.'

'Well, they've changed for Marisa. I can't think why

she's worried about me. I'm no beauty. And don't bother to give me a polite answer or I'll thump you.'

'Right. You're no beauty. I heartily agree,' he said, trying to sound casual. He met her eyes. 'But you do have something else that's more than looks. You've got wit, and an intelligence that I find most appealing. In fact, since the day we met you've caught me out and tripped me up more than anyone's ever done before.'

'Then I'm surprised you brought me here.'

'Yes, I wonder what I was thinking of. I guess I don't mind being caught at a disadvantage—every now and then.'

'I'll remember that. I could have fun tripping you up.'

'I bet you will. There are women who conquer a man by their beauty, and those who conquer him by keeping him nervous, even scared.'

'And there's no doubt which one *I* am!' She laughed. 'But maybe I don't *want* to conquer you.'

'You won't make the effort? Then I'd feel insulted. Besides, you do it without meaning to.'

'You don't know that. I might have a fiendish plan going on.'

'I live in hope. But for the moment I'll say goodnight. We have a busy day tomorrow. You should beware. When we get to Rome I'm going to work you to death.'

'That's what I hoped. Anything else would be dull.'

'And let's not be *dull*, whatever we do.'

'No. Not that you could ever be dull here,' she murmured, glancing around at his bedroom. Like the rest of the house, it was lavishly decorated in a medieval style.

'This was my father's room,' he said.

'And now it's yours because you're the Count? Do you think you can be grandiose enough?'

'I'll try to be. I've never thought of myself as grandiose, but I suppose everything is going to be different now.'

'Yes,' she murmured. 'That's true. You won your battle

tonight. Marisa saw us, which is exactly what you wanted. From now on you'll be a free man.'

'A free man?' He looked into her eyes. 'I wonder just what that means?'

She met his gaze, suddenly confused. 'You'll find out gradually. I'm here to help you.' A sudden impulse made her say. 'It's getting late and I'm tired. I think I'll go to bed now. Goodnight.'

'Goodnight. And, Jackie—thank you for everything.'

She smiled and fled. It had suddenly become vital to escape him quickly and take refuge in her room.

Once there, she paced the floor, trying to understand the conflicting thoughts and feelings that struggled for supremacy inside her head.

It was madness to be upset, she told herself. Vittorio was a man of good looks and charm. Any woman would be thrilled to be taken into his arms. And for a brief moment she had known that delicious excitement. To feel his lips caressing hers, sense the tremors in his body—those pleasures had consumed her. He had wanted her, and the blissful knowledge had driven her to a response that had been almost beyond her control.

But then, like a warning blast, a voice in her mind had warned her to take care. To guard her feelings. He'd embraced her in order to deceive Marisa, then released her when Marisa had no longer been able to see them.

He was only pretending, she thought. He'd pretend for just long enough to get what he wanted and then she'd have outlived her usefulness to him. Just as if she fell in love with him he'd find it useful. And that was all he wanted of her—to be useful. Useful in the department store, useful about the money problem, useful about Marisa.

She'd do well to remember that falling for Vittorio would be extremely hazardous to her health. Mind you, he'd be as a big a fool to fall for *her*!

* * *

With Jackie gone Vittorio stood without moving for some moments, trying to cope with conflicting feelings. This had been his father's bedroom, and it still contained many memories.

Here they had spent their last few moments together, and Franco had revealed the secret that had set Vittorio on a new path. Putting right his father's wrongs had seemed like the right thing to do—and a simple thing.

But before that there had been other talks. Some of them about Vittorio's mother. He knew that both his parents had been unfaithful in their brief marriage. Adele, his mother, had married for the title—something which Franco, deeply in love, had not suspected until it was too late.

Looking at the surroundings where his father had made his last confession, he found that another scene came back to him. Then, too, Franco had lain there, dizzy with suffering, driving himself to tell the painful truth to his son, who had knelt beside the bed.

'I lost track of all the men she had…' He'd sighed.

Filled with fear, Vittorio had asked quickly, 'Do you mean that I'm not your son?'

'No, you're mine. When you were born I had a DNA test done to check, and the result was all I had hoped. But the fact that such a test was needed—' He had given a deep groan before adding wretchedly, 'And the other child…'

'What other child?'

'Do you remember how we lost your mother when you were twelve? She died giving birth. The baby also died. It wasn't mine. We hadn't made love for a long time, so I knew. She had never loved me as I loved her. I would have forgiven her, because I so much wanted her to stay with me, but then she was gone.'

'But how could you have kept her with you, knowing what you knew?' Vittorio had asked desperately.

'Yes, it's madness, isn't it? But love *is* a kind of madness. When you love a woman so much that you'll forgive her anything as long as she doesn't leave you, it's as though you cease to be yourself. I should have divorced her years before. I'd have been safer without her there to torment me. But I couldn't do it. I told myself I stayed with her for your sake, because you needed a mother. But the truth was I couldn't bear to let her go. So we stayed together…she kept living her riotous life. And then she died.'

Vittorio hadn't been able to reply. He'd dropped his head down into the bed, close to his father's, feeling only despair.

Franco had touched him. 'I pray that your life may be filled with more hope,' he'd said. 'Don't give your love to a woman who deceives you. Be cautious, my son. Don't trust too easily. Keep your love to yourself as long as you can.'

The advice had touched Vittorio's heart. Only recently he'd quarrelled with a young woman who'd briefly inspired his trust and affection before turning to another man. Everything in him had accepted that his father had been right, and that he must be cautious.

But then he'd met Jackie—frank, honest, different from any other women he'd met. Or so he'd thought until his growing attraction to her had begun to alarm him. Holding her in his arms, he'd felt a surge of feeling that was not merely desire, but also tenderness. And the awareness of her trembling in his arms, the fervour with which she'd kissed him, had left him feeling stunned.

She'd called it efficiency, claiming to have done no more than follow his lead. But the memory of her response lingered…delightful, alarming, warning him that the road ahead led into mystery.

It was unbearable not to know the answer. He went out into the corridor, looking to see if there was a light under her door. But there was none. Had she really gone to sleep?

Or was she lying in the darkness, facing a confusion as great as his own?

He stood outside her door, listening to the silence inside, trying to decide whether to call her or knock. But after hesitating a long time he backed away, sensing that this was not the right moment.

Next morning Jackie awoke early and took a shower. Standing under the water, she wondered what she would see in Vittorio's eyes this morning. She'd felt sure he would call on her the previous night, but nothing had happened.

She'd heard a faint sound, as though his footsteps had approached her room, but then there had been only silence. Unable to bear the tension, she'd leapt out of bed and pulled open her door. But the corridor outside had been dark and empty, with no sign of him. She had gone back to bed and lain there fretting until she'd managed to fall asleep.

This morning her thoughts were still troubled—even more so because her attraction towards Vittorio made her feel that she was failing her father again.

Somehow, somewhere, there must be a way to do the right thing. If only she could find it.

She dressed and went downstairs into the hall. Through an open door she could see Vittorio sitting at a desk.

He glanced up and waved to her. 'We'll be going in to breakfast in a moment,' he said. 'And then we can—'

The sound of the phone interrupted him, making him curse slightly and then answer it. Jackie went to stand by the window, gazing out at the grass and trees, entranced by their beauty. Clearly it was a magnificent estate, and she was curious to see more of it.

Glancing around, she saw that he had his back to her, absorbed in the call. Yielding to temptation, she slipped out of the door into the garden. For a few moments it was delightful to run across the lawn to where she could see a seat under one of the trees. She sat down on it and leaned back, closing her eyes and breathing in the cool air.

When at last she opened her eyes she found herself gazing at the building that reared up so magnificently, beautiful and luxurious. But the sight caused sorrow to fall over her heart, as it had done so often since she'd arrived here. This had been the home of the man who had cheated her beloved father, reducing him to poverty and despair.

In her mind's eye she saw her father again, his head sunk in misery when his wife had left him.

He had nothing, she thought. *And the man who lives here has everything.*

She could feel tears pouring down her cheeks and ducked her head, seizing a handkerchief to wipe them away. But there were more tears, followed by sobs. She sat there shaking, trying vainly to control her grief.

'Jackie— *Jackie?*'

The voice from overhead made her look up to see Vittorio standing there. At once he sat down beside her, reaching out to her.

'Come here,' he said.

'No!' She pulled sharply away. 'Go away. Leave me alone.'

'But I—'

'I said leave me alone. I don't want to talk to you.'

She jumped up, fleeing away from him until she plunged into the trees. When she felt safely out of sight she leaned against a tree trunk and abandoned the effort to control her tears.

Suddenly she felt a pair of strong arms go around her, pulling her against him.

'I'm sorry,' he said. 'I don't mean to crowd you, but stay with me a while. Let me help you.'

She couldn't answer. The feel of his chest was warm

and comforting, giving her a pleasure she hadn't thought to know. She trembled and felt him draw her even closer.

'Cry,' he said. 'You need to. Don't fight it.'

It felt incredible that she was letting this man, of all men, comfort her. But the feel of his arms about her was unlike anything that had ever happened to her before.

'Let's go inside,' he said. 'We'll have breakfast and then go into the city. We've got a lot to do.'

'Oh, yes,' she said wryly. 'I'm going to give you all that expert opinion—if I can think of anything. I really felt very awkward when you were telling your aunt how good I am.'

'You played your part beautifully.'

'But I don't even know what I'm supposed to be expert *about*.'

'That's why we're going into town. By the time we've finished you'll be able to give me your orders.'

She rubbed her hands. 'Roll on the day!'

'Well, I've been meaning to tell you—' He stopped, realising that he no longer had her attention. She was looking about her at the medieval beauty of her surroundings as though something had suddenly struck her, 'What's the matter?' he asked.

'Nothing. It's this place,' she said. 'I just have to keep looking at it. It's wonderful how history seems to live here all around us, as though your ancestors were still alive.'

'I know the feeling. I've felt them with me all my life, and if I want to meet them I go to the gallery, where their portraits hang. Would you like to see it?'

'I'd love to.'

He led her into a great room at the back of the house. Portraits hung all along the walls, of people dressed in clothes that spoke of past centuries.

'And *all* these are your ancestors?' Jackie mused in wonder.

'Not all. Have a look at this one.'

He drew her to a full-length picture showing a young woman in a horse-drawn chariot. With one hand she controlled the horses, in the other she held a sword. On her head she wore a military helmet.

'That's Bellona,' Vittorio told her. 'The Roman goddess of war.'

'You have a *female* deity of war? Surely—?'

'Surely it should be a man?' he said, grinning. 'In any other society it probably would be. But in Rome we like strong, powerful women.'

'Unless they happen to disagree with you?' she teased, her eyes challenging him.

'Ah, well, let's not go into that.'

'Very wise,' she said with mock solemnity. 'Just think of all the awkward things I could remind you of.'

'And how you'd enjoy doing it.'

Tania had slipped into the room behind them and was listening to them with pleasure.

'You'll have a chance to meet Bellona,' she said. 'We celebrate her festival every year. You'll probably enjoy that.'

'Yes, you two have a lot in common…' Vittorio observed.

'Vittorio!' Tania protested. 'I hope you're not being rude to our guest.'

'Don't worry, Aunt. Jackie's not offended. And here's someone else you should meet,' Vittorio said, turning her towards a picture of a man in a suit of armour. 'He was the very first Count Martelli. And the two men in the next picture are his sons. The elder one died and the younger one inherited the title.'

Along the walls they went, with Vittorio describing his ancestors one by one, introducing them as though they still lived with him.

One portrait especially seized Jackie's attention. It showed a man in the luscious garb of the seventeenth century, with long curling hair falling over his shoulders. But it was his face that claimed her attention. It was Vittorio's face that had come down the centuries.

'He was my great-great-great-great-grandfather,' Vittorio said.

'Yes, I can see. It's incredible. You're really one of them. Hey—what's that?'

Her attention had been seized by another picture, a few feet along. It showed two men dressed in the attire of ancient Rome. One of them also had a face similar to Vittorio's.

'He must be another ancestor of yours,' she said. 'Who's the man with him?'

'Julius Caesar—the Roman Emperor.'

'One of your family was a friend of *Julius Caesar*? They even had their portraits painted together?'

'Not at all. There's a common belief that one of my ancestors was part of Caesar's court, but that picture was painted hundreds of years later. It's just a fantasy. There are several fantasies like that in this gallery. Over here is Napoleon. When he was Emperor of France he annexed Rome, but when he was defeated we regained our freedom.'

The picture had been carefully designed to show Napoleon regarding his companion with admiration and respect. The companion's face also bore a notable resemblance to Vittorio's.

'It's marvellous, isn't it?' said Tania.

'That face—it's *him*!' Jackie exclaimed in wonder.

'Yes, you can't get away from me even a few hundred years later.' Vittorio laughed.

'Have you shown Jackie the picture of Lady Nanetta?' Tania asked.

'Not yet, but I'm looking forward to doing it.' He guided her across the room. 'Nanetta is a family legend,' he explained. 'She was a magnificent woman, but also an alarming one.'

He paused before a full-length picture of a tall, slender woman.

'She had dozens of suitors,' he said, 'but she rejected them all. Legend says that she was a witch. It's never been proved or disproved, but she inspired a lot of fear.'

'Why did she reject them all?' Jackie asked. 'Didn't she ever fall in love?'

'Never. She had a great fortune and she believed that was all men wanted of her. She said no man could be trusted, nor was ever worthy of love.'

'How sad to believe that,' Jackie murmured. 'How could anyone endure life with nothing to believe in?'

'Is love the *only* thing to believe in?' he asked wryly.

'Of course there's always money.'

'But you don't believe in that, having turned down so much.'

'If you mean your million pounds, I turned it down for love—of my father.' She saw tension come into his face and added, 'There's more than one kind of love.'

He hesitated before saying, 'You're right, of course.'

She went to stand before the woman's picture, trying to see if her face revealed anything. But Lady Nanetta stared into the distance, concealing her secrets.

'I wonder what taught her so much distrust?' Jackie said.

'She saw a lot of evidence to distrust in her life. She was hugely rich.'

'Which was why so many men wanted to marry her?'

'Probably. Of course they may have been attracted to her as well.'

'I doubt that,' Jackie said, studying the picture. 'She was no beauty.'

Vittorio considered the picture before glancing back at her. 'That matters little,' he said. 'A woman doesn't have to be a great beauty to intrigue men. Her moods, her wit, the hint of mystery she can carry—those can lure men as keenly as mere good looks.' After a thoughtful moment he added, 'Sometimes more so.'

He was giving her a look that might have been significant. She tried to be cautious about understanding it, but there was a glint in his eye she couldn't ignore.

She called common sense to her rescue. 'If you say so,' she said cheerfully.

'I *do* say so.'

'Then I'll have to believe it—however unconvincing.'

He chuckled and put his arm around her. 'Let's get going—we have a busy day ahead of us,' said Vittorio. 'But first we'll have breakfast.'

They ate quickly, and when breakfast was over he led Jackie out of the palace to a garage around the side. He regarded her curiously as she took out her purse and examined its contents.

'Need some money?' he asked.

'No. Thank you, but I'm quite independent. I can use my bank card to draw money from my English account, can't I?'

'If you've got the pin number, yes.'

In a few moments they were on their way to Rome.

'What are we going to see first?' she asked.

'My department store. I need to see how it's managing. And I'll be interested in your opinion. After that, I'd like to show you some of the city.'

At first the road wound through the estate, and Jackie watched from the window, charmed by the green fields and forests, until finally the estate was behind them and they were heading along the motorway that led to the city.

Once in Rome, Vittorio drove straight to an area where there were shops, restaurants and commercial buildings. He parked the car and led her through the streets, letting her absorb the atmosphere until it was time to visit his department store.

It was a huge place, selling goods from many different countries and a vast range of sources. There were departments for furniture, glass, hardware and jewellery.

Jackie walked through it in a daze of delight. Everywhere Vittorio introduced her to the staff as 'my expert from England'. In the glass and china department he explained that she was to be in charge, and she was treated with great respect.

When he was called away for a moment the staff crowded round her, full of eager questions. Their English was efficient, as was her Italian.

'There are some products I'd like to show you,' she said. 'I'll need a computer.'

One was immediately made available, and she went online to show them the many sites where she found products that made them exclaim with admiration. It was clear that her visit was a success.

At last she looked up to find Vittorio regarding her with amused satisfaction.

'Found me any new stock?' he asked.

'One or two things I think might go well.'

She indicated several choices. He nodded in agreement to all of them, and a staff member began making purchases.

'We'll leave him to it while we look around some more,' Vittorio said. When they were outside he said, 'I wish you could have seen your face while you were giving everyone instructions. I think that's your idea of heaven.'

'If you mean that I'm a bully—'

'Only the kind of bully that I need working for me,' he said with a grin. 'You promised to make profit for me, and I can see that you will. Well done!'

'Thank you. After all, you did promise me authority.'

'I must have known by instinct that authority is your default position.'

'You might have a point there,' she said with a brief laugh. 'I must admit I *do* enjoy being the one to give the orders.'

'After the way you had to put up with Rik, I'm not surprised.'

'Not just Rik. I used to annoy my father a lot by arguing.' She regarded him cheekily. 'I'm a very difficult character.'

'Well, I already knew *that*.' He took her hand in his and gave it a comforting squeeze. 'I can put up with you if you can put up with me.'

She squeezed back. 'I'll do my best—however hard it is.'

'I've got a feeling we're going to be a big success.'

Coming to Italy was proving to be everything she had dared to hope, thought Jackie. Here there were opportunities and a chance for the kind of new, more adventurous life that had once seemed impossible.

Suddenly she stopped.

'I didn't realise that your store stocked clothes.'

'Of course—it's our most popular department. Come and look.'

Jackie was soon in heaven! Vittorio introduced her to the staff and she watched, entranced, as boxes were opened to reveal costly gowns. She examined them, trying to imagine her dull self in any of the exquisite dresses.

'Perhaps—' she began, turning to Vittorio. 'Oh, where's he gone?'

'He was summoned to his office,' said Donna, the head assistant. 'Do you like our stock?'

'Oh, yes, it's all so beautiful. Especially this one.' She gazed admiringly at a black satin evening gown.

'Yes, it's one of our new range. Would you like to try it on?'

'I'm not sure… It looks very sophisticated, and I'm not really like that.'

'But you might be if you saw yourself in it.'

'Oh, go on, then—let's try.'

Donna's advice was good. The dress was tight-fitting, and clung perfectly to Jackie's slender figure, giving it a drama and mystery she'd never been aware of before.

She turned back and forth, enjoying the sight of her new self in the mirror. Totally absorbed, she failed to notice the middle-aged woman who had arrived, and was watching her with pleasure.

'Is that dress for sale?' the woman asked Donna.

'Yes, Contessa. It's part of the stock that's just arrived.'

'It would suit my daughter perfectly. I'll buy it.' The shopper turned to the man who had just appeared beside her. 'You're really extending your talents in this store. Doesn't your model look lovely?'

'Yes,' Vittorio murmured, 'she does.'

He backed away quickly before Jackie could notice him. After a moment the Countess joined him. She was beaming.

'Now you have a satisfied customer,' she said. 'That dress looked so good on your model that I just *had* to buy it. Donna says it can be delivered tomorrow.'

He replied politely and escorted her away, before returning to the dress department. Jackie was still there, once more in her own clothes. For a moment Vittorio had a dizzying sensation that briefly she had become a different Jackie.

'It's time to move on, Jackie. We have a lot to fit in today.'

'Oh, that's a shame. I've had an amazing morning, and your store is magnificent.'

'No, no,' he said quickly. 'You mustn't say that. You're going to tell me how to bring it up to standard.'

'Suppose I think I can't?'

'Hush, don't say such a thing. Never admit failure.' He gave her a cheeky grin. 'You're here as an expert, giving me your lofty advice.'

'And you'll *take* my advice? I don't think so.'

'Then you can call me some suitable names. *Stupido, idiota, buffone.* You understand Italian well enough to take your pick.'

'I'll try to remember. Where to next, then?'

'I'd like to take you to my other shop. This one is much smaller. It could do with expansion, and I'd value your opinion.'

CHAPTER SIX

A SHORT STROLL brought them to the 'other shop', which she examined with interest, making notes. She was enjoying herself.

After a couple of hours they left.

Wherever they went Vittorio was instantly recognised. Even in the street people addressed him respectfully as 'Signor Conte', and regarded her with curiosity.

She could guess why she fascinated them. Word of her arrival had obviously spread fast, and she was clearly being regarded as the latest candidate for the position of Countess.

Me, she thought hilariously. *Plain, dreary me. Whatever next?*

'What's so funny?' Vittorio asked.

'Sorry—what?'

'You suddenly started laughing. People don't usually find Rome funny.'

'It's not Rome that's funny. It's me. Haven't you seen the way everybody is staring at me?'

'Sure—you've really got their attention.'

'And why? For the same reason Marisa is troubled by me. I'm seen as the latest candidate for your hand.'

'And that's funny, is it?'

'It is from the proper angle. Look.'

She pointed him towards the window of a shop they were passing. Turning, they looked at their reflections: Vittorio splendidly handsome, herself ordinary.

'Ever since the moment I came here,' she said, 'I've felt like Cinderella arriving at the ball.'

'Really? Does that make me Prince Charming?'

'Prince Charming or Prince Charm*less*. It depends on your mood.'

'You don't pull your punches, do you? Are you trying to lure me in or put me off?'

'What do *you* think?'

'I think you're trying to scare the life out of me. And succeeding.'

'That's all right, then. As long as you don't think I'm trying to lure you into marriage.'

'I promise never to think that.'

Vittorio wondered what he should have understood from her words. If she ever did set her sights on him he doubted he'd guess. She was too clever to be obvious. But the conversation had amused him too much to be troublesome.

'I'd better go into the bank while I'm here,' he said. 'The one across the road is the one I use.'

Inside the bank, she saw him treated with the same intense respect she had noticed before—which she guessed told her everything about the size of his bank balance.

'It would be easier if you banked here also, since you'll be living and working in Italy from now on,' he said. 'Tell them you want to transfer your London account.' He added lightly, 'Unless, of course, you're planning to dash back to the joys of working for Rik.'

'No chance!'

'Wise woman.'

He came to the counter with her and spoke in rapid Italian.

'There'll be bank cards for you in a couple of days,' he said at last. 'And now it's time for some lunch at last. This way.'

He led her to a little restaurant on the next corner.

As she looked through the menu he said, 'What would you like?'

'I don't know; I can't decide. I'll let you order for me.'

He regarded her with amused suspicion. 'You trust me to order for you? That's not like the Jackie I've come to know. Are you trying to catch me off-guard?'

'Well, I've got to do *something* to worry you, haven't I?'

'Don't bother. You worry me quite enough as it is.'

'In that case, please do your duty and order for me.'

He instructed the waitress, and in a few minutes a dish was set before her. It was a bowl filled with tiny lumps of meat and a few vegetables.

'It's called lamb *tagliata*,' he said. 'I remembered that you like lamb.'

'But that was the lunch we had in the hotel in London,' she said, astonished. 'You remembered from then?'

'Of course. I'm a businessman. I make efficient notes about my business associates and use them to my advantage.'

But he winked as he said it, and gave her a grin which she returned.

The food tasted magnificent. She devoured it with pleasure, aware that he was watching her closely.

'Mmm...lovely,' she said. 'You choose food well. I must put that in my own notes about *you*—along with a few other things.'

He nodded, implying that he understood her perfectly. 'Of course,' he said, 'my observations will have to include how careless you are about doing your job.'

'What?'

'You were supposed to be giving me an expert opinion of my store. So far all you've done is eat. I want to lodge a complaint.'

'I said it was magnificent!'

'But you were just being polite.'

'I'm *never* polite. Haven't you learned that yet? Hmm… I'll have to give you a few lessons.'

'I'll look forward to it. But, in the meantime, you didn't really *mean* magnificent, did you?'

'Suppose I say yes? Would that make me disappointing?'

'Come on, Jackie. Criticise. It's what you're here for.'

'Well, I *did* notice one thing missing. You have a huge range of things from all over the world, but I saw nothing from England.'

'That's because we've never had any real English expertise—until now. I did the right thing, kidnapping you.'

'You didn't exactly *kidnap* me,' she insisted. 'I wanted to come.'

'Suppose you hadn't? Do you think that would have made any difference?'

'No, I guess not.'

'You did a great job in the shop—especially when you modelled that dress.'

'Modelled—? You saw me?'

'Yes, I keep turning up when I'm not wanted, don't I? I was there with Contessa Valierse. She liked the sight of you so much she bought the dress for her daughter. I seem to gain from everything you do. As soon as I realised that, I decided that you must belong to me.'

'And if I resist?' she teased.

'It won't make any difference. When an efficient businessman finds something that suits him he takes possession of it, ignoring all distractions.'

'And you think nobody can successfully fight you?'

'That's right. I always get my own way. Make a special note of that.'

'Yes, I think I will.' She took out a scrap of paper, then discovered a problem.

'Damn! I haven't got a pen.'

'Here.' He handed her a pen.

'I wonder if I should accept that…' she mused.

'You mean because you're about to write something critical about me? Go on. Be brave.'

'Thanks.' She took it and scribbled, *He always gets his own way*, adding a little swirl afterwards.

'What's that squiggle at the end?' Vittorio asked.

'It's code. It means, *That's what he thinks.*' Jackie chuckled.

'Hmm… At least you're honest.'

'Well, I'm not sure you get your own way as much as you think you do.'

'You will be. In time.'

Despite the seemingly harsh words, the atmosphere was teasing and friendly.

'Of course it doesn't do for a guy to be too self-confident around you,' he said. 'He'd pay a heavy price.'

'Or *I* would,' she said wryly.

He considered her. 'Is that the voice of experience?'

'There was a man I was once fond off. Just fond. His name was Peter. I wasn't passionately in love, but when he mentioned marriage I was interested.'

'What went wrong?'

'My father became ill. I was looking after him and Peter didn't like that. It made him feel that he came second.'

'*Did* he come second?'

'Yes, I suppose he did. He wanted me to put Daddy in a care home, but I couldn't do that. It would have broken his heart.'

'And Peter was angry about that?'

'We had a quarrel. I told him that he couldn't give me orders and that was that. In my admittedly limited experience I've discovered that men like to be in charge.'

'Surely that isn't aimed at *me*? You have as much control as I do.'

'Not as much. Maybe a bit.'

'We'll agree to disagree. So you sent him away with a flea in his ear?'

'Yes. He couldn't believe I meant it, but I wasn't going to change my mind. How about you? Have you never been tempted to settle down with any of the beautiful women who seem to throw themselves at you at any given opportunity?'

He made a face, but said nothing.

'I'm sorry,' she said. 'I didn't mean to pry. Your love life is none of my business.' She added cheekily, 'But perhaps you don't *have* one. Perhaps you live on a pinnacle of lofty indifference.'

'If only I did. There was one woman who taught me to be careful, and it was a strong lesson that I've never forgotten.'

'Was she after your title?'

'She was. But at first she played her role so convincingly that I didn't realise the truth. I was completely taken in—until the day I found her in bed with another man.'

'What? How *could* she?'

'The man was heir to a dukedom. His social standing and personal fortune were therefore much greater than my own. That told me everything I needed to know. Her fine words and loving behaviour towards me had been because she wanted my title. When a better title came along I ceased to exist as far as she was concerned.'

'She pretended to love you—?'

'It was a good act. Fooled me.'

'And you loved her?'

He hesitated, and she could tell that he found this hard to answer.

'I thought I did. But it was a useful lesson. I've never been deceived again. I keep my suspicious side working.'

His words were cool, but she had a sense that they concealed feelings he didn't want to admit. This deceitful woman had caused him a lot of pain—some of which had never completely abated.

'What a dreadful thing to happen,' she said. 'Can you ever trust anyone again?'

'Probably not. But it's safer that way. What about you? After this guy you sent away—has there been anyone since?'

'No, I've had too much to think about. First my father died, and after that I set my heart on saving up enough money to escape my miserable existence, start a new life.'

'But you could be doing that now, by taking the money I offered you. Why did you turn it down?'

'For Daddy's sake. It would have felt like insulting him—saying that his suffering didn't matter as long as I gained the money.'

'But he wouldn't know.'

'Maybe—maybe not. But I still value his opinion. What he would've thought about things is of paramount importance to me. What about you and *your* father's wishes? Don't you take *his* views into account when you make decisions? Isn't that what you were doing in trying to give me that money?'

Jackie was exactly right, he realised. His father was still there in his mind and his heart. At times it was as if he could hear his voice in his ear. And clearly the same was true of her. It was almost alarming.

'And do you feel that *he* would know whether you've managed it or not?' she asked.

'I don't know, of course,' he said quietly. 'But *I* will know.'

'And so will I. That's why I can't give in and take your money. I feel that it would break his heart.'

'And I have to keep my word to *my* father. If I don't, that would break *his* heart.'

'If only they could have talked to each other while they

were still alive,' she said wistfully. 'They could've sorted it out without us.'

He took her hand between his. 'Instead we must honour their memories and do right by them both.'

'Yes. I'm glad of that.'

He squeezed her hand. 'So am I.'

A waiter approached, making him release her quickly.

When he'd ordered some coffee he said, 'Let's discuss the store. You said it needed more stuff from England. Tell me exactly what you mean…'

After lunch they were soon in the car, heading back through the country to the Castello Martelli. As darkness fell she saw the building's lights from a distance, and marvelled again at its magnificence and beauty.

Tania was waiting in the hall.

'Shall I get you some supper?' she asked.

'No need—we've enjoyed a late lunch,' Vittorio told her cheerfully. 'And now we have something to celebrate. This way, Jackie.'

His arm around her waist, he guided her into his office. Tania regarded them wryly. After a moment she went to the office door and stood watching while Jackie worked on the computer, accessing one English website after another while showing Vittorio her ideas for supplying his stores.

'Can you go back to the last one?' Vittorio said. 'I like those metal ornaments. Yes, that's it. Zoom in on that one. Great. Yes, I'll have that.'

He became aware of Tania stood in the doorway.

'Come and look, Aunt. Jackie's doing a wonderful job for us.'

'So I see,' Tania said, coming forward, smiling. 'You really seem very knowledgeable, *signorina*.'

'Please call me Jackie.'

'Jackie. Yes. Now, if my nephew is going to work you to death can I get you some coffee—or tea? A glass of wine?'

'I'm okay—thank you, Tania.'

'I will take a wine, please, Aunt Tania,' said Vittorio.

The other woman smiled at them both and headed to the kitchen. Jackie sensed that Tania was still undecided about her, but her manner was pleasant.

Once Tania was gone, Jackie's attention was brought back to the computer screen.

'I want to go back to town tomorrow,' announced Vittorio, 'but tonight I want to see some of those websites again.'

'I'll get started now,' Jackie said.

He sat with his attention fixed on what she was doing. Suddenly he said, 'Let me look at that.'

She enlarged the picture, which was of a metal vase with elaborate engraving.

He studied it for several minutes before saying, 'Fine. I'll buy some of those.'

He purchased the items online, studied more websites and purchased several more things. By the time they were finished he'd spent a thousand euros and was in good spirits.

'Fantastic job!' he said. I'd never have found that stuff without you. And tomorrow there'll be more. We must make an early start.'

'Then I'll have an early night,' Jackie said, rising.

He rose too, but she signalled for him to sit down. Tania had just returned to the office with Vittorio's drink, and Jackie got the sense that she wanted to talk with her nephew privately.

Vittorio nodded, gave her a gentle kiss on the cheek, and let her go.

When they were alone Tania poured him a glass of wine. 'It's been a good evening,' she said.

'Yes. I knew bringing Jackie here would be brilliant. She really knows her stuff.'

'And she makes sure you realise it,' Tania observed lightly.

'You sound suspicious. I thought you liked her?'

'In a way, I do. That's what makes it confusing. I want to believe in her but—' She sighed.

'But what?'

'What exactly is she *after*?'

'Nothing.'

'Oh, my dear boy, be realistic. Every young woman you meet is after something. Usually money.'

'No, that's one thing I can be sure of. She's not after my money. I offered her money and she refused it.'

'Obviously it wasn't enough.'

'I offered her in excess of a million English pounds.'

'A million—? Are you out of your mind?'

'In a way, yes. I've been partly out of my mind since Papà admitted on his deathbed that he'd cheated Jackie's father out of a million years ago.'

Tania gasped. 'No, that's not possible. You've imagined it.'

'It's true. He told me he and George Benton both placed a bet. Benton's paid off, but Papà stole the winnings before Benton knew. I've been desperate to put it right by paying back the money. I was going to give it to George Benton, but he's dead. So I offered it to Jackie and she turned me down.'

Tania gasped. 'She actually refused to take a sum like that? I don't believe it.'

'It's true. I'm not lying.'

'No, I mean I don't believe her refusal was genuine. She wants you to think her honest so that you'll be lured in further—perhaps even marry her.'

'I don't believe that.'

'No, because you've formed a high opinion of her—exactly as you were meant to.'

'So you don't really like her after all?'

Tania hesitated before saying carefully, 'I'm not sure. She makes me cautious. But she's so clever and sharp-witted I wonder if she might be the right woman for you, because *she* could be the one who could make you stop your nonsense.'

This seemed to strike him. He considered thoughtfully before saying, 'My *nonsense*? I think you two must be in cahoots.'

'Why? Has she called you out on your nonsense too?'

'Not outright, but she implies it every time she opens her mouth.'

'Good for her.'

'Today she called me Prince Charmless.'

'Indeed? She actually said that?'

'Without any hesitation.'

Tania chuckled. 'Now I'm *really* beginning to like her.'

'I like her too,' Vittorio admitted. 'In some ways. But not in others. It comes and goes, and the feelings get intertwined.'

'You mean you have opposite feelings at the same time?'

'Yes—it's hard to know what to think of a woman with several different aspects.'

'That can be the best kind of woman,' Tania observed.

'Certainly the most interesting,' Vittorio murmured. 'And now I think I'll have an early night myself.'

'I hope you're not going to go knocking on her door.'

'I wouldn't dream of it. She and I are just friends. We've both made that very plain.'

'As long as you're both realists.'

'Not a doubt of it. Goodnight, Aunt.' He gave her a friendly peck on the cheek and departed.

Despite retiring early, Vittorio found that his need for sleep deserted him as soon as he went to bed. After tossing and turning for a while he rose, pulled on some jeans and a T-shirt, and went downstairs, then out into the garden.

He couldn't be certain what had disturbed him. Although he knew his aunt's words had touched a nerve, he was unwilling to admit how that touch had agitated him.

We're just friends. We've both made that very plain.

Was that being realistic? Despite her lack of conventional beauty, Jackie held an attraction for him that was unsettling—all the more so because he doubted if she felt the same way.

He walked for a long time before returning to his room and going back to bed. But still sleep evaded him, and he lay there restlessly for several hours until he nodded off just before it was time to get up.

Bad news was waiting for him when he went down for breakfast. Leo, the permanent driver he employed, was feeling poorly.

'He can't drive you to Rome,' Tania told him. 'He isn't well enough.'

'No matter. I'll drive.' But he said it reluctantly. His disturbed night had left him feeling less than his best. But the trip was necessary, and he was sure he could be strong.

He reckoned it was the right decision as he observed Jackie on their journey. She had clearly done some research and knew where she wanted to visit.

'I'd like to see some more of the smaller shops,' she said after a few miles. 'The department stores are impressive, but a little shop can sometimes take you by surprise.'

'Yes, it can,' he said. 'I remember a little shop in London that took me *completely* by surprise. It was being run by a really prickly woman who trampled me underfoot, chucked me out and called me all kinds of names. And a few days later I was fool enough to bring her home with me. I can't think why…'

'I guess you just like being ill-treated,' she teased.

'That's right. And I'm sure she's got some more up her sleeve.'

'Never mind. If you fight back she'll probably make a run for it.'

'Don't you dare! Now I've got you here I'm going to keep you. You're my prisoner. Don't forget it.'

They laughed. And then they were in town, travelling the back streets where Vittorio discovered small businesses that impressed him in unfamiliar ways.

He watched as Jackie examined them, made notes, and drew his attention to things he hadn't noticed.

'You really *do* know your stuff,' he said at last as they got back into the car. 'I'm impressed.' He glanced around and said suddenly, 'Wait here, I'll be just a moment.'

On the far side of the road was a branch of the bank where he'd taken her the day before. He went in, stayed a few minutes, then returned to her.

'I've got something for you,' he said. 'Here.' He handed her a bundle of banknotes.

'But what—?'

'Now you're working for me, and that's your first commission.'

She flicked through the notes, astonished at the amount.

'It's more than I was expecting.'

'You're doing a good job. It's ten per cent of what I spent online under your advice.'

'We didn't actually agree my wages.'

'No, and if I was anything like the last man you worked for I'd cut the amount in half and defy you to challenge me. I wonder how far you'd get…'

'I never got anywhere arguing with Rik until you came and defended me,' she admitted.

'Right. But you're my employee now, and I don't expect you to work for nothing.'

'Well, if you put it like that—'

'You've *earned* that money, Jackie. Now, I'm starving,' Vittorio said. 'Just round that corner is a hotel with one of the best restaurants in Rome. Let's go. Unless you want to be difficult about that too?'

'No, I've had enough fun for today. Let's go.'

CHAPTER SEVEN

'YOU MEANT THAT about fun, didn't you? That's how you get your kicks—driving me mad.'

'Some people are more fun to drive mad than others.'

'You'd better watch out,' Vittorio said. 'It might be *my* turn to have fun.' He swung into a car park. 'Here we are.'

He escorted her inside the hotel and headed for the restaurant. When they were settled inside, Jackie's eyes widened at the sight of the menu.

'Best Roman cuisine,' Vittorio said. 'Does it tempt you?'

'Yes, it looks delicious.' He summoned the waiter and they ordered their food.

'Would you like wine?' he asked.

'Not really.'

'Me neither. I've got to drive us home. Let's have sparkling water.'

When the water arrived he filled both their glasses.

'To a successful business arrangement,' he said.

They clinked glasses.

'Here's the food,' he said with relief as the waiter approached them.

The dishes that were laid before her looked delicious, and tasted that way too.

'Lovely!' she said.

'Good.'

He paused, and she had a strange feeling that he was summoning up his courage. When he spoke again he sounded uneasy.

'The fact is I wanted us to spend a little time together. Because I feel we need to talk.'

Jackie stared at him, puzzled. 'Do we?' she asked softly. 'You might say that we're the last people to want to talk.'

'But that's wrong. We connect because I'm the only person who knows exactly how you feel.'

'I don't think you *do* know how I feel. You can't imagine how all your money and luxury depresses me.'

'Because of your father and what was done to him? I understand how that makes you feel, but I wasn't the man who did it.' He took a deep breath. 'Why do you hate me, Jackie?'

She gave a brief ironic laugh. 'I guess it's because you're the one who's available to me. I can't chastise your father, because he isn't here. But you are, so I can—' She gave a slight shrug.

'Well, that's honest, anyway. So when you kick me in the teeth you just pretend you're kicking him?'

'I guess you're right.' She sighed. 'I keep telling myself to be reasonable, but then I remember Daddy's face looking the way I saw it so often. His life was terrible at the end. He'd lost everything.'

'He hadn't lost you. He had a daughter who cared for him.'

'Yes, but I couldn't fill all the empty spaces in his life. Even now I'm still trying to do my best by him.'

Vittorio closed his eyes. 'I can't describe hearing how my father had cheated his friend, stolen from him—what that did to me. I'd always admired him, practically worshipped him as a man to be trusted and honoured. Suddenly to discover that there was another truth about him—that he was capable of such a terrible action—'

Jackie was dismayed to see that he was shaking. She reached out and took his hand. 'It's not your fault,' she said.

He opened his eyes, gazing straight at her. 'I never thought to hear you say something like that,' he said.

'Well, it's true. You didn't steal the money.'

'But I lived on it. I grew up in luxury that I had no right to. And when I started out in business my father supported me financially. He couldn't have done that if he hadn't had that stolen money. The knowledge tortured me, but I had to keep my feelings to myself. I couldn't let him know while he was dying. And there's been nobody else I could talk to. Until now.'

'And talking helps, doesn't it?' she murmured. 'I never thought to say this, but in a strange way your loss has been greater than mine. My father remains in my heart just as he always was—loving, gentle, sweet-natured. That will never change. But you've lost the father you loved and admired. He's vanished and been replaced by another father who horrifies you. I do understand how that must be a miserable loss to you.'

From the way he stared at her she could tell she'd taken him completely by surprise.

'How did you…?' he murmured. 'However did you…?'

How did she know? she wondered. Perhaps it was connected with the fierce sympathy for him that had risen in her so unexpectedly.

'You must have a gift for seeing into other people's hearts and minds,' he said.

She wasn't sure how to answer that. He was the last man in the world whose heart and mind she would have expected to see into.

'What is it?' he asked, looking at her face. 'Have I said something to disturb you?'

'No. I'm just thinking of the day we left England and Rik tried to stop me—the way you dealt with him. You said you'd do anything necessary to make him sorry he'd opened his big mouth, and that if he didn't get out you might do something you'd both regret. You were really scary.'

'And you thought that was the real me?'

'No—well, I did then. But now…'

He smiled. 'We all have different sides to our natures. I do have a side that's brutal, cruel, unforgiving, but I save it for creatures like him. Don't worry. You won't see it.'

'I'm not afraid,' she said, not entirely truthfully. 'As you say, we all have different sides. My own cruel, unforgiving side is lurking somewhere.'

'Hovering about *me* a lot recently, I guess?'

'I must admit I had it all geared up and ready for you. But now I know how different you are from what I expected…'

'You think perhaps I'm human and not an unfeeling robot?'

'I never thought you an unfeeling robot.'

'Liar.' But the word was said gently, and with a touch of humour.

'I guess I deserved that,' she said. 'If you were unfeeling you couldn't be suffering about your father as you do. You've really taken me by surprise.'

'I think we've taken each other by surprise.'

Vittorio rubbed a hand over his eyes, suddenly feeling wrung out by the emotions swirling in his head.

'Perhaps it's time we left,' he said.

His weariness was growing by the minute, and the tension of the evening was becoming more than he could cope with.

He signalled to the waiter, who approached with the bill.

Watching him, Jackie was struck by the heaviness in his manner, and the way he kept closing his eyes. Alarm began to grow in her.

At last the bill was paid.

'Time to go home,' he said.

'No.' She laid a hand on his arm. 'Vittorio, I don't think leaving is a good idea. You're in no fit state to drive.'

'But I haven't drunk any alcohol. You know that.'

'I know, but you're shattered. Your head's spinning.'

'You're right. I didn't sleep well last night.'

'You didn't sleep at *all*. You spent most of the night wandering in the grounds.'

'How the devil do you know that?'

'I saw you from my window—several times.'

'Yes, I suppose I was pretty obvious. I kept meaning to go inside and get some sleep, but somehow I couldn't make myself do it. I should have done. It's left me tired. But that's not the only thing. This evening—I've never talked about all this before.' He met her eyes. 'With you, it's different. You understand things that nobody else could, and I've said far more than I meant to say. It's hard to cope with what I… Things I said that I didn't mean to.'

She laid her hand over his. 'Can't I help you?'

'You've already helped by being you. At first the past seemed to make us enemies, but it's also—' Words seemed to fail him.

'It's also opened a door of fellow feeling that we never imagined,' she said softly.

'Yes. Suddenly everything in the world seems to be different—I'm confused, but I'm also glad.'

'Perhaps it means that we really have managed to become friends?' she suggested tentatively.

He gave a wry smile. 'My best friend. Who would ever have imagined that?'

'Friendship can come out of the strangest places.'

'They don't come much stranger than ours.'

'And now, because I'm your friend, I'm telling you not to try to drive home tonight. It wouldn't be safe.'

'Don't panic. It'll be all right.'

'I don't think so.'

'You think I can't be trusted to drive properly?'

'I think you're not well enough. I've seen how you keep closing your eyes the way people do when their head's aching. You're in a bad way, and you could collapse at the wheel.'

'I promise not to. Now, let's go.'

Jackie took a deep breath. What she was about to say was momentous. 'No. Vittorio, if you get into that car I'll call the police.'

He stared at her. 'Did I hear you right? That's the act of a *friend*, is it?'

'Yes. A friend who's trying to protect you from harm. I guess that's something you're not used to.'

'I'm certainly not used to people telling me what to do.'

'Don't worry. Now *I'm* here you'll get used to it.'

'So what's going to happen? Will *you* drive us home?'

'No way. I'm not a confident driver, and I couldn't handle the Italian roads at night.'

'Then what are we going to do?'

'This is an hotel. We can stay the night and leave tomorrow. I'll go to Reception and book us two rooms.'

She tried to rise but his hand tightened on hers.

'I'll see to it,' he said.

He summoned the waiter and spoke in Italian. The waiter nodded and departed.

After a few moments he returned and addressed Vittorio, also in Italian.

'Oh, hell,' Vittorio groaned.

'What did he say?' Jackie asked. 'He spoke too fast for me to follow.'

'They don't have two rooms available. Just one. A double room.'

'Then take it,' she said. 'You need to go to bed. I can sleep in the car.'

'Why would you do that? Don't you trust me to behave decently?'

'Of course. It's just that— Well—'

'It's just that I'm on the point of collapse. I couldn't seduce you if I wanted to. You're quite safe.'

He rose to his feet.

Suddenly he staggered, reaching out to grasp at something. But there was nothing there. Jackie leapt to her feet, just managing to catch him in time to stop him falling.

She supported him to the reception desk, where he booked the double room. The receptionist cast curious glances back and forth between them, but said nothing.

'I wonder what he's thinking,' Jackie observed as they went up in the elevator.

'I imagine we can guess what he's thinking,' Vittorio growled. 'I planned to tell him you were my wife, but—'

'You're too well known around here to get away with that one,' she supplied. 'It wouldn't have worked. Much better for him to think I'm your latest lover.'

'That doesn't worry you?' he asked curiously.

'Why should it? Who cares about *my* reputation?' She gave a teasing chuckle. 'Yours is another matter. But I expect they're used to you appearing in this situation. All right—don't answer that.'

'You're enjoying this, aren't you?' he demanded.

'Well, I admit the sight of your face just now gave me a little cheeky pleasure.'

Cheeky, he thought wryly. If ever a word described someone that one described her. And she loved it.

Not for the first time he reminded himself to be on his guard. But his guard never really protected him against her.

At last the elevator reached their floor, stopping with a shudder that disturbed his balance again. Instinctively he seized hold of her. She clasped him in return, leading him out into the corridor.

'Room thirty-seven,' he gasped.

A notice on the wall gave her the direction of the room, which luckily wasn't far away. He reached into his pocket for the key and opened the door.

The room was large, dominated by a double bed. Slowly she led him across the floor so that he could slide onto it. He lay down with relief.

'Let me pull the duvet back so that you can lie underneath,' she said.

'No, I'm fine as I am. Thank you for getting me here.' He squeezed her hand. 'You're a life-saver. I'm sorry to do this to you.'

'No need to be sorry. Friends help each other.'

'I thought I'd be able to cope…'

'But what was there to cope with?'

Vittorio struggled to find the words to tell her about how his own thoughts and feelings had overcome him. But they were taking him over again.

'Forgive me…' was all he could say.

'There's nothing to forgive. We all have bad spells sometimes.'

'But I didn't handle it very well, did I?'

It was true, but she guessed he wasn't used to this kind of burden.

'Go to sleep,' she said. 'You need it.'

'I should call Tania first. She'll be expecting us home.'

'Yes, but tell her we can't come home because you've met a business associate and need to talk to him. We have to stay until your serious discussion is over. I'll be taking notes—like a secretary.'

'But where are we supposed to be sleeping?'

'You in here. Me in another room down the corridor.'

'But there isn't one.'

'Tania doesn't know that.'

He managed a smile. 'I guess you're right.'

She picked up the phone. 'Give me the number and I'll call her.'

Tania answered at once. Jackie immediately handed the phone to Vittorio, who managed to assume a vigorous, cheerful voice. Jackie couldn't follow every Italian word, but she could just about understand that he was doing as she'd advised.

'Thank you,' he said, hanging up at last. 'That's bought us a little time. You're a great organiser. Perhaps I really *should* go into business with you—not as an employee, but as a partner.'

'You never know. We might surprise each other.'

'I'm sure of it. Heavens, but my head is aching.' He closed his eyes and rubbed his hand over them.'

'Go to sleep,' she said. 'You'll feel better in the morning.'

'Where are you going to sleep?'

'There's a sofa over there.' She pointed to the sofa beneath the window.

Vittorio looked at it in concern. 'You'll never be comfortable there. It's too narrow and not long enough. Sleep here. This is a king-size bed. We can each take one side.'

'Not while you're lying diagonally on it,' she said. 'It doesn't leave me any room.'

He made some awkward movements to the side, but they seemed to tire him.

'It's no good,' she said. 'You need the whole bed. Stretch out and get comfortable.'

'But what about you? Who'll look after *you*?'

'I'm fine. You're the one who needs looking after. Shall I get something to cover you?'

'No, I'm warm enough. You go and lie down.'

He watched as she backed away and lay on the sofa. He felt as though he was sinking into a different world, overtaken by another self—one who was reaching out to her for safety. He frowned, trying to understand the mystery, but suddenly all thoughts vanished and a warm darkness descended on him.

Watching him, Jackie saw the exact moment when Vittorio fell into sleep. At last, she thought with relief. Now he could find a little peace.

But almost at once he began muttering in his sleep, then tossing and turning as though driven by some inner torment. It troubled her to see him floundering towards the very edge of the bed. At last one agitated movement brought him so near that he started to slide off, and she hurried across to hold him just in time.

'Steady,' she said.

'Mmm…' he murmured.

She couldn't tell if he'd heard her, or even knew she was there. His eyes were still closed but his hands grasped her, as if clinging to safety.

'Move back,' she urged him.

'Mmm?'

'Move back before you fall right off.'

He edged backwards, still holding her. She followed, joining him on the bed but not getting too close.

Suddenly he turned, throwing an arm over her. His eyes were closed, and from his deep breathing she sensed that he was still asleep. She tried to nudge him away gently, but his arm tightened, drawing her close until his head rested on her shoulder.

Instinctively she wrapped her arms about him completely. She was amazed at the feeling that swept over her. This man, who always seemed so strong and determined, had aroused in her an instinct to protect. She knew that he needed the safety she could give him.

'Goodnight,' she whispered. 'Sleep well.'

His answer was a soft murmur. She couldn't make out the words, but she felt the movement of his lips against her neck and tightened her arms at the sensation that went through her. At once she felt his arms tighten in response.

He lay still for a while, but soon his lips began to move again. She leaned closer, trying to hear what he was saying, but the words were indistinguishable.

She could make out only one.

'Elena,' he murmured. 'Elena— Elena—'

Then he was silent again, leaving her wondering.

Who was Elena? Was she the woman he'd spoken of? The one he'd found in bed with another man? Or was she some other ghost that haunted him?

He spoke again. 'Jackie— Jackie—'

'It's all right,' she said. 'I'm here.'

She wondered if he'd heard, and perhaps understood. Now he lay still. She listened intently for anything else he might say, but there was no more mention of Elena.

Who *was* she? And why was she with him in his head at this moment?

At last she felt her own body relax.

Her last thought before she drifted into sleep was that somehow this was perfect.

Vittorio had the sensation of being in another world. As time passed thoughts and impulses disturbed him more, driving sleep away, so that at last he opened his eyes.

He had no idea where he was. He only knew that he was being held in an embrace so comforting that blissful feelings streamed through him. But gradually everything became real and he discovered that he was lying in Jackie's arms.

At first he couldn't believe it. It was a dream. It must be. But her warmth against him, the feel of her breasts beneath his head, were sensations of such sweetness that he was filled briefly with pleasure—and then with alarm.

How could he have let this happen? With what crazy

lack of caution had he yielded to the desire to enfold her in his arms?

But at least she was asleep. If he was very cautious she might never know.

Moving with great care, he edged away, holding his breath lest she awake and discover how vulnerable he could be where she was concerned. That was something that must never happen. Inch by inch he drew back his arm and then his head, retreating to the safety of the far side of the bed.

There he lay tense and still, watching her for any sign of wakefulness. To his relief there was none. After a while he turned over and lay facing away from her, trying to get his thoughts and feelings in order. It wasn't easy…

Submerged in peaceful silence and sleep, Jackie was unaware of passing time until she felt herself returning to the world and opened her eyes. Memories were there of holding Vittorio in her arms, feeling him cling to her. But now she lay alone, and his back was turned to her.

A faint sense of disappointment was followed by a stronger feeling of relief.

He'd claimed her as his friend, but they didn't yet fully trust each other—and if he knew how she'd embraced him while he was unaware he might feel suspicious.

And he would not be pleased, she was sure. She remembered that he'd told her he wouldn't seduce her even if he wanted to.

He didn't want to. There was no doubt about that. If he'd woken to find himself in her arms he would have been embarrassed. Luckily fate had saved her from that disaster.

But then she remembered how she had enjoyed the sensation of holding him, the feel of his body against hers. And she knew there was another disaster that threatened her.

He stirred and turned to her. 'Ah, you're awake,' he said. 'Did you sleep well?'

'Perfectly, thank you.'

'No disturbing dreams?'

'Not a thing.'

'That's all right, then.'

She thought she detected relief in his voice. He couldn't have said more plainly that there was nothing between them but practical matters.

CHAPTER EIGHT

THE BEDSIDE PHONE RANG. Vittorio answered it and found himself talking to Tania, who sounded agitated.

'Are you *mad* to have that woman in your room?' Tania demanded.

'I told you we were both staying here.'

'But not in the same room. I just called the hotel to speak to her and they told me where she is. Have you *no* common sense?'

Vittorio ground his teeth and spoke quietly, hoping Jackie would hear little and understand less. 'There was only one room available. We had no choice.'

'Can you assure me you haven't lost control?'

'I'm not even tempted. She doesn't like me, and our relationship is strictly business.'

'So she hasn't even tried to put her arms around you?'

Vittorio ground his teeth. 'No,' he said. 'She hasn't. Goodbye, Aunt.'

He slammed down the phone.

'What's she so upset about?' Jackie demanded. 'I could hear her yelling even over the phone.'

'She's shocked because we're in the same room. She's concerned for your virtue.'

'Concerned for *yours*, you mean. Does she think I lured you into a double room because I have a scheme in mind?'

'We both know that you didn't want to share my room, disliking me as you do. I've reassured her that you don't want me.'

'But can she believe that *any* woman wouldn't seize the chance to seduce you and perhaps become a countess?'

'I guess not.'

Jackie began to chuckle. 'I can't believe this is happening. The idea of me acting the role of *femme fatale* is ludicrous.'

'Don't put yourself down,' he told her. 'You've got your attractions.'

'Not the kind likely to appeal to a man who can have any woman he wants,' she said cheerfully. 'I'm a realist. How much did you tell your aunt about what happened?'

'Nothing. She asked if you'd put your arms around me. I told her you hadn't.'

'Well, that's true. It was you who put your arms around *me*.'

He stared. 'Did I?'

'Don't worry. You didn't know what you were doing. I came over to the bed because you were close to the edge and I was afraid you'd fall. You were flailing wildly about and suddenly you grabbed hold of me. I couldn't get away.'

'Didn't you thump me hard enough?'

'Damn! I never thought of thumping you. Stupid of me.'

'Want to try now?'

'No, I'll save it and get some practice first. When I finally thump you—oh, boy, will you know you've been thumped!'

He grinned, but it soon faded.

'So we just lay there all night? Did I do anything? Say anything?'

She was tempted to ask him about Elena, but she backed away from the thought. Some deep instinct told her that she would be better not knowing.

'You muttered a load of nonsense,' she told him cheerfully.

'In other words typical me?'

'I didn't say that.'

'You didn't have to. What about you? Did you talk to me?'

'A little. You seemed so agitated that I told you it was all right.'

Suddenly he could hear exactly what she had said then. *It's all right. I'm here.* Again he felt the peaceful sensation that had overcome him earlier, as he'd lain in her arms. Everything had been all right because *she* was there.

So she knew that they had clung to each other by chance, but not how they had lain together so gently. It was a relief that she didn't recall the moment and blame him for it, but also disappointing that she didn't share the memory of it with him.

He rose and went to the door. 'I'll go and sort the bill downstairs,' he said. 'Then we can leave.'

'Let's have some breakfast first,' she said. 'We don't want you falling asleep at the wheel.'

Turning to leave, he gave her a wry grin. 'I'll forget you said that.'

He closed the door softly behind him.

Somehow she must banish from her mind the sweet memory of lying in his arms. A shared memory would have been lovely, but he seemed not to know everything that had happened between them. So it would be dangerous for her to brood on it lest her feelings riot out of control.

After that it seemed best to be businesslike. Downstairs they ate breakfast, discussed sensible matters and left the hotel.

Vittorio's headache had gone and he was relieved to find himself driving at the height of his ability. That was what a restful night did. It was a reason to thank Jackie, but he mustn't tell her, he warned himself wryly . She would be sure to turn it against him in a cheeky challenge. There was just no way of coping with this infuriating woman.

But she was more than infuriating. Alarming, troublesome, teasing, tempting, alluring. And never more than one of them for five minutes at a time.

They were almost home before Vittorio broke the comfortable silence between them. 'I hope we haven't got another problem waiting for us.'

'What kind of problem?'

'Tania. How do we cope with her suspicions about last night?'

'That's easy,' Jackie said. 'We assume indifference.'

'You mean we don't speak to each other? As if we've quarrelled?'

'No, that would only convince her she's right. When we get there, just follow my lead.'

As he'd been doing for the last few days, he reflected ruefully.

At last the car drew up outside the castle—and there was Tania, standing by the door.

As they headed towards her Jackie said, loudly enough to be heard, 'You're quite wrong about this, Vittorio. It would be a very poor purchase and not worth the money.'

Catching on quickly, Vittorio enthusiastically joined the conversation. 'Of course I respect your opinion, Jackie, but I think that item would be a good buy.'

They continued this back and forth until they were at the front door, where Tania was still waiting to greet them.

'What are you two arguing about now?'

'Ask her—*she's* the expert,' Vittorio said. 'I don't even understand.'

'Do you *ever* understand?' Jackie demanded. 'That thing looked good, but you're too easily fooled.'

'What thing?' Tania asked.

'Let *her* tell you,' Vittorio said. 'I'm going to get a drink.'

He vanished, leaving the two women regarding each other.

'What thing are you arguing about?' Tania asked.

'I can't even remember. We've seen so many things that he might buy, but he's being awkward.'

'Has he been misbehaving?' Tania asked.

'Only in one sense. He thinks he knows everything about business, but he doesn't understand as much as he thinks he does. And if you dare tell him he's got it wrong he gets insulted.'

'Then perhaps you shouldn't tell him.'

'Oh, I think I should,' Jackie declared. 'It's not good to let a person think they're always right about everything. Of course, certain people are *always* going to be convinced of that, no matter what.'

'It's lucky he can't hear you saying that,' Tania observed.

'He's heard me say worse. He knows I'm not afraid to condemn him. Luckily he doesn't care about my opinion any more than I care about his.'

'I was rather worried about you two being in the same bedroom last night.'

'Don't be. Nothing happened.'

Tania still looked unconvinced.

'Look, Vittorio doesn't want anything from me except efficiency in business. And I don't want anything from him either. So don't worry. I'm not trying to drag him up the aisle.'

Tania gave her an amused look. 'Am I supposed to believe that?'

'Believe it. All the others may yearn to be a countess, but I don't. He's quite safe from me.'

'Has he told you about how lively things are going to get soon?'

'No. Why? What's going to happen?'

'Every June we give a ball. Everyone comes from miles around. It's a huge, exciting event. You'll have great fun choosing something to wear.'

'Do people wear fancy dress?

'Some of them. Some wear conventional ball gowns and some wear historical costumes. We even have a Lady Nanetta costume you could wear.'

'I'll really look forward to this ball.'

'And I want you to enjoy it. Ah, there's Gina. Please excuse me, Jackie, but I must get on.'

After Tania had left Jackie headed up to her room, intending to type up the notes she'd made in Rome. But after a few minutes there came a soft knock on the door. She found Vittorio standing there, and stood back to let him in.

'That was a brilliant idea of yours,' he said. 'If we're arguing about business there can't be anything else between us.'

'I promised her I wasn't trying to drag you up the aisle.'

'I know. I heard you.'

'You—? You were *listening*?'

'Of course. Just behind the door. You're more fun to eavesdrop on than anyone I know. Nobody else complains about me with as much imagination as you do. But I seem to have improved in your estimation. Saying I always think I'm right isn't as bad as saying I'm cold and arrogant.'

'All right—enjoy your laugh. I have to be tough on you in front of Aunt Tania so that she knows I'm not one of the crowd chasing you. That way you can use me as a defence.'

He nodded. 'And you're the perfect defence.' He hesitated before saying, 'Are you all right after what happened last night?'

'*Nothing* happened last night,' she said firmly.

'No—of course nothing did. I only meant— Well, it was nice to be in your arms.'

So he *did* know, she thought.

'Yes,' she agreed. 'It was nice and friendly.'

He regarded her for a moment before saying softly, 'Just friendly?'

'I don't know,' she murmured. 'It's hard to say.'

He didn't answer at first. Then he placed his fingers under her chin and raised it, before dropping his head to brush her lips with his own.

'I'm sorry,' he whispered. 'I shouldn't have done that. I just wanted to know—'

'Yes,' she said. 'But it's not possible. We *can't* know.'

'Can't we?'

'It's too soon.'

'Too soon can be the best time—when you're learning about each other and want to know more. Am I offending you? Do you want to push me away?'

'No—no—'

He lowered his head again, placing his mouth on hers more intensely than before, although not enough to alarm her. She responded with pleasure, moving her lips gently against his and relishing his instant reaction. She felt his arms tighten and a tremor go through his body.

Where was this leading? Control was slipping away from both of them.

And then— 'I'm sorry,' Vittorio said, releasing her. 'That was thoughtless and selfish of me.'

He stepped back, leaving a clear gap between them.

'Was it?' she asked, bewildered.

'You're vulnerable. I should have remembered—'

'But—'

'Forgive me, Jackie. I didn't mean to— Just forget it ever happened.'

'Forget what? How can I forget something that didn't happen?' she said in a freezing voice.

He backed further away. 'You're right—it didn't. It couldn't happen because we have to understand— I'd better go.'

He turned and abruptly left the room.

Jackie stood motionless, possessed by such a fury that

she was tempted to hurl something at the door. She restrained the impulse, lest he hear and realise how he had affected her.

She could hardly believe how intensely she had responded to him. The touch of his lips, the feel of his embrace had started an excitement that had spread swiftly through her, igniting a fierce response.

The best part of it had been her awareness of a response in *him*. In one blazing, beautiful moment she'd known that he wanted her as much as he'd managed to make her want him. But then, in an assertion of strength, he'd silenced his own desire, rejecting her with a pretence of chivalry that didn't fool her for a moment.

Did he *know* that he'd inflamed her passion before rejecting her? Or didn't he care about her feelings while he was protecting his own?

No, she thought bitterly. He didn't care. He didn't care about her at all. To yield to his own needs would have meant letting her know that she had a kind of power over him. And that was something that he wouldn't risk.

All the power had to be on *his* side. He'd left to protect himself, not her.

Well, two could play the power game!

The next morning Jackie went downstairs to find only Tania waiting for her in the breakfast room.

'Your argument must have been fiercer than it seemed,' she said. 'Vittorio's gone away on estate business.'

'Doesn't he often have to do that?'

'Sometimes. There's a tiny village on the far side of his land, and he needs to stay there for a couple of days.'

Before Jackie could reply her cell phone rang. Answering it, she found herself talking to Gary, a salesman who had frequently called in to the shop in London, usually with good products to offer. They were on friendly terms.

'Hello, Gary,' she said cheerfully.

'It was quite a shock to find you missing. Are you going to be over there long?'

'Hard to say.'

'Well if you return to England, don't forget me.'

'Not a chance. It'll be nice to see you again.'

She hung up.

Tania was arranging things on the breakfast table.

'That looks lovely,' Jackie said, regarding the food. 'When I've had breakfast it's time I started attending to some business.'

'What business?'

'Vittorio has left me in charge of a new department in his store. There's a lot to do, and I must go into Rome and get to work.'

'You don't have to if you don't want to,' Tania said.

'But I *do* want to. He's paying me well and I'm going to work hard and earn it. I'm really looking forward to it.'

It was true. Taking charge of the new department could be exactly the kind of pleasure she would most enjoy. But instinct warned her of another aspect.

After what had happened in the hotel Vittorio had gone away in order to avoid her. Well, if he thought she was going to play the rejected woman—watching for his return, wondering when he would find time for her—he was mistaken.

Tania called her a taxi and she was soon on her way to Rome. Entering the store, she wondered what reaction would greet her. Had Vittorio really declared her authority as definitely as she'd believed he had?

Her fears were eased at once. The staff in her department greeted her respectfully—especially Lisa, the chief assistant.

'We have some new stock just delivered,' she said eagerly. 'We were about to start unpacking it.'

'Splendid. Let's get going.'

The next few hours were delightful. The new arrivals were glass items, elegant and expensive, not just dishes but also small statues of animals.

'These are incredible,' Jackie said, lifting one up to study it. 'I think this is a lion...'

'Yes, and this one is a tiger,' Lisa said. 'Over here we have a horse and a bear.'

'All made of glass and *so* lovely. Where shall we put them?'

'I think we already have buyers,' Lisa said suddenly.

Jackie looked up to find a husband and wife descending on them. They were entranced by the statues and insisted on buying every one.

'I can't believe that really happened,' Jackie said in a daze. 'One minute we'd unpacked them—the next moment they were gone.'

'You must have bought the right thing,' Lisa said brightly. 'We'd better replace them quickly.'

In a moment Jackie was back on the computer, contacting the manufacturer and concluding another purchase.

'I've ordered three times as many,' she said. 'And they'll be delivered tomorrow.'

Her staff cheered. Jackie wondered if she had ever known a happier occasion in her life. To be in charge, to see everything work out so well, to know that she was more than capable of handling the situation—all this inspired a pleasure and a satisfaction that was almost beyond her understanding.

She plunged back into work, loving every moment. When the time came to leave she was almost reluctant.

'I know the store's closing, but I've got so much I want to do,' she said, indicating the computer.

'You could stay the night,' Lisa told her. 'Signor Vittorio has a place where he sleeps.'

'Then I'll use that.'

Jackie called Tania, wondering if Vittorio had arrived home yet. But she told her he wasn't expected for another day.

'I'm staying here at the store tonight,' she said.

'But are you sure?' Tania asked. 'I can arrange a taxi—'

'I must stay. There's so much work to do that I can't leave. Vittorio gave me this job so that I can make money for him, and I mustn't neglect it.'

'Very well. I'll explain to him when he returns.'

A tiny bedroom, almost as small as a cupboard, was attached to Vittorio's office. Clearly this was an emergency refuge, for use only when he was so submerged in work that nothing else mattered.

The bed was narrow, but comfortable. Jackie had worked late before retiring for the night. Now it felt good to brood over the success of the day. She looked forward to displaying everything to Vittorio.

She was up early next morning, greeting the staff, watching closely as their work got under way.

'The delivery is here,' Lisa said excitedly.

'Great. We'll get it displayed at once.'

'But there is so much!' Lisa protested. 'Where can we put it all?'

'Over there,' Jackie said, pointing to a large cabinet. 'Move the stuff out of that and we'll have room for everything.'

They got to work. Jackie watched, delighted at the way everything was changing for the better—not just in the store but in her life.

'It's going to look wonderful,' Lisa declared. 'We'll have to move some more things but—'

Lisa checked herself, clearly distracted by something she'd seen a few feet away.

Turning, Jackie saw Vittorio. After a glance at his grim face Lisa scuttled away.

'Tania told me I'd find you here,' he said. 'She says you stayed all night.'

He was scowling, and he sounded angry.

Jackie regarded him, puzzled. 'That's right,' she said. 'I got so involved in my work here that I wanted to concentrate on it, so I was here all night. I'm sure you're glad to know I've been working hard.'

'I'm not sure I'm *glad* about what I'm seeing. You've taken over and changed a great deal here. I don't remember us discussing it.'

'We didn't discuss it. There was a lucky chance—new stock that sold well. I've simply bought some more.'

'Which I can see is being delivered now. When did you order it?'

'Yesterday.'

'Surely not. It can hardly have been delivered so soon.'

'Let me show you.'

She accessed the computer, bringing up details of the order, which Vittorio regarded with growing shock.

'Look at the price of that stuff!' he breathed. 'You've bought so *much* of it, and paid all that extra money for a fast delivery. And you've done it without consulting me. Are you trying to make me bankrupt?'

'Are you saying you can't afford it? This from the man who tried to bribe me with a million pounds?'

'Don't dare say that. I didn't try to *bribe* you. I just want to pay you what you're entitled to. This is quite different. It isn't about money. It's about you trying to push me aside and take over.'

'I'm not *taking over*. I'm just exercising the authority you gave me.'

'I never meant it to be like *this*.'

Her temper rose. Everything had seemed so wonderful before, and now he was ruining it.

She faced him with blazing eyes. 'You said I'd be in

charge of my own department. That I'd have a team who would take my orders. I thought you meant it—but perhaps I should have understood you better.'

'What the devil do you mean by *that*?'

'I should have realised that you're a man who says what suits him but doesn't mean a word of it. When I ask you to live up to your promises, you object. When I stand up to you, you can't cope.'

His face tightened. 'We've made jokes about you being a bully,' he snapped, 'but it's *not* a joke. That's what you are.'

'I do *not* bully my staff.'

'No, but you're trying to bully *me*.'

'Then we're equal. We're both bullies. That's why we can never get things right between us.'

'Don't tempt me to fire you!' he snapped.

'You don't need to. I resign here and now. It's over. Finished.'

'No, wait— Jackie—'

'I mean it. I *won't* put up with you dictating to me. It's not what we agreed.'

'We didn't agree about you meeting men behind my back, but that didn't stop you.'

'*What?*'

'That's why you're here, isn't it? This guy named Gary called and you hurried here to meet him yesterday. And you stayed the night,'

'Did Tania—?'

'Yes, she heard you talking to him. Where is he?'

'In England.'

He paused to give her a bitter glance, before turning away and heading for his office, where he wrenched open the door to the tiny bedroom. He saw that it was empty.

'*Where is he?*'

'He's in England,' Jackie said furiously. 'He never came here and I haven't seen him. I came here to get on with some *work*. Vittorio, you're out of your mind. It was pure chance that he rang when he did.'

'And you said you looked forward to seeing him.'

'Only when I go back to England—which will now be soon. I'm finished here. I can't work for you any more. You're impossible.'

He took hold of her at once. 'I don't want you to go.'

'I didn't ask what you want. I'm going.'

'You're not.' His grip tightened. 'We made an agreement—'

'Which *you* have broken.'

'That's not true. I promised you status and authority—'

'And you didn't mean a word of it.'

'You think so? Let's see if I can change your mind.' He glanced out through the door, where Lisa could just be seen. *'Lisa!'*

Lisa entered the office, looking back and forth between them with a puzzled frown.

'I want to talk to the other staff,' Vittorio said. 'See how many of them you can get in here.'

'Some of them are busy serving.'

'Just get the ones who are free. I have an important announcement to make.'

When Lisa had gone Jackie asked, 'What are you going to tell them?'

'Wait and see.'

'But isn't it something I need to know?'

'You mean I need your *agreement*? No way. Listen to what I have to say, and then you'll know everything.'

'But you can't—'

'Don't tell me what I can and can't do. I'm your boss. Whatever I say, you'll have to accept it.'

She could have screamed with frustration. His meaning was all too clear.

Rather than let her embarrass him by resigning, he was

going to shame her by dismissing her in front of an audience. She'd thought him better, more generous than this.

The rest of the staff were coming into the room. Vittorio's grip on her arm remained firm as he greeted them.

'Gather round, everyone. I've got an announcement to
make which will probably surprise you, but it's the inevitable result of Jackie's actions over the last two days.'

Jackie tensed in anguish. Could this *really* be happening?

'You've all seen how she's plunged herself into work,'
Vittorio continued. 'Increasing the stock, changing the arrangements. I reckon there's only one response I can make
to everything she's done...' He took a deep breath. 'So I've
decided to promote her. From now on she'll have a place on
the leadership team and a significant payrise.'

A friendly cheer broke out, backed up by the sound of
applause.

Jackie barely heard. She was staring at Vittorio, trying
to believe the words that were spinning in her head.

He met her eyes, his own gleaming with ironic humour
and something else that she wasn't sure she could understand. He leaned down, murmuring, 'Now you know what
I wanted to say. Do you have any objections?'

'I don't know.'

Everyone crowded round her, patting her, congratulat-
ing her.

'I don't *think* I have any objections,' she said.

He leaned down again and whispered in her ear. 'Think
about it and tell me later.'

'Yes,' she agreed.

Like everything else between them, it would have to be
decided on later.

CHAPTER NINE

'WE'LL SETTLE THE details later,' Vittorio told his employees. 'For the moment all you need to know is that Jackie is a great power.'

He took Jackie's hand so that she had no choice but to follow him out of the building to a small restaurant nearby. 'Now for something to eat,' he said. 'After that I need something to boost my strength,' he added when they were settled at the table.

'So do I. You really enjoyed catching me on the wrong foot, didn't you?'

He turned, regarding her with an indignation that amazed her.

'*What* did you say?' he demanded. 'You think I caught you on the wrong foot? No way. You threatened to leave and I responded by improving your position. Who won? I'd say *you* did.'

'Oh, come on—'

'*You* come on. You've transformed the department to suit your own ideas. When I ventured to protest you reduced me to silence. Let's be clear who's the strong one— and it's not me.'

His tone was almost light, yet she detected a hint of definite annoyance.

She smiled at him. 'For a moment I thought you were really angry,' she said.

'No, I know how to accept defeat.'

'I wasn't trying to defeat you—'

'We'll have to disagree about that. But the sight of your face when I said you were promoted is something I'll always remember.'

'Did you really mean it?' she asked. 'It sounds so incredible.'

'Then you'll have to prove I got it right, won't you?'

'I'll try. And, however it may seem, I really *am* grateful. I thought you were going to dismiss me—'

'No way. You're far too valuable for me to risk throwing you away. You're going to make me a big profit.'

'But think of the money you've risked by doubling my salary.'

'True. I shall have to work you twice as hard.' He grinned. 'Perhaps you should be afraid.'

'The one thing I *can't* imagine is being afraid of you.'

'Is that true?' he asked ironically.

It wasn't, but just now it seemed better to be tactful.

'True enough,' she said. 'Thank you for what you did today. I'm really grateful.'

'So we're friends again?' he asked.

'I guess we are.'

He smiled and began to lean towards her. For a moment she thought he meant to kiss her, but suddenly his face lit up.

'Stefano!' he cried. 'Fancy finding you here!'

Looking around, Jackie saw a good-looking man in his thirties standing a few feet away. The man approached the table and sat down in the chair that Vittorio had pulled out for him.

When they had clapped each other on the shoulder Vittorio said, 'Jackie, let me introduce you to my great friend—Barone Stefano Fedele.'

She shook his hand. 'Signor Barone.'

'Call me Stefano,' he said, kissing her hand theatrically. 'A friend of Vittorio's is a friend of mine.'

'Come and eat with us,' Vittorio said.

'I would love to, but I'm in a hurry. I'll see you at the ball.' He grinned cheekily. '*If* I'm invited.'

'You know you are. Always!'

'It'll be a great evening. As always. Now, I must go, but I look forward to seeing you.'

He hurried away.

'What a nice man,' Jackie said.

'Yes, he's got a lot of charm. Too much sometimes.'

'Too much?'

'A bit of a flirt. Did you notice how he kissed your hand?'

'Yes. Charming…'

'His name means "faithful". And never did a man have a less appropriate name. He's what is politely known as a playboy. The impolite version you can probably imagine.'

'Okay, you've warned me. I won't go falling for him.'

'Do you *ever* fall for any man?' he asked with a touch of humour.

'That depends on the man. Sometimes I have to be wary of a man because he's nice enough to tempt me. Others don't fit the bill.'

'How long does it take you to decide which category a guy fits into?'

'It varies. Sometimes ten seconds is enough, and sometimes I have to give him a chance.'

She sounded well experienced in dealing with unwanted men, Vittorio thought. He wondered in which of the two categories she would place himself, and was briefly tempted to ask her—in a jokey manner. But caution made him resist the temptation.

He was still troubled by the memory of the kiss he had ventured to give her two days ago, and how it had affected him so intensely that he'd backed off in fear—rejecting her and rejecting his own inner self that had started to make him aware of things that troubled him.

He longed to know if the memory haunted her too. But he had an uneasy feeling that perhaps it amused her.

They barely spoke on the journey home. Once there, he returned to work in his office and she joined Tania, who was deep in planning for the ball.

'Things are building up,' she said. 'We've started receiving replies to the invitations. All acceptances. Nobody ever refuses.'

She showed Jackie the guest list, on which some names had been marked with a tick to indicate acceptance.

'You can tick Baron Stefano Fedele,' Jackie said. 'We met him this afternoon and he's looking forward to it.'

'You met him? Tell me more.'

Beaming, Tania listened as Jackie described the meeting.

'He's a good friend,' Tania said. 'And we need some of those to counterbalance the crowd of women who'll turn up and flaunt themselves. I wish we could keep them out, but they come from notable families and we have to invite them all out of good manners. We can't tell them to leave their daughters behind!' Tania sighed. 'By far the worst woman we will be forced to endure is the woman who betrayed my nephew in the past.'

'She's actually *invited*?' Jackie gasped. 'After what she did?'

'Her husband is the Duke of Revendo. His family have always been part of high society, invited to all notable occasions. If they were left out everyone would know why. And the gossip would be terrible. Vittorio simply can't risk having people giggle about how he was rejected by the Duchess because he wasn't noble enough.'

Jackie was stunned. In her mind Vittorio was the stern, determined man who had rescued her from Rik and used his strength to defend her. They had shared occasional jokes, and the night he had collapsed in the Rome hotel had shown her a gentler side to him. But never for a moment had he seemed as vulnerable as Tania's words now suggested.

Had something changed for him that night? Had there been a moment when he'd dreamed the woman lying beside him was the beloved he'd lost? Had she, Jackie, looked different to him ever since?

She couldn't tell. But suddenly, with all her heart, she longed to know.

Tania hesitated before asking quietly, 'Is everything all right between you and Vittorio—about that other man?'

'There isn't another man. I know you heard me talk to Gary on the phone, but I didn't go into town to meet him. He's in England.'

'Oh, dear. I'm afraid I told Vittorio about his call and…' She sighed helplessly.

'And he thought the worst because he thinks no woman can be trusted. Why is he so sure of that? I know about this woman who deceived him with another man, but surely he's had time to grow out of that?'

'You're right. It's not just her. It was his mother too. He adored her. They were very close, and he felt he was the centre of her life until she deserted him.'

'She ran away with another man?'

'No, she died in childbirth—but the baby came from an affair with another man. The baby died too. They're buried together. I once saw Vittorio looking at that grave, and what I read in his face was heartbreaking. He loved her so much, and had always felt she loved him, and yet she lay there with another son in hers arms for ever.'

'But that's terrible,' Jackie said. 'How could he bear it?'

'It still causes him great pain. To be fair, I can't entirely blame his mother. His father was never faithful. He slept with dozens of other women and she took refuge in affairs of her own. They did it to get back at each other, but it was their child who suffered.'

'And it's still with him, even now?'

'Yes. If even his *mother* couldn't be trusted, then he believes no woman can be trusted.'

'And then there was this girl who betrayed him?'

'Worst of all is our being forced to receive her at the ball. But now I suggest an early night,' Tania said. 'From now on we will have a mountain of work to do.'

As they left the room Jackie and Tania continued to discuss the ball for a while longer before Vittorio joined them. Tania was talking enthusiastically about the costume she planned to wear before turning to Jackie.

'Jackie, I really think you should wear Lady Nanetta's gown. What about you Vittorio? Modern evening dress?'

'No, if Jackie agrees I will be taking my costume from the guy in the picture next to Lady Nanetta. Let's have a look at him now.'

Vittorio and Jackie went to the gallery to find the picture he was talking about. Jackie studied it with fascination. He was a tall man in Regency attire. The trousers were white, the jacket dark blue.

'You're going to wear *that*?' Jackie asked.

'If I can get into it. I think I probably can.'

'All the women who want to be in your harem will love it.'

'If I wanted a harem I'd be flattered by that remark. As it is, I'll remind you that you're here to protect me.'

Tania appeared in the doorway of the gallery then, beckoning Vittorio over. He went to talk to her and Jackie went up to her room. She wanted to be alone to get her thoughts together.

She had been troubled before by a guilty feeling that she was enjoying this luxury at the expense of her father's suffering.

She reached into her bag. After few moments she found what she was seeking and took it out to study it. It was a photograph that she had taken of her father ten years ago. There was George's face, gazing back at her, his eyes as gentle and warm as she remembered them.

'That's a nice picture,' said a deep voice.

Turning, she saw Vittorio standing close. He had slipped in through the half-open door and come over to her without her realising.

'It's my father,' she said.

'I know. I recognise him from the picture my father had of him.'

'You have a picture of my father? Oh, please, let me see it.'

'I'll get it.'

He left her room, heading across the corridor to his own. Impulsively she followed him, and saw him going through a drawer, turning out papers. He handed a photograph to her, and she stared at it in astonishment.

'Yes, that's Daddy. And the other man is your father.'

'You say that as though you've seen him before.'

'The day after we met I went online to look up the Counts of Martelli. I was curious about you.'

'And you wanted to know if I was who I'd said I was, or whether I'd been telling you a pack of lies?'

He spoke cheerfully, without resentment, but she felt self-conscious enough to say, 'I didn't know you so well in those days.'

'And now you know me better you trust me even less?' he said, in the same light-hearted voice.

'It depends on the circumstances. Sometimes I think you're the biggest fraudster ever. At other times our minds seem to connect so well that...' She paused.

'That you don't believe me to be so bad after all?'

'You probably knew that already.'

'Well, whatever you think of me it's pretty obvious that our fathers got on well. This picture says a lot, don't you agree? It was taken in Italy. You can see that they were good friends.'

The two men faced the camera, grinning, arms raised exuberantly, clearly rejoicing in each other's company.

'They *do* look happy together,' she murmured.

'Yes, they do. There's no hint there of what was to happen later.'

'No. I don't think I ever saw Daddy enjoy himself so much.'

'Nor me. My father was a serious man, and an honourable one—or so I once thought. I don't recall ever seeing him bouncing with glee like this.'

In silence they met each other's eyes. Each knew what the other was thinking, but neither spoke. No words were necessary.

At last she said, 'Do you have any more pictures of your father?'

He rummaged in the drawer and produced a head shot. It depicted what Vittorio had described—a serious, honourable man, who looked incapable of any shameful action.

Jackie gazed at him, hoping her desperate emotion couldn't be seen on her face.

You did it, she thought. *You ruined my lovely father's life and got away with it. And your son thinks he can put it right with money because he can't understand that nothing can ever put it right.*

She handed the picture back.

Vittorio put it aside and clasped his hand over hers. 'I'm sorry,' he said.

'Don't be. He did it. Not you.'

'If only there was something you would let me do—'

'Stop it. *Stop it!*' she said quickly. 'Don't talk about it again.'

'Yes, it's dangerous ground, isn't it? Jackie, will we ever be able to risk treading that ground?'

'I don't know. Sometimes I think not—but how can we know?'

'We can't know,' he said. 'We can only hope.'

'Yes,' she murmured. 'But for the moment hope will take time.'

She hurried away, escaping to her own room and locking the door. She seized her father's picture again and looked at it for a long moment.

'Oh, Daddy,' she whispered, 'what shall I do? Please tell me?'

But if his loving eyes were sending her a message she could not understand it.

The next morning Tania departed to visit friends overnight. Jackie and Vittorio returned to Rome. She had noticed a small empty shop on a corner, and become fascinated by the idea of taking it over.

'It might be useful as a showcase for people who don't want to go to a huge store,' she said.

'That's an interesting idea,' Vittorio replied.

They spent some hours in the shop, which belonged to the man who lived above it. Vittorio made an offer that he accepted and the deal was quickly settled.

He finished the day by taking her into a nearby jeweller's shop and buying her a diamond necklace.

'That's—that's very generous of you,' she stammered.

'You've more than earned it. And if anyone asks you, tell them it was a gift from me.'

Thus supporting their pretence of being a couple, she thought. It was a severely calculated act, and there was nothing emotional about the gift, but she had to admit that it was beautiful and looked lovely about her neck.

'I need to call in to the bank,' he said. 'I won't be long.'

He was back in a moment, with an unusual, slightly mischievous look on his face that puzzled her.

'What's happened?' she asked.

'It'll tell you when we get home.'

'Why do you have to make a mystery of everything?'

'Because when a man knows he's doing the right thing he has to make sure nothing can get in the way.'

'Am I *likely* to get in the way of the right thing?'

'Let's say we don't always see eye to eye about what the right thing is.'

She longed to press him further, but felt it would be wise to wait until their journey was over.

At last they arrived home and he followed her to her room.

'Tell me,' she said, smiling with anticipation.

He produced a piece of paper from his pocket and handed it to her.

'You'll find the answer there,' he said.

Eyes wide, she opened it. In a moment she was overtaken by shock.

'What—what is this?'

'It's your bank statement.'

'But—how come—?'

The statement clearly indicated receipt of over a million British pounds converted to euros.

'How does that money come to be there?' she demanded.

'I put it there. You're entitled to it.'

'But I told you I wouldn't take it. You have no right to force it on me.'

'And you have no right to refuse it. It was something I *had* to do, Jackie.'

'Why? So that you can feel better about your thief of a father? I told you *no!* If you could have given it to Daddy that would have been right, but he's dead and it's too late. You can't ease his suffering now and you can't buy me off.' She looked at the statement again. 'When did you do this?'

'Yesterday. I called the bank and instructed them on the phone.'

'You dared to—?'

'I told them to take that money out of my account and transfer it to yours.'

'But I've told you a dozen times not to do anything like that,' she snapped.

'Don't *my* wishes count for anything?'

'Not when they make so little sense.

'No, it doesn't make any sense to you that I loved my father and can't forgive what was done to him. If he was alive and could accept the money himself, that would be fine. But he can't. And now it's your own feelings that matter to you. And your father's.'

'Jackie—'

'Listen to me, Vittorio, and try to understand. The only thing that would ever make things right would be if you gave back the money not to me but directly to Daddy.'

'But that's impossible!'

'Yes. It's impossible. And that's why we'll never agree about this. When you put that money in my account you did something bad and arrogant.'

She came to stand before him, regarding him with a cynical face.

'What trick did you play to get a copy of my bank statement? Do people obey you in everything?'

He seemed uneasy. 'Not everything, but they do know me at the bank. I told them that you're my fiancée.'

'You told them what?'

'I said we were going to be married.'

'And what happens when they find out you were lying?'

'I wasn't lying. Marriage would be the best thing for us, and I count on your good sense to make you see it.'

'Are you out of your *mind*? We're the last people in the world who should think of marriage.'

'On the contrary. We're the first. From the moment we met we've understood each other—'

'*No*. It's seemed like that sometimes, but all you understand is wanting your own way. This isn't about *my* father's suffering—it's about *your* father. You want to restore your image of him as a decent and honourable man. And I can't let you do that because of how guilty it would make me feel to let you buy me off. You don't understand how I could actually turn down your money. Tell me, Vittorio, has anyone in your whole life actually refused to let you buy them?'

'No,' he said, white-faced. 'People are sensible about money.'

'But I'm not sensible and hard-hearted. I'm human. I've got feelings. What would you know about that?'

'And what would *you* know about feelings?' he raged. 'The only one you have is hatred.'

'Just for you.'

'All this because I asked you to marry me?'

'But you *didn't* ask me. You told me that the decision had been taken—after you'd informed the rest of the world. Well, now you'll have to tell them that you got it wrong, because I'd sooner die than marry you. I want nothing from you—not your money *or* this.'

She seized the box containing the diamond necklace.

'Take it,' she said.

But he backed away, holding up his hands to ward her off. 'Jackie, please don't do this.'

'*I said take it.*'

She wrenched open the box, tore out the necklace and hurled it at him. He managed to seize it in time to stop it hitting his face, and tossed it back into the box.

'We won't talk about this now,' he said. 'Not while you're in such a state. When you've calmed down you'll see matters more rationally.'

'Don't fool yourself. I know what you mean by "rationally". It means me seeing things from your point of view. Well, that will never happen. I can't stand the sight of you, I can't bear to be in the same room as you, and I never want to be with you again, you monstrous bully. Now, get out. I'm leaving.'

He left at once, anxious to get away from the hate-filled atmosphere.

Jackie watched him go and locked the door. At all costs he must not be allowed to return.

Oh, how she hated him. Once she might have loved him, but not any longer. Not now that he'd insulted her with an offer of marriage and money. It might seem crazily illogical, but this man had inflamed her feelings and then tried to take possession of her as a business venture.

Now there was only one thing left that she could do.

She had to get out of here. To get away from him and fast.

She threw her things into her suitcase and checked to be sure she had her passport and purse.

It would be a long walk to Rome, and briefly she considered asking Leo, the chauffeur, to drive her. But she abandoned the idea as risky. She must walk.

Before leaving, she wrote a note to Vittorio.

I'm sure you realise why I have to go. It wasn't working between us and it never would.

She slipped it under his bedroom door. Then she went to the back staircase, where she could descend unseen. At the bottom she found herself near the back door. She would be able to slip out unnoticed.

She began to walk. Her best hope lay in reaching the main road, where she might get a bus or a taxi the rest of the way. But her walk went on and on with no sign of hope.

The light was fading, and when a hut appeared in the

distance ahead of her she could only just make it out. It had started to rain. Just a soft drizzle at first, but it had swiftly become a downpour. She began to run, heading for the hut, hoping to reach it quickly, but she was already soaked when she got there.

Opening the door, she saw that it was shabby. In the poor light she could see little else, but there was at least a bed where she would be able to rest until light broke next morning.

She stripped off her clothes, seizing the small towel she'd brought with her, and drying herself as well as she could. She put on some basic items from her suitcase and lay down.

Gazing into the darkness, she wondered at herself for choosing this way out.

Might she not have stayed in the *castello* with the man who had once seemed to be winning her heart? Did she *really* have no chance of winning his?

Maybe she was being cowardly, running away, but what choice did she have? How could she stay with Vittorio knowing she could never win his love when he was so determined not to let her? No, she'd served her purpose. He'd paid the debt, assuaged his guilt, and now he'd surely be relieved to see her gone. Besides, she was glad to get away from him—wasn't she?

CHAPTER TEN

FOR WHAT FELT like hours Vittorio sat at his desk, trying to concentrate. At last he threw down his pen and faced facts. As so often before, the infuriating woman had wiped everything except herself from his mind.

If they were to have a future together she'd have to learn that he must sometimes think of other things. And the sooner they sorted it out the better.

He went to her bedroom and opened the door.

But she wasn't there.

Downstairs, he searched room after room without finding her. Tearing his hair, he went to the kitchen to find Gina.

'Do you know where Jackie is?' he asked.

'I saw her go out an hour ago.'

'Go out? Where?'

'For a walk, I think. She was carrying a case, but she couldn't have been going far or she'd have asked Leo to drive her.'

'Did she leave a message?'

'No, Signor Conte.'

So now Gina knew he'd been deserted, and suddenly it was unbearable that she should see him at such a moment.

In fury and despair he ran upstairs to his bedroom. There on the floor he found Jackie's note, and read it with mounting disbelief.

Downstairs he confronted Gina again. 'Which direction did she go?'

'In that direction.' She pointed through the window.

The path she indicated led to the main road and ultimately to Rome. Given the note Jackie had left him, the meaning was obvious.

'Poor Jackie,' Gina said. 'It's raining so hard now. How terrible for her. Shall I tell Leo to go after her?'

'No need,' Vittorio said through gritted teeth. 'I'll go myself.'

The rain seemed to get heavier as he headed for the car. What on earth had possessed her to do this?

The only possible answer appalled him.

She was heading for Rome—perhaps the railway station, perhaps the airport. Whichever it was, she was on her way back to England, leaving him with her cruel message and nothing to hope for.

Through the darkness the car's headlights flooded the road ahead, showing no sign of her. But she *must* be somewhere near here, he thought frantically. In the time she'd had to walk she couldn't have got much further than this.

Then he saw the hut, and pulled up quickly.

There were no lights on inside, but he had a torch in the car and took it with him.

He opened the door tentatively, unable to see much. 'Is anybody there?' he called.

The response was a choking sound. Turning his torch to the far wall, he saw Jackie lying on a bed.

'Jackie!'

He rushed forward and knelt beside the bed.

'What the hell are you doing, leaving like this?' he demanded. 'Are you mad?'

'Yes,' she murmured. 'I had to get away from you.'

'Because I'm a monstrous bully. That's what you called me, and you were right. I'm a bully and I'm about to prove it. I'm taking you home with me. Don't argue. You're coming with me whether you want to or not—because you're soaking wet and I'm not leaving you here to get pneumonia. If you refuse then I'll be forced to carry you.'

'You think I'm just going to give in to your bullying?'

'Why not? When we were in that hotel you bullied *me* to stop me driving home and I gave in, didn't I?'

She rubbed a hand over her eyes. 'Then I guess I can't say no...' She sighed.

'Wise woman.'

He helped her to her feet. At once she swayed, making him seize her urgently.

'I'd better carry you anyway,' he said.

'No, I can manage.'

'Jackie, please—'

'I said I can manage. Let me go. I don't need your help.'

He released her, but stayed close, keeping his hands only a few inches away, so that she could cling to him if necessary. She managed to get to the door without needing him, but then let him support her the last few yards.

She had insisted that she didn't need his help, but as he eased her into the car she had to admit that she wasn't sorry to be returning to warmth and comfort.

Ten minutes brought them back to the house, where Vittorio parked the car before helping Jackie out.

'Go up to bed,' Vittorio said. 'I'll send Gina to dry you off and make sure you're well.'

It was lovely to snuggle down in the comfortable bed, and even lovelier to reflect on what had just happened. True, Vittorio had shown his authoritative side, insisting that she return. But he'd also shown his kinder side, looking after her carefully as he'd driven home.

It was the same old confusion. Which man *was* he? The coldly authoritative one who would tolerate no disagreement? Or the gentle, concerned one who kept a kind eye on her needs?

He was both, she decided.

There was a tap at the door.

'Can I come in?' he asked.

'Yes, come in.'

'I had to see how you were.'

'I'm very sleepy, but I don't feel too bad.'

'Then you must have a nice long sleep.'

He reached out for the blanket and drew it up over her shoulders. She snuggled down blissfully.

'I'm sorry if I caused you a lot of trouble,' she said. 'It was just—'

'I think I know what it was.' He sat down on the bed. 'When you're better we must have a talk to see if we can sort out all the ways we misunderstand each other. It's strange when you remember how many times we've noticed how well our minds connect. Yet sometimes the connection fails.'

'It comes and goes,' she mused, 'but will we ever really understand each other? We're so different.'

'*Are* we different? Haven't we found a hundred ways in which we're the same?'

'Yes,' she murmured, 'I guess so...'

As she spoke her eyes closed. Vittorio watched as her breathing grew deeper, more peaceful. When he was sure she was asleep he took a gentle hold of her hand.

'It's been a lesson for both of us,' he said. 'And there's still some way to go. But we'll get there, won't we?'

When she didn't reply he leaned down and whispered in her ear.

'We will, because we must. We really must, Jackie.'

He laid his lips softly against her cheek and left the room quickly, before she could wake.

Jackie slept well that night, and the next morning went downstairs to find Vittorio already eating breakfast.

'How are you this morning?' he asked.

'Fine.'

'Good. We must get things sorted out.'

'What things?' she asked cautiously.

'We've got the ball to think about. It wasn't very kind to Tania, the way you dashed off. Hate *me*, if you want to, but don't take it out on her.'

'I don't hate you.'

'Really? You could have fooled me.'

'That was because you'd forced that money on me. You're so sure you can buy me off, aren't you? But you can't. I want you to take it back.'

'No way.'

'If you don't take it back I'll be out of here tomorrow.'

'You'll—? After all we—? Surely we agreed on that?'

'No, you *thought* I'd agreed because I shut up about it. But I still feel the same. If I accept that money I'll be saying that my father's suffering doesn't matter. But it *does* matter. It matters more than anything in my life. It would be an insult to him that I couldn't endure. Why do you want to make me suffer?'

'The last thing I want is for you to suffer,' he said, speaking the truth.

'Then what are you going to do?'

He picked up the phone, dialled a number and engaged in a sharp-sounding conversation in Italian.

When he'd put the phone down he said, 'I've told the bank that transferring that money to you was a mistake and they're to transfer it back.'

'Will it work? Won't they say that since it's in my account I have to tell them myself?'

'Perhaps they should—but they'll do what I tell them. Let me show you.'

In his office he switched on a computer, logged in to his bank and showed her that the money had immediately been transferred.

He stared at the screen, feeling blank despair at what it told him. He'd promised his father to return the money to Jackie, and felt glad when he'd managed to do so. But now he'd yielded, taken it back, and in his heart he'd betrayed his beloved father.

Jackie was also staring at the screen, trying to take in the incredible sight that she could see.

'They just obeyed you,' she murmured. 'However did you persuade them?'

'I've got a place on the board.'

'Of course. Why didn't I think of that? Is there anywhere you *don't* have power?'

Suddenly his temper rose. 'Are you out of your mind to say that? You just told me what to do and I did it. Who obeyed whom? And you dare to accuse *me* of having all the power.'

'I'm—I'm sorry,' she stammered. 'I didn't think—'

'Do you *ever* think? You've got it so firmly fixed in your mind that I'm a controlling bully that you never look at our relationship closely enough to see how often it's the other way around. You told me to get on to the bank and transfer the money, and I did it straight away!'

'Yes, I'm sorry. I didn't see it that way—'

'No, because it doesn't fit your convenient picture of me. Heaven help me if I do something that doesn't fit your expectations. You'll wipe it out of your mind the way you tried to wipe *me* out.'

'Stop it,' she cried, suddenly weeping. 'Please stop.'

Tears had come without warning. She turned her head but it was too late. He'd already seen them.

'Hey, come on, there's no need for that.' His rage vanished and he took her into his arms, resting her head on his shoulder. 'Don't cry,' he said kindly.

She pulled herself together and drew back.

'You're wrong,' she said huskily. 'I *do* know you can be nice.'

'However hard it is for you to admit it?' he said, smiling.

'I'm sorry.'

'Enough of that. It's good that we're talking. We can sort everything.'

'Can we? There's so much to be sorted.'

'I know. But we can do anything if we try. Come here.'

He drew her close and placed a kiss on her mouth. It was gentle rather than passionate, and it warmed her heart.

'Sit down and have some coffee with me. Then we can plan what we're going to tell Tania.'

'She doesn't know about what happened yesterday?'

'Nothing happened. As far as she's concerned you didn't dash off and banish me into the wilderness.'

'I certainly didn't banish you into the wilderness!'

He regarded her wryly. 'That depends on what you mean by "wilderness".'

He guessed she had no idea of the bleak desert in which he'd found himself when he had found her gone. It had felt like the worst kind of wilderness. And that had alarmed him because clearly there was no wilderness for her.

'We'll have to get to work on the ball,' he said. 'Tania's counting on our help.'

'Yes. You're right. I should have thought of that before I left. I was selfish.'

He touched her face. 'You're not selfish. You just panicked at the thought of being stuck with me for life. We all panic.'

'You? Surely not. I can't believe you *ever* panic.'

Briefly he recalled the wild churning of his stomach when he'd found her goodbye note.

'You're right,' he said quickly. 'Not me. Ever. Now, let's—'

He was interrupted by a beep from the computer.

'It's an email I've been waiting for,' he said.

He did a quick check and opened the new message.

'It's from the store,' he said. 'Some stuff we ordered has started to arrive. I need to be there.'

'I'm coming with you. We'll go to the store and then on to the railway station to meet Tania.'

They drove into town, straight to the store, where they found a mountain of new arrivals. Jackie was briefly nervous, lest they be more of the glass statues that had caused their row, but these were different items. They had come from England and they pleased Vittorio.

'Great,' he said, looking at them. 'Well done, Jackie. I did the right thing promoting you and doubling your salary. You're really benefitting the store.'

She smiled and thanked him, but at the back of her mind was a sense that his action was rooted in their disagreement over money that constantly haunted them. It was always there. When he couldn't give her money one way he found another way to lavish it upon her. Would this nightmare ever go away?

Another thought troubled her. She knew the need to fulfil his father's wishes was so vital to Vittorio that he would seek to keep her close to him until he'd achieved what he sought. Was it anything but that? When he had eased his pain would he feel able to dismiss her?

For another half-hour they worked in his office. Then a knock on the door made him look up to see Donna from the clothes department.

'I've brought what you ordered, Signor Conte.'

Carrying a large parcel, she advanced into the room, laid it on his desk, and departed.

'Have a look,' he said to Jackie. 'It's yours.'

Puzzled, she opened the parcel—and stared at what she found there.

'The dress!' she gasped. 'The one—'

It was the black satin dress she'd tried on when she'd first visited the store.

'It's a gift,' he said.

'You're *giving* this to me? You mean that?'

'You can wear it at the ball.'

'But Tania says I'm supposed to be Lady Nanetta.'

'That's up to you. You *can* be Lady Nanetta—severe, rigorous, terrifying every man she meets. Or you can be a different woman...the one I saw in this gown the other day.'

'And what is *she* like?'

'I'm not quite sure. I'm still waiting to find out.'

In truth, he felt he already knew. When he'd chanced upon her wearing the seductive gown, its satin clinging to her figure, he had discovered something startling about her and how she could affect him. The time had not yet come when he could speak of it, but the moment *would* come. He promised himself that.

'I'll wear it with the diamond necklace you gave me,' she murmured.

'And you'll be the belle of the ball.' He paused. 'You know, it would help me if we could seem like we're even more of an item. Maybe engaged? And it will help you look the part. I don't want Marisa and the others to think I'm in need of a wife!'

'Okay, I'll do my best,' she agreed simply, knowing if she said much more she would start grilling him about exactly what he was looking for.

And she didn't even know what she wanted as the answer. Did he want a bride—just not Marisa? Or did he not want a bride *ever*?

'Come now,' he said, interrupting her thoughts. 'Let's take this with us and go to meet Aunt Tania at the station.'

When the train drew in an hour later they were there, waiting for Tania.

'Lovely to see you both,' she declared when they had

all embraced. 'How are you getting on? Not strangled each other yet?'

'We're saving that until after the ball.' Jackie chuckled.

'Splendid. Nice to know that you can put important things first. We've got a mass of things to do...'

From the moment the next day dawned it was clear that Tania had been right. The castle was buzzing with preparations.

Over the next few days quantities of extra food were delivered and temporary staff were hired. A television company had even made contact.

At last the great day arrived. In her room, Jackie donned the black satin gown.

'Can I come in?' Vittorio called.

'Yes.'

He entered the room. 'How's this?' he said.

He was wearing the historical costume of the man in the portrait of Lady Nanetta. Jackie stood back to survey him, hardly able to believe her eyes. As had been fashionable at the time, the white trousers were tight-fitting, emphasising the fact that Vittorio's legs were long, slim and attractive.

And sexy, she thought, against her will.

'What do you think?' he asked, turning to give her a better view.

'I think that costume is very...efficient,' she said coolly.

'Yes. Luckily it fits me. And I think *you* chose the right dress. That one will lure every man in the room.'

'*Every* man?' she teased. 'Every single man?'

'Well, you can't ignore me tonight, can you? Not when everyone's expecting to hear that we're engaged.'

'No, I promise to do whatever you want.'

'Do you *know* what I want from you?'

She looked up at him with shining eyes. 'I'm sure you'll let me know.'

'You can count on it. Now, we must make everything perfect. Why aren't you wearing the necklace I gave you?'

'I've tried to put it on but I can't fasten it. It's too difficult.'

'Give it to me.'

He took the necklace and moved behind her, reaching around her neck to position the jewels. She tensed at the feeling of his fingers brushing her flesh.

At last he turned her so that he could look at her face. 'Are you all right?' he asked. 'Nervous?'

'I'm fine.'

From outside they heard the noise growing.

'People are beginning to arrive. Let's take a look.'

Going to her window, they looked out. They could see cars arriving, discharging their passengers. Wide-eyed, Jackie looked at the costumes that were appearing.

Some were obvious fancy dress—clowns, animals—others were historical costumes.

Tania appeared behind them.

'You look very fine,' she told Jackie. 'You'll be a big success. *Oh!*'

The exclamation was drawn from her by the sight of a splendidly attired couple whose arrival had caused others to stare in admiration.

'Whoever are *they*?' Jackie asked in astonishment.

'The Duke and Duchess of Revendo. I must go down and welcome them in.'

Tania vanished, leaving Jackie staring down at the couple.

So *that* was the woman who had broken Vittorio's heart by dumping him for a loftier man. She turned her head to look at Vittorio. He was looking down at the Revendos but his face revealed nothing at all.

It never does, she thought. *Whatever he's feeling, he*

doesn't want anyone to know. It's almost as though he's afraid of the world.

She gave a brief gasp of laughter.

Afraid of the world. He'd be so mad at me if he knew I was thinking that.

But it was true. Vittorio didn't trust anyone. Even her.

'What's funny?' Vittorio asked sharply.

'Nothing. Why?'

'You laughed. Why? Is the crowd below so funny?'

'Some of them.'

'Meaning Elena Revendo? I expect Tania's told you about her, hasn't she?'

'Yes,' she said reluctantly. 'But you told me about her first. How can you bear to invite her?'

'Why not? She did me a great favour. Because of her I know things about female deceit, ambition and greed I might not have learned soon enough to be useful. As it is—'

'As it is you learned that lesson in time to distrust every woman you ever meet. Good for you. What would life be like if you made the mistake of *trusting* a woman?'

He regarded her wryly. 'There *is* one woman I trust,' he said. 'One who isn't greedy for money or a title, who's intelligent, honest, and brave enough to express her opinion even when it annoys people.'

The gleam in his eyes made it obvious that he meant her. It might be unwise to feel flattered by such ironic praise, but she couldn't help it.

'You mean when she annoys *you*,' she said. 'Does she annoy anyone else as much as you?'

'I doubt it. Infuriating me is something she's brought to an art form.'

'She sounds like a nightmare,' she observed lightly. 'For safety's sake you should avoid her like the plague.'

'I try, but she has a habit of popping up in my mind when I'm not expecting her.'

'Then the answer's obvious. Expect her all the time. She's so awkward that it'll make her stay away just to confuse you.'

He grinned. 'Yes, she enjoys confusing me.'

From below, they could hear the orchestra start to play.

'It's time we went down,' he said.

Offering her his arm, he walked with her, out and along the corridor to the top of the stairs.

As soon as they appeared there was a squeal from below. Everyone looked up to enjoy the sight of their elegant entrance. Some of them laughed, some cheered, some applauded.

Jackie had no difficulty seeing Marisa's face. She was at the front, staring up at them with an expression that could not hide her dismay.

Wondering if Vittorio had noticed, she gave him a sideways glance. He returned it, smiling. She smiled back, happy to know they were in this together.

Marisa, watching them from below, scowled.

Most of the guests had heard about Jackie, and eagerly crowded forward to be introduced to her. It was clear she was the star of the evening, and every guest, male and female alike, seemed to be charmed by her.

Vittorio revelled in the attention Jackie was receiving, but soon enough was enough. He wanted her to himself for a while.

'Shall we dance?' he asked.

Together they proceeded to the ballroom, where the orchestra had just started a waltz.

'We've fooled them,' he said, turning her gently around and around. 'Let's give them a bit more.'

'By doing what?'

'Can't you smile at me as though I'm your heaven on earth?'

'But what would that prove?' she asked. 'Only that I'm

one of the crowd chasing you. Now, if *you* smiled at me that would be better. But don't worry. I understand why you don't want to.'

'Don't I?'

'Heaven on earth? *Me?* More like purgatory, driving you mad.'

'Which is just how you like it.'

'I can't deny that.'

They laughed together. Those dancing near them observed them and assumed that they were in perfect accord and exchanged significant glances.

'Now we've *really* given them something,' she teased.

'And if they were to hear me tell you that you look wonderful tonight they'd enjoy that even more.'

'No, don't say that. Some of them already want to murder me.'

'But I *want* to say it.' He raised his voice. 'You're lovelier than I've ever seen you.'

'Hush, don't overdo it.'

They laughed again. Then he whirled her around and around until the music came to an end.

'That was a great dance,' he said. 'I hope we can have another one before the night is over.'

'I'm sure we can. But now you have your duty to do with every hopeful woman here.'

'Yes, ma'am.'

Turning away, she found herself facing Vittorio's Baron friend—the one she had recently met in the city.

'Stefano,' she said happily. 'How lovely to see you.'

'And you, *signorina.* I remember our meeting with great pleasure. Since then I've hoped to meet you again. Shall we dance?'

'That would be lovely.'

He put his arm around her waist, drew her close, and began to spin her into the dance.

CHAPTER ELEVEN

STEFANO WAS AN expert dancer, and Jackie found her own moderate skills rising to meet his. It was an exhilarating experience. With his help she discovered her feet could move faster and in more complex movements than she had ever dreamed.

'That was great,' he said as the music ended. 'Now let's waltz together.'

'Yes, let's,' she said, moving into his open arms.

The gentle movements of the waltz made it easier for her to look around at the other dancers. One couple stood out. Vittorio was dancing with the Duchess of Revendo.

'Oh—' she gasped.

'What is it?' Stefano asked. 'Are you feeling unwell?'

'No, I'm fine. Everything's fine.'

'I'm not sure I believe you. When people say it like that things are never really fine.'

'Yes, they are,' she said quickly.

This was something she couldn't bear to talk about. She tried to catch a glimpse of Vittorio's face, to see if it revealed any emotion. But as he whirled around with the woman who had once meant everything to him there was only a blankness in his face that might have meant indifference, or an emotion too strong to reveal.

But then he smiled. And his partner smiled back at him. And suddenly they seemed magically connected.

It lasted only a moment before they turned away, out of

Jackie's sight. She took a deep, troubled breath, wondering what life was doing to her and what it would do next.

'You're not going to have any trouble finding partners,' Stefano said as the dance came to an end. 'Look at them all, watching you.'

He was right. There was another offer for her to dance, and then another. She accepted two partners, and then Stefano came forward and claimed her again.

'You're the belle of the ball,' he said as they twirled.

'Only because I'm dancing with the best dancer in the room!' she said. 'I gather you've got quite a reputation.'

'For dancing?'

'Only partly,' she teased.

She recalled what Vittorio had said about Stefano and his reputation as a playboy.

He was handsome, delightful, and he could make her laugh. Many women would have fallen for him, but these days Jackie was too wise. All sorts of new feelings had grown within her now, protecting her from a man as obvious as this.

But to spend a few minutes dancing with him was an innocent pleasure.

'How are you coping with Vittorio?' he said.

'He's not easy, but I don't manage too badly.'

'Everyone knows he's in love with you and heading for the altar.'

'Nonsense,' she said firmly, remembering Vittorio's face as he'd danced with the Duchess.

'Apparently he told someone at the bank that you were engaged.'

'Oh, that—oh, no. That was just a careless mistake.'

He chuckled. 'Who do you think you're kidding? If there's one man who would never make that kind of mistake it's Vittorio.'

'Yes, but—I'm not one of those women chasing him.'

'Of course you're not. That's why you've caught him.'

'Oh, nonsense. I haven't.' She thought for a moment. '*Have* I?'

'Don't you think you have? Or didn't you want to?'

'I haven't quite decided about that yet.'

A burst of laughter overcame him and Jackie joined in, unable to help herself.

Feeling her shake in his arms, Stefano grasped her more firmly. 'Steady,' he said. 'Don't lose your balance. Hold on to me.'

She did so, and felt herself once more whirled dramatically across the floor,'

Standing near the door with Vittorio, Tania was regarding them with her head on one side.

'The man Jackie's dancing with,' she said. 'Isn't that Stefano?'

'Yes.'

'I hope you warned her about him. Women lose their hearts to him so easily.'

'Not Jackie,' Vittorio observed. 'She never loses her heart to *anyone*.'

'Is that personal experience talking?' asked Tania curiously.

'It could be.'

'But you haven't decided yet? Perhaps you should take your own advice.'

'What advice is that?'

'You once told me that a shrewd businessman never lets a good deal escape him. Seize it while it's going, you said. Perhaps *there's* your deal.'

'A businessman?' he murmured. 'Is that all I am?'

'At one time you'd never have doubted it.'

'At one time I was a different man.'

As they watched the dance ended. At once another man appeared to claim Jackie, who went happily into his arms.

The two of them waltzed contentedly until the music ended, at which moment two more young men approached her, both trying to claim her. All around them the other dancers paused to enjoy the sight.

'Don't let a good deal escape,' Tania urged.

'You're right,' he said. 'Time I acted.'

He strode out onto the floor, arriving just as the two hopeful men were getting deep into argument.

'Sorry to break up the party,' he growled. As he spoke he put his arms around Jackie, drawing her close in a clasp too firm for her to resist. 'But the lady belongs to *me*.'

'Do I?' she asked lightly.

'You do. And if you don't know it now you soon will.'

Vittorio knew a strange feeling as he took her into his arms. Only a few minutes ago she'd been dancing with a well-known charmer, gazing up into his face, collapsing with delighted laughter, and then whirling away with him as though aiming for another world.

Now she was in his own arms, looking coolly up into his eyes and thinking—

Just what *was* she thinking? What lurked behind her gaze?

'I warned you not to fall for Stefano,' he said.

'I didn't. I was just being polite.'

'Polite to him *and* every other man in the room—thus making me look an idiot.'

'Why should it affect you?' she asked lightly.

'Because there's a rumour that we're engaged.'

'A rumour *you* started, for your own convenience. You just wanted to get the better of me about our disagreement.'

'And yet somehow you're the one who always finishes on top,' he observed. 'Isn't that strange?'

'Not strange at all, seeing that I've got right on my side,' she said.

'You *always* think that, don't you?'

'Sure—it's something I learned from you. Oh, boy, the things you've taught me! Get your own way at all costs. Never ask anyone else's opinion, and if they dare to offer one tell them to shut up.'

'I didn't ever tell you to shut up,' he protested.

'Not in words, but you don't need words. Why are you complaining? I had a few dances…enjoyed some innocent fun. It didn't do you any harm. We're not really a couple. We just made a bargain.'

He didn't answer. He had an uneasy feeling that the bargain was slipping away.

'Vittorio, listen to me. You claim that all women are deceitful liars, playing one man off against another. So what are you saying now—that I'm just one of them? Am I no better than the Duchess?'

'Leave her out of this.'

'How can I when you made such a point of dancing with her?'

'That was a courtesy. I danced with her to show that she doesn't trouble me. She did once, but now when we meet things are different.'

'Different? That could mean anything.'

'It means that my heart no longer belongs to her. It belongs to someone else—but I shouldn't have to tell you that. You should know without words.'

'Perhaps,' she whispered. 'But sometimes words can help.'

'Or they can make things worse—which they often do with us. Why are you so determined to quarrel with me, Jackie?'

'*I'm* determined to quarrel?'

'You know how badly I want to sort things out between us. Maybe I was clumsy about the money, but I was desperate to put things right between us, to make you stop hating me because of your father. You can see that, but you won't yield an inch.'

'Why *should* I? Stop this, Vittorio. You talk of putting it right, but nothing will *ever* put it right for my father because he isn't here any longer. If I took the money from you his tragedy would still be the same as it always was. The only difference would be my conscience, tormenting me because I'd benefitted from his suffering, knowing that after all his lovely treatment of me I'd just shrugged my shoulders and said it didn't matter.'

'Would he have blamed you for that?'

'No, he'd have told me to put myself first.'

'Then *listen* to him.'

'I can't take advantage of his sweet nature. I owe him better. But, Vittorio, this is no time to venture over such dangerous ground.'

'You could be wrong.' His arms tightened, drawing her closer. 'Perhaps the best way to tread on dangerous ground is in each other's arms.'

'Perhaps,' she agreed.

'Sometimes I think "perhaps" is the most troublesome word in the world. *Perhaps* I have feelings for you that frighten me. *Perhaps* you have the same, but you fight them off.'

'Perhaps…' she said, giving him a challenging look.

They were dancing slowly past a large open door. Suddenly he whirled her through it and into a dark corridor.

'What are you *doing*?' she demanded.

'Finding out what "perhaps" means.' His voice became intense. 'There's something I need to know. Jackie.'

'What?'

'This.'

He dropped his head so that his mouth covered hers. For an instant she tried to resist, remembering their last kiss which had ended in rejection. But the feel of his mouth was thrilling, devastating. Her mind sought to reject him, but her flesh warmed and trembled with pleasure.

Her arms seemed to go about him of their own accord, drawing him closer, seeking something that only he could give her. She moved her lips against his, revelling in the excitement of his response. She had the sudden devastating conviction that he was hers. He belonged to her because that was what he had chosen.

And with shattering conviction she knew that if she weakened she would belong to him. But how weak did she dare to be?

He raised his head a little. Her mouth was free but she could still feel the whisper of his breath against it.

'Well?' she murmured. 'Did you find the answer you wanted?'

'Perhaps…perhaps…' he said softly. 'There was just a hint. But you're not going to let me guess too soon, are you?'

Her smile teased and challenged him. 'If it's true you shouldn't need to guess. You should *know*.'

'Only if you'll *let* me know. You like to keep me wondering, don't you?'

'It can be fun,' she said.

'There's more in this for us than fun, Jackie. Can't you feel that?'

'I'm not sure *what* I feel. I'm still waiting for you to teach me.'

'Devil! Witch! Stop playing games with me.'

'All right,' she whispered, and drew his head down again until his lips touched hers.

She knew at once that she'd taken him by surprise, and a sudden determined impulse made her embrace him with greater fervour, enveloping him with her desire and rejoicing in his responding passion.

'Vittorio—'

'Jackie— Jackie—'

There was something in his voice that made her heart soar. But suddenly it was all over. He released himself from her and stepped back.

'Why do you torment me, Jackie?'

'I don't—'

'Don't deny it. You knew what you were doing tonight would drive me mad. That's how you get your pleasure, isn't it?'

'I've told you—'

'Did you enjoy dancing with them knowing what the sight of you was doing to me?'

'But I *didn't* know. How was I supposed to know you cared either way? You don't care about me. You pretend to for the sake of our audience, but it's all an act—'

'And *that's* why you hate me? Oh, yes, you've made yourself very plain about that. You hate me because I gained from what my father did to yours. You say all those polite things about how *he* did it, not me. But I see the truth in your eyes every time you look around this place. You see him, don't you? You see your father standing there. And he tells you to hate everything—including me.'

'Yes, he's here for me, but he doesn't tell me to hate. Hatred was never his way. All I feel is his love, which will always be with me.'

Before he could answer there was a shriek of laughter from further along the corridor. Instinctively they both backed off.

'Do you want to go back to the ball?' he asked.

'Not yet—I'm not quite ready.'

'Nor I. Let's stay away together for a while.'

'I'd like to go and have a cup of tea.'

'Tea? Not coffee? Ah, yes, you're English aren't you? Come along.'

Smiling, he offered his arm and they went along the corridor to the kitchen together.

But a surprise was waiting for them. There were already several young women in the kitchen, and as they neared she heard one of them say, 'What a shock Jackie must have given you all!'

The reply came in Italian, causing the first woman to say, 'I don't understand Italian. You know I don't.'

'*Scusami*. In English you would say Signorina Jackie is fooling herself. She thinks she can win Vittorio, but she doesn't know him. Jackie hasn't got a chance, but she's too stupid to realise that. Vittorio will take her to his bed, have what he wants, then throw her out. And *we'll* all have a good laugh.'

Jackie began to shake. To hear all this with Vittorio standing there, hearing it as well, was a nightmare.

'Are you sure he'd do that?' someone asked. 'He might really be in love with her.'

'Get real. Vittorio's *never* really in love with anyone. I've seen the way he looks at her,'

'So have I,' said a voice that sounded like Marisa's.

Jackie tensed as the voice continued.

'And *I've* seen the way he looks at any woman he's trying to seduce. That special expression he can put in his eyes—he's brilliant at that. Fools them every time.'

'I shouldn't think Jackie's easily fooled. I reckon she's tougher than that.'

'That just makes her more of a challenge. It'll make it all the funnier when she realises what a fool he's made of her.'

'But there's a rumour that they're engaged. Apparently he told someone at the bank.'

'I'll bet *he* didn't tell anyone. *She* told someone, trying to back him into a corner.'

'Wasn't he supposed to be engaged to *you*, Marisa? I remember when everyone was talking about it.'

'People talk about everything,' came Marisa's voice. 'What does it matter?'

'Perhaps you should think about Dino Norese,' said someone else. 'He's mad about you.'

'Dino's all right. Nothing special.' Marisa's reply was cool and lofty.

'Let's get out of here fast,' Vittorio murmured in Jackie's ear. 'We don't want them to see us.'

He drew her along the corridor until they were out of danger.

Her head was whirling with what she had heard. The world saw her as a woman foolishly trying to enjoy an impossible conquest and making herself absurd. And Marisa was trying to gain from this too, seeking to reclaim Vittorio.

Some of her words came back to her.

'I've seen the way he looks at any woman he's trying to seduce. That special expression he can put in his eyes...'

That special expression. She had seen that expression in his eyes, and it had pleased her more than she cared to admit.

He wanted her. She wanted him to want her. And there lay danger.

Suddenly Vittorio stopped, taking hold of her shoulders and looking determinedly into her face.

'You're not taking any notice of that nonsense, are you?' he demanded. 'Do you *really* believe I'm trying to lure you into bed for the pleasure of dumping you afterwards? Is that what you think? *Is it?*'

'No,' she protested. 'But obviously it's what everyone else thinks. It makes me look like the biggest fool on earth. I've got to get out of this place—and this time I'm going to leave for good.'

'Jackie, please think straight. If you leave again you'll make *me* look like the biggest fool on earth.'

'Can't you understand? They think I'm so desperate to marry you that *I* spread the rumour we're engaged.'

'And if I know one thing about you it's that you're *not* desperate to marry me. This is my fault, for what I said at the bank. And I have to put it right.'

'Fine. Go back there and tell them the truth.'

'What truth?' he demanded. 'We have so many truths, and some of them contradict each other.'

'The truth that we fight all the time—that we don't trust each other and can't talk without hurling accusations.'

'That won't convince them that we're not going to marry. Quite the reverse. Some of the most successful couples I know keep up their battle from morning till night. I'm beginning to think we're perfectly suited to each other.'

'Very funny.'

'True—it *is* funny. I like a laugh. The thought of laughing with you for the rest of my life has a certain appeal.'

'But laughter fades after a while,' she said. 'We've got to be sensible.'

'Sensible? Us?'

'Yes, it doesn't sound likely, does it? But I think it's time to put things right.'

'How do you want to do that?'

'We return to the ball separately. We're very polite to each other—'

'You mean with the kind of frigid politeness people use when they actually want to murder each other?'

'Yes. But I've had that temptation often enough to know how to overcome it.'

'Okay, I'll obey your orders. We act indifferent, but I think we should have a polite dance with each other.'

'To confirm the indifference,' she said.

'Right. Let's make a start.'

'You go first.'

He went in ahead of her. Jackie waited several minutes

and then she too returned to the ballroom, going at once to where coffee was being served, and talking politely to the guests she found there.

On the far side of the room she could see Vittorio dancing again, talking cheerfully to his partner. He seemed oblivious to her presence—but that was the polite distance they had promised each other.

'Will you dance with me, *signorina*?'

The man standing before her was a duke. Extending his hand, he led her onto the floor, silently announcing to the world that he had heard the rumour of their engagement and she was accepted in Vittorio's high society.

After him she was claimed again and again. There was no doubt that she was a success.

Across the floor she could just make out Marisa, approaching Vittorio, speaking to him intensely. From her expression she seemed displeased, and clearly his reply did not improve her mood.

So he'd made her understand that she had no hope, Jackie thought. But what had he told her about their imaginary engagement?

Her mind was spinning with everything that had happened that evening. Between herself and Vittorio things seemed to change from moment to moment, leaving her permanently confused.

And now came the moment for which she had been waiting. Vittorio advanced towards her, hand outstretched, and asked theatrically, 'Will you do me the honour, *signorina*?'

She went into his arms, feeling them close around her as they went spinning across the floor. Even as they whirled she was acutely aware of the curious faces following their every movement.

'They've heard the rumours of our engagement,' he said. 'They're trying to decide how true it is. Time to tell them.'

As the music ended he raised his voice.

'Can I have your attention?'

All around them couples slowed to a halt, staring at him curiously.

'I think you know Jackie,' he said. 'Ever since we came here as a couple everyone has wondered about her. Are we lovers? Are we going to announce our engagement soon? Guess what. We've wondered that ourselves. We have our disagreements—sometimes too often. And we've told ourselves—and each other—that these troubles made it impossible for us to be together.'

Jackie turned wild eyes on him. What was he thinking of, to let strangers into their private lives? This way he would make her look more foolish than ever.

'But there's something more important than troubles,' Vittorio declared, still speaking loudly to the crowd. 'And this is it.'

Before Jackie realised what he was doing he pulled her into his arms and laid his mouth passionately over hers. At first she was too stunned to react, but the feel of his lips caressing hers soon took possession of her mind, her heart and her flesh.

From all about them came cheers and applause. Everyone was delighted.

'It's time we gave them the message finally,' he whispered.

'How do you mean?'

Suddenly his arms released her and he dropped down to one knee.

'Jackie, will you marry me?' he called, loud enough for everyone to hear. 'Will you make me the luckiest man on earth? Will you make me unbelievably happy?'

He looked up at her.

'Do I get an answer?' he said.

'Do you really want one? Aren't you just fooling?'

'No, I'm not fooling. Will you marry me?'

'Then my answer…' she took a deep breath '…is yes.'

The cheers were riotous.

She had the dizzying sensation of having won a triumphant victory for the first time in her life. Plain, dull Cinderella had won Prince Charming.

Well, perhaps Prince Charmless, she thought. But she wasn't complaining.

Tania came forward, arms outstretched to embrace her.

'What a lovely thing to happen!' she declared, loud enough for everyone to hear. 'I'm so glad.'

Everyone got the message that despite her low birth Jackie was being welcomed into the Count's family. It was all settled happily and the ball could continue to the end of the evening.

Together Jackie, Vittorio and Tania bade the guests farewell, and at last the castle was empty.

Tania kissed them both.

'He has made the right choice,' she told Jackie. 'It's so lovely to see that just for once he's got it right.'

'Just for once?' Jackie queried comically. 'Surely he gets things right more often than not?'

'You'll find out about that—but hopefully not too soon. Wait until after the wedding before you discover what a clown he can be. Then it'll be too late for you to escape.'

'Thanks a lot, Aunt.' Vittorio said wryly. 'What would I do without you?'

'You'd have married one of those stupid debutantes. As it is, you've got a woman who'll keep your feet on the ground and make you act sensibly.'

'Hush,' said Jackie urgently. 'He doesn't *want* to act sensibly.'

'That's what I like to hear,' Vittorio said, slipping his arm around Jackie's waist. 'A woman who understands me.' He laughed. 'And now I think I'll go to bed. It's been

a heavy day. Jackie—we'll celebrate tomorrow. I'll buy
you a ring.'

'Lovely,' she said, smiling.

She doubted if he was really tired. He simply wanted to
get away from her to sort out his thoughts. She understood,
because it was the same with her.

They left the ballroom together. As they went upstairs
she waited for him to say something about that devastating scene, but he was silent.

At her door he said, 'We'll talk tomorrow. We have much
to say.'

In her room she stripped off the black satin dress, hanging it up with great care. From now on she would treasure
it as a sign of the new Jackie.

But who *was* Jackie now? she wondered.

Suddenly she no longer knew.

Was Jackie the woman whose heart reached out to Vittorio despite her sensible resolutions?

Tonight should have been a delight. He had declared his
longing for her before the world.

Yet deep within her there was still the suspicion that he
wanted to marry her not for love but to silence the troubles
that still disturbed him. He longed to make things right with
his father's memory. Other people would have found that
strange and incredible, but to Jackie, also intent on keeping her father's memory alive, it made sense.

Suddenly there was a slight sound from outside, followed
by a click as the door was opened.

'Can I come in?' Vittorio asked.

'Yes.'

'I thought I should come and apologise,' he said. 'It must
have been a shock when I sprang that proposal on you. I
just got a bit carried away.'

'It's all right. Don't worry. I'm not actually expecting
you to marry me.'

'Everyone else is.'

'Meaning Marisa and the other women? Soon she'll grab herself a husband and we can pretend until then.'

Vittorio gazed at her incredulously. 'I said you were a woman who understands me, and I was more right than even *I* knew.'

'I understand you well enough to know you don't want to get married—so don't worry.'

He gave a brief, wry laugh. 'You're only half right about that. Sometimes I'm not keen on marriage, but sometimes I feel that you're the one person who could tempt me.'

She regarded him with her head on one side. 'Temptation is there to be resisted,' she said. 'Be sensible.'

'According to you, I always resist being sensible. Maybe I'm right. Perhaps it's something we should think of.'

'Think of *marriage*?'

'Unless this is your way of rejecting me. Is your answer no, Jackie?'

'I don't know,' she said slowly. 'Everything is so confused between us. We're often friends, but we hover on the verge of being enemies.'

'I know. But somehow enmity just doesn't work. We always return to being—well—'

'Friends?'

'That too, but friendship is too simple.'

'Don't you feel friendship for me?'

'I feel all sorts of things for you that I don't want to feel. I try to fight them, but they fight me back.'

She nodded. 'I know what you mean.'

'Do you remember that night we spent together in Rome?'

She considered. 'I'm not sure we actually spent it *together*. We were on the same bed, but in different worlds.'

'There were some very close moments. I can remember lying in your arms. I wasn't sure how I got there, but it felt wonderful—warm and safe, and as though the whole world had changed and become kinder.'

His gentle tone revived her memory of waking with him, looking into his face and seeing it vulnerable as it had never seemed before. The sight had touched her heart, arousing a feeling of protectiveness towards him that had never entirely faded.

'Yes,' she murmured. 'The world was different.'

'We can make it different, if that's what we want.'

'If we want it badly enough.'

He stroked her face with tender fingers. 'I know what I want, and how badly I want it. But is it what *you* want?'

'Perhaps,' she whispered.

'Ah, yes—perhaps. The word that we said could decide everything. Perhaps we need to know more.'

He drew her closer, placing his mouth over hers.

He was right. They needed to know more. They needed this.

She moved her mouth against his, telling herself that she was merely seeking information, and what she learned sent shivers of delight through her.

But then she was invaded by a thought that made her draw back.

'What is it?' he asked. 'Am I doing something wrong? Don't you want me?'

'Perhaps…' she said, echoing their significant word.

'Is that your way of keeping me doubtful?'

'No, it's my way of saying I want to be sure if you really want me. Have you forgotten that time when you began to kiss me and then backed off, saying I was too vulnerable? You might be going to do that again.'

He groaned, and dropped his head so that she could no longer see his face.

'Why did you do that, Vittorio? Why did you reject me?'

'I didn't reject you. Believe me, Jackie, I didn't. I *forced* myself to let you go. I wanted you so much that I didn't dare go on any more.'

'But why? What would have happened if you'd gone on?'

'We would have made love, and then you would have known—everything.'

'Would I? Do we ever know what "everything" is?'

'Not really. We think we do, but there's always something—' He gave a sigh. 'I meant everything about *me*—how I feel, the power you have—'

'What power? I don't have *any* power. You could turn your back on me and leave at any minute.'

'Could I?'

'Go on—prove it. Reject me.'

He regarded her for a moment with a curious expression, as though he was trying to be quite certain of how she was manipulating him. At last a knowing smile took over his face.

'You know I can't reject you. You're just demonstrating your control and my weakness.'

'Then prove me wrong. Go on. Toss me aside.'

'If I could, I would. But I can't. You have me. I'm yours. Now you can crow with triumph.'

'I don't think I'll do that,' she said, sliding her hands around his face. 'I think I'd rather enjoy exercising my control.' She smiled. 'Kiss me. That's an order.'

He obeyed at once, touching his lips to hers. She waited for the kiss to grow more forceful, but that didn't happen. The soft touch continued, filling her with a sensation of sweetness that made her want to weep with pleasure.

Then he increased the pressure, and suddenly the kiss was as forceful as she could possibly have desired. She responded joyfully, urging him on further, and felt his embrace grow more intense as he moved towards the bed and drew her down beside him.

His hands began to explore her body, pulling away her

clothes. Her heart beat more strongly as things progressed to their inevitable conclusion.

When it was over peace descended on her as they lay together.

'Are you all right?' he asked, gazing anxiously down into her face. 'Did I do wrong?'

'Do you *think* you did?'

He shook his head. 'Having you in my arms feels more right than anything has ever felt before. Do you mind if I stay?'

'For as long as you like.'

He gave a sigh of pleasure and eased down so that his head lay on her breast.

She enfolded him with an instinctive protectiveness that overcame her to her own surprise.

Who would ever have thought this man would need her protection? Yet instinct told her that he did, for reasons that he himself had never suspected.

'Go to sleep, my love,' she whispered. 'I'm here. I'll always be here for you, as long as you need me.'

He didn't move, but she felt his breathing grow deeper.

'And you *do* need me,' she murmured.

He slept almost motionless for the rest of the night, and awoke looking lively.

'That was a great night's sleep.' he said. 'No bad dreams. What about you? Did I keep you awake, lying on you in that position?'

'Not at all,' she said cheerfully.

In truth she was feeling slightly stiff, but the pleasure of giving him a peaceful night was stronger than anything else.

'I'd better go before anyone sees me here,' he said, rising quickly.

At the door he turned to look at her anxiously.

'Jackie, things *are* all right between us, aren't they?'

'Perhaps,' she said.

'Perhaps?' He laughed. 'You know, that's a perfect answer. Bye, now. See you later.'

He vanished, closing the door behind him. Jackie lay back, closing her eyes, relishing memories of the night before, wondering where they would lead.

CHAPTER TWELVE

SHE WENT BACK to sleep and overslept, and was late going downstairs. Vittorio wasn't there, and only arrived half an hour later. From the frown on his face it was clear that he was displeased.

'I need a word with you,' he said.

'Has something happened?'

'Yes. I've been in touch with the bank. I wanted to return your money, but I can't. It seems you've put a block on your account so that nothing can be put in it. Did you do that?'

'Yes.'

'Why?'

'Why did *you* try to put the money in again, against my will? You *know* how I feel about it, yet you've tried to force it on me again.'

'So you fought back by blocking your account against me?' he snapped.

'I didn't fight—'

'Didn't you? Isn't that we do?'

'Only when there's no choice!' she cried. 'Why did you try to make me accept that money again?'

'Because it's the right thing to do.'

'The right thing? To ignore my feelings and make me accept something that hurts me? That's the *right thing* to do?'

'I didn't mean to hurt you—'

'No, you just don't care whether you hurt me or not.'

'I'd hoped to help you understand that you're making a fuss about something that doesn't matter.'

'My feelings don't *matter*? Thanks. I was beginning to understand that anyway.'

'Jackie, please talk sense. Why has this issue of money become so important to us?'

'It's not the money itself. It's what it *means*. You want me to take it for your father's sake, and to comfort you, but it wouldn't comfort *me*. The pain would stay with me. And if you had any feeling for me you would understand that. But you don't, and if we stayed together this would be with us all our lives, spoiling everything we might have had. I love you, but I'm beginning to think I could never be happy with you, and I could never make you happy.'

'How can you *say* that? How would you know what makes me happy?'

'Look ahead down the years, Vittorio. Can you really see happiness when we feel so differently about the things that matter?'

'We can make it happen. We don't have to give in just because we have a disagreement.'

'This isn't just a disagreement. It's more important than that. It's a difference that could last all our lives, poisoning everything. It was only because of a disaster that we met in the first place. Perhaps we were never meant to.'

'Stop it!' he said savagely. 'Don't talk like that. *Stop it.*'

'Yes. There's no point in talking, is there?' she said.

She fled the room, desperate to get away from a conversation that was breaking her heart. Against all likelihood Vittorio had claimed her love. Now, before her loomed a vision of a future without him.

He still didn't understand. He thought it was about money, but it wasn't. How could they ever be united as one when they saw life so differently?

In her own room she switched on her laptop, seeking

the distraction it could sometimes give. She forced herself to concentrate on the emotionless screen, hoping to control all feeling before she yielded helplessly.

An email had arrived. Opening it, she read it.

Things are chaos at the shop without you. Rik has managed to sell it and the new owner is desperate for staff who understands the place. Gary.

This was it. The sign she'd been waiting for—her chance to put the past behind her. Vittorio, Rome—everything she wanted to forget.

It had to happen. They weren't right together. She'd thought she could make it work because she loved him, but maybe sometimes love wasn't enough.

Going downstairs, she found Vittorio, as she'd expected, in his office, buried in paperwork.

'I have something to tell you,' she said. 'I'm going back to England.'

'Will you be away long?'

'I'll be away for ever. I'm saying goodbye, Vittorio.'

'Goodbye? So you really think we no longer have a chance?'

'Did we ever have a chance? We thought we'd got things right at last, but it was an illusion. Let's be honest. We need to forget that we met—and especially forget *how* we met. That has always been a kind of poison between us. Now it's time for us to face the truth and part. And you need never worry that I'll start any legal action. I promise I never will.'

'Is that what you imagine has been troubling me all this time?' he demanded angrily.

'I don't know *what's* been troubling you. I don't think I'll ever understand you any more than you will understand me. It's best that we say goodbye now.'

He gave a bitter laugh. 'Perhaps I should have expected this. You've meant more to me than any other woman because the others were after my title and my money. I valued you because I thought you wanted only me. But you don't want me. So you're right. Let's call it a day.'

His words were like a blow to her heart. If he had said he loved her everything would have changed. But he wanted her only for reasons of pride.

'Yes, let's,' she said. 'I'll call the airport now.'

'Let me do it for you.'

He immediately got on the phone.

After making a few notes he said, 'There's a flight at midday tomorrow. I'll book you on it.'

A few minutes were enough to do the job. Then all was settled.

'I'll print your ticket off for you,' Vittorio said. 'And I'll arrange a taxi to get you there in good time.'

'Will you see me off?'

'Yes, I'll come to the airport and make sure you get on the right plane. We don't want you to get lost, do we? Don't worry. Everything will go well.'

But nothing was going well, she thought sadly. They were parting, and all he cared about was arranging things properly. His insistence that she'd meant more to him than any other woman had been just empty words. She meant nothing to him.

But as she lay in bed that night she managed to find a little hope. There had been times when he'd treated her with something that might have been affection. Perhaps when they were at the airport tomorrow he might show some feeling. Perhaps he'd ask her to change her mind and come back. She would kiss him goodbye and then— *oh, please*—let him kiss her back. Let him discover that they really loved each other. Surely she could make him want her?

Still clinging to hope, she finally fell asleep.

She awoke early, dressed quickly and hurried downstairs, full of hope and determination. She would not give in. Today she would open her heart to Vittorio and persuade him to open his heart to her. It would be a day of victory.

She was smiling as she went into the kitchen.

But there a shock awaited her. There was no sign of Vittorio.

Tania was sitting alone at the table. She looked up and smiled at Jackie.

'Have a good breakfast,' she said. 'Vittorio said you'd be leaving early for the airport. He asked me to tell you goodbye for him.'

'He—what?'

'He got called away to an important meeting. He says he's sorry, but he couldn't help it.'

Jackie drew a sharp breath, fighting back the desire to cry out.

It was over.

He had abandoned her without a word of goodbye, and in doing so he'd made plain his indifference to her.

'I'll leave at once,' she said. 'Goodbye.'

'Must you go?' Tania asked. 'I've so liked having you here.'

'Thank you, but the sooner I go the better. I've turned into a different person here—one I'd better get rid of.'

'But why? It's true you've become another person, but she's very attractive. She's bright and witty, always ready to join in the fun.' Tania smiled fondly, adding, 'She's a true Roman.'

'That's very kind, but my *other* self is actually rather stupid. She's easily taken in because she believes what she wants to believe. Now it's time for her to face facts.'

'But does she know which are the right facts to face?'

Tania asked, regarding her curiously. 'Sometimes one makes mistakes about these things.'

'Not this time,' Jackie said with a sigh. 'I got it wrong at first, but now I've seen the light and—well, that's all that matters.'

'But there might still be things you should know.'

Jackie managed a smile. 'If there are, I think I'll discover them at the right moment. Now, I must go and finish my packing.'

She made a quick escape. Tania's unease told its own story. Vittorio's aunt knew that he was up to something that would hurt Jackie badly, and she was unsure what to reveal.

But Tania didn't need to tell her, Jackie thought. Vittorio was angry with her for daring to leave him.

Jackie hurried upstairs. The sooner she was out of here the better.

Tania waited until she was out of earshot, then picked up the phone and dialled a number.

'Vittorio? Is that you? Oh, good. Listen—she's just been down here. I told her that you'd been called away early— no, I didn't tell here where you've really gone. I kept quiet about that, as we agreed. My dear boy, are you sure you're going about this the right way? I know she's an attractive young woman, but she can also be very difficult— All right, I suppose you're right to take the chance, but you might have to duck for safety when she finds out what you've actually been up to today.'

The flight to London seemed to take for ever. Jackie tried to tell herself that one stage in her life was finished and she must prepare for the next. But no common sense thoughts could heal the pain in her heart.

Her love was over—which meant that her life was effectively over. And she didn't know how she would endure it.

Arriving in London, she headed straight for the shop. It seemed strange when she arrived—more restricted, less interesting.

Perhaps she could find a job here. The place apparently needed her.

Going inside, she saw nobody—until a man appeared from the back.

'Can I help you?'

'I'm looking for a job,' she said. 'Are you short-staffed? Do you need anyone?'

He shook his head.

'I'm afraid I can't give you a job. Only the owner can do that.'

'Then can I talk to the owner?'

'I'll fetch him.'

He went deep into the back of the shop and she heard him call, 'Can you come here, sir?'

After a moment a man appeared, the sight of whom made Jackie gasp.

'Vittorio!'

Smiling, he came towards her and laid his hands gently on her shoulders.

'But what are you—?' she gasped. 'How did you get here?'

'I booked you on the midday flight, but I booked myself on the flight at six in the morning. That's why I'd already gone when you woke up. I needed to get here well ahead of you.'

'So *you're* the new owner?' she said, stunned.

'No. You'll find the owner's name here.'

He drew out a piece of paper bearing the owner's name, and showed it to her.

'But that—it's *my* name there.'

'That's because you're the owner,' he said simply. 'Just as your father would have wanted.'

'But Rik—'

'I contacted Rik from Italy and persuaded him to sell to me. A lawyer here finished the formalities, and when I arrived I went straight to the lawyer and transferred the property to you. That's why I needed to get here well ahead of you.'

'But—how am I going to run this place? Are you telling me that it's all right for me to move back to London?'

'No, I'm telling you that you're coming home with me, because I'm not letting you go—now or ever. I hope you agree to that, or I'll be forced to bring my bullying side to the surface.'

There was a gleam of humour in his eyes, but also something else that might have been an anxious plea.

She gave him a warm smile, saying, 'Perhaps you should beware. I might have to bring my bullying side to the surface.'

'And we both know I don't cope with that very well. But it's lucky you're a great businesswoman, because you can organise this place while living with me in Rome. Please, Jackie. *Please.*'

She touched his face. 'I guess it would be heartless of me to refuse. We'll do it your way.'

He smiled and kissed her hand.

'I've taken over the apartment upstairs, where you used to live. Come up with me. I've got something to show you.'

It felt strange to be climbing the stairs to her old home— like moving back in time. Inside she found it much the same as she remembered: plain and basic.

While he made her a cup of tea she studied the papers that made her the owner of the shop.

'However did you do this? And how can I accept it?'

'You can because I've got something else for you— something that will solve the great problem that has always come between us. I mean the money. We will never be at peace over that until we find a final decision that feels good to us both.'

'But is there such a thing? How could there be?'

'I think I've found it. Look at this.'

He handed her a letter that she read with mounting astonishment. It came from a charity and was addressed to her father.

'It says he's donated a quarter of a million pounds,' she gasped. 'But how could he?'

'Easily—with a little help.' Vittorio handed her several more letters. 'Look at these.'

The letters were from three more of her father's favourite charities, each one thanking him for the gift of a quarter of a million pounds.

'*You* did this?' she breathed.

'Let's say I was your father's messenger boy. I told you I'd find a way of handing over the money in a manner that you couldn't resist, and I've done it. It's really just a way of forcing you to do what I want, selfish bully that I am. You said I couldn't understand why this was so important to you, and at first you were right. But then I started to fall for you and the more I came to love you the more I saw it through your eyes.'

'You can *do* that?' she cried joyfully. 'You really understand now?'

'I knew you didn't want the money yourself, but it was painful to you to know that I had it. You told me that we needed a way to return it to him without involving you, but that didn't seem possible.'

'You found one,' she breathed. 'You found it. Look what it says about him.'

She read from one of the letters. '"After his magnificent gift George Benton will be celebrated as one of our greatest benefactors—a man whose generosity knew no bounds and for whom no admiration and respect would be enough."' She looked quickly through the other letters. 'All four of them say something like that. Look!'

He took the papers from her, gazing with a pleasure that matched her own.

'They do him justice,' he said. 'That's the best we could hope for.'

We. The joyful word echoed through her brain. They were together in this.

'We,' she breathed. 'You said "we".'

'It's "we" because now everything matters the same to both of us. We're a team, and we always will be. Forgive me, my darling, for taking so long to see the light, but now I have seen it. I was desperate for a way to reach out to you and prove that my heart understood yours. I knew nothing else would ever make you love me.'

'And you're right,' she breathed. 'I thought you'd never understand the truth about what was keeping us apart, but you do. And now you've actually found a way—' She seized the letters. 'This is brilliant. I've never been so happy in my life.'

'Then why are you crying?' he asked anxiously, for tears had begun to pour down her cheeks.

'I can't help it,' she wept. 'Suddenly—'

Suddenly she was invaded by an emotion more powerful than any she had ever known.

Vittorio put his arms around her. 'Hold on to me,' he said. 'You're safe now. I'll never let you go.'

'Never? Promise me?'

'I promise. What greater tribute could I pay to your late father than by promising to love, protect and care for his daughter for the rest of her life?'

He kissed her. She returned the kiss joyfully, then rested against him, feeling the warmth and sweetness of knowing he was hers for ever.

'Did you always mean to give me the shop?'

'Of course. A man should give his bride a wedding gift. And this is mine to you.'

'A wedding gift?'

'We're getting married. You promised to marry me ages ago and I'm holding you to that promise. I won't take no for an answer. Say yes. Say you'll marry me and accept the shop.'

The words sounded forceful, but he said them with a gentle smile that ended all her fears. Now she could only do what her heart urged.

'All right,' she said softly. 'I'll marry you. *And* I'll accept the shop.'

Now that they understood each other perfectly she could sense that everything was different. They had reached their destination at last and there was no more to fear.

They spent the night together—not making love, but lying peacefully in each other's arms.

In the darkness of the night Jackie awoke to find Vittorio standing at the open window, looking up into the sky.

She went to stand beside him. 'I think our fathers would be overjoyed that we've found each other. They'd be even more delighted that we've finally begun to love and understand each other in the way they always wanted.'

He put an arm around her. With the other he reached up to the heavens. She followed his gaze to where the stars glittered and the moon glowed.

'They're up there too,' he said. 'Can't you tell?'

'Yes,' she breathed. 'And I think—I think they're shaking hands to congratulate each other.'

'That's what I think too,' Vittorio said.

Then he drew her closer, enfolding her in an embrace that would protect them all their lives.

"It all could have gone so terribly wrong."

"But it didn't."

She caught her lower lip between her pretty white teeth. "I was so scared."

"Hey." He brushed a hand along her arm, just to reassure her. "You're okay. And Munch is fine."

She drew in a shaky breath and then, well, somehow it just happened. She dropped the purse. When she reached out, so did he.

He pulled her into his arms and breathed in the scent of her skin, so fresh and sweet with a hint of his own soap and shampoo. He heard the wind through the trees, a bird calling far off—and Munch at their feet, happily panting.

It was a fine moment and he savored the hell out of it.

"Garrett," she whispered, like his name was her secret. And she tucked her blond head under his chin. She felt so good, so soft in all the right places. He wrapped her tighter in his arms and almost wished he would never have to let her go.

* * *

The Bravos Of Justice Creek:
Where bold hearts collide under Western skies

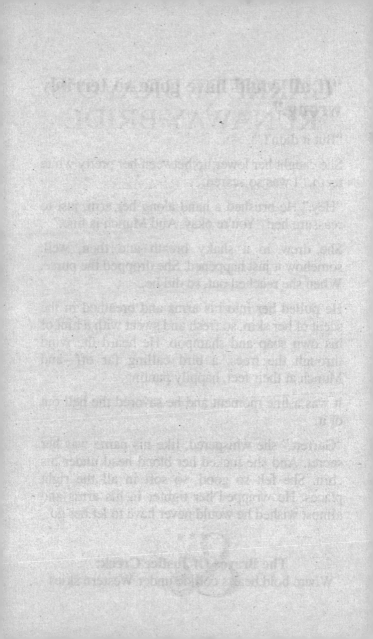

GARRETT BRAVO'S RUNAWAY BRIDE

BY
CHRISTINE RIMMER

First Published in Great Britain 2017
By Mills & Boon, an imprint of HarperCollins*Publishers*
1 London Bridge Street, London, SE1 9GF

© 2017 Christine Rimmer

ISBN: 978-0-263-92337-7

23-1017

Christine Rimmer came to her profession the long way around. She tried everything from acting to teaching to telephone sales. Now she's finally found work that suits her perfectly. She insists she never had a problem keeping a job—she was merely gaining "life experience" for her future as a novelist. Christine lives with her family in Oregon. Visit her at www.christinerimmer.com.

For MSR.
Always.

Chapter One

When the battered bride staggered into the circle of firelight, it was after nine at night, and Garrett Bravo was sitting outside his isolated getaway cabin slow-roasting a hot dog on a stick.

For a weirdly suspended moment, Garrett knew he must be hallucinating.

But how could that be? He'd never been the type who saw things that weren't there. And he'd only had a couple of beers.

His Aussie sheepdog, Munch, let out a sharp whine of surprise.

"Munch. Stay." He glanced sternly down at the dog, who quivered in place and stared at the apparition on the other side of their campfire.

Garrett looked up again. She was still there.

He opened his mouth to speak, but nothing came

out. Finally, with a ridiculous shout of confusion and lingering disbelief, he jumped to his feet. The sudden movement knocked his hot dog off the stick and down to the dirt. He gaped at it as it fell. Munch cocked an ear and glanced up at him expectantly. When he failed to say no, the dog made short work of the fallen treat.

"Oh, really," said the tattered vision in white. She came around the fire toward him, waving a grimy hand. "You don't need to get up. It's worse than it looks, I promise you."

It looked pretty bad to him. Leaves decorated her straggling updo and nasty bruises marred her smooth bare shoulders and arms. Her left eye was deep purple and swollen shut. The poor woman's big white dress was ripped in several places and liberally streaked with mud. And her bare feet? As battered as the rest of her.

"My God," he croaked. "Are you sure you're all right?"

She blew a tangled hank of blond hair out of her good eye and shrugged. "Well, I've been better."

How could she be so calm? Had her groom gotten violent? If so, the man deserved a taste of his own damn medicine—and speaking of medicine, she needed a doctor. He should call for an ambulance, stat. He dropped his hot-dog stick on top of the ice chest by his chair and dug in a pocket for his phone.

But the phone wasn't there. Because he'd left it in the cabin. Up here on the mountain, cell reception was nil.

Garrett let out a long string of bad words and then demanded, "Who did this to you?"

The bride remained unconcerned. She hitched a

thumb back over her shoulder. "Little accident back down the road a ways."

"Your groom…?"

"Oh, he's still in Denver. Some stranger ran me off the road." As he tried to process that bit of news, she added, "Camilla Lockwood. But please call me Cami." She offered a scratched, dirty hand.

Numbly, he took it. It felt cool and soft in his grip. *And real.* She was definitely real. "Garrett. Garrett Bravo."

"Good to meet you." A frown tightened the skin between her eyes. "You okay, Garrett? You look a little pale."

He looked pale? "How will I call you an ambulance when my phone doesn't work?"

"You won't." She reached up, clasped his shoulder and gave it a reassuring squeeze. "It's fine, really. I don't need a doctor."

"But—"

"Take my word for it, I would know. You think this looks bad?" She indicated her body with graceful sweeps of both hands. "I've been through worse. Lots worse—and who's this?" She dropped to a crouch, her giant dress belling out around her, and held out a hand to his dog. Munch made a questioning sound. "Come on, sweetie pie," she coaxed. When Garrett made no objections, Munch let out a happy little bark and scuttled right over. "Oh, aren't you the cutest boy?" She scratched his ears, rubbed his spotted coat—and glanced up at Garrett with a beaming smile. "Beautiful dog. Such pretty markings." Garrett dipped to her level, took her arm and pulled her to her feet again. "Hey!" She tried to jerk free. "Ease up."

"We need to get you down the mountain."

"No, we don't."

Ignoring her protests, he started pulling her toward his Jeep Wrangler Rubicon on the far side of the cabin.

"Garrett. Stop, I mean it." She dug in her heels.

"Camilla, come on now."

"I said, call me Cami. And no. Just no. I'm not going anywhere." As she whipped her arm free of his grasp, he debated the advisability of scooping her up and carrying her bodily to the Jeep. But even with all the scratches and bruises, she seemed to have a lot of fight left in her. And say he did manage to get her over there and into the SUV. How would he convince her to stay put while he ran into the cabin for the keys?

Maybe he could reason with her. "You need a doctor. I only want to take you down the mountain to Justice Creek General."

"No means no, Garrett." She braced her hands on her hips and narrowed her one working eye to a slit. "And I have clearly said no."

So much for reason. "Will you at least sit down? Rest for a minute?"

She flipped that same tangled hank of hair off her forehead. "Sure."

Before she could change her mind, he caught her elbow and dragged her over to his chair. "Here. Sit." She dropped to the chair with a large huff of breath, her big dress poofing out as she landed, then quickly deflating. Slowly and gently, he explained, "Relax, okay? I'm just going to go into the cabin and get the first aid kit."

"First aid can wait."

"But—"

"Please, Garrett." She picked a twig from her hair and tossed it over her shoulder. "I need water. My tongue's just a dried-up old piece of leather in my mouth, you know?"

That tongue of hers seemed to be working pretty well to him. But yeah. Water. He could do that. "Stay right there?"

"I won't move a muscle." Munch, always a sucker for a pretty girl, sidled close and plunked down beside the chair. For the dog, she had a tender smile. "Hey, honey." She stroked his head. "What's his name?"

"Munch."

"Cute," she said. And Garrett just stood there, staring down at her as she petted his dog. Finally, she glanced up at him again and asked hopefully, "Water?"

"Right." Against his better judgment, he left her alone with only Munch to look after her as he ran for the cabin. At the door, he paused with his hand on the knob. What if she took off?

Well, what if she did? If she insisted on wandering Moosejaw Mountain in the dark barefoot in her torn-up wedding dress, far be it from him to try to stop her.

He went in, filled a tall insulated bottle with water, grabbed the dish towel and ran back out.

She was still there. "You're a lifesaver," she said when he handed her the bottle.

He flipped open the cooler, grabbed a handful of ice and wrapped it in the towel. "For your eye."

She took a long drink and then let out a happy sigh. "Thank you." Only then did she accept the ice. Pressing it gingerly to her bad eye, she frowned. "Don't tell me I stole your only chair." She started to rise.

"Relax." He patted the air between them until she

dropped back into the seat. "I've got a spare." He grabbed the extra camp chair from where he'd left it leaning against a tree, snapped it open and set it down on the other side of the cooler from her.

Now what?

Awkward seconds struggled by as they just sat there. She sipped her water and iced her eye and he tried to decide what he should do next.

Maybe she needed food. "Are you hungry, Cami?"

She gave a long sigh. "Starved."

He could help with that at least. "How about a hot dog?"

She rewarded him with a radiant smile. "A hot dog would really hit the spot about now."

A half an hour later, the beat-up bride had drunk two bottles of water and accepted three hot dogs, each of which she'd shared with Munch. The dog remained stretched out beside her. Periodically, he would lift his head from his paws to gaze up at her adoringly.

Garrett still felt bad that he hadn't convinced her to let him drive her to the hospital. She could have at least allowed him to get out the first aid kit and sterilize a few of those scratches.

He asked glumly, "Do you have a head injury?"

She repositioned the makeshift ice pack on her injured eye. "And you need to this know why?"

He shrugged. "I was going to offer you a beer. But if you've got a concussion, maybe not."

That earned him another dazzling smile. "A beer would be so perfect."

Apparently, she was never going to answer the head

injury question. But she seemed reasonably clearheaded, so he flipped open the cooler and passed her a beer.

Tucking the ice pack into the cup holder on her chair, she popped the top and giggled like a happy kid when it foamed. He watched her throat move as she swallowed, after which she settled back in her chair and stared up at the star-thick Colorado sky.

She really did seem okay. And at the moment, he couldn't think of any more ways she might let him help her. He settled back, too.

Somewhere in the trees, a night bird twittered.

Cami made a soft, contented little sound. "Got to hand it to you, Garrett. This is the life."

He completely agreed. "Yeah. Munch and I have been up here for almost two weeks now, only driving down the mountain twice for food and supplies. The first few days were tough. I kept worrying about work. But eventually, I got over that and started enjoying the quiet and the big trees. Overall it's been great."

"So you don't live up here?"

"No. I'm on vacation. I've got three more days. Wednesday, I have to head home."

"To?" She stared up at the sky, the beer can dangling from one hand as she idly scratched Munch's back with the other.

"I live down in Justice Creek."

Cami said dreamily, "I've been to Justice Creek a couple of times. Such a pretty little town."

"I grew up there. My sister and I run a construction company."

"What's your sister's name?"

"Nell. She's a pistol." He rolled his head Cami's way

again and found her watching him. Otherworldly, the gleaming blue of that good eye. "You would like her."

Cami's dirty angel's face looked wistful. "A pistol, huh?"

"Oh, yeah. Nell never did a damn thing she didn't want to do. She's unpredictable, but you can count on her, too. I always know she has my back."

"She sounds amazing." Cami turned her face to the stars again. "I wish I could be like that." Garrett was about to tell her she was more than unpredictable enough, when she glanced down at her torn dress and said in a small voice, "I'm thinking you've already guessed that I ran out on my wedding." She slanted him a glance. At his nod, she faced the sky again and continued. "Biggest wedding of the season. Everyone who's anyone in Denver was there. I was going to go through with it up to the very last moment—which means, I didn't plan my escape." She wrinkled her nose at the stars. "That's me. No planning. I never think ahead. When I can't take it anymore, I just freak and run. Today, that happened during the wedding march. My bridesmaids were already on their way down the aisle. The wedding planner signaled me out of the bride's room…" Her voice trailed off.

He prompted, "And then?"

"And then I just grabbed my purse off the vanity table and sprinted out the back door. The door opened on the parking lot and I'd made my dad drive me in my car for the ride to the church." A low, sad chuckle escaped her. "Okay. I confess, I may have done a little planning, after all. Because I had a spare set of keys in my purse. I jumped in my BMW and took off with no plan after that whatsoever and nowhere in particular to go." She paused for another sip of beer.

When she settled back again, she continued. "Eventually I got out on the highway. I took an off-ramp. I saw the sign to Moosejaw Mountain. I took that turn. It's one twisty road getting up here, Garrett, but my 750i handled like a dream. I would still have that car if some idiot in a green pickup hadn't come barreling down as I was going up. Ran me right over the side of the road and into a very steep ravine."

"My God." Had she been knocked out, then? He probably shouldn't have given her that beer.

She raised the beer in question toward the distant moon and took another swallow. "I admit, it was scary while it was happening."

"Were you knocked unconscious?"

"No. But the airbags deployed and somehow, I got smacked in the eye. When the car finally stopped rolling, I couldn't get the door open. And that, along with everything else—how messed up my life had gotten, the way I'd run out on my wedding that never should have been happening in the first place—well, it all just made me tired. So I took a nap."

"A nap," he echoed disbelievingly. "In a wrecked car at the bottom of a ravine?"

"That's right." She was defiant. "I closed my eyes and went to sleep—and you should see the way you're looking at me. Same way my parents do. Like you wonder how much brain damage I've sustained. And you don't even know about the coma."

He gulped. "There's a coma?"

She waved a dismissing hand. "That was six years ago. Yeah, there are scars. But I'm fully recovered—

well, I mean, as much as anyone can recover from an experience like that. Anyhoo, back to the ravine. Whoever was driving that green pickup didn't bother to stop or call for help, so when I finally decided I really had to make the effort to get out of the car and get back up to the road, I was on my own."

"That driver should be arrested. Did you get a plate number?"

She gave him a look of great patience. "Sorry, Garrett. I was kind of busy trying to keep from rolling off the side of the road. And then I did roll off the road. And then I just gave up for a while and took a nap. When I decided to get moving again, it took me a long time to get the car door open. And scrambling up out of there? That's where most of these scratches and bruises came from. It was not the most fun I ever had, believe me. But I finally got back up to the road. I stood there and thought, down or up? I'd already been down, so I started climbing. I just kept walking until I got here."

"We should be calling the police on that guy in the pickup. Leaving the scene of an accident is a crime."

"Too bad your phone doesn't work." She didn't sound the least regretful.

He tried one more time to get through to her. "If you'd just get in the Jeep, we could—"

"Uh-uh. I really am okay, Garrett. And I like it here. I'm free at last and I'm not going anywhere until I'm ready to go. No one runs my life but me. Not ever again." She offered another toast with her beer can. "From this day forward, I decide where I go and when I'm leaving. Okay, I didn't handle my escape very well. Yes, I ran away like I always do. I left Charles at the altar and I'm sorry about that."

"Charles is your fiancé?"

"*Was* my fiancé. Charles and I grew up together. His parents and my parents are good friends. He and I are both vice presidents at my family's company, WellWay Naturals."

Garrett had heard of WellWay. Their products were in all the big grocery stores. "The vitamin company?"

She nodded. "Vitamins, supplements and skin care products. Charles has been after me for years to marry him. I kept telling him no. Eventually, though, he wore me down. I messed up, I know it. I handled the whole thing really badly, but at least I didn't marry him, and someday he'll thank me." She blew out a weary breath. "And yes, I ran away again. But this time, I *own* it. This time, I'm laying claim to my future. I'm going forward now, not back."

"Forward to…?"

"When I figure that out, you'll be the first to know." She drank, plunked the empty can on the cooler between them and granted him another gorgeous smile. "So then." She grabbed the ice again and reapplied it to her eye. "You know my story. What brings *you* to this beautiful neck of the woods, Garrett?"

Is she actually out of her mind? he wondered. Could be. But for some reason, he *liked* her. He went ahead and told her the embarrassing truth. "I'm kind of hiding out."

"I can relate. Who are *you* hiding from?"

"My mother."

"What did she do to you?"

"It's what she's *trying* to do. The past few years, she's been obsessed with seeing me and my sisters and brothers happily married. Nell and I are the only ones still single. Even my mother knows better than to try to tell Nellie what to do. So lately Ma's been pestering *me*."

"Pestering you, how?"

"Demanding I come see her and then browbeating me when I get there about how it's time I found love and happiness at last. Introducing me to very nice women I don't want to go out with. Lecturing me about 'trying again' every chance she gets."

"Again?"

"I was married. Years ago. It didn't work out. I suck at relationships." Cami chuckled. He shot her a frown. "That's funny?"

"It's just the way you said it…"

"What way?"

"Really fast, like you wanted to get it over with and you didn't want me to ask you any questions about it."

"I did. And I don't."

"Duly noted." She poked at her black eye, wincing a little, and then iced it some more. Her ring finger was bare.

"You lost your ring."

She shook her head. "Before I left the church parking lot, I took it off and stuck it in the glove box. I'm guessing it's still there. Go on, about your mother and your needing to get away?"

He shrugged. "Long story short, I'm kind of a workaholic and I needed a break from everything, my mother most of all. So I'm here where my mother would not be caught dead—roughing it in a one-room cabin on top of a mountain. And she can't even call me because there's no cell service."

Cami clucked her tongue, chiding him. "You seem way too pleased with yourself when you say that."

"I kind of am. Unfortunately, to appease her, I did promise her I'd have dinner with her the night I get back to town. But I'll deal with that when it happens. For now, Ma's off my back and I'm up here in the great wide-open, taking a breather, trying to figure out what to change up to get more out of life."

"Well, Garrett. What do you know? We have stuff in common."

For the first time since she'd materialized out of nowhere, he allowed himself to laugh. "I guess we do."

"And I sure am glad you were here." Cami was picking bits of crushed, dried leaves out of her hair with her free hand.

"You look tired." At his softly spoken words, she made a cute humming sound that might have been agreement. He asked in a coaxing tone, "You ever gonna let me patch you up a little?"

Cami worked another leaf free of her tangled hair. He accepted that she wouldn't answer. But then she did. "I would kill for a bath about now."

"That can be arranged."

Cami decided she loved Garrett's cabin.

On the outside, it was simple, of weathered wood with old-fashioned sash-type windows and a front porch with stone steps.

Inside, it was cozy and plain, just one big living area with the kitchen on one wall, the bed on another and a sofa under the front window.

When he ushered her ahead of him into the dinky

bathroom, she grinned and brushed a finger along the wooden rim of the tub. "It's half of a barrel."

"That's right, a whiskey barrel." He hung back in the doorway. There wasn't enough room for both of them in there. "A full-size tub wouldn't fit." He was tall and broad-shouldered with beautiful light brown eyes that made her think of melting caramel. Definitely a hottie, with a few days' worth of scruff on his lean cheeks, dressed in old jeans, dusty hiking boots and a faded brown denim jacket over a white T-shirt. He was so easy to be with. Already, she liked him a lot and had to keep reminding herself that she hardly knew him.

"I put in the tub and hot water up here this spring," he said. "Before that, it was sponge baths or nothing."

She glanced around at the vintage sink, the milk-glass light fixture and the knotty-pine paneling. "I like it. It's super rustic."

He indicated the metal caddy hooked on the outside of the tub. "Soap and shampoo are right there. Towel and washcloth under the sink. There's a new tooth-brush and a comb you can use in the medicine cabinet. I'll go back out to the fire and leave the window over the sofa open. Give me a holler if you need anything."

"Would you undo the hooks at the back of my dress before you go?"

"Uh, sure." He took a step into the tight space and she backed up to meet him.

Gentle fingers brushed the skin between her shoulder blades and then worked their way down. She pressed the dress to her chest to keep it from falling off. "All done," he said after a minute.

She looked over her shoulder and met those melty

eyes. "Take this thing?" To her, the dress represented all that was wrong in her life. It wasn't even her style, so poufy and traditional. Her mom had coaxed her into choosing it. "I don't think there's room for both it and me in here."

He had soft lips to go with the melty eyes. Those lips turned up slightly. "Uh. Sure." He was looking at her kind of funny, like he still didn't quite know what to make of her—which was nothing new. People often looked at her that way. Maybe he was thinking she shouldn't be so quick to take off her dress in front of him.

Well, maybe she shouldn't. But then again, why not?

She trusted him. He'd been nothing but kind to her, helping her all he could while at the same time respecting her wishes. Never once had he bullied her to do things his way. This man was not going to make a move on her—or if he did, he'd already proven that he understood the word *no*.

Cami dropped the dress. It plopped around her feet like a parachute, belling out, then collapsing. Underneath, she wore a tight white satin bustier that ended in ruffles at her hips. She'd thrown her silk stockings away back down the mountain somewhere. There hadn't been much left of them after she dragged herself up to the road. As for her five-inch Louboutins and her giant half-slip covered in a big froth of tulle? She'd dumped those during the trek up out of the ravine.

The bustier, with satin panties underneath, covered her as well as a swimsuit would. It also showed the long, pale scar cutting down the outside of her right thigh—but she'd never been the least sensitive about that. She considered it a war wound, proof of an earlier attempt to escape a life that was always a prison for her.

Stepping free of the acres of dirty white lace, she held it up to him. "Burn it, will you?"

He took it gingerly. "What will you wear?"

"I don't even care." Unfortunately, she'd left her suitcases in Denver—turned them over to Charles yesterday to load into the limousine. She had nothing but the dress and her underwear, but she would go naked before she put that thing on again. "Burn it."

"Up to you." Garrett backed into the main room and shut the door.

Cami turned to the barrel tub and flipped on the taps.

Garrett had just doused the fire for the night when he heard the cabin door open.

Munch ran up the steps to greet their surprise guest as she emerged from inside wrapped in a towel. The light from the cabin outlined her curvy shape in gold as she knelt to give Munch the attention he'd come looking for.

As Garrett mounted the steps, she rose. "Thank you. Really. I feel so much better now."

"Good—and it's past midnight. You think you could sleep?" With a soft sound of agreement, she turned and went back inside. He and Munch followed her. Garrett shut the door.

She faced him with a sigh. "Did you burn it?"

"It's nothing but ash." He dropped to the old bentwood chair by the door and started taking off his boots.

When he looked up again, she was still standing there wearing a wistful smile. "Thanks."

"Any time. You want one of my shirts to sleep in?"

Her smile turned radiant. "Yes, please."

He got a faded Pearl Jam T-shirt from the dresser and handed it over.

"Thank you. Again." She disappeared into the bathroom, emerging in the shirt that covered her to midthigh.

There was another awkward moment and it came sharply home to him that he didn't know this woman at all. They were two strangers about to share the same sleeping space.

"I'll just take my turn in the bathroom." He eased around her, went in and shut the bathroom door. Hanging on the back of it next to his sweats was that sexy corset thingy of hers. It struck him all over again how bizarre this whole situation was.

When he came back out wearing the sweats, she'd already stretched out on the couch. She was settling his old afghan over herself.

He moved a few steps closer. "Cami, take the bed."

"No way." She wiggled her toes under the blanket and adjusted the thin throw pillow under her head. "This couch isn't big enough for you and we both know it. Your feet would be hanging off the end." Munch made himself comfortable in the space between the rickety coffee table and the sofa. She put her hand down and stroked his spotted coat. "Don't look at me like that. I'm not budging."

"Suit yourself."

"Oh, yes, I will. From this day forward, I will be suiting the hell out of myself, just you watch me."

He got the extra pillow from the bed and gave it to her. "You're allowed to change your mind. If you can't sleep on those lumpy cushions, I'll trade with you."

She yawned hugely. "'Night." Pulling the afghan up under her chin, she shut her good eye.

In the morning, her black eye had opened to a slit and she refused a fresh ice pack for it. "It'll be fine," she assured him. "I'm a fast healer."

He put a couple of logs in the woodstove to get the coals going again and made coffee and scrambled eggs. She shoveled it in like she hadn't eaten in weeks, and he felt ridiculously pleased with himself to be taking good care of her.

But then he said, "After breakfast, I'll drive you down the mountain."

She guzzled some coffee. "You said you were staying for three more days."

"Cami, you really need to—"

"Uh-uh." She showed him the hand. "Don't say it. Don't tell me what I need. For the rest of my life, *I* decide what I need. And what I need is to stay here with you and Munch until you have to go."

"But you—"

"Not going. Forget it. I need a few more days up here in the peace and the quiet before facing civilization and calling my parents to say I'm all right."

"They're probably really worried about you."

"I know." She chewed on her plump lower lip and looked away. "And I feel bad about that. But right now, I need this—you and me and Munch up on this mountain with nothing to do but breathe the fresh air and appreciate the big trees." He marshaled his arguments, but then she leaned across the rough surface of the table and begged him, "Please, Garrett. Please."

And he could not do it—could not tell her no. "Damn it," he muttered.

"Thank you," she replied, extra sweet and so sincere.

He got up to pour them more coffee. "So then, what *do* you want to do today—besides breathing and staring at trees?"

She dimpled adorably. "I'm so glad you asked. See, I left the church without my suitcases, but I did have my purse, with my credit cards and my driver's license. I don't know what I was thinking when I finally got my car door open and started climbing up to the road. I left my purse behind. I was hoping we might go back for it."

Garrett gave her his flip-flops, another shirt and a pair of his jeans to wear, with an old belt to keep them up. She wore that corset thing under the shirt for a bra. He knew this because he was a man and thus way too aware of what went on beneath a woman's shirt.

They piled in the Jeep, with her riding shotgun and Munch in his favorite spot all the way in back. More than halfway to the state road at the base of the mountain, she said she thought they'd passed the place where she went into the ravine. He turned around the next chance he got.

She found it on the way back up, recognizing a Forest Service fire danger sign a few yards from where she'd gone off the edge. There was enough of a shoulder to park by the sign.

Before he could tell her to leave the dog in the Jeep,

she let him out. Panting happily, Munch followed her to the edge.

"This is definitely the place," Garrett said, taking in the skid marks. He came up beside her and peered over the edge. Her car had flattened everything in its path as it went down. It seemed impossible that she'd survived the crash and the tumble into the ravine. "You were lucky to be driving that Beemer."

She made a sound of agreement. "Handles like a dream and one of the safest cars around. I'm going to miss it."

"I can see the car." The vehicle was half-buried in underbrush, but twisted metal and shiny red paint gave it away. "What's that?" He pointed at something white and poufy halfway down.

"My slip. It was hard enough climbing with the dress. I kept tripping, so I took it off and left it."

"You want it?"

She looked at him, her expression severe. "No, I do not."

The incline was close to eighty percent. It would be steep going, but there were lots of trees and bushes to hold on to. He figured he could make it down there, get whatever she wanted from the car and get back up without too much trouble. "Anything else you want besides your purse?"

"There's a notebook and some pens in the glove compartment. I would really like to have those—oh, and my engagement ring should be in there, too. I should give it back to Charles."

"Anything else?"

"My old red hoodie might be in the trunk. I could use that, if we can get it open—oh, and there's a hatch through to the trunk in the back seat, so maybe…" She let her voice trail off on a hopeful note.

"I'll try. Take Munch and wait in the Jeep."

"What?" She set her stubborn chin. "I'm going with you."

Had he expected that? Yeah, pretty much. "Not in my flip-flops that don't even fit you. Your poor feet are cut up enough already."

"But I—"

"Stop, Cami. It's not a good idea and I think you know it's not."

"It just seems wrong to make you go alone."

"I'm dressed for the job and you're not. It'll be simpler and safer if I do this myself."

She mouthed a wistful thank-you at him and turned back to the Wrangler. "Come on, Munchy." With a happy whine, the dog jumped in.

"This shouldn't take long," he reassured her as she climbed up to the seat and pulled the door shut.

He started down. It was not only steep, the ground was thick with roots, rocks and debris. Past her big, white slip, he found one white satin shoe and then the other. The soles were red, the high heels covered in dirty rhinestones. Cami hadn't asked for them, so he left them where they lay.

The car was upside down and badly bent and battered, the driver's door gaping open, the trunk crushed in. The cab, though, was intact. He pushed the deflated air bags out of the way and looked for a purse, finding it easily—on the ceiling, which was now the floor. Most of the contents had escaped.

Checking not only the ceiling but under the up-side-down seats, he found the latest model iPhone, a hot-pink leather wallet full of cards and cash, plus loose makeup, a comb, a brush, a tin of Altoids and all the other random stuff a woman just has to cart around with her wherever she goes. He shoved it all back in the purse.

The glove box popped right open for him, spewing its contents, including the pens and notebook she'd mentioned. He found her registration and proof of insurance in there, too. He even found her fancy ring. It had a platinum band and a large, square-cut diamond. The ex-fiancé might not have been the guy for her, but at least he wasn't a cheapskate. He stuck the ring in his pocket.

Finally, he managed to crawl into the back seat and get the trapdoor to the trunk open. After a little groping around back there, he got hold of the hoodie she'd asked for.

The purse was more of a satchel, big enough that he could stick the notebook, pens and car documents in there, too. He tied the sleeves of the hoodie around his neck, shoved the straps of the satchel up his arm as far as they would go and crawled from the wreck.

He'd made it halfway back up to the road when he heard Munch frantically barking, followed by a bizarre, pulsing cry.

Adrenaline spurting, every nerve on red alert, Garrett froze in midstep. He knew that strange cry. Black bears made that sound when you stole their food or otherwise pissed them off.

Chapter Two

Dropping the purse, grabbing for branches to pull him forward, Garrett scrambled as fast as he could up the hillside. Somewhere up ahead Munch barked like crazy and the bear's angry vibrating yowl continued.

Then Cami's voice joined in. "Shoo! Back! Get out of here, you!"

Garrett grabbed the slim trunk of a cottonwood sapling and hauled himself higher, finally getting close enough that he could see them through the brush. They were maybe ten yards below the road. Cami had lost the flip-flops but had found a long stick. She held off the bear with it while Munch ran in circles around them, barking.

With no weapon handy, Garrett grabbed a rock and threw it at the bear, striking it on the rump. The bear turned and let out a quick growl in Garrett's direction, but then went right back to chuffing and growling at Cami, pawing the ground.

She yelped in response and kept jabbing with her stick. "Back! Go!" Munch continued circling them, barking frantically.

Garrett scuttled closer and threw a bigger rock.

That did it. The bear turned on him. Black bears could move fast when they wanted to. And that one flew down the hill straight at him.

"Garrett!" Cami's terrified scream rang through the trees as Garrett lunged to the side, counting on gravity and the bear's forward momentum to drive it right past him.

It worked. The bear saw him move but couldn't stop in time. It lost its footing and started to roll.

A split second later, Munch zipped by, too.

"Munch!" Garrett shouted. "Stop!"

But the dog was already out of sight down the ravine. He heard the bear make that threatening sound again. There was scrabbling in the brush and grunting from the bear.

And then a loud, startled cry from his dog.

The bear gave another angry grunt. Brush rustled and branches snapped. Garrett caught a flash of dark fur through the undergrowth—the bear running off.

And then there was silence.

"Omigod!" Cami came sliding down the bank toward him. "Munchy! Oh, no!" She toppled.

Garrett caught her before she could fall. "Hey now. Hold on." With a gasp, she blinked up at him. He asked, "You all right?"

"Let me go." She tried to break free. "I have to—"

"No," he said softly. When she kept struggling, he shouted it. "No!"

A whimper escaped her. "But Munch…"

He took her by the shoulders. "Go back to the Jeep."

"I can't—"

"Look at me, Cami. Look at me now." She moaned, but she focused. "Whatever happened down there, it's over. Don't believe what you see in the movies. Black bears as a rule aren't aggressive and that one's already run off."

"But where's Munchy?"

"I'll go see."

"Oh, Garrett. I was going to stay in the Jeep, I promise. I'm so sorry." Tears filled her good eye and seeped from the injured one.

"It's okay. Just let me—"

"God, I feel so terrible. Munchy started barking. He jumped right over me and out the open window."

"He probably caught the bear's scent. We had a couple of bears messing with our trash on a camping trip once. Munch was only a pup, but he chased them away. Just doing his job, that's all."

"If anything has happened to him, I'll never forgive myself."

He gave her shoulders a gentle shake. "Look at me. Listen. It's not your fault."

"But I—"

"I'm sure he's fine." No, he was not sure. But he had to say something to settle her down. Last night, he would have sworn that nothing could shake her, but right now he feared she might lose it completely. "I need to get down there and see what's going on, okay?" She swallowed hard. And then, finally, tear tracks shining on her too-pale cheeks, she nodded. He instructed, "I want you to wait right here. Do that for me. Please?"

"Yes." The agreement came out of her on a whisper of sound. And then more strongly, she added, "Okay."

"Come on now. Over here..." He guided her to a boulder that poked up from the bracken and slowly pushed her down. "I'll be right back," he promised. She just stared up at him, tears dripping from her chin.

What else could he do? He took her hoodie from around his neck. It zipped up the front, so he wrapped it around her. "You going to be okay?"

She sniffled and stuck her hand in a pocket of the hoodie. "Go," she commanded, pulling out a rumpled tissue and dabbing her eyes. "I'm fine."

He wasn't so sure about that, but he turned anyway, and started down the bank, passing her purse where he'd dropped it. Several yards farther on, he spotted Munch's tail sticking out of a clump of brush.

His whole body went numb, a strange coldness creeping in, freezing him in place. He'd worried that Cami might break. Now, the sight of that unmoving tail almost broke *him*.

And then that tail twitched.

"Munch?" He practically fell the rest of the way.

Landing hard on his knees, he shoved the brush aside.

The poor guy was just lying there, as though he'd stretched out on his side for a nap.

"Munch?"

There was a weak little whine. And then, woozily, Munch lifted his head.

"Munch. Munch…" For some reason, Garrett couldn't stop saying the mutt's name. He bent close. No blood that he could see.

The dog whined again.

"How you doing, boy? Where does it hurt?" Garrett ran seeking fingers over head, neck, back, belly and down the long bones of each leg. He checked the paws, too.

Nothing.

About then, Munch gave his head a sharp shake.

"You okay, buddy?" The dog wriggled his way upright and started wagging his tail.

Relief poured through Garrett, bringing another wave of weakness. He plunked back on his butt in the brush and grabbed the dog in a hug. "Guess you're all right, after all, huh?"

For that, he got sloppy doggy kisses all over his face.

Laughing, Garrett caught Munch's furry mug between his hands. The dog whined sharply. Garrett felt it then, a bump behind the right ear. Carefully, he stroked the sore spot. "You think you can make it back up to the Wrangler?"

The dog let out a sound that just might have been *Yes!*

Garrett rocked to his feet and straightened with care. His legs still felt shaky, but they were taking his weight. "Well, let's go, then. Heel."

Munch obeyed, falling into step at his left side. Eager to reassure Cami that the dog was okay, Garrett climbed fast, pausing only once to grab her purse as they passed it.

A moment later, he caught sight of her waiting on the rock where he'd left her, wearing the hoodie, looking like a lost Little Red Riding Hood, tears shining on her soft cheeks. She spotted him. Batting tears away, she sat up straighter. And then she saw Munch. With a gasp, she shot to her feet. "He's okay?"

Garrett gave her a nod. "Go ahead. Show him the love."

"Munchy!" she cried. The mutt raced to greet her and she dipped low to meet him.

Garrett waited, giving her all the time she wanted to pet and praise his dog. When she finally looked at him again, he explained, "The bear must have whacked him a good one. When I found him, he was knocked out, but I think he's fine now."

She submitted to more doggy kisses. "Oh, you sweet boy. I'm so glad you're all right…"

When she finally stood up again, he handed over the diamond ring and that giant purse.

"Thank you, Garrett," she said very softly, slipping the ring into the pocket of the jeans she'd borrowed from him. "I seem to be saying that a lot lately, but I really do mean it every time."

"Did you want those high-heeled shoes with the red soles? I can go back and get them…" When she just shook her head, he asked, "You sure?" He eyed her bare feet. "Looks like you might need them."

"I still have your flip-flops. They're up by the Jeep. I kicked them off when I ran after Munch." For a long, sweet moment, they just grinned at each other. Then she said kind of breathlessly, "It all could have gone so terribly wrong."

"But it didn't."

She caught her lower lip between her pretty white teeth. "I was so scared."

"Hey." He brushed a hand along her arm, just to reassure her. "You're okay. And Munch is fine."

She drew in a shaky breath and then, well, somehow it just happened. She dropped the purse. When she reached out, so did he.

He pulled her into his arms and breathed in the scent of her skin, so fresh and sweet with a hint of his own soap and shampoo. He heard the wind through the trees, a bird calling far off—and Munch at their feet, happily panting.

It was a fine moment and he savored the hell out of it.

"Garrett," she whispered, like his name was her secret. And she tucked her blond head under his chin. She felt so good, so soft in all the right places. He wrapped her tighter in his arms and almost wished he would never have to let her go.

Which was crazy. He'd just met her last night, hardly knew her at all. And yesterday she'd almost married some other guy. She could seem tough and unflappable, but she'd had way too much stress and excitement recently. The last thing she needed was him getting too friendly with her.

Gently and way too reluctantly, he set her away from him. Biting that plump lower lip again, she gazed up at him, her expression both hopeful and a little bit dazed.

"Now, listen." He ached to stroke a hand down her

pale hair, to cradle her soft cheek in his palm, but he didn't. "What do you say I take you back down the mountain? We'll be in Justice Creek in less than an hour and you can—"

"Stop." In an instant, that dazed, dewy look vanished. Her soft mouth pinched tight. Without another word, she grabbed her purse and headed for the Jeep, Munch at her heels.

Garrett followed at a distance as she climbed up to the road. He gave her time to stick her feet in his flip-flops and usher the dog in on the passenger's side. When she jumped up to the seat and slammed the door, he circled around the front of the vehicle.

As soon as he got in behind the wheel and pulled the door shut, she commanded, "Take me back to the cabin or I'll say goodbye right here."

He let the silence stretch out before coaxing, "Come on. Don't be that way."

Her tight mouth softened a little. "I'm sorry. I'm just not ready yet to deal with all the crap that's waiting for me back in the real world."

"I meant what I told you," he warned. "I'm going home Wednesday."

She turned her gaze from him and stared blankly out the windshield. "I understand."

"Cami, when I go, I'm not just leaving you alone in that cabin. You don't even have decent shoes to wear."

"I know." She looked so sad.

And he had that need again, to touch her in a soothing way—to clasp her hand or pat her shoulder. Or better yet, to pull her into his arms where she felt so good and fit just right. But he kept his hands to himself.

He spoke firmly. "If I take you back to the cabin

now, you have to agree that you'll be ready to go down the mountain with me on Wednesday."

"I'll be ready." She met his eyes then. "I'll go when you go. I just need a few more days on this mountain of yours where no one can find me."

He eyed the faded, baggy T-shirt he'd given her to wear, the jeans she had to hold up with a battered old belt and the too-big flip-flops that had to be a real pain to walk in. "How 'bout this? We drive down to town and get you some clothes that fit you, then come right back up to the cabin?"

Her lush mouth got pinchy. "Nice try. I'm not going down there till Wednesday. I'm just not. I want this time away from everything, Garrett. And I'm going to have it."

"We can use my credit card if you're worried they'll—"

"No."

"Well, then, I could take you back to the cabin and then go down myself and get you some better clothes."

"Better clothes can wait till Wednesday." Her pinched look had softened. "Please. Will you just let it go?"

He figured it was about the best deal he was going to get from her. "Fair enough," he said gruffly. And he had to hand it to her. She'd picked the right place to disappear. No one was likely to come looking for her up here.

She was smiling again, her good eye a little misty. "You are the best."

"Sure."

"I mean it. You are."

"So how come I have so much trouble telling you no?"

"Don't be a grump about it." She slapped at him playfully. "I happen to love that you can't tell me no. My parents and Charles never had a problem with no when it came to me. It was always 'Camilla, no' and 'Camilla, don't' and 'Camilla, behave yourself and do what *I* say.' I've spent my whole life doing what other people think I should do, interspersed with the occasional attempt to escape their soul-crushing expectations."

Again, he had to quell the urge to reach for her. She was the cutest thing, with her black eye and her scrappy attitude. "Well, you're running your own life now."

"Oh, yes, I definitely am."

"And we have an agreement. We're at the cabin till Wednesday and then you'll let me drive you home."

"Got it." She stuck out her hand and they shook on it.

At the cabin, he had firewood to split.

She volunteered to help so he got the maul ax, his goggles and two pair of gloves and led her out to the chopping block behind the cabin. "I've never chopped wood," she said cheerfully.

He put on his goggles. "And you're not starting now. Not in flip-flops." A slip of the maul and she could lose a toe. "You can stack the split logs, if you want to." He pulled on his work gloves and handed her the extra pair. "But take it slow and be careful."

"I will."

For a couple of hours, he worked up a sweat with

the ax. He tossed the split logs away from the chopping block. She gathered them up and stacked them against the back wall of the cabin. Then when lunchtime approached, she went inside to make sandwiches. He washed up at the faucet behind the cabin and joined her on the front steps where she had the food waiting.

They ate without sharing a word, but the silence was neither tense nor awkward. Just easy. Relaxed. After lunch, he went back to splitting wood.

When he came to check on her later, she was sitting in one of the camp chairs drawing pictures in her notebook.

He peeked over her shoulder at a pencil sketch of Munch snoozing at her feet. "You're good at that."

"I wanted to go to art school," she said as she shaded in Munch's markings, the beautiful spots and patches of his blue merle coat. "I always dreamed of studying at CalArts. But my father prevailed. I went to Northwestern for a business degree and took a few art classes on the side. Then, the summer I graduated from college, I knew I had to do something to make a life on my own terms."

"But your dad wasn't going for it?"

"No, he was not. I tried to make him understand that I didn't want to work at WellWay, that I needed a career I'd created for myself. He just wouldn't listen."

"What about your mother? She wouldn't step up and support you?"

"My mother never goes against my dad." She shaded in Munch's feathery tail, her pencil strokes both light and sure. "And she basically agrees with him, anyway."

"So you went to work at WellWay, then?"

"No. I tried to get away again."

"Again?"

"There were several times I ran before that. The time I ran after college, I packed up my car and headed for Southern California—and was rear-ended by a drunk driver on I-70 in the middle of the night."

Garrett swore low, with feeling.

"Yeah. It was bad. I almost died."

"That coma you mentioned last night...?"

She nodded but didn't look up from her drawing of Munch. "I was unconscious when they pulled me from the wreck and I stayed that way for two weeks. You probably wondered about that scar on my leg? Another souvenir of that particular escape attempt."

"But you made it through all right."

"Thanks to the best medical team money could buy and a boatload of physical therapy, yes, I did."

He had that yearning again to touch her. To pull her up into his arms and comfort her, though she didn't seem the least upset.

He was, though. Just hearing about how bad she'd been hurt made something inside him twist with anger—at her father, who wouldn't let her live her own life. And at her mother, too, for not supporting Cami's right to be whatever she wanted to be.

"When I was well enough to go home, I moved back in with my parents." She kept her head tipped down, her focus on the notebook in her lap. "My father insisted. And I was too weak to put up a fight. There was more physical therapy—and the other kind, too, for my supposed mental and emotional issues. And when I'd completely recovered from the accident and finished all the therapy, I moved to my own place at last—and started my brilliant career at WellWay."

He clasped her shoulder and gave it a squeeze, because he couldn't stop himself.

She didn't lift her head from her focus on the sketch, but she did readjust the sketch pad on her knees enough to give his hand a pat. "It's okay, Garrett. I'm all better now."

Feeling only a little foolish, he let go.

She sighed. "Mostly, I like to create my own comic strips." She flipped the sketchbook back a page to a cartoonlike sequence of sketches where a cute little bunny with a ribbon in her hair used a stick to fight off a bear with the help of a patch-eyed Aussie dog. A boy bunny in jeans and a T-shirt similar to Garrett's ran toward the girl bunny wearing a freaked-out expression on his face.

"I'm guessing that's me?"

She slanted him a teasing glance. "Okay. I took a little artistic license. You didn't look *that* scared."

"Maybe I didn't look it, but *that* scared is exactly how I felt."

A giggle escaped her. "Yeah. Well, it's not like you were the only one." She flipped the page back and continued working on the drawing of Munch. "I have a whole series on the bunny family. Unlike my real family, the bunny family works on their issues. They respect each other and try to give each other support and enough space that every bunny gets what she wants of life."

"Wishful thinking?"

"Oh, yeah."

He watched her draw for a while. But there was

more wood to split, so he went on around back and got busy with the maul.

Later, he showed her how to lay and light a campfire. They had steaks and canned beans. When they went inside, he taught her the basics of how to use a woodstove.

She took another bath. When she came back out to the main room, she smelled of soap and toothpaste. "Anything good to read around here?"

He pulled a box full of paperbacks out from under the bed. "Help yourself."

She chose a tattered Western and stretched out on the couch with it. When she fell asleep, he pulled the afghan over her and turned out the light.

The next day was pretty much the same, quiet and uneventful. She drew cartoons in her notebook. He split wood.

Beyond getting the wood in, he'd been planning an overnight hike and some fishing for these last couple of days on the mountain. But now that he had Cami with him, he didn't want to leave her alone for too long.

Strangely, it was no hardship to have to stick close to the cabin for her sake. There was just something about her. He felt good around her, kind of grounded. She pulled her weight and she didn't complain about the rustic living conditions.

They went for a walk up the road—not too far, about a mile. With only his flip-flops to wear, her feet couldn't take a real hike. They stopped at a point that looked out over the lower hills, some bare and rocky, others blanketed in pine and fir trees.

"Kind of clears your mind, being up here." She sent

him one of those dazzling smiles and he marveled at what a good time he was having with her. He would miss her after he dropped her off in Denver.

Was he growing too attached to her?

Oh, come on. He'd known her for less than forty-eight hours. No way a guy could get overly attached in that time.

That night, he tried to offer her the bed again. But she insisted she was comfortable on the couch.

After he turned out the light, he could hear her wiggling around, fiddling with her pillow, settling in. "You sure you're okay over there?"

"Perfect." She lay still. The cabin seemed extra quiet suddenly. Outside, faintly, he heard the hoot of an owl. There was a soft popping sound from the stove as the embers settled. "Garrett?"

"Hmm?"

"Tell me about you."

He smiled to himself. It was nice, the sound of her voice in the dark. "What do you want to know?"

"Well, your parents. What are they like?"

So he told her about his father, Frank, who'd had two families at the same time—one with his wife, Sondra, with whom he had two sons and two daughters. And the other with Garrett's mother, Willow. "Ma had three boys, me included, and two girls with dear old dad. And then, when Sondra died—the day after her funeral as a matter of fact—my dad married my mom."

"Ouch—I mean, wow, that was fast."

"No kidding. Everyone was pissed off about it, that my dad couldn't show just a hint of sensitivity to Sondra's memory, that Ma couldn't wait a little longer after all those years of being my dad's 'other woman.' At the time, we were all pretty much at war, me and my mother's other kids on one side, our half siblings on the other."

"It sounds awful."

"Yeah. But eventually we all grew up and realized it wasn't *our* fault that our parents couldn't manage to behave responsibly and respect their marriage vows. Now we're tight. We all like getting together, looking out for each other, knowing we can count on each other, all that family stuff. My half siblings are even nice to my mother, which I find really impressive. Not only is she the woman my dad cheated on Sondra with, she's not a friendly person. She's distant, hard to get to know."

Cami made a low, thoughtful sort of sound. "Are your mom and dad still together?"

"They were until he died six years ago. Now, when she's not traveling, which she does a lot, she lives alone in the mansion he built for Sondra, just her and the housekeeper."

"That sounds kind of sad."

"You'd have to meet her. She's not someone people feel sorry for. Like I said, she comes off kind of cold and superior. And then there's the whole matchmaking thing I mentioned the other night. She's driven us kind of crazy with that crap lately."

"Because she loves you and wants you to be happy."

He grunted. "Right. I'll keep telling myself that."

"And I did the math. Your dad had nine kids total?"

"That's right." Garrett laced his hands behind his

head and stared up at the shadowed rafters overhead. "You sound impressed."

"I kind of am. And jealous, too. I always wanted at least a sister. Preferably two. And I would have loved to have a brother. I truly do believe that if my parents had only had more kids, they wouldn't have been constantly on my case to do things their way. More kids keep the parents busy, you know? The parents have to chill a little and accept that they don't have absolute control."

"But you've finally broken free, right? You're going to do things your way now."

"Oh, yes, I am." She said it gleefully. "I'm finally going to find work that makes *me* happy. And I'm fortunate that I won't have to take just any job to get by. My trust fund matured three years ago, when I was twenty-five. I have my own investments and a good chunk of change in savings, too. My life is my own from now on."

"You really think your dad might have tried to cut you off just to get you to do what he wants?"

A silence from her side of the room. From the rug by the sofa, the tags on Munch's collar jingled as he gave himself a scratch. The sound was followed by a soft doggy sigh.

When Cami finally spoke, she didn't really answer his question. "Well, it doesn't matter if he would or he wouldn't. He can't. My money is my own. I'll be able to support myself while I figure out what *I* want to do with my life from now on." She sounded both wistful *and* determined.

He wanted to get up and go to her, pull her into

his arms and promise her that from now on her life was going to be downright amazing. He wanted to...

He cut the thought off before he got to the end of it.

He liked her. A lot. But she was going home to Denver and he was going back to Justice Creek. This, right now, in the cabin, just the two of them? It was only one of those things that happened sometimes. She'd needed some help and he was willing to give it.

They got along great and he enjoyed her company.

But that was all there was to it. Day after tomorrow, he would drive her down the mountain and that would be the end of it.

Tuesday pretty much flew by.

And that night in the dark, they talked some more.

She said she liked it on the mountain so much, she just might find a getaway cabin of her own. "Eventually. You know, after I figure out where I want to live and what to do with my life."

Garrett opened his mouth to tell her she could use the cabin any time she wanted to—and then caught himself before the words could escape.

It only *felt* like he'd known her forever. Tomorrow, he would take her home. Maybe he'd talk her into giving him her number. Who could say what would happen from there?

For now, though, offering her the use of his getaway cabin whenever she wanted it was going too far.

In the morning after breakfast, they loaded up the Jeep with Garrett's clothes, his camping stuff and the leftover food. He turned off the hot water, drained the tank and shut off the water to the cabin, too, just in case he didn't make it back up the mountain before winter set in. He unplugged the fridge and braced the door slightly open. Then he locked the cabin up tight.

At the Jeep, Cami paused to take in the plain, unpainted structure with its narrow front porch and red tin roof. "I'm going to miss this place."

Garrett couldn't stop himself from reaching out a hand to cradle the side of her face. Her black eye was open now, most of the swelling gone, though it was still a startling blend of black, brown and purple fading into green. She gazed up at him solemnly.

"I've loved having you here," he said.

Her throat moved as she swallowed. Her soft lips parted. He had no idea what she was going to say.

And he decided it would probably be wiser not to find out. "Come on. Let's get moving." He dropped his hand from her cheek and opened the door for Munch to hop in.

She didn't say much on the drive down the mountain. That surprised him.

He realized he'd been bracing for some kind of resistance from her. But she was quiet and accepting, her thoughtful gaze focused on the winding dirt road ahead.

Was she *too* quiet?

He hoped she was okay, that she hadn't started to stew over what would come next.

"So, Denver, then?" he asked when they approached the turnoff.

"You know," she said casually, "just take me to Justice Creek, if that's okay."

"But I thought—"

She cut him off with an airy wave of her hand. "No, really. I'll rent a car and drive myself back when I'm good and ready. But for now, I think I'll try Justice Creek for a while."

"Uh, you will?" Not only was he surprised at her abrupt change of plans, but he was suddenly ridiculously happy, which alarmed him a little.

"Yeah. I'll get a hotel room. Do you know a good place?"

He eased onto the state highway going west, toward Justice Creek. As he made the turn, he decided he couldn't just leave her at some hotel. "How about this? Come to my place first. We'll drop Munch off and put the food away and then we can, you know, talk about your options…"

The smile she gave him made the sunny day even brighter. "That sounds like a great idea. Your house, it is."

Cami's heart swelled with gratitude.

Garrett Bravo was not only hot and way too handsome, he was a good guy. A real-life hero, a hero who'd been up there on Moosejaw Mountain just when she needed a hero the most. Someday she would figure out how to repay him.

No, she had no idea where she was going or what she would do when she got there.

But so what? She was finally playing life by ear and loving every minute of it, following her instincts for once, the way she'd always longed to do.

Her condo in Denver was already on the market. At some point, she'd have to pack everything up and move it all to wherever she ended up living. But none of that had to be done right away.

First things first. She needed to get going on the rest of her life.

Whatever that might turn out to be.

The state highway became East Central Street as they entered the town of Justice Creek. They passed the town hall and Library Park on the right. Charming shops lined the street on either side.

Cami had always thought Justice Creek was a great place. With Denver only a ninety-minute drive away, the pretty little town at the edge of the national forest made a perfect day-trip destination. Cami had visited several times. She'd caught the summer rodeo once and shopped the annual Christmas fair the last four years running.

Every time she'd come to town, she'd felt right at home.

And now, today, with her life wide-open in front of her, Cami saw Justice Creek for what it was: a perfect jewel nestled in its own small valley, surrounded by spectacular mountains. The kind of place where a person like her might be happy to settle down.

They passed the turn to Oldfield Avenue. She glanced out her side window and saw the white walls and red tile roof of the world-famous Haltersham Hotel. It was perched on a rocky promontory with gray, craggy peaks looming above it.

Right then, with the magnificent old hotel in her sights, Cami experienced a moment of great clarity.

No wonder she'd ended up with Garrett and Munchy on Moosejaw Mountain. Her subconscious had been leading her right here to Justice Creek the whole time.

This town…

Oh, definitely. *This* was the town for her.

It was all so simple, so perfect and clear. The question of where she would live the rest of her life was already answered, had *been* answered long ago. The truth had only been waiting for her to be ready to see it.

Justice Creek would be her new home.

Chapter Three

A curving pebbled driveway led up to Garrett's house on Mountainview Avenue in Haltersham Heights not far from the hotel. The exterior was weathered cedar and shingles and silver-gray stone, with lots of big windows.

Inside, those windows let in plenty of light. The modern kitchen and dining room opened onto the living area. Two sets of glass doors led out to a low deck and a patio, complete with a fire pit.

"What a beautiful house." Cami set a box from the cabin on the gorgeous granite counter. It had a swirling pattern of cream, brown and silver. "Kind of modern and rustic, both at once." The vaulted wood ceilings had log accent beams.

Garrett opened the glass door by the table to let Munch out. "I had it built it a few years ago, when Bravo Construction really started making money."

She watched Munch bound off the deck and into the yard. "He won't run off?"

"There's a fence. He's fine."

Together, they brought in all the food. Garrett said he didn't mind her looking in his cabinets to see where things went, so she got to work putting the food away while he unloaded his clothes and a bunch of random camping equipment.

"I'm just going to get a load of laundry started," he said and vanished down the hallway off the kitchen.

Cami put boxes of crackers and cold cereal in an upper cabinet and then made herself march to the end of the counter where she'd dropped her Birkin bag on the first trip in from the garage. With a grimace of dread, she took out her phone. She'd fully charged it at the cabin and turned it off when they left.

As soon as she turned it on, there would be a flood of frantic calls, texts and messages to deal with. Up on the mountain, it had been so easy to tune out the real world. Not anymore. The time had come to deal with everyone she'd been trying not to think about. They were going to be very upset with her when they found out that she had purposely avoided dealing with them since Saturday afternoon.

She was still standing there with the powered-off phone in her hand when Garrett emerged from the laundry room.

"That is not a happy face." He put his arm around her.

She leaned into his solid strength, breathed in his woodsy scent and made herself smile up at him. "I think I'll just go out and sit on that back deck while I make a few calls."

"Anything I can do to help?"

Take me back up the mountain. We'll stay there forever, just you and me and Munchy. "Thanks, but I think this is something I need to deal with myself."

Garrett got busy putting his gear away in the garage.

When he returned to the kitchen, she was still outside, pacing back and forth across the wide patio tiles, the phone to her ear. Munch, panting anxiously, trailed along behind her. Garrett stood at the glass door admiring the shine to her thick gold hair. How could she be so pretty even in his ill-fitting old jeans and faded shirt?

When she glanced over and saw him watching her, she gave him a quick wave and went back to her pacing. It looked like the phone calls were going to take a while.

He finished putting the kitchen stuff away and made them some sandwiches. When she finally came inside, she went straight to the end of the counter and stuck her phone back in her giant purse.

"You made lunch," she said, her eyes worried, her smile way too bright.

"Come on." He pulled out one of the high padded chairs at the kitchen island. "Everything will look better after you eat."

She got up on the stool. "Yum. I'm so hungry."

He let her polish off half of her turkey on rye before he asked, "So. Want to talk about it?"

She gave a tiny shrug. "My parents are furious. They demanded I return to Denver immediately. I told them I'm not coming back except to close up my condo and pick up my stuff."

He touched her arm in reassurance. "I'm sorry, Cami."

"Yeah." She forced another sad little smile. "Me, too."

"How was it with Charles?"

"Not much better—scratch that. Worse. He said he had to see me immediately, that we *had* to talk."

"Don't let the guy bully you."

"I'm not. I told him I needed to think about the whole face-to-face idea. I made it clear that I wasn't coming back, so there really was no point in us meeting. He was calling me bad names when I hung up."

"What an ass."

"Well, I did leave the guy at that altar, after all."

"And now he wants to talk about that? What's the point?"

Now she was the one putting her hand on his arm. It felt really good there. "I don't know, Garrett. I mean, I love that you're on my side, but I do feel guilty about running away. It had to be pretty awful for him."

"Talking about it with him isn't going to fix anything."

"I know you're right. But as I said, I haven't decided whether to talk to him or not."

"If you do decide to see him, meet him here."

"Why?"

"I should be close by, just in case."

She patted his arm and then picked up the other half of her sandwich. "At least my maid of honor was understanding. She promised she'd call my other bridesmaids and tell them I'm okay. It's so weird." She stared thoughtfully down at the triangle of sandwich in her hands. "I *like* my maid of honor, but I never felt all that close to her. It's as if, in Denver, I was just going through the motions, acting out living a life that wasn't really mine—oh, and, apparently, I'm a missing person, so I guess I need to go see the police and explain how I'm not so missing, after all."

"That, I can definitely help you with."

"No way. You've done enough."

No, he hadn't. Not if she still needed him. And clearly, she did. "My brother-in-law, Seth Yancy, is the county sheriff. I'll take you to the justice center."

She crunched a tortilla chip. "Uh-uh. You have been beyond amazing, but I've got to start cleaning up my own mess. I'll go myself. There's a car rental place in Justice Creek, right? I'll call them and have them bring me a car. Then I'll go visit your brother-in-law the sheriff and explain that I'm not missing. Once that's handled, I'll get a hotel room. And *then* I'm going shopping so you can have your jeans, shirt and flip-flops back."

"Keep them." He took a bite of his pickle. "They look better on you, anyway."

She gave a cute little snort of laughter. "They look awful on me and we both know it."

Her laugh eased his concern for her a little. "So... You're staying here in Justice Creek?"

She studied the sandwich for a moment, then set it back down. "Yep. I've been trying to figure out how to tell you because it sounds kind of crazy, but I made my decision an hour ago, as we were driving along Central Street. In a blinding flash of insight, I realized that I love it here and that Justice Creek is the place for me—and you're giving me that look, Garrett."

"Which look is that?"

"Like you're wondering if I'm a few fries short of a Happy Meal."

Was he? Well, maybe. A little. He'd never met anyone like her, that was for certain. "I'm just surprised, that's all. But hey, I love my hometown, too. It's a good place to live."

Garrett got that she needed to start somewhere if she really was going to make a whole new life for herself. And why not Justice Creek? She would probably be very happy here.

And the more he thought about it, the more he disliked the idea of her checking into a hotel. He had four bedrooms and three of them were empty. Also, he felt protective toward her—which was perfectly natural, given the circumstances. He'd looked after her on the mountain and he wasn't ready to stop yet. She had a great attitude, but creating her life all over again from scratch would be challenging.

He had to keep her close for a while, to be sure she was handling things all right and be ready to step in if she needed his help. Especially if the ex-bridegroom showed up. She would have to have backup for that.

"Garrett?"

"Hmm?"

"What exactly are you thinking?"

He put it right out there. "Stay here at my house. I've got plenty of room."

She nibbled another chip. "I don't know. Didn't we just go over how I've taken way more than enough advantage of you already?"

"No, you haven't. Besides, what will Munch do without you?" The dog, stretched out on the floor near his food bowl, flapped his tail against the floor and gave a hopeful whine right on cue. "See? You're not even gone yet and he's already sad about how much he'll miss you."

"I'll miss him, too, but I have to go sometime."

Not yet, she didn't. The more he thought about it, the more sensible her staying with him seemed. "How 'bout this? Just play it by ear. Stay over tonight and decide tomorrow if you want to stay longer."

She answered his question with one of her own. "You finished?"

"All done." She grabbed both their plates and took them to the sink. Before she could trot out more reasons to leave, he said, "Give me your phone."

"Because?"

"We need to trade numbers."

She flicked on the faucet and gave the dishes a quick rinse. "It's in my purse."

He got the phone and sent himself a text, thinking how strange it was that he'd slept in the same room with her for the past four nights and he was just now getting her number. "Okay. We're set. Now let me show you your room, then I'll get you a key and write down the alarm code."

An hour later, Garrett had left to check in at Bravo Construction and the nice guy from the car rental place had just dropped off a cute little silver Subaru Forester.

Cami checked the car over and gave the guy her credit card to run through his reader. Another car pulled up and the guy from the rental place got in and left.

She was about to hop into the Subaru when she remembered that she hadn't locked the front door or armed the alarm, so she ran back up the steps to deal with that.

Munch was waiting just inside the door. He whined and wagged his tail. After a minute, she realized he was trying to lead her back to the kitchen. When she followed, he went straight to the glass door.

"You want to go out, Munchy?" He whined and panted up at her. She opened the door and out he went. Right then, the house phone on the end of the counter started ringing. There was absolutely no way it could be for her, but she checked the display, anyway.

Willow Bravo.

Garrett's mother...

Cami snatched the phone from the base because... well, she wasn't exactly sure why. Sometimes she didn't know what got into her lately. One moment she'd get a little down about all the ways she'd messed up her life. But then, in an instant, all this lovely new freedom had her feeling bold and ready for anything, and that had her doing things she wouldn't ordinarily do.

Like answering Garrett's phone for no reason except that she was curious about his mother. "Hello?"

For a moment, the line was silent. Then a cool, slightly husky voice said, "Hello, who is this?"

"My name is Cami Lockwood."

"Do I have the right number? I'm calling Garrett Bravo."

"Yes, this is Garrett's house."

"Put him on the line, please. Tell him his mother is calling."

Cami debated how much to tell the woman, given that Garrett had run off to his cabin partly to get a break from her. "I'm sorry. He's not here right now."

Another silence from Willow. Then she said, "Cami—it *is* Cami, right? I don't believe we've met. Are you from the cleaning service?"

"Yes, it's Cami. And no, I'm not the maid. I'm a friend of Garrett's."

"Oh, really?" Willow's tone had perked up. Given what Garrett had told her, Cami knew why. Willow thought she was Garrett's girlfriend. "A *new* friend, I'm guessing."

"A *special* friend," Cami added; she had no idea why, except that her friendship with Garrett *was* special. Just not in a romantic way.

"I'm so happy to hear that." Willow's tone said it all. Garrett's mom was making assumptions. Cami ought to stop her. But she didn't. Willow said, "I can't believe he's never mentioned you before."

"Yes, well, as you said, we, um, only got together recently." She was making it worse and she knew it.

But somehow, she couldn't stop.

"Cami, I can't wait to meet you. Do you live here in town?"

"I'm originally from Denver, but yes. For the time being, I'm staying with Garrett."

"Wonderful." The cool alto voice had warmed considerably. "Then he's home from the cabin today as planned?"

"Yes. We just got back a couple of hours ago. Now he's gone to check on things at Bravo Construction."

Willow actually chuckled. "You stayed at the cabin together? I had no idea."

"Well, it was sort of a spur-of-the-moment decision."

"But he never takes anyone up to the cabin."

"He didn't take me. He went on his own."

"But you said you were there together." Willow sounded confused. Understandably so.

Cami explained, "I, um, joined him a few days ago. And I do love it up there. It's so peaceful. I hated to leave." It was nothing but the truth. Just not *all* of the truth.

"I don't get the appeal of roughing it, frankly." Willow sounded downright chatty, as though she and Cami were already BFFs. "Give me a luxury resort with all the amenities, if you don't mind. But I do realize that any special friend of Garrett's would have to enjoy all that outdoorsy stuff—and listen, I won't keep you. The reason I called was to remind my son that we're having dinner tonight. Would you be sure to tell him that I'll expect him here at the mansion at seven?"

"Of course, I'll tell him."

"And, Cami, I have a great idea." Willow paused and then asked coaxingly, "Why don't you join us for dinner tonight?"

Cami opened her mouth to decline—but then again, she was living by her instincts now, wasn't she? And her instincts told her that if she played this right, she could repay Garrett just a little for everything he'd done for her. Because, come to think of it, what better way to get his mother off his back on the matchmaking front than for Cami to go to dinner with him? Already, Willow believed that she and Garrett were together in the romantic sense.

And okay, pretending to be Garrett's girlfriend would be dishonest. But in the end, who, really, could it hurt?

"Hello? Cami, are you still with me?"

"Right here."

"Perfect. We're on, then. See you both at seven."

She really did need to talk to Garrett before saying yes to that. "I... Wait. Willow, I'm not sure if... Hello? Willow?" But Willow had already hung up.

Cami set the phone very carefully into its cradle and then considered snatching it up again and calling Willow back.

Instead, she got out her own phone and called Garrett.

He answered on the second ring. "Hey. Everything okay?"

"Define okay."

"Cami." His voice was suddenly harder. Darker. "Just tell me. What's going on? Is it that idiot, Charles?"

"No, really," she rushed to reassure him. "It's nothing about Charles."

"Well, then?"

She dragged in a big breath and let it all out in a rush. "Your mom called to remind you of dinner at the mansion at seven tonight. I told her I was staying here and that I am your special friend and then she invited me to dinner tonight, too."

There was a pause. A significant one. Finally, he asked, "Where *are* you?"

"I'm still at the house. I dealt with the car guy and came back in to set the alarm and your landline rang—and I know, I know. I had no right to answer it, but I did. And then, well, things just sort of seemed to take their own course. You know, conversation-wise."

"'Special friend' as in girlfriend?"

"Well, kind of, yes."

"You told Ma that we're a thing."

"Um. Not in so many words."

"Cami." He said it in a slightly pained way, but at least not in an angry way. "What are you up to?"

She went ahead and confessed. "I was just thinking that it's not a *bad* thing if your mom believes we're together, because if she thinks we're together she'll stop matchmaking you. I figure that if we convince her that you're with me, she'll leave you alone for at least six months." She paused, hoping he would jump in with reassurances.

Dead silence from him.

Finally, she offered sheepishly, "All righty, then. I'll just call her back and straighten things out with her."

"Absolutely not." He said that with zero hesitation. "You're in it now, Cami."

That didn't sound good. "In it, how?"

"You're going to my mother's with me tonight."

She brightened. "Excellent."

"You say that now, but you haven't met my mother."

Cami laughed. "I just talked to her. We had a nice little chat."

"Nobody has a nice little chat with my mother."

"Well, *I* did. And I'm very curious to meet her in person." And to see the mansion that had originally belonged to Willow's rival, Frank Bravo's first wife.

"I'm glad you're curious, because you *are* meeting her. We'll tell her tonight that she misunderstood about you and me."

For some unknown reason, Cami felt disappointed. "Fair enough."

"Okay, then—and I know you have a lot to do today." His voice had gentled. He sounded more like the Garrett she'd known on the mountain. "You think you can get it all finished in time to be home and ready at six forty-five?"

Home. She glanced around the beautiful kitchen and realized that she did feel very much at home there. "I'll be ready."

"Call me if you need anything."

"I will."

"And, Cami?"

"Yeah?"

"I know you were only trying to help me out." He said it low, with real affection. She felt warm all over. Someone spoke to him on his end. He said something back and then spoke to Cami again. "Gotta go."

"Bye…" Grinning, she ended the call.

"That was her?" Nell, Garrett's baby sister and business partner, popped a cherry Life Saver into her mouth and sucked on it thoughtfully. Nell wore dusty jeans, combat boots and a soft gray Bravo Construction T-shirt with the sleeves pushed up onto her shoulders. The shirt showed off the half sleeve of ink that covered her left arm from shoulder to elbow.

Garrett dropped the phone on his desk and chuckled to himself. "She let Ma think we're a thing."

"But you're not?" Nell gave him a sideways look.

"I told you, I like her a lot. She's going through some challenging stuff and I'm here to help her however I can. We're *friends*."

"The operative words being that you *like* her a *lot*." Nell tossed her long red hair.

"Don't even start with that crap. Please."

"Fine." Nell put up both hands. "Sorry. You like her a lot. But you don't *like* her a lot."

"You always were a pain in my ass."

"Go ahead. Be thickheaded. It kind of suits you."

"Brat."

She slouched back in her chair. "So. Will you take over with Deck?"

Declan McGrath had been Nell's high school boyfriend. He'd broken her heart back in the day. Now, more than a decade later, he'd decided he wanted another shot with her. Nell kept refusing to go out with him, but Deck wouldn't let it go. His latest move had been to approach her to build him a house.

Garrett shook his head. "The guy obviously wants to work with you, personally."

Nell leaned forward and braced her elbows on her knees. "Think of it this way. Deck is going to get someone to build him a new house. That someone should be us. And even though I don't want to deal with him *personally*, there's no reason that *you* can't. He's rolling in money now." Deck had done well for himself. He owned and ran Justice Creek Barrels. Apparently, there was big money in repurposing wine and whiskey barrels. Nell went on. "He's going to want the best and that's what we'll give him. Everybody wins. It's a no-brainer, big brother."

"He wants *you*. You hand him off to me, he's not going to be happy."

"Too bad. He wants a house. You can help him with that. The two of you get along fine."

"Nellie, come on. I bought the barrel tub up at the cabin from him. That doesn't exactly make Deck my best friend."

"Speaking of the cabin," Nell began way too casually. "Who held down the fort here while you were up on the mountain hiding from Ma? Why, I believe that might have been me, your long-suffering, hard-working sister and business partner."

Garrett gave up. "Point taken. I'll call Deck and set up a first consultation."

"You are my favorite brother."

"I know—well, aside from Carter and Quinn and James and Darius."

"Ha. When do I get to meet Cami? I have a feeling I'm going to love her."

Garrett had no doubt on that score. "She really is something. Gorgeous, definitely. But even better, she's so easy to be around and she's smart and funny. And tough, too, at heart. Nothing gets her down."

"So what you're saying is, when it comes to Cami, what's not to love?"

"Exactly."

"And I know you mean that in a purely friends-only kind of way."

He tried a scowl. "Get off my case, Nellie."

"I'm still not really clear on how you and Cami met…"

"It's a long story." He made a mental note to ask

Cami how much of that story she wanted shared. For now, he played it vague. "I think I'll let her tell it."

Nell gave him a wink. "You be sure to say hi to Ma for me tonight."

At the Broomtail County Justice Center, Cami asked for Garrett's brother-in-law, Sheriff Seth Yancy. The sheriff, a big guy with kind eyes and a confident manner, ushered her into his office and listened to her story.

He quizzed her about her black eye and the healing scratches on her face and arms and asked if they were all from the accident. When she confirmed that they were, he said he wanted to have a look at the scene before anyone disturbed it, just on the off chance they might get a lead on who ran her off the road. He promised he would call her and let her know when they'd "released the scene" so that she could arrange for a tow.

Her phone was ringing in her purse as she left the justice center. She checked the display.

It was Charles.

"Not talking to you right now," she muttered under her breath. Setting the phone to Silent Page, she put it away.

Then she headed for Central Street, stopping first at a stationery and art supply store, where she stocked up on sketch pads, colored pencils, pastels and several packages of colored paper. Art supplies soothed her soul. They also helped her brainstorm ideas. And she needed ideas for her future, because not only was she going to make her home in Justice Creek, she also planned to find herself a career that would include her love of drawing and art.

What career exactly? She had no clue. Sooner or later, though, she would figure it out.

After the stationery store, she wandered from one boutique to the next buying clothes, shoes, makeup and toiletries. It took hours. She could probably have returned to Denver and cleared out her closet at the condo in the same amount of time.

But she wasn't ready to face going back. Not yet. Plus, there was something hopeful and liberating about getting everything new. She felt grateful to have the money to do that, to buy brighter colors than she used to wear, to choose clothes in an easier, less structured style than before.

She found a lingerie store and bought a boatload of underwear, some filmy nighties she didn't really need and a couple of cute sleep shirts. It was a truly great moment to finally take off her wedding bustier and put on a comfortable bra for a change. A block from the lingerie store, she stuffed the bustier in a trash can and congratulated herself on the fact that she would never have to look it—let alone wear it—again.

By five, when she headed back to Garrett's, the Subaru was piled high with shopping bags and she'd decided that when she did go back to Denver to pack up her condo, she would donate all her designer clothes to Goodwill.

When Cami emerged from her bedroom in a little white dress printed with bright red cherries that clung to her curves, Garrett had one word for her.

"Wow."

She giggled in that happy way she had and twirled around. "I went shopping." Her blond hair was sleek and shiny to her shoulders and she wore red sandals with delicate high heels.

"I can't even tell you have a black eye."

"It's the magic of makeup, Garrett." She bent to scratch Munch behind the ears. "Hey, handsome. You be good while we're gone." Munch gave a happy whine in response. "You look very handsome, too." She nodded approvingly at his blue knit shirt and khaki pants.

It felt a little strange, he realized, to be taking her to his mother's. In fact, it felt a whole lot like a date.

But it wasn't. And they would clear that up with Ma when they got to the mansion.

Out in the garage, he led her to the Ferrari-red 1969 Mustang Grande he rarely drove. He'd decided on the Mustang because the Jeep was dusty and spattered with mud, not because he wanted to impress her or anything.

"Gorgeous old car," she said as she settled into the leather seat.

He explained that his older brother Carter customized cars for a living. "He fixed this one up just for me."

The ride to the Bravo mansion was a short one. Cami gave him a rundown of her visit with Seth at the justice center and all the stuff she'd bought that afternoon. "I know it's self-indulgent to buy everything new. But I did it anyway. A whole new wardrobe." She smoothed the skirt of her cherry-covered dress. "To start my whole new life." She gave him a glowing smile, and he felt great just being with her in her pretty dress, driving with the windows down on a warm summer evening.

He'd already pulled to a stop in the sweeping turn-around in front of his mother's ostentatious white house before he realized they hadn't agreed on what exactly she was willing to say about how she'd ended up on Moosejaw Mountain with him.

Not that they really needed to discuss it in advance. He decided to follow Cami's lead. It was her story. Let her tell it in her own way.

They went up the wide steps between the two pretentious white pillars. Estrella, the mansion's longtime housekeeper, pulled the door open before he even rang the bell. "Garrett. So good to see you."

"Come in, come in!" His mother, in a pale green silk dress, her slim arms spread wide, emerged from the living room off the entry hall. Estrella stepped back, and Willow grabbed him in a hug. "I'm so glad you're here," she said softly. Her perfume, some light yet exotic scent she had made specially in Paris, swam around him. The hug kind of bewildered him. Willow Bravo had never been much of a hugger. She must really be happy that he'd finally found a girlfriend. He almost felt bad to have to tell her the truth. "And you must be Cami." She reached for Cami.

"Mrs. Bravo."

"Willow," his mother corrected as she drew Cami close. "It is simply wonderful to meet you." The women pulled apart and beamed at each other.

"Garrett's told me so much about you," Cami said.

Willow smirked. "He's complained about me, hasn't he? Go ahead and admit it."

"Never," replied Cami with a mock-serious frown.

And then the two of them laughed together, like they shared some kind of tasty little secret that no man could ever understand.

"Drinks in the library." Willow swept out a hand. "This way."

They went through the formal living room into the room behind it, where carved, built-in shelves held rows of leather-bound, gold-tooled volumes. A giant fireplace dominated one wall and the center of the room held twin damask sofas, a scattering of silk-covered chairs, carved side tables and a large, inlaid coffee table. Willow gestured at one of the sofas. Garrett sat down and Cami sat next to him, a lot closer than she really needed to on such a big couch.

But really, Garrett didn't mind her sitting close. She looked adorable in that dress—adorable and happy. That made him happy, too. And she smelled like sunshine and vanilla and some flower he couldn't quite recall the name of. Frangipani, maybe? Jasmine?

No, he didn't mind her sitting close in the least—though he did kind of worry it would reinforce his mother's incorrect assumptions about their relationship.

Willow went to the ornate drink cart between two of the chairs. "Martini?" He would have preferred whiskey or ice-cold vodka, straight, but his mother loved martinis and served them up every chance she got.

"Yes, please!" Cami replied with great enthusiasm. "Good and dirty, if you don't mind. I love the taste of olives. Just can't help myself."

"Dirty, it is," Willow replied, sounding downright gleeful. His mother. Gleeful. Would the weirdness never cease? "Garrett?"

"Sure, Ma. Thanks."

Willow expertly mixed their drinks, skipping the vermouth for Cami's and using olive juice instead.

"And I would like to propose a toast." Willow raised her glass high. "To love and happiness for both of you. I'm so pleased that you've found each other."

Garrett opened his mouth to explain that he and Cami were strictly in the friend zone, but Cami gave him a fond little bump with her shoulder and piped right up with, "To love and happiness." She clicked her glass with Garrett's first and then with Willow's. And she looked so sweet and pleased with the situation, it seemed just plain mean-spirited to argue the point now.

So he went ahead and let his mother tap her glass against his, figuring he might as well be sociable and just finish the toast. He could find another opportunity to correct the misunderstanding about him and Cami.

Garrett waited for the right moment.

But somehow, another opportunity never came. They finished their drinks, his mother rambling on about her latest trip. She'd gone to Sweden. Cami had been to Sweden twice, as it turned out. She said how much she loved the botanical gardens in Gothenburg and the Icehotel—an actual hotel made of ice—in some city with a name he'd never heard before.

When they sat down to dinner, Willow asked Cami about her family and her work. Cami managed to tell his mother the truth about growing up in Denver and the Lockwood vitamin empire without revealing that she'd recently left her groom at the altar or how, specifically, she and Garrett had met.

Garrett listened to the women laughing and chattering away and realized he was having a really good time—the most fun he'd ever had at the stuffy Bravo mansion, that was for sure. And it was all because of Cami, who had somehow turned his usually distant mother into someone warm and sociable.

He did snap to attention, though, when Cami said, "You know how these things go, Willow. Garrett and I found each other up on the mountain, and it was so special, right from the beginning, from the first moment our eyes met. We've been virtually inseparable ever since."

Inseparable? Okay, maybe they hadn't been apart until today, but still. She was definitely carrying the whole thing too far. He really did need to call a halt to this silly game before it got way out of hand.

So he opened his mouth and flatly announced, "Wait a minute. I just want to clarify. Cami's exaggerating. We are not dating. She is not my 'special' friend."

Chapter Four

Cami gasped. Willow blinked and gaped at Garrett.

Okay, maybe that had been a little abrupt. But it couldn't be helped. He needed to make the truth of their situation perfectly clear before his mother got too invested in the idea that he and Cami were a couple.

Didn't he?

And then Cami reached over and put her soft little hand over his. "Wow. That is so harsh. Garrett, you're such a mess."

Now he was the one gaping. He ought to yank his hand out from under hers and tell her to cut it the hell out.

But he didn't. Her hand felt so good touching his. And he just sat there and stared at her and wondered how a woman could be so completely impossible and so downright adorable, both at the same time.

She turned to Willow. "Clearly, he has a thousand emotional issues."

"Yes," said Willow somberly. "I'm afraid that he does. I don't know if he's told you how it was for him—for all five of my children—growing up?"

"Well, he did mention something about his half siblings and your, um, husband's first wife. And… all that."

"So then, you do understand? It was a difficult time and all the children were affected. And yes, I blame myself. Rightfully so."

"Well, but it's in the past, isn't it?" Cami asked gently.

"Yes, but I—"

"And Garrett says all nine of your husband's children get along great now. They've all moved on. You just have to forgive yourself, Willow. *You* have to move on."

"I'm trying."

"I'm so glad." Cami's full lips bloomed in a gorgeous smile. Then she frowned. "As for Garrett, well, I realize I've got a big job ahead of me, getting him to open up and give his heart freely. One minute he loves me, the next I'm 'not his special friend.' Sometimes I kind of wonder why I try. But love is like that, right? You just keep working, keep plugging away. When you love someone, what else can you do?"

Willow knocked back a big gulp of the white wine Estrella had served with the trout almondine and nodded in bemused agreement. "Yes. I see that." She echoed Cami softly, "What else can you do?"

With a final, gentle pat, Cami let Garrett's hand

go. "It's all right, sweetheart." Her eyes, of that mes-
merizing otherworldly blue, held his. "I understand."

Garrett opened his mouth to ask her if she had lost
her ever-loving mind.

And then he just couldn't do that.

She was trying to help him. And really, why was
he making such a big deal of this? What could it hurt?

If Ma wanted to believe he and Cami were a thing
and Cami wanted to play the role of devoted girlfriend, well, why the hell not?

It was almost ten, the night clear and warm, when
they got in the car and headed back down the curving driveway away from the mansion. Garrett didn't
say anything during the short drive home.

Cami leaned her head back against the seat rest and
really hoped he wasn't furious with her.

At his house, she set her purse on the kitchen table
and bent to greet Munchy, who gave her a bunch of
doggy kisses and then turned to get some love from
Garrett, too. He knelt to ruffle the dog's fur.

Cami gathered her courage and asked, "Are you
mad at me for lying to your mother and making her
think we're in love?"

He held her gaze over the wiggling body of the dog
between them. "It did kind of freak me out at first."

A nervous laugh escaped her. "I noticed that."

"But I got over it."

She couldn't resist teasing him. "For a minute
there, I was sure you were going to tell your mom
I was crazy and should probably seek professional
help."

Munchy's claws tapped the wood floor as he trotted to his water bowl to lap up a drink. Garrett stood and she did, too. "You were so determined."

"I know I should have taken the hint when you tried to put the brakes on."

There was definitely the ghost of a smile on his beautiful mouth. "But instead, you went all in with it." When the dog padded to the glass door and sat down, Garrett opened it for him. Munch slipped out.

She confessed, "I think I went *too* far with that stuff about how messed up you are. Sorry."

"Hey. You were playing it for all you were worth. And Ma wanted to believe you so badly. I didn't have the heart to keep fighting you both."

Cami slipped off her red sandals. The cool wood floor felt good against her bare feet. "I'm just glad you're not angry with me."

"I'm not." His voice was low and a little bit rough and the two of them were just standing there, staring at each other.

Good gravy, he was hot, with those melty amber eyes, those fine, broad shoulders. And that tender heart of his that he didn't even realize was so good, so true.

Was she falling for him?

Or was it only that Garrett and this bold, beautiful new life where she was finally becoming her real self were somehow intertwined for her? She had found him on the mountain and she'd loved every minute of her life since then—even the crappy ones, like almost losing Munchy to an angry bear and having to deal with her parents and Charles.

He said, "Plus…"

"Yeah?"

"Well, you were right that if she thinks we're together, she'll get off my case for a while. I wouldn't mind that in the least."

A lightness stole through Cami. "Good. I know it's not much, but it's nice to be able to tell myself that *I'm* finally doing something for *you*. And I've been thinking. Um, you mentioned my staying here?"

"The offer's still open."

"I'm glad. Because I want to stay here with you." At his slow, flirty grin, she shook her red sandals at him. "You are such a teaser. I mean, as a roomie. Of course I'll pay rent. You should think it over."

"Forget the rent."

"But, Garrett—"

"And I don't need to think it over. I want you to stay for as long as you need a place. And not because your staying helps me catch a break from Ma, either, though I've decided not to complain if it does. But the real deal is, I kind of hate to see you go." Oh, she did like the sound of that. "Life's a lot more interesting with you around."

Was he flirting with her? And was she a fool to hope so?

He opened the glass door again and Munch came back in. "Like I said, the offer's open. It's up to you." Munch fell into step behind him as he headed for the living room. "'Night, Cami."

"'Night…" He disappeared on his way to the stairs in the front hall.

She almost felt sad to see him go.

Garrett was sound asleep when he heard a soft tap on his bedroom door. "Garrett?" It was Cami's voice.

"Huh?" He came wide awake suddenly and squinted at the bedside clock—11:34.

"Garrett?" More tapping. Munch was already over there, whining and wagging his tail.

"Give me a minute!" He turned on the lamp and then grabbed the sweats he'd thrown across the bench at the foot of the bed.

When he opened the door, she looked up at him through anxious eyes. "Sorry." She wore a giant pink T-shirt with a cupcake printed on the front. And she must have noticed he was staring at the sparkly sprinkles in the frosting—or more specifically, at the soft curves of her braless breasts underneath. She looked down at the breasts in question. "New sleep shirt. I could never resist a great big cupcake, especially one with sprinkles."

"Cute," he said. Because it was—and so was she. And he was *not* thinking about her breasts, which were just right, round and full and...

Uh-uh. Not going there. No way. She seemed sad or worried about something. She'd probably come to him for comfort. The last thing she needed was to catch him sporting wood.

She patted Munch on the head. "I woke you up."

"It's okay."

"No, it's not. You're never going to want me for a roomie if I won't even let you sleep at night."

He leaned against the door frame. "Did you wake me up to say you're sorry for waking me up?"

She seemed to consider his silly question, but then she said, "I miss the cabin. I know that's crazy. I wasn't there for all that long. But I miss it anyway. I miss the way we would talk at night after you turned off the light."

He couldn't figure out her mood exactly. But something was bugging her. "You need to talk now?"

She caught her lower lip between her pretty white teeth—and nodded.

He took her hand, loving the way her cool fingers curled trustingly in his. She didn't object as he pulled her into the room and led her to the far side of the bed.

"What a beautiful bed." She touched the headboard, running her fingers along the weathered wood.

"It's repurposed, made of wood from old barns. Lie down." She jumped right up and stretched out on top of the covers. He got the extra blanket and settled it over her, then went back around and got in on his side. Munch joined them, curling up at their feet. Garrett turned out the light and adjusted his pillow under his head. "Comfy?"

He heard a soft sigh from her side of the bed. "Very."

"Now, talk."

"I feel kind of bad bothering you with this."

"Talk."

She came out with it then. "It's Charles."

"What did that bonehead do now?"

"He just keeps calling. And texting. I turned my phone down in the afternoon and ignored him. And then I powered it off when we went to your mother's. When I turned it back on an hour ago, I had three new calls and four texts from him. I've gotten zero calls from my parents, which leads me to believe my father has ordered Charles to get busy and get me back in line. Charles does what Quentin Lockwood tells him to do and that means he's not going to back off until I agree to see him."

Garrett hadn't even met the guy, but he already wanted to punch Charles's lights out. He didn't think much of her father, either. "You really believe that a face-to-face with your ex-groom is going make a difference?"

"I don't know. Not for sure. But I guess I kind of feel I owe it to him. I should have broken it off with him in person, but I knew if I did, the chances of making my escape would not be good."

"Because the guy is so damn convincing?"

"No. Because Charles would have run straight to my father and my father would have found a way to keep me from going. I can't tell you how many times my father has managed to stop me from striking out on my own, how many times I've run away and then screwed up and ended up right back where I never wanted to be. I'm not screwing up this time. I'm free and I'm staying free."

"I believe you," he said with real admiration. "What I can't believe is that you didn't get out on your own long before now."

"See? That's another thing I like about you. You think I'm strong and tough and ready for anything."

"Because you are—and what do you mean, you screwed up in the past?"

"I just mean that something would always happen and I would have to go back to Denver and the overprotective bosom of my family. I told you about that time after college, when that drunk driver crashed into me and I ended up in a coma?"

"You did. You also mentioned it wasn't the first time."

"And it wasn't. The first time, I was ten."

"Okay. That's a little young to strike out on your own."

"You're right. But I did it anyway. And I only got lost and ended up huddled in a shed in a snowstorm for two days, afraid I would die."

"My God."

Her hand brushed his shoulder, a quick pat of reassurance, and then it was gone. "Don't worry. I got through it. The man who owned the shed found me. His wife gave me some hot soup and called the police. A lady from child protective services came and took me back to my parents. They grounded me for months and made me get counseling."

"Did *they* get counseling?"

"Are you kidding? *I'm* the one with problems, remember?"

"They could have made a little effort to understand what was bothering you."

"Hmm. I think they really believe that they *have* made the effort to understand me. And what they understand is that *I'm* the one who's making the trouble, that instead of facing my issues, I run away."

"Because they won't listen to you and work with you to help you have the kind of life that suits you."

She laughed. The sound made his chest feel tight in a really satisfying way. "I love the way you think, Garrett."

He grunted, because now his throat felt a little tight, too. "So what happened next?"

"Well, in high school, I fell for a bad boy. Robbie

Rodriguez worked at Taco Bell. I went in for a chili verde burrito and got lost in his big brown eyes. We ran away together. But then it turned out that Robbie wasn't so very bad, after all. A couple of days on the road and he started worrying about his family. He said he couldn't do it, couldn't just walk away from everyone who loved him."

Garrett laced his hands behind his head and stared up at the shadowed ceiling. "So you went back to Denver."

"We did. My father was furious and my mother was worried sick. I felt just awful. I got more therapy. My counselor was patient and understanding and helped me to see that running away wasn't the solution."

Given all that she'd told him, Garrett wasn't sure he agreed with her therapist. Not in her particular case, anyway. "What *was* the solution?"

She chuckled and poked him with her elbow. "That's the problem. I don't think there is a solution when it comes to my father. Except to get away from him and stay away long enough that he finally has to accept that this is my life and I'm the one who gets to choose how to live it."

"Sounds like a plan to me."

"See?" She scooted closer. He smelled her scent of vanilla and tropical flowers. And then he felt her soft lips brush his cheek. She was back on her own side of the bed before he could do anything stupid— like grab her close and hold on tight. "That's why I need to be with you right now," she said. "Because you *get* me, Garrett. You get me in a way that no one else ever has. You make me strong."

His throat still felt weirdly tight. He had to speak around the irritating obstruction. "You *are* strong." It came out rough with emotion he didn't want to examine.

And she laughed. He didn't think he'd ever get enough of hearing her laugh. "See? That. What you said right there? That's what I'm talkin' about."

A silence descended, a companionable one. It went on for a while. It felt so good, just lying here beside her. He stared at the ceiling. His eyelids were growing heavy.

In a minute, he'd be falling asleep. And they had yet to settle the question of what she should do about Charles.

He blinked a few times to wake himself up. "So… about Charles. Are you going to meet with him?"

"Mmm-hmm. I'm thinking tomorrow. You know, get it over with. Probably someplace public."

That alarmed him a little. "Why? Are you afraid of him?"

"Not afraid, just…" She seemed to have trouble finding the right word.

He felt for her hand. When he had it, he twined their fingers together. "I'm listening. Tell me."

"Charles is always so sure he's right. He's like my father that way. Relentless in getting what he wants."

"You think he'll bully you into going back to him?"

"I'm pretty sure he's going to try. That's why I plan to meet him at a restaurant or something, someplace where he'll be reluctant to make a scene."

"I don't get the guy's reasoning. Even if he talked you into coming back, what kind of life would you have together if one of you just wants to get away?"

She squeezed his hand a little tighter. "It's not really me that he wants. It's WellWay. Marrying the boss's daughter is a means to seal that deal up tight."

"Wait a minute. You're saying he doesn't even love you?"

"You sound angry." She eased her hand free of his.

He had to resist the urge to grab it back. "I'm sorry. But everything you've told me about this guy just pisses me off."

"It's complicated. I mean, I'm pretty sure he *thinks* he loves me, that he *tells* himself he loves me. I'm also positive he loves WellWay more. And he's been really good for the company. He's ambitious, creative, hardworking and smart. When my father retires, Charles *should* be the one to step up and run the company."

"So then, there's the solution. You don't have to marry Charles in order for him to end up as CEO of the company he loves so damn much."

"That's not how my father sees it. It's a family company and I'm his only child. He wants me to take over from him eventually. If I marry Charles, we can take it over together. I think that's the optimum outcome as far as my dad is concerned. I marry Charles and that locks me in to living the life my father wants for me, plus it makes Charles truly one of the family. He'll be there to make sure I stay in line after my parents are gone."

"*Stay in line*? That's just scary, Cami. I'm glad you escaped."

She let out a low, sweet chuckle. "You have no idea how happy it makes me that you understand how I feel, what I need."

"But you still think you have to meet with Charles—and what is his last name, anyway?"

"Ashby. Charles Ashby. And yeah. I think I do. For the sake of closure, you know?"

"Wasn't it closure enough that you left him at the altar?"

"Spoken like a guy. Garrett, closure doesn't work like that."

"Why? Because it's not closure if you don't talk it to death?"

She softly sighed. "Eventually, I have to go see my parents, too, and try to make peace with them. But one big helping of awfulness at a time. Charles first."

"Tell him you'll meet him here at the house. I'll be here when you do. If he gives you any crap, Munch and I will come running."

She was quiet for the longest time. He wondered if she'd dropped off to sleep.

But then she confessed glumly, "I came in here hoping you'd say that. Now I'm thinking I'm a manipulative jerk to get you involved in this."

"You're not a jerk. And you didn't manipulate me. I volunteered. In fact, I volunteered back at lunchtime, remember? I said if you were going to meet with him, meet with him here."

"I know, but—"

"Stop arguing. Tell me you'll talk to him here at the house."

Another silence. Then, softly, "I will."

"Now, get some sleep." He half expected her to jump up and run off back to her room.

But all she said was, "All right, then. 'Night."

* * *

In the morning when he woke up, she was still there beside him in bed, sound asleep, looking sweet as an angel—if an angel can have a black eye.

Very carefully, so as not to wake her yet, he got up on an elbow and stared at her sleeping face, thinking that he was kind of crazy about her.

How did that happen?

He decided that how didn't matter. He liked her. A lot.

It didn't have to be a big freaking deal.

She opened her eyes and looked straight at him. "Huh? What'd I do?"

"Nothing." He fell back to his own pillow and put his arm across his face before admitting out of the corner of his mouth, "I was just watching you sleep, that's all."

He felt the bed shift as she levered up and leaned over him. "Like in a pervy way?"

He groaned. "Possibly." And then he distinctly heard her snicker. He lowered his arm enough to look at her above him as she chortled away. "That does it. If you're just going to laugh at me, I'm never perving on you again." That only made her laugh harder. She fell back to her own pillow. He muttered, "I suppose it is kind of funny…"

Okay, not *that* funny. But he couldn't help grinning. He felt good—good about everything, for some unknown reason. He started laughing, too.

For two or three minutes, they just lay there in bed, staring at the ceiling and laughing together.

Then Munch, who was already at the bedroom door waiting to go outside, gave an extraloud whine.

They got up together and let him out.

* * *

Cami called Ashby after breakfast, while they were still at the table having second cups of coffee.

The guy was a douche, no doubt about it. Garrett couldn't hear the other end of the conversation. But Cami hardly got more than a couple of words out before Ashby would interrupt her. Finally, she said she would see him that evening. He seemed to be insisting he was coming right now.

She held firm. "Seven tonight. Or tomorrow night, if that works better for you."

He must have agreed. She rattled off Garrett's address.

Ashby said something else.

And Cami started to argue again. "No, Charles. I told you—" She pulled the phone away from her ear and glared at it.

Garrett set down his mug. "What happened?"

"I do not *believe* that man. He said he'll be here in an hour and a half. And then he hung up." Her sweet mouth trembled a little and two spots of hectic color rode high on her cheeks.

"Hey." He got up and went around to her, pulled her up into his arms and stroked a hand down her hair—because he wanted to, because his touch seemed to soothe her and he really liked touching her. Then he took that fairy princess face between his hands and held her gaze. "Look at it this way. It's better to get it over with. In a couple of hours, you'll be done with him."

She stared up at him anxiously. "I'll bet you need to get to work, huh?"

"No way am I leaving you here alone for this. I'll hang around just in case you need backup."

"Now I'm messing up your workday."

He smoothed her hair behind her ear. "No, you're not. I've got lunch with a prospective client at one. Nothing important until then."

Garrett managed to convince her to let him answer the door, so that Ashby would know from the get-go that she wasn't alone, that she had someone to stand up for her if it came to that.

Ashby, who was tall, with blond hair and cool blue eyes, didn't waste a second being friendly. "Who are you?" he demanded when Garrett pulled back the door.

"I live here."

"What?" The guy was good-looking, Garrett supposed. If you liked them really lean with pointy, over-bred features. And that lightweight gray suit he was wearing looked like Armani. "Where's Camilla?"

"I'm right here," Cami said from back near the stairs. Munch, at her feet, gave a low, warning growl. "Shh, Munchy," she soothed. "Everything's okay." Then she spoke to Ashby. "Come in, Charles."

Garrett was blocking the door, but he didn't move. He seriously did not like the guy. He and Ashby spent several seconds just glaring at each other.

"Garrett," Cami said, more strongly. "Please."

Reluctantly, he moved aside and gestured the other man in.

"Camilla, who is this man?" Ashby demanded once he'd cleared the threshold. "Why are you here?"

"Mind your manners, Ashby," Garrett warned. "Or I'll mind them for you."

Ashby turned on him. "Who *are* you? I don't know you."

Before Garrett could put the pretentious ass in his place, Cami said, "Charles, this is my friend Garrett. Let's go on in the kitchen." She turned and headed through the living room, Munch at her heels. With a last glare at Garrett, Ashby followed. Garrett took up the rear.

"Sit down, Charles." Cami gestured at the table. "Coffee?"

Charles did not sit. "No coffee." He sent another chilly glance at Garrett. "I want to talk to you alone. I think you owe me that."

Munch growled again. Garrett was about to inform the arrogant idiot that Cami didn't owe him squat.

But she caught his eye first. "It's okay. I do need speak with him in private."

Garrett didn't think she needed any such thing. But it was her fight. He got that. "Fair enough." He marched to the door on the other side of the island, the one to the hallway that led to the laundry room.

Ashby muttered something under his breath and Munch growled again.

"Hush, now," Cami soothed the dog. And then she looked at Garrett again. "I think you'd better take Munchy with you."

Garrett clicked his tongue. "Munch. Come." With one more watch-yourself growl for good measure, Munch followed him out. Garrett closed the door behind them.

Then, feeling no shame whatsoever, he pressed his ear to the door.

* * *

Cami waited until she heard Garrett shut the kitchen door before trying to settle Charles down a little. "Come on, Charles. Have a seat and we'll talk."

Charles shot his cuffs and stood straighter. "I'll stand. What's happened to your eye? Did that guy—?"

"Please. Garrett would never lay a finger on me."

"But if he's—"

"I had a little accident, that's all. I wrecked the Beemer."

"What in the…? How could you?"

"Actually, the accident wasn't my fault."

"You have a bruise on your chin. Have you been to a doctor? I don't believe this. What if you have internal injuries? Are you sure you don't need—"

"I'm perfectly fine. You really need to calm down a little, Charles."

"Calm down? *I* should calm down? I don't even know how to start with you, Camilla. You've been in a *car* accident?"

She waved a hand. "Like that hasn't happened before. I told you, I'm fine. Will you please let it go?"

"You left me at the church. I can't believe you would humiliate me that way. And now you've moved in with some strange guy in this nowhere little tourist town? You've always been a little too quirky and unusual for your own good, but as of this moment, I'm starting to think you've gone stark-raving nuts." He finally paused for a breath.

And she asked mildly, "Well, then, I guess it's all worked out for the best, hasn't it?"

"The best? What are you talking about?"

"Charles. It was a bad idea, you and me getting

married. I never should have said yes in the first place and I apologize for not ending it in a more considerate way. But it's done now and we can both move on."

He made a sputtering sound. "Move on? We're not moving on. Whatever gave you that idea?"

"Well, given that I ran out on our wedding and disappeared for several days without a word, it ought to be pretty clear to you by now that what we had wasn't working for me."

"Clear? What are you saying? None of that matters."

"Charles. Wake up. It matters."

"It does not. Of course we're going to work this out. Of course I will somehow learn to forgive you. We'll return home today. The license is still good and I've spoken with the priest. We can be married this afternoon and go on as we should have on Saturday—minus the reception, with the honeymoon slightly shortened." He raked his fingers through his pale blond hair. "So get whatever things you have here and I'll take you home now."

Cami knew she wasn't getting through to him, but she refused to become discouraged. She tried again. "Stop. Think. You have to know it would be a disaster. We'd only end up divorced."

"That's not true."

"You need to face facts here. I don't love you, Charles. And you don't love me, either."

He winced. It was only the slightest tightening around his mouth and eyes, but Cami saw it. And then he insisted woodenly, "Of course I love you."

"No, you don't. You love WellWay and you want to be president and CEO someday."

He looked pained. And she knew why. Because he did want to be president. He wanted it more than anything—even if he had to marry Quentin Lockwood's wayward daughter to get there. He said wearily, "We'll run the company together."

"No. *You* will run the company whether I'm there or not. And you deserve to run the company when my father retires. You don't need to marry the boss's daughter to make that happen."

"No, I… Cami, you know we're perfect for each other."

"That's not true."

"Of course it's true. You know that, in the end, this is all going to work out."

"Yes, it *is* going to work out. But not in the way you keep insisting. It's over between us, Charles. I never should have agreed to marry you and I'm not going to Denver with you today. I'm not going to Denver at all. Not for a while, anyway."

"You don't mean that."

"And you need to stop telling me what I think and feel. Listen, I was weak. You kept asking and, well, you know my father. He kept pushing. I finally gave in. But that's all it was. Just another sad surrender to my father's relentless push to run my life. We are not a good match. We would make each other miserable. Face it. Please. You don't love me, Charles."

"Yes, I do."

"No, you don't. If you did, I wouldn't have caught you kissing your secretary the day before our wedding."

Chapter Five

Garrett, his ear pressed to the other side of the kitchen door, could hardly believe what he'd just heard.

The bastard had *cheated* on her? Why hadn't she said so? This wasn't right. The argument on the other side of the door shouldn't even be happening. Ashby didn't deserve any damn closure if he'd been fooling around behind her back.

Garrett threw the door wide and headed for Ashby, Munch at his heels.

Cami whirled and put her hand out. "Garrett, don't."

"Do you *mind*?" Ashby demanded from the far side of the table. "This is a private conversation."

Munch gave a long, low growl and Garrett took another step toward the cheating SOB Cami almost married.

But then she reached out and grabbed his arm. "I mean it, Garrett. No."

"But he cheat—"

"Please." Her eyes were so soft, her tone way too anxious. "This is for me to handle." She moved in closer and pressed her hand to his chest. He smelled her sweet perfume, wanted to grab her fingers, pull her behind him and face that rich-boy punk across the table for her.

But those beautiful blue eyes told him no.

Beside him, Munch let out another growl. "Come on, boy." Garrett bent enough to get the dog by his collar and led him back into the hallway, pulling the door closed behind him again.

Cami watched the door close on Garrett's face and realized she was totally falling for him. He was a true friend.

And more. So much more. He was everything she'd begun to think she'd never find in a guy. Funny and helpful, bighearted and smart. Not to mention, way hot.

But how she felt about Garrett wasn't the issue right now.

Right now, she needed to finish this sad thing with Charles.

She turned on her heel and went back to face him across the table. "All right." She even managed a smile. "Where were we?"

His lip curled downward, a frown that was also partly a sneer. "Get your things. We are leaving."

A shiver raced up her spine as she realized how much he sounded like her father. Thank God she hadn't married him. "No, Charles. *I'm* not leaving. Yes, I admit that I've been a coward. But not anymore. If I had loved you, walking in on you kissing someone else would have devastated me, but all I felt was a kind of numb disbelief that I was marrying you the next day and we didn't even love each other."

"Of course I love you," Charles said automatically. But he actually looked a little ashamed. "And as for that little incident with Tricia, you...didn't say anything at the time."

"Except for *excuse me*, you mean?" She'd been pretty stunned. "I didn't know what to say. So I just shut the door and left."

"I assumed you understood that it was nothing."

"Well, you assumed wrong."

"I swear to you, Camilla. It was only that one kiss. I don't know what I was thinking. Tricia is flirtatious, yes. But she's an excellent assistant and we've always kept it strictly business."

"Except for the flirting and the kissing, you mean?"

Charles raked a hand back over his hair. "Don't be sarcastic."

"Sorry, but a little sarcasm seems totally appropriate about now."

"What did you expect me to do? You would never let me near you."

Because we didn't love each other. "You felt deprived. Is that what you're saying?"

"You know I did."

"So you got involved with Tricia."

"No. Of course not. That's not what I said."

She actually almost felt sorry for him. "Charles. You were as trapped as I was. Admit it. Move on."

He drew his shoulders back, as though by standing straighter he could somehow put himself in the right. "What I'm trying to tell you is that I have never touched Tricia before or since."

She really did wish she could get through to him. "But, Charles, don't you see? If it was true love between us, you never would have touched Tricia at all."

"No. Now, that's just not so. Do you have to romanticize *everything*? I did love you—I *do* love you. And you are twisting my words. I am saying that my kissing Tricia was only one of those silly things that happen now and then. Eventually, you will stop being so ridiculously naive and realize that a meaningless kiss is nothing to get all upset about."

"Charles." She gave him a long look of great patience. "When a woman catches her fiancé kissing another woman, it is definitely something for her to get upset about—and before you start in with your denials again, I want you to understand that I do see my own part in this."

"Well, that's something at least. If you hadn't been so cold, I never would have—"

"Charles. Forget Tricia. And anyone else you fooled around with while we were engaged."

"I never—"

"Oh, please. When are you going to face that you were as unhappy with me as I was with you?"

"What? No. Of course I wasn't unhappy. How can you say that? There you go being difficult again."

"Here I go telling the truth. Again. And you know it, too. I should never have agreed to marry you. And when I finally woke up and admitted to myself that it wasn't going to work, I should have done a better job of calling it off. But still, ending it was the right thing to do and you should be grateful that I came to my senses and ran before we actually got married and made everything worse."

"Grateful?" he huffed in outrage. "I should be *grateful…*"

"Yes, you should."

"Well, I am not grateful. And this conversation is not going anywhere. I've promised your father I will bring you back today and, one way or another, that is exactly what I intend to do."

"Oh, now." She shook her head. "See? There it is. That is the real reason you're here and we both know it. You're here because my father sent you."

He didn't even bother to deny it. "We are going home now."

She took his ring from her pocket. "*I'm* going nowhere. Here's your ring." She held it up for him. "Take it and leave, please."

Fast as a striking snake, as she bent to set the ring on the table, he whipped out a hand and grabbed her wrist. "We're leaving together. Now." His grip was hard, punishing. She tried to jerk away, but he didn't release her. "Let's go."

She knew a flash of actual terror. And then she steeled herself. "Let go of me, Charles."

"We're out of here." He stepped clear of the table and yanked her toward him.

"No. Let me go!"

At her cry, the kitchen door burst open behind her, hitting the wall with a loud bang. Cami whipped her head toward the sound as a whirlwind of angry dog and furious man burst out. Munch and Garrett came flying toward her.

Charles let her go and jumped back, giving a yelp of fear as Munch latched on to the hem of his pant leg. The dog growled and the fabric tore.

"Munch!" Garrett commanded. "Sit!"

With one last, low growl, Munch released Charles's pricey pant leg and dropped to his haunches.

"Get the hell out," said Garrett.

Charles tugged on the sides of his jacket. "Your dog has destroyed a good pair of pants."

"Hang around," suggested Garrett, way too quietly, "and see what *I* destroy."

Cami breathed a careful sigh of relief as Charles swiped the ring off the table. "All right, Camilla, have it your way. We are through."

"Oh, yes, we are," she agreed with enthusiasm, catching hold of Munchy's collar before he got any more overly protective ideas.

"Out." Garrett took another step toward Charles.

"Don't you come near me." Charles backed toward the living room. Garrett followed, step for step, herding him toward the front door. "You know this isn't the end of it." Charles looked past Garrett at Cami as he continued moving backward. "You might be rid of me, because I'm done with you. But your father won't put up with this."

Cami refused to waver. "When you report to him, tell him I don't want to see him until I'm *ready* to see him and he'd better not turn up here uninvited."

Before Charles could reply, Garrett herded him out of sight. It was just as well, Cami decided as she heard the front door open and shut. She held on to

Munchy until Charles's Maserati started up outside. He peeled rubber pulling out.

"Show-off," Cami muttered to herself.

Garrett reappeared from the front hall. At her side, Munch gave a happy whine at the sight of his master.

"He's gone," Garrett said.

Her heart welling with happiness, she watched him approach. She'd faced down Charles and never wavered. And when things got out of hand, Garrett had been there to make it right.

With a glad cry, she threw herself against his broad, strong chest. His big arms went around her, banding tight. She pressed her cheek to his hard shoulder, breathed in his scent of pine and leather. He made her world feel safe and right.

"You okay?" His lips brushed the crown of her head. She felt his warm breath ruffle her hair.

And she looked up. His beautiful caramel eyes were waiting.

Did she speak his name? Or did she only hear it echo inside her with every hopeful beat of her hungry heart?

"Cami." There was an entire conversation just in the way that he whispered her name.

"Garrett." She said it out loud that time.

He made a low sound, like a question.

And she slipped her hand up his chest, over the thick, muscled curve of his shoulder, until she could clasp the nape of his neck. "Yes. Oh, yes..."

He lowered his mouth and she lifted up.

His warm, soft lips covered hers. She gave a happy cry and surged even closer. He tasted of coffee with a dollop of cream, of nights on the mountain and all the wonder and wild beauty that made up her new life. The life she'd always wanted, the life that used to seem so far away, moving ever farther out of reach.

But not anymore.

She pressed even closer, felt the evidence that he really, truly did want her.

And, oh, she wanted him, too. Wanted his kisses and his hands all over her, wanted him to scoop her up and carry her to his bedroom, where they could share a whole lot more than this perfect, tender kiss.

She wanted it all with him, for the very first time.

How strange life was. How many times had she puzzled over what, exactly, she was waiting for when it came to having sex?

Well, it all made sense now. She had waited for Garrett. He was always meant to be her first.

He lifted his head. She saw desire in his eyes. And hesitation, too. "I shouldn't—"

She stopped his words with her fingers to his lips. "Shh." *Don't ruin it. Just let it be.*

And he did. He let it be.

She said, "Somehow, I'm always thanking you." It came out in a whisper, fervent. Grateful. Overflowing with emotions she thought it safer not to name.

Yet.

He touched her chin, rubbed his rough thumb in a slow caress down the side of her cheek. "He's gone. I really don't think he'll be back."

"He was going to drag me out of here."

"But he didn't."

"Because of you."

One corner of that gorgeous, oh-so-kissable mouth of his kicked up. "Don't forget Munch, the wonder dog." At their feet, the dog in question thumped his tail against the floor.

"Never, ever could I forget Munchy."

"And you didn't tell me that Ashby was a cheater." He said it in a chiding way.

She combed the short hair at his temples with her fingers, because it felt good. Because he let her. "Charles kissing his secretary really wasn't the issue."

His eyes darkened. "It's exactly the issue. If a guy cheats, he doesn't deserve an explanation as to why a woman is done with him—and don't come back with how he didn't have sex with her. If he kissed her, you just don't know what else he was up to."

"But, Garrett, it was a good thing, the *best* thing, that I saw him kissing Tricia. It woke me up, you know? Made me finally admit that it was almost too late and I had to get out of there."

"Still. A cheater's a cheater. My dad cheated on his first wife with my mother. None of us ever completely forgave him for that. Or forgave my mother, for that matter."

"You said they're all past that."

"Okay, yeah. You're right. We do forgive. But we don't forget. We remember how their cheating hurt us, all of us. We Bravos—my generation, anyway—we don't cheat. Ever. And you should have told me what Ashby did."

"I guess I felt kind of sorry for him." At Garrett's snort of outrage, she made a low, soothing sound and pressed her hand against his cheek, just for a moment, just to watch the heat flare in those amber eyes. "Charles was my friend when we were kids. His dad and my dad were like brothers. Then his dad had some money problems and Charles had to take out serious loans just to get his education. WellWay is everything to him. It's his ticket back to the good life. He's as trapped as I ever was—more so, really. He's got no nest egg to count on if he walks away."

"Sorry. I'm not feeling any sympathy for the guy." He took a swatch of her hair and rubbed it between his fingers, tipping his head to the side in a thoughtful sort of way. "And we should talk about what just happened." He meant the kiss. She could see it in his eyes.

"Uh-uh." She tried to press her fingertips to his lips again.

But he caught them. "Cami, I kissed you."

"And I kissed you back. I liked it. A lot."

"So did I. But that's not what matters."

"Garrett. It is exactly what matters."

"You really are too tempting, you know that?" He brought her captured fingers close then and brushed his warm lips against them.

Pleasure shivered through her. "All I'm saying is don't you dare try to talk yourself out of kissing me again."

"It's what you want?" His eyes were almost golden now. "More kisses from me?"

I want it all from you. Everything. At last. "More kisses. Yes."

"More kisses will take us beyond the friend zone." It was a warning.

"Great. So what are we waiting for?"

He was trying really hard not to smile, but she saw the telltale twitch at the corner of his mouth. "You need to think about it." He made his voice deadly serious. "You need to consider all the crap you've been through and whether it's a good idea to get something going on the rebound like this."

Feeling perfectly serene, she gave herself a slow count of five before answering, "Okay. I've thought about it. It's a good idea. A *really* good idea."

He took her by the shoulders and set her away from him. "Think about it some more."

She didn't argue. There was no need. The man was hers. He just couldn't let himself admit it.

Yet.

Chapter Six

Half an hour after Garrett left the house that morning, Cami got a call from her mother. The call didn't surprise her. Charles would have reported to her dad and her dad would have turned right around and sicced her mom on her.

Cami's mom was actually a nice woman. If not for Cami's dad, Hazel Lockwood would long ago have backed off and let Cami lead her own life.

The conversation went pretty much as expected. Her mom gently pleaded for her to be "reasonable" and return home immediately. Cami calmly explained that her home was now Justice Creek and she fully intended to make a new life there. She repeated what she'd told Charles, that she was not coming to Denver for a while and she did not want any visits from her parents. She asked that her parents respect her wishes and let her be for now and hung up feeling sad that it had come to this, but reasonably confident that they would leave her alone—for a while at least.

For the rest of the morning, she sat out on the deck, filling blank pages with sketches and ideas. She needed to focus on her next step in the process of creating a new and more satisfying way of life and she did her best thinking with a sketchbook in her hand.

When she got hungry, she made a sandwich from stuff left over from the cabin. Garrett's cupboards were looking kind of bare, so she texted him that she would get groceries and he should let her know anything specific he wanted. He texted back the usual guy-type items: beer, boxed cereal, chips, cheese and hamburger.

She replied, I'm cooking myself dinner. Should I make enough for you?

Absolutely. I'll be back by seven.

She was grinning to herself at the hominess of it all, the two of them texting each other about groceries and dinnertime, when her phone rang in her hand. It was the sheriff calling to let her know that she could go ahead and have her car towed out of the ravine.

Ten minutes later, feeling strong and capable and ready for anything her new life might hand her, she jumped in the Subaru and headed out to take care of business.

"Deck, I really don't know what to tell you, man." Garrett took a small sip of thirty-year-old scotch. It went down smooth with just enough heat. Normally, he didn't drink at lunch, not with a whole afternoon of work ahead of him. But Declan McGrath had ordered scotch. To be sociable, Garrett had said he'd have one, too.

They sat in a quiet back booth on the ground floor of McKellan's Pub, which was owned and managed by a family friend, Ryan McKellan—really, Rye was more like an actual member of the Bravo family. His brother Walker had married a Bravo cousin, Rory. Rye and Garrett's half sister Clara were lifelong best friends and had almost gotten married once. And four years ago, Rye had hired Bravo Construction to build a couple of loft apartments in the empty third floor above the pub. Rye lived in the front loft now with his new girlfriend, Meg. Nell had the one in the back.

"I can't catch a break with her." Deck meant Nell. Shaking his head, he turned his drink in a slow circle. "Why won't she act as the general on my new house? It's just business, right? What's wrong with my money, that's what I want to know?"

Garrett tried kidding him. "Dude. Nell doesn't want to run the project for you, but we'll still take your money."

Deck only grumbled, "Is that supposed to be funny?"

Might as well give it to him straight. "Nell says no, Deck. If we build your house, she's not running the project. And when Nell says no, you'd best take her word for it."

Deck raised his glass and knocked back a mouthful. "Well, I'm not giving up. One way or another, I'm going to get her to see that I know how wrong

I was and I'll do just about anything for one more chance with her."

Garrett sipped scotch and wondered idly what the deal was with Deck, to decide he had to try again with the high school sweetheart he'd dumped all those years and years ago? But Garrett didn't ask. He liked Deck and wanted his business, but no way was he ending up running interference between his sister and her old flame.

Nope. Not getting involved in their drama. Deck was one determined guy. But when Nell made up her mind about something, no mere man was likely to change it. They would have to fight this out on their own.

The waitress came with club sandwiches. They spent a few minutes concentrating on the food. Garrett's mind wandered a little—to Cami and that bone-melting kiss she'd given him earlier. He probably shouldn't have kissed her. It only made him want to kiss her some more and that wouldn't be wise. She needed a friend now, not more romantic complications.

And he needed to keep his grabby hands off.

He smiled to himself. She'd texted that she was cooking him dinner. The thought of that, of her in his kitchen whipping up a meal, made him smile. He did love having her around.

Did he love it too much?

No, he decided. He just needed to watch himself around her, keep it friends-only, and everything would be fine.

Deck said glumly, "So I'll bring the architect's plans by your office tomorrow morning? You can work up a contract for me."

Garrett swallowed a bite of sandwich. "You sure about this?"

"What? Nell or my new house?"

Garrett grunted. "Either. Both."

"Yeah. I'm sure. As for Nell and me, I'm not giving up. And even if she won't work with me personally on it, I still want Bravo Construction to build my house."

By six-thirty that night, Cami had chicken in mushrooms and wine bubbling on the stove.

Garrett got home right on time. It was a warm evening, not a cloud in sight. They ate outside on the deck. He praised her chicken and she slipped more than one bite to Munch, who sat by her chair, soulful eyes begging her. Garrett talked about all the work he had to catch up on at Bravo Construction.

She tried not to be jealous that he had work he seemed to love. "Lucky you. I'm still doodling all day, trying to decide what to do next."

"You'll figure it out." He said it with confidence, so certain she would not only come up with a job that made her happy, but when she did, she would be amazing at it.

He made her feel capable and special. Her life just somehow made complete sense when Garrett was around.

Was she falling and falling hard for the guy? Oh, yes, she was.

And who was she kidding, really, with the whole "falling" routine?

She'd already fallen. She loved him—was *in* love with him.

So what if she'd just met him five days before?

Love was love, no matter how fast it happened. So-phisticated people, people who thought they knew better about how the world worked, how relationships worked—people like her father and Charles—they thought love at first sight was some silly romantic notion, that you had to know someone forever to even begin to call it love.

And okay, maybe there was some truth to the way others viewed love. She was willing to give them that. *Some* truth, but not all.

Because life and love were bigger than any one person's perception of them. And some people did fall in love at first sight. They fell and they kept falling, deeper and deeper, as they continued to discover the rightness of that love.

Some people were perfect candidates for love at first sight. And Cami knew now that she was one of those people, someone who was finally getting her chance to follow her heart, instead of trying to be what others thought she should be.

Looking back on that first night at the cabin, the truth came crystal clear to her now. She'd seen the light of his campfire through the darkness and fol-lowed it. From the first moment she saw him, when he bolted straight up out of his camp chair and dropped his hot dog in shock at the sight of her, she'd *known* this was the man for her.

Was she going to tell him that?

Not for a while. Not until he was ready to hear it. Garrett was an amazing guy but kind of a slow learner when it came to love and romance. She wouldn't push him. She would give him all the time he needed to realize he loved her, too.

As they finished up their meal, she considered bringing up the subject of kissing and when they would be doing more of that. But she was kind of hoping he might bring it up first—or maybe kiss her again, which would be way better than just talking about it.

He did neither.

They cleared the table, and he loaded the dishwasher. Then he said he had work to catch up on. He disappeared into his home office at the front of the house.

She got ready for bed. All comfy in yoga pants and a sleep shirt, she settled on the couch in the living room to watch TV and fill up more pages with doodles and drawings.

At half-past ten, he still hadn't come out of his office. It was just her and Munch streaming the second season of *Orphan Black*. She could almost start to suspect that he might be avoiding her. That only made her smile. He liked her too much to avoid her forever. And that kiss this morning? It had told her everything she needed to know. He not only liked her, he was into her. She would love to move on from the friend zone right now.

But if he needed time, she would just have to give it to him.

At some point, she must have dropped off to sleep.

When she woke up, Garrett was all around her, his powerful arms cradling her. They were moving, going up the stairs. She could hear the tapping of Munch's claws on the hardwood floor as he followed behind them.

She wrapped her arms around his neck and snuggled in against his broad chest. "Take me to your room. I want to sleep with you."

"Cami," he said. Just her name and nothing more, in that chiding tone that told her everything—that he wanted to take her to his bed with him.

But he was telling himself he shouldn't.

He stopped at the door to her room. She could feel his hesitation. He felt he should take her in there and put her in the bed he'd assigned to her.

But he didn't want to do that, not really. He only *thought* that he should, because of what had happened that morning.

Because of the kiss.

Because they were just friends and he thought they ought to remain that way.

Wrong.

"Please." She breathed the word into the warm crook of his neck. "I promise not to try to kiss you."

A low sound escaped him. She felt the rumble of it in his chest. He was trying not to laugh.

And she snuggled in closer. Yeah, okay, she was shameless. She was also enjoying herself immensely. She had a new life to live and a fabulous man to seduce.

In time. When he was ready.

For now, though, she only wanted to sleep with him every night, to be close to him in the dark, where it would be easier to continue the bedtime talks they'd shared at the cabin. Easier to reveal the secrets of their hearts.

He stood there at her door for a minute or two that seemed to stretch out into eternity. She pressed her lips together to keep from coaxing him some more.

If he really didn't want her in his bed for whatever reason, she needed to accept that. Somehow.

But then at last, he continued on down the hall to the master suite. Happiness surged through her as he carried her in there and around the bed to the side she'd slept on the night before.

So gently, he laid her down and tucked the extra blanket around her. Munch jumped up and took his place down by the footboard.

Garrett disappeared into the bathroom. She heard the toilet flush and water running in the sink. Her eyes felt deliciously heavy. She shut them again and let sleep carry her away.

When Garrett came out of the bathroom, she was sound asleep, turned on her side, hands tucked under her cheek, a little smile on those plump lips of hers, his own scrappy little angel.

His own.

She wasn't, not really. He kept trying to remember that. But she was so adorable. Irresistible, really.

Whatever she wanted, all she had to do was ask. And he would scramble to get it for her.

He kept trying to remember all the reasons he shouldn't let her get too close. But somehow, with Cami, all the reasons added up to nothing. With Cami, half the time he couldn't even remember what those reasons were.

Ordinarily, he was a distant guy, a careful guy. A guy who mostly tried to keep interactions on a casual level. He got along with people just fine by not getting in too deep.

When it came to women, he liked a good time—in

and out of bed. A good time and not a lot more. After his marriage ended, he'd learned to keep things light. He'd accepted the fact that he didn't have what it took to make a real relationship work, that he was somehow emotionally disappointing, lacking in whatever it was a woman needed most from a man.

But then along came Cami.

With her, everything was all turned around. He felt scary-close to her. He loved just hanging with her. He *wanted* her living in his house.

Just look at him, *sleeping* with her without ever having had sex with her. What was that even about?

Her bruised eye opened halfway and she yawned. "You know it's weird that you're just standing there staring at me, right?" When he didn't answer immediately, she took one hand out from under her head and beckoned him down. "It's late. Come to bed."

Something happened inside him, a rising, warm sort of feeling. He didn't trust where this was going.

But so what? He was having a great time with her and helping her out a little, too. If she wanted to sleep with him, he wouldn't say no. She felt right in his bed, whatever they did or didn't do there.

And as far as keeping a little distance, keeping from getting *too* close, well, that would happen naturally. He worked long hours, after all. They would have plenty of time apart. And she would be busy making a whole new life for herself. It wouldn't be like on the mountain, just the two of them and Munch, together around-the-clock. The intensity of what they'd shared at the cabin would fade as time went by.

"Come to bed…" She said it even more softly that

time, on a sigh. Her hand was back under her cheek and her black eye had drifted closed.

Feeling eager to be closer to her and much too happy to have her sleeping in his bed, he switched off the lamp and slid in beside her.

Garrett left for work at seven the next morning. Cami barely had time to pour herself a first cup of coffee before he was out the door. About fifteen minutes later, the doorbell rang.

Cami peered through the window beside the door before opening it, just in case it might be Charles—or worse, her dad. Nope. A gorgeous redhead in jeans and heavy boots with bright tattoos on one arm saw her and waved. Something about the woman reminded Cami of Garrett. One of his sisters, maybe. Or possibly that cousin he'd mentioned once.

Cami pulled the door wide. "I'm sorry. Garrett's already left for work."

"Perfect. I wanted to get you alone. It's Cami, right? I'm Garrett's sister, Nell."

Cami felt a smile bloom. "You're the one nobody messes with."

"That's me."

"It's so good to meet you." She ushered Nell inside.

They had coffee on the sofa in the living room, while Munch snoozed on the rug in a wedge of early-morning sun.

Nell asked how she got the black eye and Cami ended up telling Garrett's sister everything—or, at least, most of everything, including the real story of how she and Garrett had met, from fleeing her wedding to the accident on the steep road, to wandering up Moosejaw Mountain barefoot in her wedding gown until she stumbled on Garrett and Munch at the cabin. "I'm starting my life over, I guess you could say. Garrett's helping me with that. He's invited me to stay here for as long as I need a place."

"He's nuts about you," Nell said.

Cami's heart did the happy dance. "He told you that?"

"No." Cami's face must have fallen. Nell explained, "He didn't have to tell me. I've known him all my life. He wouldn't invite just any woman to live with him. And when he talks about you, he gets that look." She made a silly face. "The man is gone on you."

Cami might be in love with the guy, but he wasn't there yet and she needed to respect that, so she downplayed what she felt for him. "We're good friends."

"Oh, I'll just bet you are." Nell chuckled.

Cami couldn't resist adding, "Your mother thinks we're a thing."

"Why am I not surprised?"

"Garrett tried to set her straight, but I didn't let him. I told her we were together—I mean, *really* together. I seriously got into it, too. Until he gave up and let me lie to her. I suppose I should feel guilty about that."

"Are you kidding? Why?" Nell laughed. "And whatever it is between you and Garrett, I'm glad. Ma drives us all batcrap crazy half the time, but she's right about Garrett. He's gotten to be way too much of a loner the last few years. He's a charmer and a good guy and most people don't even realize he never really gets close."

"But he does get close, Nell. *I* feel close to him."

"And you have no idea how glad I am to hear that."

Before she left, Nell invited Cami out for happy hour that evening at McKellan's Pub. Cami wanted to start meeting people in her new hometown, so she said yes.

"I'll make some calls," Nell said, "see how many of my brothers and sisters I can scare up. It'll be Bravos for days." Nell got out her phone and they exchanged numbers.

"I'll call Garrett," Cami said, "and invite him, too."

"Go for it."

As soon as Nell was out the door, Cami sent him a text and then waited with the phone in her hand, half expecting him to text her right back. He didn't. And she refused to feel let down as she slipped the phone into her purse. She put on enough makeup to cover her black eye and took Munch for a nice walk.

When she got back, she checked her phone. He'd answered, Sorry. On the run all day and then an early dinner with a wholesale carpet rep. Doubt I'll make McKellan's. Have fun.

So then. They wouldn't be having dinner together, either. He hadn't been kidding when he said he worked a lot. She tamped down her disappointment and texted back, All right. I'll just go have fun without you, then. See you later tonight.

She also had a voice mail from her dad. It was the usual, brief and unpleasant.

"Camilla, your behavior is completely unacceptable. I want you to come home and work things out with Charles. We don't need to discuss this. You just need to remember your responsibilities and start to live up to them. Call me immediately to tell me you're coming home."

The voice mail just made her want to ignore him and get on with her day. Too bad there was still a good girl lurking down inside her ready to ask, "How high?" when Quentin Lockwood said, "Jump." That girl would be edgy all day if she didn't reply.

However, talking to her dad never seemed to go well.

She settled on a text: Got your message. I live here in Justice Creek now and Charles and I are not getting back together. I will let you know when I plan to come to Denver. I'm not going to reply to any more of your demands, Dad. I love you and I'll be in touch.

Her heart beat a harsh rhythm under her ribs and her hands were shaking a little as she hit Send. She did love her dad and she knew he loved her, too. But the life he wanted for her, the life he'd so insistently seen she was groomed for, just wasn't a life that worked for her.

Really, she hated defying him. But if defiance was the price of her freedom, she would defy the hell out of her father until he finally saw the light.

She grabbed her keys and headed out the door.

Garrett worked in the office all morning. He met with Deck McGrath, discussed his house plans and promised him a bid within the next few days. Nell came in later from a renovation she was running up in Haltersham Heights.

"I stopped by your house and met Cami this morning," she said. "I like that girl." A buzz of annoyance sizzled through him. What made Nell think it was a good idea to go dropping in on Cami out of the blue?

Nell asked, "She get with you about coming to happy hour tonight at McKellan's?"

"Yeah." He stared blankly at his laptop screen and kept his voice noncommittal. "I don't think I'll make it."

Nell plunked her butt on the edge of his desk. "Why not?"

"I've got dinner at five with the new guy from Clarkson's Carpeting."

She leaned closer and peered over the top of the screen at him. "Reschedule with the carpet guy—or bring him along. C'mon. It'll be fun. And Cami's your girl. You really ought to be there."

His girl? No, she was not.

True, he couldn't seem to stop thinking about her and he'd already let her convince Ma that there was more going on between them than there was.

But that didn't make her his girl in any real sense.

She *wasn't* his girl. And he was putting a little distance between them as a way of reminding them both that they were just friends.

Because he really did need to draw the line somewhere. Didn't he? "What do you mean, *my* girl?"

Nell just stared at him, eyes like green daggers, for a few never-ending seconds. "You know exactly what I mean."

"What did Cami say to you?"

And then Nell smiled—a smile so sweet a guy could get a cavity just looking at it. "She said you two are friends. The *best* of friends."

"What the—?"

"Chill. She made it clear that it's friends-only, if that's what you're working up steam about."

He should have felt relief, right? But no. Now he felt sad and deflated to learn she *hadn't* tried to tell his sister that she was his girl.

Something was wrong with him. Cami had been so right when she told Ma he was messed up.

"We are," he said flatly. "Friends. Just friends."

"Well, great, then. Jacob Selby said he'd be there." Jacob was one of their subcontractors, a custom cabinet maker they used whenever possible for high-end builds and renos. The guy was six-six with long hair and a beard—and a striking resemblance to Chris Hemsworth. "I'm going to introduce them. You never know. They might hit it off."

No effing way. "Why?"

"Garrett." Nell's eyes twinkled with challenge. "Jacob's a sweetheart, which means the real question is, why not?"

"She doesn't need more complications in her life right now."

"I get that. And Jacob wouldn't be a complication. He's a total gentleman in the old-school sense of the word."

Garrett shut his laptop so he could glare at his sister unobstructed. "You are really pissing me off."

"And you've got your head up your butt. You've got a thing for that girl and you might as well just admit it, go with it. Who knows what might happen? Maybe something good."

"You're starting to sound like Ma now. It's not cute. And while we're on the subject of people with their heads up their butt, why have you got me running interference with poor Deck?"

Nell jumped off the desk like it was on fire. Her

red hair fanned out as she whirled on him. "That's low. You know it is."

"Why not just go with it?" He threw her own words back at her. *"Who knows what might happen? Maybe something good."* Yeah, he was acting like a ten-year-old. And right now, he didn't even care.

"Really? Seriously?" Nell demanded. "You're going *there*?"

"You bet I am."

"And you'd better stop. Deck already ripped my heart out of my body and ate it for lunch. Twice. I don't need that. Never again."

"That was in high school. Deck had it rough in high school."

"Didn't we all?"

"Don't. Yeah, we had our big family drama. But it was nothing like Deck's situation. The poor guy didn't know where his next meal was coming from—and whatever happened with you two back then, you're both different people now."

"Not that different. Let it go, Garrett."

"Then get off my back about Cami."

Nell pressed her lips together and seethed. But only for a moment. Finally, she gave it up. "Sure. Have it your way."

And don't you even try to set her up with Jacob. The words burned his tongue trying to get out, but somehow he held them back.

Nell left.

He had his assistant, Shelly, bring in takeout for lunch and ate at his desk as he continued to plow through the mountain of work that had piled up in his absence. In the afternoon, he made the rounds of current Bravo Construction projects. He met with his sister-in-law Chloe, an interior designer who was staging the model condo on a just-completed twelve-unit project on Aspen Way and had to read the riot act to a drywall subcontractor who was two weeks behind schedule on two BC jobs.

The whole time he was feeling like a complete jerk because he'd lied to Cami and to his sister. There was no early dinner with the carpet guy and he could definitely make it to McKellan's for drinks.

Hell. He *wanted* to meet Cami for Friday night happy hour.

He'd just had this feeling he ought to put the brakes on a little. But lying was a lousy way to do that.

If he really wanted to get some distance from her, he ought to try not carrying her to his bed at night. Or hey. What about just saying he was sorry, it wasn't working out for her to stay with him, after all? She'd made it clear that she could afford a place of her own. She didn't *need* to stay with him.

But again, he wanted her in his bed, whatever the two of them did or didn't do there. And he didn't want her to move out.

He wanted *her*. A lot. So much it scared him, so much he was mucking everything up. So much he was lying to her, fighting with Nellie about her, obsessing all day over her.

One way or another, this crap had to stop.

Dressed in tight white jeans, a flowy boho top and green suede cutout lace-up stilettos, Cami felt more like her new, freer, happier self than ever as she entered McKellan's Pub at five that night. So what if

Garrett wouldn't be there? She looked like a million bucks and she was going to meet some Bravos and have a great time.

Nell found her at the door, got her a drink and introduced her around. She met two of the Bravo brothers and Nell and Garrett's half sister Clara. Clara owned a restaurant over by the library. Her husband, Dalton Ames, was the president of Ames Bank.

Dalton, who was tall and dark-haired with killer blue eyes, knew Cami's parents. He said that before he moved to Justice Creek, he used to run into them now and then at charity events in Denver.

"Are you involved with WellWay, then?" he asked.

"Not anymore," she replied. "And never again."

Cami met the owner of the bar, Ryan. Rye was blond and hunky, one of those guys who could really turn on the charm. He joked that he and Nell were not only family in every way that mattered, they were next-door neighbors, living in adjoining loft apartments on the top floor of the building.

"Meg!" Nell signaled one of the bartenders, a tall, curvy woman with light brown hair. Meg stepped up on the other side of the bar and Nell introduced her to Cami.

Rye announced proudly, "Meg is with me." He caught Meg's hand where a diamond engagement ring glittered. "We're making it legal. I'm the happiest man in Colorado. She just said yes."

Meg held the ring up for Cami to see.

"It's beautiful. Congratulations."

Rye and Meg shared a glance full of love and desire and simple, open affection.

"Let's get a table," Nell suggested. She led Cami

to a deuce at the base of the stairs leading up to the second-floor bar.

Once they were seated, Nell explained that, until Meg, Rye had never gotten serious about a woman. "Except for Clara, back in the day. But Clara's happily married now and Rye's been, well, the way Rye's always been, which is one pretty girl after another. Until about a month ago, when Meg Cartwell's '56 DeSoto broke down a few miles east of town. Rye was driving back from Denver and stopped to help her out. Meg had left Denver herself, as it turned out. She was on her way home to Oregon, to this little seaside town right near the Washington border called Valentine Bay where—wait for it—her BFF since childhood is named Aislinn. Aislinn Bravo."

Cami laughed in delight. "A relative?"

Nell nodded. "A cousin. Aislinn's dad and my dad were brothers—so anyway, Rye talks Meg into sticking around for a while. With him." She pointed at the ceiling. "Upstairs. Meg had worked as a bartender, so he offered her a job. The man's totally in love and so is Meg. I never thought I'd see the day. It's happening fast. He proposed last night. I didn't even know she'd said yes until about an hour ago."

"Wow. That is pretty fast."

"I know. But fast just works for some people."

"Oh, Nell. I so agree. My life has been way too controlled, everything laid out, planned ahead. Never making a move without considering every angle. Every decision reached with long deliberation. I like life a little more on the fly, you know? Especially when it comes to love. I mean, you may not really be able to love a person at first sight. But you can know if you *could* love them. You can see the potential. And I would take it even further. I would say that when it comes to love, sometimes your heart just *knows*."

"Yes!" Nell raised her hand, palm out, above the table. Cami slapped hers against it in a high five. Then Nell said, "I never thought Rye would ever find the one for him. It wasn't like he was looking for someone, if you know what I mean. But then he met Meg. That was it. She's the one. They both seem really sure. I think it's going to work out for them."

Cami was nodding. "Seeing them together, I have to agree."

"They're getting married at Christmastime. I can't wait. I already love Meg like one of my sisters. And you gotta know that cousin Aislinn will be coming out from Oregon to be Meg's maid of honor. We might have a mini Bravo family reunion along with a holiday wedding."

"It's so romantic." Cami thought a little wistfully of Garrett, who couldn't be here tonight because he had a date with a carpet salesman. She shouldn't be so disappointed not to have him here—and she *wasn't*. She refused to be. She focused on enjoying the moment, on being with Nell, girlfriends together, having a good time on Friday night.

Nell waved at a big, long-haired, bearded guy in jeans, lumberjack boots and a flannel shirt. "Jacob! Over here." She grabbed a chair from the next table.

The big guy came and loomed above them. "Nell." He saluted her with a tall glass of dark beer. "How's it going?"

Nell patted the chair and Jacob sat down. She introduced him to Cami. Jacob had warm hazel eyes and a friendly smile. He was a carpenter, he said, and did work for Bravo Construction.

Nell spotted one of her brothers over by the bar. "There's Carter. I'll be right back."

And off she went, leaving Cami with Jacob, who was really nice and seemed to be flirting with her. He asked her how she liked Justice Creek.

She told him just how she felt about the place. "I love it here, Jacob. I've decided I'm not leaving. I'm making Justice Creek my home."

"A woman who knows what she wants." He leaned a little closer. "I like that." He asked her more questions.

She didn't get into too much detail, but she told him the basics, that she was staying in Justice Creek and looking around for business opportunities. He talked about his work. His dad, he said, had been a carpenter before him.

Jacob was easy to talk to. She was starting to think that maybe she'd made a new friend.

And then she glanced up and spotted Garrett. Her skin got all shivery and her heart gave a happy little lurch beneath her breastbone. "Garrett!" She stuck up her hand and waved him over.

Not that she needed to. He was already on his way, staring straight at her, the corners of his sexy mouth turned down in a grim, angry line.

Chapter Seven

Jacob turned in his chair to see Garrett coming toward them—and Garrett's hostile expression morphed instantly into something borderline friendly. Jacob got up. "Garrett. Hey."

"Jacob." The men shook. When Jacob sat back down, Garrett took the chair Nell had left vacant.

Cami regarded him across the table. She was so glad to see him here—and yet suspicious, too. Something strange was up with him, scowling one minute, then putting on a smile. She just didn't get it. "No dinner with the carpet guy, after all?"

Garrett answered offhandedly. "Yeah, didn't happen."

Jacob frowned and glanced back and forth between her and the infuriating man across the table. "Carpet guy?"

"Cami wanted me here tonight." Garrett's gaze stayed locked with hers. "But I had a business dinner."

Wanted? Well, yeah. She had. She *did*. But the way he said it made it sound like she'd begged him to come.

She glared right back at him. "I *invited* you."

"Because you *wanted* me."

This was getting really weird. Cami felt angry and kind of turned on, both at once. She really had no idea what to say next.

And poor Jacob. He looked like he just wanted out of there. Fast. Cami so didn't blame him.

"Okay, guys." Jacob put up both hands. "Is there something I'm missing here?"

Cami tried a laugh. It came out sounding strained. "Garrett and I are good fr—"

"Cami and I live together."

Talk about a conversation stopper. Cami actively resisted the burning need to give him a good, sharp kick under the table. Could he be any ruder? Let alone more confusing?

Above his beard, Jacob's cheeks had flushed dark red. Apparently, he really had been flirting with her. And now Garrett had made him feel like a fool. "Look, guys. I'm not here to make any trouble. Nell didn't tell me you two were a couple."

Garrett gave a lazy shrug. "You know Nell. She loves to stir things up."

Cami should have jumped in right there and insisted that Nell hadn't stirred anything up and she and Garrett *weren't* a couple. But then again, being with Garrett was just what she wanted, so denying that they were a couple would be counterproductive to her own heart's desire.

In the end, she said nothing. She just sat there with her mouth shut, feeling all turned around, half of her gleeful that Garrett seemed to be claiming her. And half of her pissed off that he had to be such a complete douchenozzle about it.

Jacob had had enough. "Looks to me like the two of you need to talk." He stood.

Cami gazed up at him. He seemed like such a good guy, with his kind eyes and that gentle, friendly way he had. She liked him—but he wasn't Garrett. And she and Garrett really did need to talk. "Great to meet you, Jacob."

The big man gave a nod and left them alone. The minute he was gone, Garrett shifted to stand. "Want another drink?"

"Don't you dare run off now." She pinned him with her hardest glare until he sank back into the chair.

"I was just getting a drink." He said it so mildly. Apparently, mean, surly Garrett had vanished. In his place sat easygoing, evenhanded Garrett, aka the amazing man she'd met on the mountain.

"Drinks can wait." She sat back in the chair and crossed her arms over her chest. "You realize you just made me look like a cheater."

"A cheater?" He put on a look of great surprise.

"Yes. A cheater. That is what I said."

"Cami, what are you talking about?"

"Oh, please. You're trying to tell me you honestly don't get it?"

"Get what?"

"You are really pushing it, you know that? But

just in case you actually do need help with this, allow me to explain. Before you got here, Jacob was flirting with me."

"Yeah." Now he sounded surly again. "I picked up on that. Loud and clear."

"Jacob was flirting with me and I was letting him—because *you* have made it painfully clear to me that you and I are *not* together. Feel free to correct me if I've got that wrong."

"Cami, hey…" He leaned in and folded his beautiful, strong hands on the table. Faint white scars marked his knuckles, testament to the hard work he'd done with those hands. She wanted to touch them, to touch *him*. All over. Too bad at the moment she also wanted to jump up and walk out. He gave her the melty eyes. "Don't be pissed at me."

"But I *am* pissed at you." She leaned across the table, too, folding her hands on it, same as him. "You had better start being honest with me, Garrett Bravo, or I am getting up from this chair and walking out of here."

He looked down at the table, then over at the bar, then across at the retro neon beer sign on the opposite wall. Anywhere but at her. She waited, giving him one more chance to start making things right.

And then, at last, he confessed, "I felt like we were getting too close."

She clasped her hands tighter—to keep them from reaching out to him. "Got that. Keep going."

"When you texted me about tonight, I wanted to meet you here. I wanted it bad. To be out with you, us together, and not just as friends."

Joy burned through her, silvery and fine. "I wanted that, too."

"But I was afraid. So I lied and made up the dinner meeting with the carpet guy."

Her joy kind of fizzled as disappointment dragged on her, that he'd fabricated a business dinner in order to put distance between them. "I appreciate that you're admitting you lied to me. But Garrett, if you want a little space or whatever, you need to just say so."

"But that's just it. I *didn't* want space. I wanted to get closer and that freaked me out. And you're right about the lying. It's not a solution to anything. I never should have lied to you. I am sorry, Cami." He held her eyes as he said it.

And that did it. She forgave him.

Why hold out against him? She'd wanted him to come with her tonight, and now, here he was, admitting at last that there was more than just friendship between them. She wasn't exactly thrilled with how they'd gotten here.

But at least they *were* here.

She gave him a slow nod. "I accept your apology." Her fingers just wouldn't stay still. They inched across the smooth wood of the tabletop until they touched his. She waited, breath held. And then his big hand closed around hers, warm and rough and so very right. Her heart was just galloping away inside her chest. She asked, "What are you afraid of?"

He didn't answer right away. She started to think he would blow off the question. But then he said, "Right now, you don't need a new boyfriend. You need someone you can count on. We're supposed to be friends and I'm supposed to be helping you. Instead,

I'm thinking all the time about getting you naked—and *you're* not helping *me* to remember what a bad idea that would be."

"But Garrett. It wouldn't be bad. I happen to think it could be very, very good."

He glared at her. "See? Like I said, you're not helping."

"Garrett, I want to be with you, *really* be with you. And since you want that, too, we don't even have a problem except for the one you've made up in your head."

"What if it all goes to hell?" He regarded her warily now. At least he'd stopped glaring. "I don't have the best record when it comes to the whole romance thing. I'm no good at relationships."

"Who told you that? Wait. Let me guess. Your ex-wife?"

"Yeah, and my ex and I didn't agree on a lot of things, but about this, she was right."

"Sorry, not buying that. And come on, lighten up. We like each other. A lot. I want us to take the next step together, that's all. It's not like I'm asking for a lifetime commitment." *Not yet, anyway.*

"You're impulsive."

"I know." She allowed herself a slow grin. "I love that about me. Taking things slowly? Thinking everything over in advance? If that floats your boat, more power to you. But to me it's just an excuse not to reach out and grab hold of what you really want."

He was still looking grim. "At least one of us should be considering the consequences."

"But I *am* considering the consequences. And the way I see it, whatever happens in the future, we have something good, you and me. We have something good and I want to go with it, to see where it takes us."

"You know who you sound like?" He was still way too serious. "Nell. She came in the office this morning and got on me about you, about how it was obvious I wanted you and you wanted me. She said that I should go for it with you."

Cami crowed out a happy laugh. "Okay, just for the record, I love Nell." He actually smiled. At last. And then she demanded, "What else did Nell say?"

"She threw Jacob into the mix, told me how she was going to introduce you two tonight. I said she'd better not try it. And she started in about how Jacob's such a prince and if I don't want you for myself, what do I care if she introduces the two of you?" He lifted her hand off the table and put his other hand around it, too, surrounding her in the thrilling heat of his touch. "I was miserable all day."

"Serves you right," she said tenderly.

"And then, well, here I am now because if I was a woman I would go out with Jacob. I couldn't stand the thought of him making a move on you." He asked glumly, "You would have said yes, right?"

"No."

He brightened. But then he scoffed, "Oh, come on. He's a great guy and he looks like Thor. Anyone would go for him—I mean, anyone who's into guys."

She wanted to kiss him, but for the moment she kept her lips to herself. "I like him. But that's all. I wouldn't have gone out with him. Can we please stop talking about Jacob now?"

"Works for me—and the thing is, I *wanted* to be here with you. Even if Nell hadn't threatened to dangle some serious man candy in front of you, I don't think I would have been able to stay away."

"I'm so glad." She leaned as far as she could across the table.

He looked at her as though he would never look away. "Cami..." And then he leaned in, too, just enough for a kiss, a sweet kiss, a swift, perfect brush of his lips across hers.

She sank back to her chair with a happy sigh.

They stayed on at McKellan's long past happy hour. Garrett kept her close and Cami loved every minute at his side. She met more Bravo brothers and sisters, wives and husbands, and family friends, too.

Garrett's mother showed up. Everyone seemed blown away that Willow had a guy with her, a lean, good-looking older man with thick white hair. She introduced the guy around. His name was Griffin Masters and he lived in San Diego.

She'd met him on one of her cruises, she said. "Griffin's staying for a few weeks."

Garrett looked a little stunned. "What? You mean, with you, at the mansion?"

Willow seemed to be restraining herself from rolling her eyes. "Yes, Garrett. With me."

As soon as Willow led her new boyfriend away, Garrett said, "I don't believe this. Ma with a guy. I don't think she's been with anyone since Dad died. I never thought she would."

Cami didn't get it. "Would what?"

"I don't know. Be with anyone who wasn't Dad."

"Didn't you say it's been six years since your father died?"

"Yeah. So?"

"So then, she's moving on, slowly getting over the loss of her husband. That's a good thing, don't you think?"

He looked kind of stunned. "You don't get it. She started with my father when she was eighteen. There was never anyone else for her." Over at the bar, Willow lifted her martini and touched it to Griffin's glass. The glance they shared sizzled with heat.

Cami gently suggested, "Well, it looks like there's definitely someone else now."

Garrett grabbed her hand. "There's a bar upstairs. Let's go up there."

She hung back. "Um. Because?"

"She's my mother. She's always made me crazy, what with her stealing another woman's husband, all the yelling and carrying on when we were kids and then marrying my dad when Sondra was barely dead. Not to mention taking Sondra's mansion and everything in it and making it her own. And then lately with all the matchmaking. And now *this*." He tipped his head toward his mother and her boyfriend, who were sharing a kiss. "Look at that. I didn't need to see that." He pulled Cami toward the stairs.

She followed, arguing, "Garrett, she's a vibrant, beautiful woman. You should be happy for her."

He only muttered, "I think my eyeballs are scarred for life," and led her up the steps.

At the upstairs bar, there was more excitement.

Nell was giving some serious grief to a big, hot-looking guy in a suit. "You don't fool me, Declan McGrath. I know what you're up to and it's not going to work."

The big guy answered mildly, "Sparky, get over yourself. I'm just having a drink."

Cami pulled Garrett closer. "Sparky?"

He put his wonderful warm lips to her ear and explained, "Pet name from the old days. They used to be together years ago. He wants another chance with her. Nell says no, but Deck won't give up."

Nell had more than no to say. "You don't need to get your drinks here." He sat with his back to her, facing the bar. She leaned over his shoulder. "Go to some other bar."

"Relax." He slowly sipped what looked like whiskey, neat.

"Damn you, Deck. I *live* here."

"This is a bar. I'm what is known as a customer. You live upstairs."

"You are harassing me and I am sick of it."

Elise Walsh, one of the Bravo sisters, came up on Garrett's other side. She suggested out of the corner of her mouth, "You take Deck and I'll take Nell."

"Crap," said Garrett wearily. "Sure."

"I'll go in first."

"Have at it."

Elise, looking cool and professional in a pencil skirt and silk top, glided to Nell's side. She took Nell's arm and whispered something in her ear. Nell scowled, but she did let Elise pull her away as Garrett grabbed a chair for Cami.

"Sit here," he said. "I'll be right back with drinks."

She took the chair and grinned up at him. "No hurry. I'll just enjoy the show."

But apparently, the show was over. Garrett slid onto the stool beside the man named Deck. He leaned close and said something. The big man muttered something back, threw some bills on the bar and left.

"Life with the Bravos is so exciting," Cami said when Garrett returned with fresh drinks. "I love this town. Did I mention I'm never going to leave?"

"I think you did, and more than once." He bent close and kissed her and she thought, *This is happiness.* Together with Garrett on a Friday night.

Around eight, they ordered burgers. Rye and Meg joined them. Then later, Nell invited the four of them upstairs to her loft, which was gorgeous and open, all modern and sleek.

It was after midnight when Garrett walked Cami to her Subaru in the parking lot in back.

At the car, he framed her face in his hands. "Tonight was good." His woodsy scent tempted her and his warm breath touched her cheek.

"More than good. Because we were together. Really together, for the first time."

He kissed her, a slow kiss, a kiss that got hotter and deeper the longer it went on. She heard footsteps behind her somewhere. A woman laughed low. A car door opened and then shut. All that was nothing compared to the pleasure of Garrett's mouth on hers. She felt the lovely, hard ridge of him, wanting her, pressing into her belly.

When he finally lifted his head, she let her eyes drift open and gave him a slow smile. "A good-night kiss…"

A low rumble of laughter escaped him. "Except it's not good-night because you're coming home with me."

"Where's your car?"

"Two rows over." He smoothed a hank of hair behind her ear.

"I'll wait for you."

He kissed her again, even deeper than the first time, his body so hard and hot, pressed against her. Most of her life, she'd felt she was missing out on the good stuff somehow.

Not anymore. She had her arms around Garrett now. And she was following him home.

At the house, they greeted Munch and took him out into the yard. He bustled around, sniffing the bushes, chasing after shadows. She and Garrett sat together on the end of the low deck. The moon was a full silver ball floating above the mountains, the stars a little faded-looking, paled by the lights of town.

Garrett put his arm around her and pulled her in close. She rested her head on his shoulder. It seemed to her the best place to be in the whole world—on the deck with Garrett, the moon so big and magical, shining in the sky.

He said, "It's a week tomorrow night since you appeared out of nowhere up on my mountain."

"Only a week? Not possible. It seems like forever that I've known you."

He ran his hand down the outside of her arm, a slow caress that set a thousand fluttery creatures loose in her belly. "I want to take you to bed with me. And not just as roomies."

"Yes."

He nuzzled her hair and teased, "You are so easy."

"Yes, I am and proud of it." She put her hand on his chest, felt his heartbeat, strong and steady beneath his shirt, under warm flesh and sturdy bone. "Tell me about your ex."

He chuckled low. "Now, there's a mood killer."

She poked him, just a little, with her elbow. "Come on. I want to know."

"I don't know what to tell you."

"How about her name, to start?"

"Miranda Hale. She's a teacher."

"Does she still live here in Justice Creek?"

"No. She moved to Milwaukee after our divorce. Her family's there. But when I met her, she was teaching third grade at Justice Creek Elementary. Nell and I were just getting Bravo Construction off the ground. Miranda hired us to remodel her kitchen."

"And you asked her out?"

He nodded. "We got married about a year later. She was pregnant." Cami blinked in surprise. It was the first time he'd mentioned having children. "I wanted the baby," he said. "And I wanted Miranda."

A baby. Cami had a thousand questions. Did Miranda take the child away from him? But how? That would be so awful. But the alternative was even worse.

She asked, "Were you happy—I mean, at first?"

"On and off. We always had issues, I guess you could say. I don't like drama, don't like it when things get messy and emotional. Miranda claimed that I was never 'emotionally available.' Her words. 'Garrett, you're just not emotionally available and I have no clue how to reach out to you.' She also used to say that there was no 'there' there with me."

Cami pressed a little closer to his side. "Your ex-wife was wrong."

"No. She was right. Ask anyone. My bet is they'll

say that they like me well enough. But they don't know me very well." He chuckled. The sound didn't have a lot of humor in it. "And I have no idea why you want to hear about Miranda and me. Believe me, I'm not the hero of that story."

"You're a hero to me. And I want to know the things you wouldn't tell just anybody."

He toyed with the filmy sleeve of her shirt and then carefully smoothed it down over her arm. "A few weeks after the wedding, Miranda said she knew I never would have married her if there hadn't been a baby. I lied and said that wasn't true. But she wasn't fooled." He fell silent.

Cami tipped her head up to look at him. He was staring at the moon.

Eventually, he spoke again. "At four months along, she lost the baby."

Oh, no. She pressed her hand to his heart again and sought his gaze through the darkness. "I'm so sorry, Garrett."

His eyes were full of shadows. But he brushed his lips to her temple in a tender little kiss. "I didn't know what to do about that, how to comfort her, you know?"

Cami allowed herself a small sound of understanding, but no more. He was talking to her, *really* talking. She would not miss a word.

He went on. "She tried to get me to go into counseling, but I said no. I worked even harder than usual, eighteen-hour days sometimes. She'd always said I didn't spend enough time with her. After we lost that baby, she said she hardly saw me at all. I would promise to be home more. And then there would always be some crisis that kept me working late.

"Then, three years after we lost the first baby, she got pregnant a second time. She cried when she told me. She said she shouldn't have gotten pregnant again, that it wasn't going to work with us, that just being with me made her lonely. And then, at five months along, we lost that baby, too."

Cami didn't know what to say. It was such a sad story. She ached for him. And for his ex-wife, too.

He gathered her closer against his side. "A year later, I came home from work one night and Miranda was gone. She left me a note. One line. *'Without the babies, what's the point?'* She sent me the divorce papers and I signed them. That's it. The story of my marriage that was probably doomed from the start."

Munch came and sat on his other side, settling in close, as though the dog knew his human needed support.

Cami said, "You blame yourself that it didn't work out." It wasn't a question.

And he didn't say she had it wrong. Instead, he fiddled with her hair, smoothing it, then wrapping a curl around his index finger. "I did marry her mostly because of the baby. I didn't love her enough. And she was always so emotional. Her tears didn't reach me—they only made me shut down, made me want to get away."

She gazed up at him, at his handsome face silvered in moonlight. She wanted so much to understand. "Because?"

"My childhood, I guess." He avoided meeting her eyes and stared off toward the dark humps of the mountains. Somewhere near the back fence, a night bird twittered. A slight breeze stirred the bushes and made the branches of the pine tree a few feet from the deck whisper together.

"You said tonight at McKellan's that your mother was emotional when you were growing up."

"Yeah. She likes to play it civilized and sophisticated now, with her martinis and the big, fancy house that used to be Sondra's. Now, she travels first-class and never raises her voice. But she wasn't always like that. When I was growing up, she was constantly carrying on, kicking my dad out of the house, then taking him back. I never wanted to live like that, with the endless shouting matches, the ongoing drama. And now..." He seemed to run out of words.

"Now, what?" she prompted.

"Now, looking back on the years with Miranda, I see that, yeah, she was emotional. But really, she was just trying to reach out to me and I kept pushing her away."

Cami stared up at the moon, too, thinking about all he'd just said. His honesty touched her. But he'd been too hard on himself, she thought. And she could guess why. "So you *are* saying it's your fault that your marriage failed, that you didn't love your wife enough and you were a terrible husband?"

"Yeah. That's about the size of it."

"Well, I don't agree with you."

He gave her a wry smile for that. "Cami. You get that it's really not up to you, right?"

"You lost *two* babies, Garrett. That's so awful. And not just for Miranda. For you, too. Sometimes a marriage just can't stand the weight of losses like that. And okay, I never met your wife, but I'll bet if I talked to her, she might have a few regrets about her part in what happened. I'll bet she wouldn't let you have *all* the blame."

He was actually smiling. "About that new career you're looking for? Maybe you ought to consider going into family counseling."

She didn't smile back. "Don't try to make light of what happened to you—and to Miranda. It seems to me that you grew and changed from it, that you see your part in what went wrong. I admire that. What I *don't* like is that this story, what you just told me, it's like a warning, isn't it? You're trying to scare me away."

"You *should* be scared." He was sounding all gruff and grumpy again.

She took his warm, beard-stubbled face between her two hands. "Stop trying to protect me from you. I don't *want* to be protected from you. I'm having the best time of my life with you and I don't want to stop. I *want* you. Now, tonight. And the only question right now is, do you want me, too?"

He looked at her for the longest time. And then, at last, he answered, "You know I do."

"Perfect." She threw her leg across him and climbed into his lap.

He groaned. "God. Cami…"

It was the sweetest, sexiest moment. She could feel him growing harder, right there at the core of her, and she had his unforgettable face tipped up to her.

Cami did what came naturally. She wrapped her arms around his neck and pressed her mouth to his.

Chapter Eight

Did she fear he would refuse her?

A little, yeah.

But he didn't. Instead, he gathered her closer. He wrapped his wonderful arms so tight around her and took the kiss deeper. She lost herself in it—in all of it. In his thrilling hardness and heat, in the wet, hot tangling of their seeking tongues and caressing hands.

And then his touch strayed down her back, dipping into the curve of her spine, sliding out over the flare of her hips, until he cradled her bottom. Holding her firmly, he shifted forward.

"Oh!" She wrapped her legs around him good and tight, hooking her stilettos at the small of his back as he rose.

And then they were kissing again, a dizzying kiss that went on and on as he strode across the deck to the glass door that led into the living room. When he got there, still kissing her, he reached out and shoved the door wide. Munch bumped through ahead of them. Garrett carried her in and she stuck out a hand to slide the door shut.

For a moment, he paused there just inside the door, holding her close to him, kissing her as though he couldn't get enough of the taste of her mouth. She kissed him right back, as hungry for him as he was for her.

And then he was moving again, across the living room into the front hall and on up the stairs.

He broke the kiss at the door to his bedroom. "Munch," he commanded. "*Your* bed. Lie down." With only one plaintive whine, Munchy trotted over to the dog bed in the corner and climbed in.

Garrett carried her into the room, over to the gorgeous barn-wood bed and on around to the side she already thought of as hers. Carefully, he lowered her until she stood on the rug. She swayed on her feet when he let her go.

He steadied her. "Okay?"

"Garrett, I am so far past okay. I'm splendid. I'm downright spectacular."

"Oh, yes, you are." His voice was a low rumble, his eyes low and lazy, just eating her up. She felt his gaze as a touch that burned and beckoned. "Do. Not. Move."

Staring into his beautiful eyes, she caught her lower lip between her teeth and nodded.

He turned, grabbed the covers and threw them back.

It sent a hot shiver all through her to see the white

sheets revealed. Tonight, there would be no blankets to separate them. Just the thought of the two of them naked together made her knees go all shaky in the most delicious way.

And seriously, before they went any further, she needed to tell him that she hadn't exactly done this before.

But then he commanded, in a voice so low and intimate, "Sit down. Right here." He bent and patted the sheet.

She couldn't drop to the bed fast enough. Never had she felt quite like this—breathless, her skin supersensitized, her face flushed with heat.

Garrett knelt at her feet. He wrapped his hand around the back of her calf. Even through her jeans, she felt his cradling touch so acutely, his fingers molding, caressing, as his hand glided down the back of her leg, stirring a chain of delicious shivers as it went.

He stopped at the spot where her heel met the back of her lace-up stiletto, cradling her foot as he undid the laces. "These are some dangerous shoes you got here, Camilla."

"Cami," she corrected a little more sharply than necessary, reaching out to brush her fingers through his hair. It was so thick and unruly, the richest brown color, warm and alive.

His head was tipped down, but she saw the corner of his mouth lift. "It pisses you off when someone calls you Camilla?"

"Yeah."

"Well, that gets me hot." He looked up and locked eyes with her again as he slid off that sandal. "But about these high-heeled shoes…"

"Hmm?"

He set the sandal neatly upright beneath the night table. "These shoes make a man want to see you wearing them with your legs in the air."

"Oh!" It came out on a goofy little gasp.

"Maybe I'll get to see that sometime."

"I... Sure," she answered dazedly. Because her mind was a hot stew, every neuron blazing. All he'd done was take off her shoe and suddenly she had no mental energy left to form coherent verbal responses.

But then again, it wasn't only the shoe. It was the searing looks he gave her, the way he'd carried her in here with her all wrapped around him, the endless, sizzling-hot kiss they'd shared.

He got busy with the other sandal, untying the laces, sliding it off. And finally setting it side by side with its mate under the nightstand. Then he rose to stand above her again. "Up, now."

She felt...hypnotized. Mesmerized. By his caramel eyes, by his rough-tender commands. She stood.

And then he was taking her filmy shirt and lifting it. "Raise your arms." She raised them. He pulled the shirt up and off. "So pretty..." He brushed a finger against the satin bow in the center of her lacy purple bra.

She just stared at him, eager and yearning and suddenly totally out of her depth. It was time—past time. She knew it. She *had* to open her mouth and tell him.

He cradled her breast.

It felt so good. She let out a tiny moan. "Um. I..."

He leaned closer. His warm breath touched her cheek as he whispered, "Beautiful," and slipped his thumb beneath the cup of her bra.

She made another sound. It wasn't a word, just a tiny squeak of pleasure as he brushed his thumb back and forth across her nipple.

And then he took her mouth. He kissed her slow and deep. His hands got busy. They roamed all over her, rubbing her shoulders, caressing her back, molding her waist and wrapping both hands around her bottom again, stroking, squeezing…

She returned his kiss eagerly. It felt so good, nothing better. He must have popped the hooks at the back of her bra. She lowered her arms and the bra fell away and vanished.

Poof.

She sighed as he cupped her bare breasts, one in each hand.

"Since that first night," he said low and rough in her ear as he touched her, caressing her, rubbing her nipples between his thumbs and forefingers. "You've been making me crazy. You, in that white corset thing, standing in the bathroom by the tub, and then on the porch after your bath in only a towel. Looking so good, so hot. Even with your eye bright purple, swollen shut, and most of you covered in scrapes and scratches, I wanted to eat you right up."

Did she moan out his name? It seemed that she might have.

"Kiss me, Cami."

Eagerly, she offered her mouth and he claimed it all over again, his hands on the move once more, straying down to the placket of her white jeans. The kiss took her over. She gave herself up to it—to him, with his skilled mouth and talented hands, his rough-tender words and the manly, clean scent of him that she would know in a room full of strangers, with all the lights off.

I should tell him, she scolded herself as he undid her fly and took her jeans down.

I need to tell him, she thought in a vague, distant way as he knelt and trailed a line of worshipful kisses along the white scar that ran the length of her thigh.

But she didn't tell him. He ruled her senses. And she really couldn't bear it if he stopped. And what would it be but a mood-killer, to tell him now that this was a first for her?

Uh-uh. She wanted this with all her heart and soul. She wanted *him*.

She did not want to stop now. And she knew him, she really did. Knew him to his soul already, in the space of a week. So what if that was impossible? It was also true.

If she told him, he would stop.

There would be talking. There would be slowing down and taking time and, well, she just didn't need time.

She needed him. She needed *this*. To be swept away, taken over, kissed and touched and claimed at last.

So she sighed and pulled him up to her and moaned in delight when he lifted her and laid her down, naked and yearning, on the white sheets of his bed.

He stripped and he was fast about it. In half a minute, he had everything off and tossed aside. Then he just stood there, unmoving, looking down at her through those golden eyes.

"Garrett..." He was so fine, with those broad, muscled shoulders, everything cut and hard and honed.

She drank him in, his square-jawed face and powerful neck, that tempting line of silky hair trailing downward from his broad chest, over his ridged belly all the way to where he was ready for her, thick and erect, big enough to scare her a little.

It would probably hurt.

But she didn't care. It wouldn't hurt for long. And she wanted him all over her, moving inside her, whispering her name.

All her life, she'd been looking. For *this* life, the life that he'd shown her, the life she'd waited too long to find. Everything was wide-open now. She could find her truest self, be the woman she was meant to be—Garrett's woman, she fervently hoped.

She reached up her arms to him.

With a slow smile, he took a condom from the bedside drawer and set it by the clock. "Cami." He said her name all rough and low, like a promise, like a secret they shared, just the two of them.

And he came down to her. She rolled to face him as he stretched out on his side. He touched her throat, smoothed her hair, whispered again that she was beautiful.

And she was perfectly, gloriously lost—in his touch, in the feel of his naked body against hers, in the rough scrape of his beard scruff, the taste of his mouth, the hot sweep of his tongue beyond her parted lips.

She could kiss him forever. Until their mouths fused permanently, never again to part.

He gave her bottom lip a little nip as he went lower, running that naughty tongue of his down the center of her throat. "You taste like heaven." He kissed the words onto the side of her neck.

And his kisses didn't stop there. On they went. He breathed one into the hollow her throat, scattered them across her upper chest until he reached the waiting curves of her breasts.

He lavished attention on one and then the other, taking her nipples into his mouth, sucking them deep.

She lay moaning in dizzy delight as he drove her wild with kisses, with slow, perfect caresses.

And no, she wasn't a complete innocent. She'd had boyfriends, fooled around. She really shouldn't let him do all the work here. She needed to take a little initiative, do more than just lie here in ecstasy, gasping and sighing, reveling in the glory of his every touch.

But she was lost in the best way, a slave to his stroking hands, to his skilled, hungry kisses.

Her breasts ached in the sweetest way as he kept kissing them, kept drawing her nipples into the wet heat of his mouth, making her clutch him close and cry out, "Yes!" and "Please," and "Don't ever stop."

He didn't stop.

He went farther. Lower.

His fingers strayed to the core of her, where she was wet and so ready for him. He stroked her, making low sounds of excitement and approval, those fingers of his strumming her, playing her just right.

He dipped a finger in. "You're so tight…"

She made a noise of agreement, self-reproach stirring. *I need to tell him…*

But she didn't. She eased her legs wider as he stroked her. She lifted her hips off the bed, inviting him, encouraging him, opening herself fully to the searing perfection of his touch.

He was just really good at this, taking his sweet time with her, caressing her so perfectly, kissing his way down her belly, so he could play her with his mouth and his wonderful fingers, together. It felt so good, exactly right.

She never, ever wanted it to end.

But he kept the pleasure building. And her climax took her over without warning.

She hit the peak, her body opening like a flower of purest sensation, pulsing as she came. The world was suddenly a bright, hot, expanding shimmer of light with her at the center, pleasure racing along every nerve ending, flying out the ends of her fingers, the tips of her toes—and then turning inward again, contracting down into the core of her, leaving her limp and satisfied, wearing a silly smile.

Garrett didn't think he'd ever seen anything as beautiful as Cami losing herself to his touch.

At the end, as she went loose and easy, he gathered her close to him and stroked her sunny, wildly tangled hair. She tucked her head into the crook of his neck and sighed in contentment.

"So good." Her soft lips brushed his throat.

And then her cool hand went roaming, her fingers trailing down the outside of his arm, along the line of his hip. A moment later, those soft fingers closed around him. He groaned, aching for more.

But he had questions that needed answering first. He caught her wrist. "Hey."

She made a questioning sound. But she did let go.

He brought her hand to his lips and kissed her sweet fingertips, lingering on the rough spot, that callus at the top inside joint of her middle finger where her pencil rested when she drew in those notebooks of hers. "You got something you want to talk to me about?"

Her sharp intake of breath said it all. And then she tipped her head back and stared at him through anxious eyes. A sweet blush crept up her slim neck and over her cheeks. "You can tell?"

"Not for sure. Not until a second ago, from that little sound you made when I asked, and the look on your face right now. And, well, you *are* really tight."

Her blush deepened. "I…didn't know how to say it. It felt so awkward just to blurt it out. And it was so beautiful, what you were doing. I thought maybe we could, you know, just go ahead and let it happen."

He hid a smile. "Get it over with, you mean?"

She winced. "I guess I should just say it right out loud instead of dancing around it, huh?"

"That would be good."

"So, Garrett." She made a show of clearing her throat. "Ahem. It just so happens that I am a virgin. And I can't tell you how happy it would make me if you would please be my first."

He kept his expression strictly serious. "Cami, I would be honored."

"Honored." She snickered. "I'll take it."

"But—"

She put her fingers to his lips. "Ugh. There are 'buts'?"

He smoothed her hair, a slow stroke and then another, to soothe her worried frown. "The other day, when Munch and I were eavesdropping on your private moments with the bonehead, the guy called you 'cold.'"

She gave a gusty sigh. "Yeah. Charles and I were engaged for two years and I just… I couldn't bring myself to have sex with him. I kept saying I wanted to wait—and I did. Because never would have been too soon with him, you know?"

"I get it. I met him, remember?"

"He really isn't a bad guy, Garrett."

"He tried to drag you out of here against your will. That makes him a bad guy in my book."

"Yeah, well. I still have some sympathy for him and the position he's in. I've known him all my life and I never thought of him romantically. But still, I caved and said yes to him. And then I let it get all the way to the altar before I called it off. What a disaster. I didn't have the guts to break up with him till the last possible minute, but I also refused to have my first time be with him. I can't believe what a coward I was, that it took me twenty-eight years to finally bust out on my own."

"Come on. Think positive. You're out now."

"Oh, yes, I am. And loving every minute of it, believe me."

"So I completely understand why you didn't sleep with Charles."

"Thank you."

"But what about that bad boy you ran away with in high school?"

"I told you. Robbie wasn't really bad. He was a great guy and I was sure it was true love with him. We fooled around a lot. But he was Catholic and he didn't believe in sex before marriage. So nope, not with Robbie. And you know, people make jokes about punching your V-card. But it's really not funny. The longer you're a virgin, the harder it gets to just go do it, you know? Because I never wanted to have sex with just anybody. And the years went by and I started to worry that maybe I would never have sex at all. I…I always wanted to be in love first."

In love?

Garrett's pulse kicked into overdrive and his mouth went dry. Yeah, okay. If he ever were to take a chance on love again, it would be with someone like her, someone honest and true and openhearted, someone even-tempered, who could show up on a mountain-top bloody and battered and just wave her hand and ask for water and a hot dog.

But he'd failed at love. In an epic way. His babies had died and his poor wife could never get through to him. Just the thought of going there again had his gut clenching and flop sweat breaking out on his brow. Hadn't he already made that painfully clear to her?

But then she gave him that glowing smile. "Or if not love, I wanted to find a really good friend I could trust absolutely."

He realized he'd inadvertently been holding his breath. He let it out slowly so she wouldn't notice. God, she was gorgeous. With eyes like blue agates and those lips that begged for long, wet kisses. All that, and a good heart. Integrity, too. "You're like no one I've ever known before."

"That's a good thing, right?" Her mouth trembled in the hope of a smile.

If a fairy princess married a unicorn, their first-born child would be Cami. "It's an excellent thing."

And she grinned full-out. "Whew." She scooted in closer.

He pulled up the blankets and tucked them in around her. "Now go to sleep." He switched off the light. "We have time. We don't have to rush it."

She made a tiny humphing sound. "Translation. You're turned off by the whole virgin thing."

"No. I just don't want to hurt you and I think we should take it slow."

"Oh." She didn't sound at all convinced, though he couldn't see her face to know for sure.

"Cami. Do you need me to lay it right out there for you?"

"Well, yeah. I kind of do."

"I think lube will help and I don't have any handy. I'll get some tomorrow."

"Um, okay."

"Go to sleep." He shut his eyes and willed his erection to subside.

And then she whispered, "But for tonight, what about you?"

"I'll be fine." It came out a little harsher than he meant it to.

She wasn't buying. He could almost feel her mind working. And then, finally, she asked, "It does turn you off, doesn't it? That there might be blood and I don't know what I'm doing."

"Wrong."

"I don't believe you."

A bad word escaped him. He captured her hand and brought it down between them.

"Oh!" Her fingers wrapped around him again and he made himself breathe very carefully. In. Out. In again… "Garrett, this can't be comfortable."

He nuzzled her ear. "It's been this way pretty much since you appeared on the mountain. Long showers help."

"It's just not fair."

"Don't worry about it. I'll survive."

"Stop arguing." And she kissed him.

She tasted like heaven and her hand started moving…

He sank into the kiss as she played him below. He knew he should stop her. But for a virgin, she certainly seemed to be ready for anything—and surprisingly skilled with that little hand of hers.

"Garrett," she whispered against his mouth, her hand working serious magic on his aching hardness.

And then she ducked beneath the covers.

"Cami, you don't have to…" He lost his train of thought completely as her warm, wet mouth closed around him. She kept those clever fingers good and tight at the base. "Cami… I…"

He what?

He had no idea. His brain had ceased to function. He fell back against the pillow and let her have her way with him. It didn't take long.

When he got right to the brink, he tried to warn her. "Cami, I'm going to…" Again, words deserted him.

But she just kept on driving him absolutely out of his mind.

And in the end, he surrendered completely. His

climax roared through him, emptying him out in the most perfect way.

When he could move again, he pulled her up into his arms and whispered, "You are incredible. I think I just might have to keep you in this bed indefinitely."

She sighed and settled closer.

He tucked the covers around them nice and tight. "Now will you go to sleep?" He breathed the words into her sweet-smelling hair.

"Yes, Garrett." Her lips brushed his throat.

A few minutes later, he heard her breathing even out into slumber. Not long after that, he faded off, too.

In the morning, he woke holding her close. She was curled into him, her legs tangled with his, her head tucked against his chest.

She felt really good in his arms, so womanly and soft. And she smelled of vanilla and sex. *Tonight*, he thought, they would take it all the way. He was going to make it good for her, so that when she looked back on what they'd had together, she would be glad she'd wanted him for her first.

He went off to work that day with a giant grin on his face. Nell gave him grief as usual and the drywall crew still hadn't picked up the pace. As always, even on Saturday, he had too much work to do. But he had tonight to look forward to, so for once it was easy to smile through every setback.

At a quarter of noon, Cami texted him. R U @ the office? I want to bring sandwiches.

She was fixing him lunch? Did life get any better? He texted back, @ a job site.

I can bring sandwiches wherever you are.

Grinning like an idiot, he sent her the address.

She showed up twenty minutes later wearing cut-off jeans, cowboy boots and a snug white T-shirt with Jessica Rabbit printed on the front. She'd put her yellow hair in matching high ponytails and she was about the cutest thing he'd ever seen.

The drywall guys thought so, too. They looked at her like they wanted to gobble her right up. At least they had the sense to keep their mouths shut. When her back was turned, he gave them the evil eye. They stopped staring and got to work.

Garrett took Cami out into the open area behind the house. She'd come prepared, with a basket of food and a blanket to sit on. He spread the blanket on the flattened weeds and she brought out turkey sandwiches, chips, apple wedges and bottles of iced tea.

"I've been thinking about my future," she said as she nibbled on a chip. "The first day I was here, I went into this stationery store. Great place. Art supplies, greeting cards, all kinds of gorgeous custom paper, everything. This morning I went by there again. The owner wants to sell. There's a workshop in the back. I've always wanted to set up a website, try making greeting cards using my own designs—and I could sell them on Etsy, too. If I bought the shop, I could run it and make the cards in back."

"Your eyes are shining."

Her soft cheeks flushed warm pink and she confessed, "I'm kind of excited at the idea. I would have the store to run right away and take my time with the greeting cards, kind of feel my way along, developing my own line."

He sipped his tea. "You should go for it."

"Yeah?"

He nodded. "You need money?"

"Nope. I roughed out the numbers and I'm good." She laughed. "Yes, my much-hated business degree is coming in handy, after all. And I have great credit. I'm thinking about a business loan, rather than spending any of my nest egg. Monday, I'm going to talk to my bank and see what they can do for me."

He wanted to grab her and kiss her. But if he did that, he wouldn't want to stop. And the drywall guys were probably peering out the windows to see what he and the hot blonde got up to. "We should go out tonight and celebrate."

For some reason, she hesitated to answer. Finally, she said, "Well, I haven't bought the store yet."

"Doesn't matter. I want to take you out. There's this great new place, Mirabelle's. I'll see if I can get a reservation. Seven good for you?"

She set down her sandwich and exhaled a slow breath. "Garrett, I really would love to go out to dinner with you…"

He finally got the message. She had other plans. Maybe they were good plans. Maybe she wanted to get going ASAP on finishing what they'd started last night. That would be a whole lot better than good— more like downright spectacular. His work jeans got tighter. He ordered the problem to subside and asked hopefully, "But?"

"This morning after you left…"

"Yeah?"

"Your mother called."

The issue in his pants vanished as though it had never been. He had that sinking feeling. She hadn't been angling for hours and hours of amazing sex, after all. Not even close. "What did Ma want and don't tell me you said yes?"

Blue angel eyes reproached him. "You don't have get all surly about it."

"Just tell me what she wants."

"She wants us to come to dinner at the mansion tonight—to get to know Griffin a little."

He stared at her for a long count of five before accusing, "You said yes."

She scrunched up her adorable face. "As a matter of fact, I kind of did."

When Garrett pulled the Mustang to a stop in the small parking area in front of the Bravo mansion, four other vehicles were already there. He recognized them all. His mother had summoned all five of her children.

"Everybody's here," he marveled aloud. "I can't believe nobody managed to back out."

Cami leaned across the console and tugged on the collar of his blue dress shirt. "You look so handsome." She kissed him, a light breath of a kiss that had him wanting to haul her close and kiss her some more. She wore a red wraparound dress with little white polka dots on it and he could not wait to get home and take that dress off her.

"We could just turn around and go back home," he suggested. Hey, it was worth a shot. "You could call Ma and say I suddenly felt sick."

She laughed. "Come on. It's going to be great."

"Dinner at my mother's is *never* great."

"First time for everything—come on, handsome. Let's go."

It was not great.

The invitation had been adults only. So it was Carter, Garrett, Quinn, Jody and Nell, plus wives and husbands—and Cami. Because Ma thought that Cami and Garrett were a thing.

And, come to think of it, they actually were. As of last night. More or less. In a friends-with-benefits sort of way.

In the library for cocktails, Ma made them all drink martinis, all but Jody, who was nursing her three-month-old, Marybeth.

Carter tried to refuse. "No, thanks. Got a beer?" But then his wife, Paige, whispered to him. And Carter grumbled, "Fine. A martini. Make mine a double."

Once the first round of drinks was served, Nell pulled Garrett aside. "Is this a nightmare? Tell me we're going to wake up soon."

"Griffin seems like an okay guy," he tried gamely.

Their brother Quinn, who owned a gym across the street from McKellan's, joined in. "He's in real estate in San Diego. A widower. He's got three grown children."

Jody had wandered close. She whispered, "Really, it doesn't seem like there's anything wrong with him. And the chemistry with him and Ma is pretty much off the charts."

Garrett put up a hand. "I could go my whole life without knowing that."

From over by the ornate fireplace, his mother called, "All right, you four, stop whispering in the corner and join the party."

So they went and sat with the others and talked about nothing in particular through the cocktail hour. Garrett sat next to Cami on one of the sofas and wished they were home, where he could unwrap that sexy dress and bury himself in her softness at last—but slowly, with care. Because she was a virgin and he couldn't believe she'd chosen him for her first.

He put his arm around her. She sent him a glance full of sweet, sexy promises and snuggled in a little closer. He felt like the king of the world. He breathed in her flowers and vanilla scent and loved the way that polka-dot dress wrapped in front creating an excellent view of her cleavage, which he could not wait to see more of later tonight.

Life was good. Even drinking a martini in the mansion library with his mother and her new boyfriend was almost bearable with Cami tucked up close to his side.

Griffin, who did seem to be an okay guy—aside from the fact that he was clearly doing Ma and that was just gross—told them proudly about his two daughters and his son, all three of whom were married and running the family business together. The two daughters had children.

Nell asked, "So have you met the Masters family, Ma?"

Willow sipped her martini. "I have and I love them." She *loved* them. Garrett tried to get his mind around that, Ma loving someone else's kids. She patted Griffin's knee. "It's been, what, Griff, two years since that first weekend at the Cabo house?" Griffin had already mentioned that he owned a vacation place in Cabo San Lucas. Ma gave the rest of them a cool smile. "Griff invited me and his children and grandchildren for a week to get to know each other."

"Wait a minute." Nell looked as stunned as the rest of them. "I'm just doing the math here. You met Griffin's family *two years* ago?"

Willow gave an airy sigh. "I told him I wasn't ready. But he insisted."

Griffin said quietly, "I know it's a shock to all of you. We should have told you sooner, too."

"No kidding," muttered Jody. Her husband, Seth, took her hand, a gesture clearly meant to soothe her.

Griffin seemed honestly regretful. "I wanted to meet you all long ago."

"I put him off." Willow waved a hand. "I just wasn't ready yet."

Jody cleared her throat. "How, um, long have you two known each other?"

"Five and a half years," said Griffin, eliciting more than one gasp. "We met on a Mediterranean cruise." Garrett wanted to throw his martini at the far wall. *Not even a year after Dad died. Unbelievable.* "My wife had passed away two years before." Griffin draped his arm across Willow's shoulders and she gave him an adoring smile.

"We decided to see the world together," Willow said. Garrett suppressed a snide remark. After Franklin Bravo's death, it had seemed like she was always off on some trip or other. They'd all thought she was nursing her perpetually broken heart. Should they have guessed she hadn't been traveling alone? "As friends-only, at the time," she added.

"Neither of us were looking for anything but friendship then," Griffin said.

"But slowly," said Willow, "it did become…more." Her voice was strangely soft—and warm, like her expression. It was bizarre to see her this way, so happy and relaxed. His mother was never happy and she'd always been much too watchful and calculating to actually relax.

"So much more," Griffin was saying. The two shared one of those smoldering looks that Garrett really didn't need to see. Ever.

And then his mother said, "That's why we've invited you all here this evening. Because you are my family and I love you all very much and I want you to know that I've found the man I intend to spend the rest of my life with."

"You're…getting engaged?" Nell croaked.

"We already are," Willow answered with pride.

"For the last year," added Griffin.

That brought a silence big enough to drive a tractor through.

Finally, Jody piped up weakly, "But, Ma, we had no clue."

And Nell said, as if it proved anything, "I never saw a ring. I don't see a ring now."

Willow gave Griffin yet another glowing smile. "I'm ready, darling. I'll take back my ring." And Griffin whipped out a ring with a diamond the size of Fort Knox. She offered her hand and he slid the big sparkler on her finger. "There," she said. "That's better. I admit I felt naked without it." She looked up from the giant rock to send an openly loving glance around the room. "I know. I should have told you all sooner. I should have introduced you to Griffin a long time ago. But it just felt so terribly awkward. I had always sworn that your father was the only man for me. And I realize you all view me as this sad, misguided, lonely figure who'd lost the only love of her life and could never love another. I know that I believed that myself. But then I met Griff. And slowly everything changed. I hardly knew where to begin, how to tell you that I had found someone new, someone so very special. I kept putting it off and that only made it harder. And now, finally, well, we're running out of time. We couldn't wait any longer."

"Running out of time?" demanded Carter. "Ma, are you pregnant?"

Willow let out a musical laugh. "Darling. Of course not."

"Then why?" Quinn, a former martial arts champ who wasn't afraid of anything, looked terrified.

Garrett felt pretty damn freaked himself. "Ma. What the hell are you telling us? Is somebody going to die?"

His mother laughed again, a totally un-Willow-like laugh, lighthearted and joyous. "No one's going to die, sweetheart. I meant that we're running out of time until the *wedding*. Griff and I have set the date. We're getting married in December at the Haltersham Hotel."

Chapter Nine

Cami got a little worried about Garrett during the drive home. He was too quiet. And he scowled out the windshield most of the way.

Twice, she reached over and brushed his arm. The first time he pulled out of his funk long enough to give her a smile. The second time, he caught her hand and pressed his lips to the back of it.

She appreciated the gesture. He was letting her know it wasn't her he was mad at.

But she knew that already. He was upset with Willow—really upset. Cami didn't exactly understand why.

Yeah, she got that the news of the wedding had come as a complete shock to everyone. Willow really shouldn't have waited so long to introduce the family to her new love.

But Griffin seemed like a great guy and he and Willow were obviously devoted to each other. And they had certainly known each other long enough to be confident it was the real thing.

Okay, maybe it was *too* much of a shock for Garrett. He couldn't actually be happy for his mother and her new love at this point. And the fact that Willow had sprung the wedding date on them right on the heels of the news of their engagement was a lot to take in.

She offered, "You want to talk about it?"

He turned the corner onto his street. "No, I do not."

At the house, they greeted Munchy and then Garrett let the dog out into the backyard.

He reached for her the minute he slid the glass door shut. They shared a kiss that curled her toes and made her belly hot and melty.

But when he lifted his head, his eyes were far away.

She reached up and stroked her fingers into the short hair at his temple. "Talk to me."

But he didn't. Instead, he kissed her again. His lips played on hers. She surrendered to that kiss, to the delicious taste of his mouth, to the woodsy scent of him that made her feel safe, protected and deeply desired. It thrilled her, to be wanted this way—for herself as she really was—by the wonderful man who had no plans to try and make her over into his idea of who she ought to be.

She heard a faint whining sound—Munch, wanting back in. Garrett broke the kiss to open the door. The dog bumped through and trotted to his water bowl for a noisy drink.

Garrett said, "Sorry if I'm grouchy. It's not you."

She took his hands and guided them to her hips. Then she clasped his thick shoulders. "I'll try one more time. Talk to me?"

He scanned her face as though committing it to memory. And then, at last, he said, "I wanted tonight to be perfect for you. I wanted to take you to Mirabelle's for a romantic meal, just the two of us. Instead, we had to go to the mansion and deal with Ma and the guy she hasn't bothered to mention to any of us for the past five and a half years." He touched the space between her eyebrows. "You're frowning. Why?"

"Well, I wouldn't say she hasn't bothered."

"I would."

"Garrett. She was anxious about telling you all. She didn't know how to go about it."

"Sorry. That's just no excuse."

"I think she really loves him. And that they're happy."

He glared into the middle distance for several seconds, and then, finally, he looked at her again. "I get that. I do. And the truth is, Ma annoys me no matter what she does."

"Ooo." She fluttered her eyelashes at him. "Honesty. I like it."

He reached out, eased his hand around the back of her neck and pulled her in close to him. There was no other place she would rather be. He kissed the tip of her nose. "It's just leftover crap from my childhood and I know it. And hey, she might as well be happy while she's annoying me, right?"

"Right!" Cami said it with enthusiasm. "And I had a great time. I love a good martini and the food was delicious."

He arched a thick eyebrow at her. "Not to mention the family tension you could cut with a dull, rusty knife."

"You should meet *my* parents. My mother's not so bad. But my father, well, I do love him but sometimes I wonder why. He's so sure he's right. Drives me insane."

He brushed a finger along her cheek, traced the shape of her ear and then trailed that finger down the side of her throat, stirring lovely, hot goose bumps in his wake. "Your father doesn't scare me. And I plan to go with you the first time you meet with him again."

Her heart went to mush. "You would? I have no idea why you would want to put yourself through such a thing. It's not going to be any fun."

"From what you've said about him, I don't really trust your dad. You need a friend to back you up."

A friend. Weren't they kind of beyond friendship now?

Again, she sternly reminded herself that she needed to give the guy time. Tonight was the one-week anniversary of the night that they'd met. And he was hardly like her—a love-at-first-sight kind of person.

His finger kept moving. He followed the V of her neckline, down over the curve of one breast and up the other to her collarbone, which he traced all the way out on each side and then back in, ending in the hollow at the base of her throat. "Did I tell you how much I like this dress? I like the way it clings to every perfect curve. And I really like how easy it will be to take off you." His voice had gone delightfully low and rough and his eyes had turned slumberous. His eyelashes were so beautiful, inky and thick as any girl's. "This dress really helped me to get through drinks and dinner. Every time I was tempted to say something rude to my mother, I would look at your breasts, which this dress shows off in a spectacular way, and feel better about everything." He cupped one, and she bit her lip at how good that felt. "Even the crappy things in life are more bearable when I can look at your breasts."

"You're welcome." She gazed up at him, wanting his kiss, wanting his hands all over her, wanting him inside her.

Tonight.

For her very first time.

He muttered something low and dirty. And then he grabbed her hand and led her toward the stairs and up them.

She followed eagerly, Munch at her heels.

In the master suite, he sent Munch to the corner bed. Then, right there at the door, he pulled her close and started kissing her again.

Deep kisses, dizzying. Beautiful in their intensity. Like a drug, those kisses of his. She was already addicted to them. She needed an endless supply. A lifetime of his kisses wouldn't be enough.

As he kissed her, he began taking her clothes away, untying the bow at one side of her dress, and then the little one on the inside that anchored the other side in place.

He eased it off her shoulders and it drifted to the floor. He took away her red lace bra and slipped his fingers under the tiny front of her matching thong.

Oh. My. Goodness. The things he did with those fingers of his, kissing her endlessly as he played with her, her needy moans echoing in her head before he swallowed them down. She could have come, just from that. His mouth on hers, his hand working the sweetest magic down below.

But she didn't come. Every time she would find herself rising to the peak, he would slow those perfect caresses, keeping her near the edge.

But never quite letting her fall.

"Shoes," he commanded against her lips.

She took his meaning and got rid of them, kicking one off and then the other, pushing them both out of the way with a couple of quick swipes of her bare feet.

"Bed." He bit the side of her throat and sucked on it. She would have a bruise there in the morning, a tender little testament to this magical, first-time night.

And then he scooped her up and carried her. He'd pulled back the covers earlier. She loved a man who planned ahead.

She loved *him*, with all her heart and soul.

He laid her down and made quick work of her thong, pulling it down and away in one long sweep of both hands. And then he straightened, his eyes molten gold as he gazed down at her. He began to undress, unbuttoning his shirt in quick, ruthless movements.

She gazed up at him, burning for him, her skin supersensitized, her heart throbbing slow and deep, her blood so thick and hot as it pulsed through her veins.

He dropped to the bedside chair to get rid of his shoes and socks and then he was up again, shoving his dress slacks and boxer briefs off, only slowing enough to ease them free of his erection. Such a beautiful man, broad and muscled, his thighs and arms thick and powerful, his eyes hot with promises she knew he would keep.

He pulled open the drawer by the bed and took out a condom and a little white bottle with a purple label, setting them in easy reach, his gaze holding hers the whole time.

"Cami," he said on a growl as he came down to her, a beautiful big bad wolf of a man ready to gobble her up, watching her hungrily through golden eyes. She opened her arms to him and gathered him close.

More kisses, perfect kisses. The kind that go on and on and on. It all blurred together in the best sort of way. His hands on her body, driving her higher, yet somehow never quite letting her fly over the edge. In time, his kisses strayed from her mouth. His lips brushed over her cheek and then lower, blazing trails of heat and wonder all along her eager flesh.

She cried out in pleasure, lost to him, to his burning kisses, his skilled and tender caresses. He just kept kissing her, touching her, sweeping her away on an endless wave of sweet sensation.

He rose above her on his knees. She blinked up at him, dazed and dreamy, and commanded, "Come back here."

"Oh, I will. Very soon." And he smiled at her, a sweet devil's smile, as he rolled on the condom and then used the clear gel from the little white bottle. He squirted more of the stuff on his fingers and held her gaze as he used it on her.

She moaned at his touch, at the coolness of the gel where she was burning up in the best possible way.

"You're so wet. I don't think you even need this stuff." His fingers stroked her.

"I don't care if I need it. It feels good. Cool. I like it a lot." He dipped two fingers in and she laughed in sheer delight.

"You think it's funny?" He made the question into a tender threat.

A threat of what exactly, she had no clue. "I think it's incredible—and I don't just mean the gel. I mean you and every naughty thing you do to me. I love it. All of it. As long as it's with you."

"Yeah?" Amber eyes glowed down at her.

"Yeah." She caught her lower lip between her teeth and moaned. And then those amazing fingers found a certain extrasensitive spot inside her. She let out a sharp cry at the bright bloom of increased sensation.

"Does that hurt?"

She shook her head hard and fast against the pillow. "Are you kidding? No way. It's good, really. So good…" And she moaned in need and excitement as he kept on touching her.

Her eyes were too heavy to stay open. She let them drift shut. She gave herself up to him, lifting her hips to him, opening her legs even wider, begging him with her body never to stop.

He bent closer. That soft mouth covered hers. She tasted her own desire on his lips, on his devilish tongue. So perfect, the weight of him, the heat and the hardness covering her.

And then he lifted his head away. She felt him, there, where she wanted him, nudging at her core. He pushed in so slowly.

"Oh!" She opened her eyes wide at the unaccustomed sensation.

His eyes were waiting. "Okay?" He hovered above her, inside her, but just barely.

"Very okay." She wrapped her arms loosely around his big shoulders.

"More?"

She nodded. "Yes, please."

With a slow smile, he gave her more.

It felt so good, the feeling of fullness, the unhurried, delicious stretching. She lifted her legs and wrapped them around him, too. "More," she whispered, holding his caramel gaze.

He groaned then, his brow crinkling, his beautiful mouth going softer than ever. "Cami…"

"Garrett…" She tightened her arms and legs around him, pulling him down.

Another strangled sound escaped him.

She took his face and captured his gaze. "Yes," she whispered. "I'm ready. Yes…"

"Sure?"

"Yes."

"Because, Cami, I…" That sentence died unfinished.

Not that it mattered. She answered his question again, "Yes."

And finally, he believed her. He pushed his hips toward her as she rose to take him. Her body gave to him easily, taking him in like he was born to be there.

Stillness. Total stillness in that perfect moment. Just the two of them, joined at last in the most basic way.

He braced his forearms on either side of her and pressed his forehead to hers. It was so beautiful, the feel of him inside her, the warmth of his breath across her skin. In that moment, there was only the two of them. She stared up at him, and he gazed back at her and she was glad.

So very glad, that she'd waited to have this with him.

He started to move then, slowly. He watched her as he rocked her, ready to stop if she needed that.

But stopping was the last thing she wanted or needed. She gasped at the sheer beauty of it, the hot, wet, perfect glide of him deep inside her, filling her, stretching her, stoking her pleasure. She pulled him closer, lifting herself toward him, whispering encouragements, sighing his name.

He moved faster. She wrapped herself tighter, closer, around him as they went on rising and falling, bobbing happily on their own private ocean of pleasure. She could have gone on like that forever.

But he'd played her too well and she was more than ready. And this time when she reached for the peak, he did nothing to slow her down.

The glow started, that shimmer of building sensation. The shimmer became a pool of light and the light became a rising flame. The flame spread, licking everywhere, until there wasn't an inch of her inside or out that didn't shudder and burn.

For a dazzling, perfect moment, there was nothing but light and heat filling her to overflowing as she hit the crest. A guttural, garbled sound escaped her.

And then he was pushing up onto his hands. "Cami." Those amber eyes blazed down at her as he started to move again, slow and deep at first, but pumping into her harder, faster, as he chased his own release.

He came, straining his head back, the powerful muscles in his neck standing out in sharp relief as he groaned his satisfaction out loud.

When he collapsed on top of her, she gathered him in. Even then, wrung out from his climax, he was careful not to crush her with his weight. He guided them over, so they were on their sides facing each other.

For the longest, sweetest time, they just lay there, holding each other. She never wanted to let him go.

But finally, he smoothed her hair and kissed her mouth and eased away. He settled the covers over her. "Be right back…"

She stayed where he left her, feeling weightless and wonderful, perfectly content, listening to the jingle of Munchy's collar from over in the corner and the sound of water running in the bathroom. Really, did it get any better than this?

When the bathroom door opened, she pushed back the blankets and got up. In the middle of the floor, he caught her. He smelled like soap and toothpaste and they shared a laughing kiss before he let her go to clean up a little and brush her teeth.

By the time she returned to the bedroom, Munch had reclaimed his favorite spot at the foot of the bed and Garrett had turned off the lamp. He held the covers up for her.

She slid in beside him and he pulled her back against his body, into the shelter of his strong arms.

Her father called the next day.

They were having breakfast and she made the mistake of answering without checking the display.

He started right in on her. "This is becoming ridiculous, Camilla. When are you coming home?"

"I don't want to get into it with you right now, Dad." Garrett looked up sharply from the Sunday edition of the *Justice Creek Courier*. She gave him a rueful shrug and said to her father, "As for coming to visit you, I'll let you know."

"Camilla, this is unacceptable. If you don't—"

"Talk to you later, Dad." He was sputtering in fury as she disconnected the call.

"Bad?" Garrett asked after a long, silent moment.

She gave him another shrug. "It is what it is. Do you have to work today?"

He turned the page. "You're changing the subject on me."

"That's right."

He looked at her over the top of the paper, melty brown eyes making purely sexual promises. "On occasion, I've been known to take a Sunday off."

A lovely shiver went through her. She felt beautiful and sexy and a little bit sore. But not sore enough to keep her from having the best Sunday ever. "Is this one of those Sundays?"

He set down the paper. "Finish your breakfast so we can go back to bed."

It was a beautiful day. They spent most of it in bed.

That night, he took her to Mirabelle's for a leisurely romantic dinner. And then, back at home, he carried her straight up to the bedroom again.

The next week was a busy one. She got the money from her insurance company to buy a new car. She also got a loan to buy her store and good advice on her new business venture from Garrett's half brother James, who was a partner in a small law office right there in town.

Every night, she slept wrapped in Garrett's arms. And on Monday, Tuesday and Friday, when he had no lunch meetings, she packed up the picnic basket and joined him wherever he was working that day.

The next week was just as good. Tuesday, she got a great offer on her condo and agreed to the sale. Her Realtor drove up from Denver to bring her the contract. If everything went as expected, they would close in mid-September.

That night when Garrett got home from work, she had a bottle of expensive champagne chilling on ice. They toasted the sale and then celebrated by going to bed early—and not to get extra sleep.

The next day, in his office, over roast beef on rye, they joked about how good they were for each other.

She said, "You're schooling me in Backbone 101."

That made him laugh. "You've already graduated. Look at you, getting rid of the cheating fiancé, saying no to your father no matter how much grief he tries to give you and building yourself a business that works for you."

Her plans to buy the stationery store were moving right along. She'd signed the papers two days before. By the end of the month, the old owner would be out. The deal had included all the stock, shelving, sales equipment and display units. Once the shop was hers, Cami would close for the month of September. She wanted to rearrange the place a bit, put her own stamp on it and set up her workshop in the back. Her

new shop, Paper Princess, would have its gala grand
opening the first Saturday in October.

In the meantime, she'd turned her bedroom at Garrett's house into a temporary workshop. For several
satisfying hours a day, she sketched out her new line
of Paper Princess greeting cards. She'd even fooled
around with some ideas for Paper Princess paper dolls.
And Chloe Bravo, Quinn's wife, had set her up with
an excellent web designer. PaperPrincess.com would
go live on the shop's grand opening day.

Life was good. And the man across the desk from
her had a lot to do with making it that way.

Cami sipped her iced tea and grinned. "Backbone
101 isn't all you've helped me with." She granted him
a wicked grin. "There's also my sex education."

"Watch it," he warned in a growl. "I'll be forced to
hold a special class. Right here on this desk."

Sex in his office? In the middle of the day? Heat
bloomed in her belly. "I'm a big supporter of continu-
ing education."

He waved the last of his sandwich at her. "Finish
your lunch and prepare to get schooled."

"Yes, Professor." She made a show of batting her
eyelashes at him. "And if *you're* teaching *me* about
the endless joy of sex and the deep satisfaction of
standing up to my controlling father, what am *I* teaching *you*?"

He ate the last bite of watermelon from the fruit
cup she'd packed for him. "Hmm. Maybe, how to take
time off now and then? The health benefits of sharing lunch with someone hot and fun and sexy? How
to deal with my mother and not want to kill her?"

Cami blushed with happy pleasure. She did love

this man and she longed to tell him so. Too bad she couldn't shake the feeling that he wasn't ready to hear it yet. "So then, Health and Life Skills. A guy needs those, right?"

"Absolutely, he does." He balled up the plastic wrap from his sandwich and lobbed it at the trash can. Then he swung his boots to the floor, stepped to the door and twisted the lock. "And now for a little higher education…"

Cami left Garrett's office that day with an extra-wide smile on her face.

Unfortunately, half an hour later, as she was playing fetch with Munchy in Garrett's backyard, her father called again. That time, she had sense enough to check the display before answering.

She let it go to voice mail and took Munch inside, where she got to work on her greeting cards. Time passed in a happy creative haze. She came up with several new card designs and cute text to go with them.

At a little after five, she knocked off. It was Garrett's turn to deal with dinner so she didn't have to figure out what do about the meal that night.

Munchy always liked a walk. He danced around in circles when he saw her get his leash.

"Sit." Quivering with happiness, he dropped to his haunches. She praised him as she hooked the leash to his collar.

They had a nice two-mile stroll. The whole way she thought about the voice mail she hadn't listened to yet.

Guilt was making her stomach knot up, so when they got back to the house, she listened to her father's message—and couldn't resist talking back to his recorded voice as he listed her sins.

"Camilla." He let out a sigh that came through loud and clear, even in voice mail. "I'm at the end of my rope here. I don't know what to do about you."

"How 'bout this, Dad?" she scoffed at the phone. "Try respecting my choices and allowing me to live my own life."

"You've hurt me deeply and broken your poor mother's heart."

She moaned. "Oh, come on."

"And what about Charles? The man carries on, but all his joy in life is gone."

"Joy? I stole his joy?" She almost threw her poor phone at the wall about then. "I don't remember him having a lot of that in the first place."

"If you won't take my calls, at least call your mother. She hasn't smiled since you vanished from your own wedding."

"Great, Dad. Thanks. Now it's all my fault if Mom is unhappy."

"I mean it, Camilla. This has gone on long enough. Stop being a spineless coward. Come to dinner at least. Let's talk this over like reasonable adults."

That night, Garrett brought takeout from Romano's restaurant. Italian from Romano's was her favorite, but Cami hardly gave the take-out bags a glance.

"What's the matter?" he asked.

"It's nothing. Let's eat."

She'd already set the table. He petted his dog, washed his hands and they sat down to dinner.

"Ma called today," he said, hoping that might rouse

her out of her uncharacteristic funk. Cami loved to
hear news about Ma and Griffin.

"She and Griffin are still in town?"

"They're living here until December. She said they
would go back to California for Labor Day and also
for a week in October. His family's coming here for
the wedding. They'll all stay at the mansion for a
week. After the wedding, Ma's moving to Southern
California—but she and Griffin will be coming back
to visit often, she said." He watched Cami take a tiny
sip of wine and tear a piece of bread in half. "But
here's the big news…"

Cami glanced up from the food she wasn't eating. "What?"

"Ma wants to deed the mansion to Sondra's children."

That seemed to perk her up a little. "Wow."

"And not only the mansion. She wants to give Sondra's kids the antiques and pricey furniture that used
to belong to their mom. Ma said she thought it was
the right thing to do. Can you believe it, Ma wanting
to do the right thing by Dad's first wife's children?
Pigs are flying, I kid you not."

Across the table, Cami managed a chuckle at least.
"You know, I do like your mom."

"I've been meaning to ask you why."

"Oh, come on. You know why. She's smart. And
she's perceptive. She has a sense for what's really
going on with people."

"I find her seriously self-absorbed."

"Stop." She faked a glare. But then the smile returned, slightly dreamy this time. "Plus, she and
Griffin? I have to tell you, it's beautiful to see them

together. They're living proof that love can find you even when you think romance and passion are long gone from your life."

"Can you not talk about passion and my mother in the same sentence, please?"

She pointed her fork at him. "You are such a prude."

"You weren't calling me a prude all spread out on my desk today."

"Well, okay," she relented, a tiny smile playing at the corner of her mouth. "You're only a prude when it comes to your mother."

As if there was something wrong with that. "You bet I am."

Cami let out a little snort of derision. "And another great thing about your mom? She makes a mean martini."

"She ought to. She's had enough practice." He launched into the rest of his story. "So anyway, Ma said she was calling all of us—her own children, I mean—to see what we thought of her giving the house to Sondra's kids. I said go for it. Nell did, too. Nell and I are a hundred percent positive that Carter, Quinn and Jody will feel the same. Nobody but Ma and Dad ever thought it was okay for him to just move Ma into the house he built for Sondra, especially when the poor woman hadn't been dead a week." He shook his head. "There's been a lot of bitterness over that house. I think all the bad feelings are gone now, but for Ma to give it back to Sondra's children..." He sipped his beer. "Yeah. It's the right thing."

Cami pushed her veal around on her plate. "You

think one of your half brothers or -sisters will want to live there now?"

"Doubtful. Maybe Clara or Elise will want the place. But it's not likely. They'll probably end up selling it. I warned Ma of that, even though I expected my saying it would piss her off."

"But it didn't."

Sometimes he wondered if Cami knew his mother better than he did. "Not in the least. Ma says if they want to sell it all and split the proceeds, that's up to them. And Estrella, the mansion's longtime housekeeper, is ready to retire, so she won't be put out of a job."

Cami raised her wineglass. "Way to go, Willow." Garrett raised his beer, reaching across to tap her glass with it. They both drank.

And then she went right back to fiddling with her food.

He'd had enough of watching her be miserable. "Do you think maybe it's time to tell me what's wrong?" When she only glanced up glumly, he added, "That's veal piccata, in case you didn't notice. Veal piccata from Romano's and you've hardly had a bite. It's a sin before God and his angels not to eat every bite of a dinner that comes from Romano's."

"You're right. Sorry." She cut a tiny wedge of the tender veal and ate it. "It's amazing. Thank you."

He set down his fork. "Look. Whatever's got you so down, I want to know about it. Will you please talk to me?"

She wiped her mouth with her napkin, which was totally unnecessary, given that she'd hardly eaten anything. "Did you mean what you said about going with me the first time I went to see my parents?"

"You know I did. Anytime, anyplace. I'm going with you."

"You're the best. I mean that. I should remember that I'm supposed to be getting an A in Backbone 101 and insist that I don't need you there. But really, I do."

"I'm there. So then, you talked to them?"

"My dad called this afternoon. I didn't answer, but I played his voice mail a few hours later. He said a bunch of mean crap. But he was right that I need to go and see them. It's been almost a month since I left."

Almost a month...

How could that be? It seemed like just yesterday that she'd appeared at the cabin.

And yet, at the same time, he felt that he'd known her all his life, that he knew every inch of her, inside and out.

Imagining a day without her in it? He couldn't. She filled up all the spaces in his world that he hadn't even realized were empty, filled them with her happy laugh and her wide blue eyes and her body that thrilled him and also somehow felt like home.

He wanted her with him, bringing him lunch in a basket, offering herself for dessert. It was way beyond friendship and that freaked him out a little—okay, fine. It freaked him out a lot.

And what about the prospect of losing her when she decided it was time to strike out on her own? It caused a physical ache in him to even consider her leaving, to imagine his bed without her in it, her seat at his table empty.

But where else was this thing with them going to

go? It wasn't forever or anything. She'd barely gotten rid of the bonehead. No way was she ready to get serious again.

That made him…what to her?

A rebound guy, that was what. Best case, he could consider himself a temporary hero at a time when she needed one. They were friends with some serious benefits going on.

He needed to quell all these feelings he wasn't even supposed to be having and live in the damn moment.

She was watching him way too closely. "You okay, Garrett?"

"Fine." He needed to get off the emo train immediately. The whole point was that he hated all the emotional back-and-forth that happened in a serious relationship—not to mention, he sucked at it.

Which was why he didn't *have* serious relationships.

Never again.

He needed to focus on loving every minute with her, on being there for her as long as that worked for her. When the day came that she was ready to strike out on her own, he wouldn't hold her back.

And what were they talking about, anyway?

Right. Her dad. "So then, you went ahead and called him?"

"Yeah."

"And?"

"He said more mean things to me. The usual ones. I'm flighty and irresponsible and I need to cut that out immediately and do things the way he wants them done—meaning the *right* way. Which is to say, *his* way."

"Cami. Is there a downstroke here?"

Her smooth brow puckered. "A downstroke?"

"I mean, I completely get that your dad's an over-bearing jerkass. But are we going to Denver anytime soon?"

"You really don't have to go with—"

"Yeah, I do. I want to. Are we going or not?"

She puffed out her cheeks on a big exhale. And then finally, she gave it up. "Saturday night at seven. Dinner at my parents' house."

Chapter Ten

From outside, Garrett eyeballed the Lockwood house at around ten thousand square feet. It sat on a slight hill in superexclusive North Cherry Creek and had two stories aboveground. Judging by the windows that gleamed below ground level, the house also included a fully finished basement.

Cami's father answered the doorbell. Quentin Lockwood was tall and very lean with a long face etched in what appeared to be a permanent scowl. Cami must have gotten her looks from her mom.

"Camilla." Lockwood's scowl deepened at the sight of Garrett. "Hello."

"Hello, Dad." Cami's voice was so cautious, so over-controlled. Garrett's exasperation with her father ratcheted up several notches. Anyone who dimmed Cami's joy and enthusiasm was a dirtball in Garrett's book.

Lockwood stepped back. "Come in."

They crossed the threshold. The soaring entry had two stories of curved windows on either side of the coffered front door.

Lockwood's surly silence and hostile staring were interrupted by a gorgeous blue-eyed blonde. She fluttered in from the next room, slim arms outstretched. "Oh, sweetheart. Here you are."

"Mom." Cami stepped forward and the two women embraced.

"At last." With a happy sigh, Hazel Lockwood pressed Cami close. "I'm so glad you came." Cami's mom seemed sincere at least. And she actually sent Garrett a welcoming smile over Cami's shoulder.

When the women pulled apart, Cami embraced her father stiffly and then took Garrett's left arm. "Mom, Dad. This is Garrett Bravo." Her face lit up with a mischievous smile. "Garrett is my *special* friend."

Her mother greeted him warmly. "It's so nice to meet you, Garrett."

And her father finally offered his hand. Garrett shook it and then Lockwood said, "Well, all right, then. Shall we go on into the library for drinks?"

Cami gave Garrett's arm a squeeze. "Just like at the mansion, huh?"

"Excuse me?" said her father.

Garrett explained, "My mother always serves drinks in the library."

"I hope you'll feel right at home, then," Lockwood replied sourly. "This way." He ushered them through a wide arch into a two-story room finished in way too much glossy, deep red Brazilian cherry. There was a parquet cherry floor, a looming fireplace with a cherry surround, cherry platform steps on three walls leading up to glassed-in cherry bookcases full of leather-bound volumes. The gracefully curving cherry staircase climbed one wall to a second-floor gallery railed in cherry.

A fat sofa with too many pillows, an ornate coffee table and three large armchairs cozied up to the unlit fireplace. Garrett and Cami took the couch. Quentin offered drinks. He whipped them up while Hazel urged them to help themselves to the giant tray of different cheeses and gourmet crackers waiting on the coffee table.

Once they all had drinks, Lockwood folded his long frame into a studded leather throne of a chair and said, "Camilla, it is wonderful to see you." At Cami's careful nod and strained smile, he added reproachfully, "Though it was my understanding you would be coming alone."

Cami's tight smile died a sudden death. "The way I remember it, you *wanted* me to come alone, but I told you that I planned to bring Garrett if he could make it."

Hazel piped up with, "Honey, we're glad you brought your friend with you." Lockwood started to speak, but she beat him to it. "Now, tell us how you've been doing. How are things in Justice Creek?"

"I love it there." Cami slid closer to Garrett. Her fingers brushed his thigh, seeking contact. He caught them and held on. She launched into a quick recap of her progress in the past month, how she'd gotten to know so many people, had begun volunteering in the community. "I work a few afternoons a week helping out at the animal shelter and I've agreed to help

a Blueberry troop make their own Christmas cards."
She told them about Paper Princess. "Greeting cards
and stationery. My store opens in October. I hope
you'll come to my grand opening."

"Expressing your creative side, right?" Hazel beamed.
"We would love to come. Wouldn't we, Quentin?"

Lockwood ignored his wife. "We need you back at
WellWay. And you could at least give Charles a call.
He's having a hard time without you."

"Dad." Cami sounded weary now. "Where to even
begin with you? I'll say it all again. I'm not coming
back to—"

"Don't," commanded Lockwood. "Please."

"You know what? You're right. I've said it too
many times. And I know you've heard me, so that's
that. We can just let it be."

Hazel chirped, "Are you sure you wouldn't like
some cheese?"

"Mom." Cami shook her head. "Forget the cheese."

"What is that you're wearing?" asked Lockwood,
eyeing Cami's yellow sundress. She looked like a million bucks in that dress. It had skinny little shoulder
straps, laces up the back and the hem went every
which way, like a bunch of yellow handkerchiefs sewn
together. "It's not your style at all."

"Wrong," said Cami flatly. "This dress is exactly
my style."

Garrett agreed. And he said so. "It's perfect on
you. *You're* perfect." Was he laying it on too thick?
Not a chance. Lockwood needed to have his eyes examined if he thought there was anything wrong with
that dress or the woman wearing it.

Lockwood knocked back a slug of scotch. "I do

not understand you, Camilla. I really thought you'd finally settled down and come to realize—"

"Well, Dad. I did come to realize a few things, now you mention it, though they are actually things I've always known. That I want a different life than you had planned for me, that I was never going to be happy trying to be who you wanted me to be."

"Happy." He repeated the word with a sneer.

"Yeah." She came right back at him. "Happy. Because happiness matters. It's even in the Declaration of Independence, in case you might have forgotten. Everybody's entitled to 'life, liberty and the pursuit of happiness.' Well, I had a life, all right. But it wasn't much without the *liberty* to decide how I wanted to live it. And there was no way I could pursue my own *happiness* with a man I didn't love and a job that made me want to run away screaming."

Garrett almost applauded. The woman was magnificent. She really didn't need him here, but he was kind of glad she'd brought him along. It was seriously enlightening to witness firsthand what a self-righteous ass her father was.

She finished with, "And if we're just going to sit here and cover the same ground over and over again, I think Garrett and I should just give up and go." She started to stand.

But her mother cried, "No. Please don't go, honey." Hazel turned reproachful eyes on Lockwood. "Quentin." This time, her voice actually held a note of steel beneath the sweetness.

Lockwood answered with a bitter edge. "All right. I'll keep my mouth shut. You don't want to hear it and I'm tired of saying it."

"Please stay," Hazel pleaded.

Garrett was more than ready to get the hell out. But this was Cami's show.

Finally, Cami nodded. "I guess we can give it a try."

So they stayed. They finished their drinks and went in to dinner, which was served in a formal dining room by a middle-aged woman in black.

Hazel tried to keep the conversation going. She asked Garrett about his work and got Cami talking about her shop some more. Mostly, though, the meal consisted of long stretches of painful silence punctuated by the clink of monogrammed silverware against fine china plates.

Lockwood hardly said a word through the meal, but his reserve was far from benign. He reminded Garrett of a long, skinny tiger crouched to strike.

Mostly though, Cami's father behaved himself. There were plenty of snide remarks and way too much scowling, but at least he was reasonably civil and the evening limped along.

The woman in black served coffee and dessert. Garrett dared to hope they would get through the final course and get the hell out before anything too awful happened.

But ultimately, Quentin Lockwood just couldn't leave bad enough alone.

Garrett had taken only one bite of his tiramisu when Cami's dad brought out the big guns. "Hazel," he said severely. "I'm sorry if I'm about to upset you, but there comes a time when a man is finally forced to draw the line."

"Quentin, I mean it." Hazel spoke fervently. "Don't you dare." Her mouth was trembling.

Cami set down her spoon. "Is this a threat of some kind, then?"

Lockwood said, "It's your last chance, that's what it is."

"Dad, I thought we already—"

He ran right over her. "I want you to return to Denver and take your rightful place at WellWay again. I don't know if Charles will be willing to take you back at this point, but I insist that you at least try to patch things up with him."

"Is that all?" Cami asked.

"Not quite. I want you to go back into therapy, where you will examine why you feel compelled to keep walking out on your own life. And I want your sincere promise that you will never run away again."

Cami just stared at him for several unnerving seconds, after which she replied quietly, "No."

Lockwood actually seemed kind of surprised. The guy refused to believe that Cami wouldn't finally cave to his will. "No, to…?"

"All of it, Dad—well, except for promising never to run away again. I can make that promise now because I'm finally where I want to be."

The frown lines in Lockwood's forehead got deeper than ever. "Meaning…?"

"That I live in Justice Creek now, and as I've said repeatedly, I love it there."

"Well, all right, then, Camilla." For the first time that evening, the man smiled. It wasn't a pretty sight. He raised his delicate china coffee cup as though to make a toast and announced, "I am disowning you."

Hazel gasped. From the expression on her pretty face, she'd had no idea her husband would go that far.

But Cami didn't even flinch. "*Disown.* See, that's the problem, Dad. You never *owned* me in the first place."

"Don't give me your clever wordplay. You know what I mean. You will get nothing. I'll cut you out of our wills, out of WellWay, out of all of it."

That single bite of tiramisu seemed stuck in Garrett's throat. And here he'd thought the Bravos had issues. "Cami." When she looked at him, he tipped his head in the direction of the front door.

She gave him the saddest little smile. "Not yet, Garrett." She turned her calm gaze on her father. "What else, Dad?"

"You think I'm bluffing?" Lockwood taunted. "I'm not bluffing."

"Quentin." Hazel's voice was hardly more than a desperate whisper this time.

He ignored her. "Sadly, Camilla, I don't know what else to do about you. You are a confused and pathetic creature who doesn't know how to run her own life, a woman who is clearly a danger to herself. Over and over, you have taken the wrong turns, made the self-defeating choices. Every time your mother and I become confident you've finally taken your rightful place in the world, you run off on some wild-goose chase again. Well, this it. You're out on your ear and I refuse to feel guilty about cutting you loose. I'm hardly leaving you destitute. You got your trust fund. Take care of the money you already have. Because the real family fortune will never be yours."

Cami said nothing. She sat very still. Even with

that stricken look on her face, she was a bright ray of sunshine in her yellow dress.

But Garrett couldn't sit still. He'd heard way more than enough. He shoved back his chair and dropped his napkin on the table. "We're outta here."

Cami stayed in her chair. "I'm sorry you had to see this, Garrett. But I'm not leaving. Not yet. Not until I've had my say."

I'm here for backup, he reminded himself. *It's her fight, not mine.* Slowly, he sank back to his seat.

Cami turned to her father. "I love you, Dad." She spoke gently, with real kindness. "I can't be what you want. If I could, I would have changed myself long before now. But I'm just…not that person. Not the Lockwood you always wanted me to be. I'm sorry. I really am. But you go ahead and do what you have to do. In the meantime, I'm going to be happy in Justice Creek, doing work I love with people I care about who feel the same for me. And I truly hope that someday you'll miss me and decide that maybe it's time you gave up trying to run my life, time to let yourself just love me as I love you. Until then, well…" She slid her napkin in beside her plate and silently pushed back her chair.

Garrett stood again and went to her side.

She took his hand and said to her father, "The sad thing is, there was a time when your threats would have worked on me. But that time is past, Dad. I won't stop hoping, though, that someday you'll find a way to accept that I finally grew up and became who I really am."

Her father threw up both hands. "All that's just nonsense. *Who you really are.* What does that even mean? I am done with—"

"Stop!" Hazel Lockwood shouted. Shocked the hell out of Garrett—and Cami and her dad, too, judging by the stunned looks on their faces. Hazel shoved back her chair and popped to her feet. "I've had about enough of this, Quentin." Cami clutched Garrett's hand tighter as Hazel rounded on her husband. "This can't go on. Cami's right. And you are wrong, my love. She's a grown woman and she has a right to make her own choices." She marched down the long table to loom above him. "Take it back," she demanded. "Apologize this instant."

Was this really happening? Garrett slid a glance at Cami. She looked as astonished as he felt. He'd spent a grim two hours with the Lockwoods. It was long enough for him to feel certain that Cami's mom had never been the kind of woman to call out her man.

Until now, anyway.

About then, Quentin got past his stupefaction that his wife had dared to stand up to him. "Hazel, what is the matter with you? I don't believe this."

She fisted her hands at her sides and insisted, "Take it back, Quentin. Take it back now."

"That does it." He jumped up. "I've said what I had to say. Camilla, do not come back. I've had more than enough of your foolish self-destructive behaviors. Good night, everyone."

And with that, he stormed from the room.

At the door, Cami hugged her mother. "Thanks for trying, Mom."

"I'll have a long talk with him. It will work out, you wait and see." Hazel's anxious eyes belied her words. "Garrett, it was lovely to meet you."

"Thanks, Mrs. Lockwood."

"Hazel. Please." She opened the door and they went down the wide stone steps and got into the Mustang.

When Garrett started up the engine and pulled away, Hazel lifted a hand in a wave.

"You doing okay over there?" he asked when they were out on the highway speeding toward home. Forty-five minutes had passed without Cami saying a word.

"I'm sad." She stared out the windshield as the dark highway fled past behind them.

"You're amazing."

"Yeah?" she asked hopefully, but she didn't look at him. Her eyes remained on the road ahead.

"Are you kidding me? Look at you. You've accomplished everything you set out to do, made a life in Justice Creek on your own terms. You've faced down your overbearing ex-fiancé and your controlling dad. No question about it. You blow me away."

Did she almost smile? He wasn't sure. She stared out at the night and said somberly, "I love my dad. He's not always a complete jerk. When I was little, he used to give me piggyback rides and play catch with me. He always treated Mom like his queen and me like a princess. I won a prize in an art show once. He was so proud. It's just, you know, I'm his only kid and he had plans for his kid." She turned to look at him then. "But I'm not going back. No way." She leaned across the console and put that fine mouth close to his ear. Her breath warmed his skin. "Thanks for coming with me."

He turned to claim a quick, sweet kiss. "What's a friend for?"

Something happened in those big blue eyes—a withdrawal, maybe? Or maybe not, because a moment later, she put a finger to his chin and turned his face her way again for another swift and tempting kiss. A low, sexy laugh escaped her. "Take me home, handsome. I want to show you what a good friend I am."

"That is by far the best offer I've had all night." He turned his eyes to the road and drove a little faster, inching it over the speed limit, eager to undo the laces of that yellow dress and explore their *special* friendship in a mutually satisfying way.

"Cami?" She heard the cautious tap of Garrett's knuckles against the bathroom door.

"Be right out." She stared at her reflection in the mirror above the sink. In a strapless bra of ivory lace and matching thong, she was all ready for seduction.

Except for the sadness that she couldn't seem to shake.

Because her dad had just kicked her out of his life.

And the man she loved kept calling her his *friend*.

Yeah, okay. That wasn't fair to Garrett. He'd taken care of her on the mountain, opened his home to her, introduced her to his friends and family, backed her up when anything threatened her. And shown her how glorious lovemaking could be. She had no right to expect him to fall in love with her just because she'd fallen for him.

Why *shouldn't* Garrett call her a friend? She *was* a friend. And if she wanted more from him than friendship and amazing sex, she had to put herself out there, to tell him what she felt in her heart.

That was the first step, after all. She needed to say, *I love you, Garrett*, and give the guy a chance to respond.

"You okay?" He was still there, waiting for her on the other side of the door.

Squaring her shoulders, she went and opened the door to him. "I'm perfect," she lied.

"Oh, yes, you are." He wore absolutely nothing and he looked spectacular that way. His eyes full of sexy promises, he reached out and touched her shoulder. "Turn around."

She obeyed, showing him her back. His clever fingers got to work. Her bra fell away. She caught it before it dropped to the floor. His fingers skated along the length of her arm, stirring hot little flares of pleasured sensation. He took the bra from her fingers. She didn't look to see what he did with it.

His warm palm glided around to cup her bare breast. He pulled her back against his chest and she went with a willing sigh, letting her head fall onto his shoulder, feeling his heat and hardness pressing into the cleft of her bottom, the head notching against the small of her back.

She whispered his name, "Garrett," in arousal and longing. In sadness and gratitude.

And most of all, in love.

He wrapped his hand around her throat, claiming it, claiming *her*, all of her, body, soul and yearning heart. She shuddered in pleasure, letting him guide her, tipping her head all the way back until their lips could meet.

A long kiss, wet and deep and thrilling. He trailed his hand down the front of her to cup her breast again and tease the nipple, but only for a moment. His fingers drifted on downward to the sensitive terrain of her belly. She moaned into the kiss as his fingers slipped beneath the barely there cover of her thong and found her waiting heat.

She cried things, desperate things, "Please," and, "More," and, "Never, ever stop," as those wonderful fingers of his played her like a song. All the while, he kept on kissing her, until her knees gave out and she came with a shouted, "Yes!"

And then he scooped her up high in his arms and carried her to the bed. He took away her thong and they were both completely naked.

My love, she thought, staring up into those amber eyes. *I love you so.*

But she didn't say it. She feared he wouldn't want to hear it. And she'd had more than enough sadness for one night. Instead, she reached for him and opened her body to him the way she longed to open her soul.

Much later, in the dark, as he slept beside her and Munchy lay curled up at the foot of the bed, she let the sadness wash over her. For the father who considered it his right to try to force her to be someone she didn't want to be.

And for her own cowardice in the face of love.

By Wednesday of that week, Garrett knew something wasn't right with Cami—something that had nothing do with the cruel thing her father had done.

How many times now had he glanced her way to find her watching him? And then, just when he would think she was going to say something important, she would look away.

He knew he should ask her what was going on.

But he didn't ask. He really wasn't all that sure he wanted to know.

On Thursday, he came home at seven to find her in the kitchen staring out the window over the sink. It was her turn to come up with dinner, but there was nothing cooking. She usually set the table. Not tonight.

She must have heard him come in through the living room, but she didn't acknowledge him. She just stood there and stared out at the thick lower branches of the Douglas fir in the side yard.

Munch wiggled over to greet him. He crouched to give the dog some love.

When he stood up again, she turned to face him. "Hey." She leaned back against the counter, her bare feet with their cute turquoise-painted toes shuffling against the hardwood floor.

Was she nervous? She kind of seemed like it.

"I'm guessing we're going out?" he asked. "How about the Sylvan Inn? I've been meaning to take you there. It's cozy and the hammer steaks and cheesy potatoes will rock your world."

Her smooth throat clutched as she swallowed. "Could we, um, sit down for a minute? I need to talk."

What about? What's going on? "Sure."

She put out a hand. "The living room, maybe?"

Now *he* was the one gulping. They stared at each other. He had that feeling again—that whatever she had to say, he didn't want to hear it.

But he followed obediently when she turned for the other room.

She dropped to one end of the sofa, curling her legs to the side and facing him.

He took the other end. "So what's this about?"

She folded her hands on her thigh, then unfolded them and stretched out an arm along the back of the sofa. "I'm just going to say it." She brought her arm down and clasped her hands again. And then she stared down at them as though she wondered how they got there on the ends of her arms.

Had something happened with her father or the bonehead? "Cami. *What?*"

And she looked up into his eyes. "Garrett. I just have to tell you. I'm in love with you. I've been in love with you since the first moment I saw you and I don't care if that's impossible, that's how it is for me. I love you. I want to be with you. I...want more than friendship with you. More than *benefits*. Garrett, I love you and I want *everything* with you."

Love.

A rough symphony of bad words played through his mind. His throat ached and the inside of his mouth felt like he'd just tried to eat a bucket of sand. She sat there with her misplaced hands, looking like an angel in blue jeans with turquoise toes.

He wanted her. More than anything. Wanted just what they had, nights wrapped around each other and lunch in a basket. Her laughter, her soft voice, her vanilla scent, those otherworldly eyes.

But love?

No. Uh-uh.

If only she hadn't said it. If only she could have

just left it alone. He didn't want to dig down into the love place. He'd been there and done that and didn't have what love took.

Uh-uh. Not doing that again.

And still, she kept looking at him, kept waiting for him to say something, to tell her what he *felt* for her, to say she was everything and he couldn't live without her, that yes, he loved her, too.

This was it. This was where he disappointed her. This was the thing he didn't really know how to do. "Cami, I…just don't know what to say."

She caught her lower lip between her teeth and looked down at her hands again. "I meant to be patient," she said in a whisper. "But I guess I'm just not the patient type. Not anymore." Her bright head came up and she looked at him, seeking something she wasn't going to find.

For way too long, they just stared at each other.

And finally, she spoke again. "I can't thank you enough for all you've done for me. You've been the best friend I've ever had. And I still want your friendship, Garrett." That didn't sound so bad. He almost let himself breathe again. But then she said, "Eventually, I hope we can be friends again."

That pissed him off. *"Again?"* He practically shouted the word. She flinched and he made himself lower his voice. "But we *are* friends. Right now. I *want* what we have." His voice got louder again. He forced it down. "I don't want to lose you."

She held out her hands, palms up, fingers wide. And then she gathered them in to rest, one over the other, in the center of her chest. "It hurts too much. I have…all this longing. For you. For your love. Right now, for me, our friendship just isn't enough."

"You can't just—"

"Yeah. Yeah, I can. I *have* to. I love you. And to be here with you when my love is just burning inside me, when all I can think about is giving that love to you and having you give it back to me from your heart…" She shook her head. "Something has to change in me. I need to find my patience again, to be willing to wait for you, hoping someday you'll be able to openly return my love. Or if not that, then I need to somehow come to accept that you're never really going to be mine. But for now, until something changes, I can't be your friend and I can't live here with you anymore."

What? She was leaving? Just like that? His heart thudded so loud his ears were ringing. His mouth tasted bitter and his skin had shrunk so he felt stuffed tight inside it. "That's wrong. That's ridiculous. Of course you can live here. I *want* you here. I don't want you to go."

"But I have to go."

"No, you don't."

"Yeah. It's time. I need to get my own place."

He strove for calm, for a reasonable approach. "I… Look. Let's go get something to eat." He rose. "And then you can sleep on it. No big decisions have to be made right this minute."

She unfolded those shapely legs and stood to face him. "Garrett." She gazed at him with tender sadness. "I've made my decision. I know what I have to do. I'm going to pack up my stuff and get out of here tonight."

"But…where are you going to go at seven-thirty on Wednesday night?"

"It's not a big deal. I'll get a hotel room. I've always wanted to stay at the Haltersham. I think I'll try there." She reached out as if to reassure him somehow—but then she let her hand drop to her side without touching him. "I will be fine." And just like that, she turned and walked away.

Chapter Eleven

He didn't know how to stop her, so he just stood there like a brain-dead fool as she headed for the stairs.

And then he couldn't bear it.

He wasn't going to be able to watch her go, so he got his dog and left in the Wrangler. He ate fast food from a drive-through, then went to his office. He left the Jeep in the parking lot and took Munch for a long walk up one side of Glacier Avenue and back down the other.

When he returned to Bravo Construction, it was a quarter of nine. Was she gone yet?

And had she needed his help carrying her stuff out to the car?

Well, so what if she'd needed him? He wasn't about to help her leave him. She would have to do that on her own.

Just in case she was still at the house, he went on into the deserted office. He made coffee and drank too much of it and signed the stack of payables Shelly had left on his desk. There was always plenty to do at BC. He spent a couple more hours plowing through paperwork.

Every time he made the mistake of glancing at his dog, Munch would stare up at him reproachfully, as if the damn dog already knew that Cami had left and it was all Garrett's fault.

Around one in the morning, he took Munch for a quick walk around the parking lot. Then he went back inside and stretched out on his office couch.

When he woke up, it was six in the morning. He and Munch returned home.

Inside, he found her keys on the kitchen counter with a scratch-paper note. She'd drawn one of her bunny characters, the girl bunny in a ballerina skirt with a pink bow between her bunny ears. The bunny wore a sad expression. She sat in a patch of grass dotted with wildflowers and waved her bunny paw at him. Beneath the sketch, Cami had written, *I got a room at the Haltersham. I will be fine. Please take care of yourself and give Munchy a big hug for me.*

Garrett went through the motions of starting his day. He fed the dog and gave him fresh water. He ate some breakfast and took a shower.

He and Munch were back at the office at a little after eight.

Somehow, he got through the day, though Nell asked him what was wrong about ten times, and each time, he lied and said there was nothing.

Lunch was bad. He didn't have a lunch meeting. Shelly ordered him takeout. He ate at his desk and tried not to picture Cami sitting in the guest chair, nibbling on apple wedges, laughing at something he'd said.

He worked late, ate at the Sylvan Inn by himself and got home at ten. That night, he crashed in one of the spare rooms. No way he could face his empty bed yet.

Friday, he got to work before eight.

Nell was waiting for him. "I want to talk to you." She followed him into his office and slammed the door so hard it hurt his head.

He put his hand to his ear. "Easy, Nellie. You'll knock that door off its hinges."

His baby sister folded her arms across her Bravo Construction T-shirt and gave him the evil eye. "What did you do to Cami?"

Alarm rang through him. "What happened? Is she okay?"

"No thanks to you. Ma, Griffin and Elise were at the Haltersham yesterday afternoon hammering out wedding plans." Their half sister Elise was a caterer and wedding planner.

"Ma's having Elise plan the wedding?"

"Elise is the best. Everybody knows it. And she's all excited that Ma would ask her—and Elise doing Ma and Griff's wedding is not what I'm talking about."

He dropped to his desk chair. "Cami." Just saying her name made his bones ache with longing.

"Yeah, you idiot. Cami. Ma spotted her in the Haltersham lobby and asked her what was going on, why was she there? She said she was staying at the hotel until she found a place of her own. You know Ma.

She got right on it, asking what was up between you two. Cami wouldn't talk about it. Ma said no way she was letting Cami stay at a hotel. If she needed a place, she could stay at the mansion. Cami thanked her but refused. Ma called me. I was finishing up at the job site, so I went right over there."

He didn't need a blow-by-blow. "So what you're telling me is that Cami's all right?"

"She wouldn't say it, but I know what you did. You broke her heart, you big jerk. If I didn't love you, I'd slap you silly about now."

"Lay off me, Nell. It's bad enough without you riding my ass."

At least that shut her up. For about thirty seconds. And her voice was marginally softer when she said, "Anyway, I convinced her to take the spare room up at my place until she finds something."

"That's good." She would be with family. It eased his mind a little.

And then whatever mental peace he'd found shattered all to hell when his sister said, "Ma wants to see you."

That wasn't happening anytime soon. "Ma can wait."

Nell made a snorting sound before adding, "Also, Cami's dad called her last night while she was getting settled in at the loft."

His gut clenched. "Can't that SOB just leave her alone?"

"Relax. It's a good thing. Her dad apologized. For everything. Evidently, her mother walked out on him. It was a come-to-Jesus moment for Cami's dad. He and her mom are back together already and he swore to Cami's mom that he would make things right, that he would give up trying to get Cami to live her life by his rules."

"So then, Cami's no longer disowned and disinherited?"

"Not anymore. They're working it out, Cami says. She's cautiously optimistic."

For a moment, the ache inside him eased a little, to learn that Cami hadn't lost her father, after all.

Nell said way too damn smugly, "You know one way or another, Ma is going find a way to get a little quality time with you."

"Yeah, well. She'll have to catch me first."

Garrett managed to avoid his mother for four full days. But then on Wednesday, exactly one week after Cami moved out, he made the mistake of going home before midnight. He'd stopped for takeout at Romano's and got home at a little after eight—and he was sitting at the kitchen island shoveling in spaghetti carbonara when the doorbell rang.

The funny thing was, he knew it was Willow. He could have just refused to answer the door.

But getting home earlier hadn't really been a mistake. He'd survived a whole week without Cami.

It was a week too long.

He had to do something, find a way to say the things he'd sworn he would never say to any woman ever again. Maybe Ma could help him with that.

But even if she couldn't, he was ready to listen to her tell him what a damn fool he'd been.

He went to the door and let her in. "Want some spaghetti?"

"I ate with Griff."

She said she'd take coffee, so he made them each a cup. It was a nice night. He led her out to the table on the lower deck. Munch sniffed the bushes for a while, then came and stretched out beside Willow's chair.

She stuck her hand down and scratched his head—and then got right to business. "You sent that sweet girl away?"

Coffee sloshed as he set his cup down too forcefully. "No. I never wanted her to go. I just want her with me. Like, permanently."

"You're making no sense, Garrett. That girl's in love with you. She wouldn't leave you unless you did something to make her go."

He moved his mug to the left and then slid it to the right again. "When things went south with Miranda, I kind of gave up on love." His mother laughed. Sometimes she was the most insensitive person on the planet. "It's not funny, Ma."

"Wait till you're my age. You'll get the humor."

"The thing is, Cami said she loved me. I told her I wasn't going there, so she moved out. She says she can't be my friend, not for a while, not till she gets over me, or whatever."

"Is that really what you want from her, for her to get over you so that she can be your *friend*?"

"I just want her, okay? I just...want to be with her, take care of her, eat lunch with her, hear about her damn day."

Ma rested her forearm on the table. That gigantic diamond Griffin had given her glittered in the fading light. "Garrett, you're in love with her."

He drank some coffee and set the cup down with a little more care that time. "Yeah. I am. I really am."

When the doorbell rang at a quarter after nine that night, Cami was alone in the loft. She assumed the unexpected guest was some friend of Nell's, but she checked the peephole just to be safe.

Her heart leaped into her throat and got stuck there when she saw it was Garrett. Hope bloomed.

And then died an ugly death.

No way could she let herself get her hopes up just to get them crushed to dust all over again.

Garrett tapped on the other side of the door. "Cami." His voice was slightly muffled, but she heard him well enough. "I know you're in there. Let me in."

She pressed her hands to the door, laid her cheek against it and shut her eyes. It almost felt like being close to him again—just to know he was on the other side.

Whatever he'd really come here for.

"What do you want, Garrett? I told you I didn't want to see you for a while."

"Cami. Come on." His voice, so gruff and deep and thrilling, destroyed her. Another shimmer of longing shuddered through her. It hurt so much it almost felt good. "Open the door."

The yearning was too strong. She gave in and pulled back the door. The sight of him broke her poor heart all over again.

She couldn't do this. Whatever he wanted, she couldn't deal with it right now.

He caught the door before she could shut it in his face. "Let me in. Please. I've got stuff to say. Just hear me out." His hair was as thick and unruly as ever. And those melty eyes turned her knees to mush. He looked kind of tired. She supposed that she did, too. Sleeping wasn't that easy without his big arms to hold her.

She stepped back, clearing the way for him, though she knew she shouldn't.

And then he was inside with her, bringing the too-tempting scent of his skin and all that electricity he generated for her, just by being him. Having him right there in front of her was so hard to bear. She retreated another step, and he shut the door.

What was she supposed to say? "You want something to drink or—?"

"Nothing. Just to talk."

"Well, all right." The living area was one big, high-ceilinged space. She led him over to the sofa and chairs near the floor-to-ceiling front windows. "Have a seat." He took one end of the sofa. She backed to a chair and sat down, too. "Now. What?"

His gaze was all over her, making slow passes from her bare feet up her legs to her cutoffs and the plaid shirt she'd tied in a knot at her waist. "You look so beautiful."

Her hand went to her hair. She had no idea why. "You came here to tell me I'm beautiful?"

He didn't answer. He just stared at her in that hungry, sexy way he had that always made her want to rip off her clothes and jump in his lap.

She demanded, "Garrett, what are you *doing*?"

He seemed to shake himself. "Nell said your dad called and he wants to make things right."

"Yeah. He, um, I think he's finally accepted that my life is my own. I'm meeting him and Mom for dinner next week and they will be coming to my grand opening in October."

"That's so great. I'm glad."

They stared at each other. Her heart raced and her breathing sounded ragged and way too loud. She clutched the chair cushion to keep from leaping up and throwing herself at him. "Please. What's this about?"

He didn't answer right away. She was about to ask the question again when he finally said, "It's been a week since you left me."

"I know that. I've lived through it, too."

"You were right to leave."

"Seriously, Garrett? You think I needed you to come here and tell me that?"

"Probably not. But it's been a week of hell. I work and I work some more and then I fall into bed and I can't sleep. Munch is really pissed at me."

"Is he okay?"

"He'll live. He just misses you. *I* miss you. It's killing me. But I... You were right to go because you deserve the truth from me and I wasn't willing to give you that a week ago. I was holding on to old garbage and I needed to let all that crap go."

"What garbage?" It came out as a croak.

"The garbage that I wasn't going to go there again, that I would never try to love someone again, because I'm so bad at it and I would only mess it up. I didn't want to mess it up with you, Cami. But somehow, I went and did it anyway. I messed it up and all for nothing. Because I lost you *and* I love you. And I think I always will."

She realized she'd stopped breathing. "Excuse me. What did you just say?"

"I said I love you, Cami. God, you have no idea how much. It feels like I've loved you since the first minute I saw you, standing there in your poufy white dress looking like you'd just gone a few rounds with Muhammad Ali. I saw you and I was finished, done for, just like in all those corny romantic movies. You're the one for me."

"I… You… Garrett, did you hear yourself? You just said you love me."

"Because I do. I love you, Cami. I belong to you. Please come back to me. Please be mine and I'll be yours and we won't let anything ever tear us apart."

That did it.

With a cry of sheer gladness, she leaped from her chair. He got up, too.

"Garrett, you mean it? I can come home?"

"Please, Cami. Please come home." And he held out his arms to her.

It was all the encouragement she needed. She threw herself at him. He caught her in flight. She wrapped her arms and legs around him good and tight and pressed a big smack of a kiss on his scruffy cheek. "That does it. You'll never get rid of me now."

"Excellent." He looked at her with such tenderness, with the same love and longing she felt in her soul. "Because I don't want to live without you. I want you there in our bed when we wake up in the morning. I want to bring home the takeout and share it with you. I want it all with you, Cami. I want a lifetime, you and me."

And then he kissed her.

Oh, the feel of his lips on hers. Nothing could ever

compare to that. She surrendered to that kiss with her whole heart, holding nothing back.

And when he lifted his head, she said, "Forever? You really mean it?"

"I do."

"What about kids? I do want kids someday."

"I never thought I would again. But now, with you…" He gave her that slow smile, the one that set the butterflies loose in her belly. "Yeah. Kids. I want them, too."

"You would? Really?"

"Cami, with you, I want what you said you wanted a week ago—everything." And then he said, "Marry me."

And she said, "Yes."

He demanded, "Right away."

"Absolutely. I want it outdoors, Garrett. I want it easy and casual. With a picnic reception after."

He kissed her again, long and slow and sweet. And then he nuzzled her ear and whispered, "I know just the place."

They were married on Moosejaw Mountain eleven days later, on the second Saturday in September.

The whole Bravo family drove up to the cabin for the ceremony. The Lockwoods came, too. It was a beautiful day, warm for September. The endless Colorado sky was cloudless and a slight breeze stirred the evergreens.

Cami wore a white sundress with a handkerchief hem and white flip-flops on her feet. She had a crown of flowers in her hair and carried a bouquet of black-eyed Susans. Her father walked her down the make-shift aisle between the rows of folding chairs to where Garrett waited for her, so handsome in jeans, a white shirt and a tan vest. Munch, looking dapper in a black satin bow tie, sat proudly at his side.

Garrett held out his hands to her. She took them. Facing each other, hands clasped, they said their vows—to love, to honor and to cherish, for the rest of their lives.

As the minister declared them husband and wife, Cami knew that running away from marriage to the wrong man had been the smartest thing she'd ever done. Now she would never have to run away again. She had found her true home at last in Garrett Bravo's loving arms.

* * * * *

Nell Bravo is the only single Bravo left
in Justice Creek, Colorado.
But not for long. Declan McGrath is determined
to claim her, even if he has to break a few rules
to make her his.

Don't miss the final instalment of
THE BRAVOS OF JUSTICE CREEK,
MARRIED TILL CHRISTMAS,
coming in December 2017
wherever Mills & Boon books
and ebooks are sold.

And catch up with the rest of the Bravo family:
THE LAWMAN'S CONVENIENT BRIDE
A BRAVO FOR CHRISTMAS
MS. BRAVO AND THE BOSS
available now from Mills & Boon!

MILLS & BOON®

EXCLUSIVE EXTRACT

Beautiful, young widow Noelle Fryberg is determined to
show her Christmas-hating boss, millionaire James
Hammond, just how magical Christmas can be…Could she
be the one to melt his heart?

Read on for a sneak preview of
CHRISTMAS WITH HER MILLIONAIRE BOSS
the first book in the magical THE MEN WHO MAKE
CHRISTMAS *duet*

He'd lost his train of thought when she looked up at him,
distracted by the sheen left by the snow on her dampened
skin. Satiny smooth, it put tempting ideas in his head.

Like kissing her.

"Don't be silly," she replied. For a second, James thought
she'd read his mind and meant the kiss, especially after she
pulled her arm free from his. "It's a few inches of snow, not
the frozen tundra. I think I can handle walking, crowd or no
crowd. Now, I don't know about you, but I want my hot cocoa."

She marched toward the end of the aisle, the pom-pom
on her hat bobbing in time with her steps. James stood and
watched until the crowd threatened to swallow her up before
following.

What the hell was wrong with him? Since when did he
think about kissing the people he did business with? Worse,
Noelle was an employee. Granted, a very attractive, enticing
one, but there were a lot of beautiful women working in the
Boston office and never once had he contemplated pulling one
of them against him and kissing her senseless.

Then again, none of them ever challenged him either. Nor did they walk like the majorette in a fairy band.

It had to be the drone. He'd read that concussions could cause personality changes. Lord knows, he'd been acting out of character for days now starting with agreeing to stay for Thanksgiving.

It certainly explained why he was standing in the middle of this oversized flea market when he could—should—be working. Honestly, did the people in this town ever do anything at a normal scale? Everywhere he looked, someone was pushing Christmas. Holiday sweaters. Gingerbread cookies. One vendor was literally making hand-blown Christmas ornaments on the spot. Further proof he wasn't himself, James almost paused because there was one particularly incandescent blue ornament that was a similar shade to Noelle's eyes.

The lady herself had stopped. At a booth selling scented lotions and soaps wrapped in green and gold cellophane. "Smell this," she said, when he caught up with her. She held an open bottle of skin cream under his nose, and he caught the sweet smell of vanilla. "It's supposed to smell like a Christmas cookie," she said. "What do you think?"

"I like the way your skin smells better."

Don't miss
THE MEN WHO MAKE CHRISTMAS:

CHRISTMAS WITH HER MILLIONAIRE BOSS
by Barbara Wallace
Available November 2017

SNOWED IN WITH THE RELUCTANT TYCOON
by Nina Singh
Available December 2017

www.millsandboon.co.uk

MILLS & BOON®

Why shop at millsandboon.co.uk?

Each year, thousands of romance readers
find their perfect read at millsandboon.co.uk.
That's because we're passionate about
bringing you the very best romantic fiction.
Here are some of the advantages of
shopping at www.millsandboon.co.uk:

* **Get new books first**—you'll be able to buy
  your favourite books one month before they
  hit the shops

* **Get exclusive discounts**—you'll also be
  able to buy our specially created monthly
  collections, with up to 50% off the RRP

* **Find your favourite authors**—latest news,
  interviews and new releases for all your
  favourite authors and series on our website,
  plus ideas for what to try next

* **Join in**—once you've bought your favourite
  books, don't forget to register with us to rate,
  review and join in the discussions

Visit **www.millsandboon.co.uk**
for all this and more today!

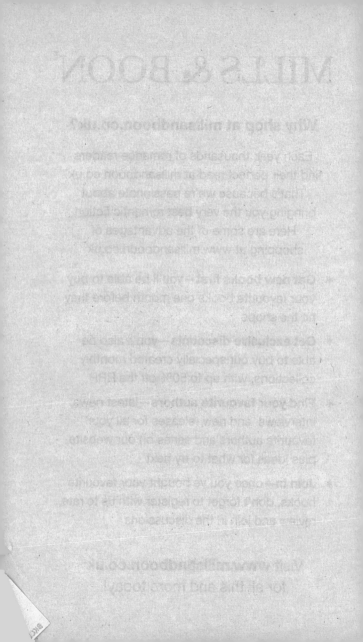